The Unfading Lands

Katharine E. Hamilton

ISBN-10: 0692335765
ISBN-13: 978-0692335765

The Unfading Lands

Copyright © 2014 by Katharine E. Hamilton

All rights reserved. Except for use in any review, the reproduction or utilization of this work in whole or in part in any form by any electronic, mechanical or other means, now known or hereinafter invented, including xerography, photocopying and recording, or in any information storage or retrieval system, is forbidden without the written permission of
Katharine E. Hamilton.

www.katharinehamilton.com

Cover Design by Kerry Prater.

This is a work of fiction. Names, characters, places and incidents are either the product of the author's imagination or are used factiously, and any resemblance to actual persons, living or dead, business establishments, events or locales is entirely coincidental.

DEDICATION

Dedicated to my Meemaw, Pat Hamilton. Thank you for giving me the confidence and nudge to step out in faith and give this writing thing a shot. I love you.

ACKNOWLEDGMENTS

There are so many people I wish to thank for helping and supporting me with this project. I hope I did not miss anyone, but if I did, I'll make sure you make the second book.

My husband, Brad. Thank you for being a sounding board, giving me ideas, and for also NOT thinking I'm completely crazy... or if you do, you keep it to yourself. Ha! I love you.

My family. This envelopes a large group of people, but most importantly - Momma, Daddy, Jared, and Kerry. Thank you for supporting me and always encouraging me.

My PreReader audience: Megan Wellborn, Janet Wells, Sherrill Crisp, Kerry Prater, Debra Machen, and Erin Davis. Thank you for taking the time to read my ROUGH manuscript and providing me with feedback. Your enthusiasm and excitement helped me shape the manuscript into what it is.

My editor, Lauren Hanson. Thank you for making me look good... seriously. Ha!

Dr. Samuel Maroney. Thank you for providing me with your knowledge to develop key scenes. It's nice to talk to someone about... (spoiler alert avoided)... and it be a completely normal conversation.

Kerry Prater. For all the amazing cover designs and website designs she created for me, and for truly bringing The Unfading Lands to life.

The Script and Ed Sheeran. Because every writer needs good jams to listen to while they write, and these always helped get my creative juices flowing.

Tulip and Cash, my furry friends, for always snuggling and listening to me as I read the same scenes out loud over and over again. Thank you for continually acting interested.

My Readers. Thank you for transitioning from my children's books to this one. Thank you for supporting me and encouraging me. I hope you guys enjoy the book, and I cannot wait to hear what you think about it!

The Unfading Lands

Katharine E. Hamilton

# PROLOGUE

The morning was dark. Dreary skies with thick, rolling clouds that seeped mist and fog over the early morning landscape. Gray. Everything was gray. And depressing. His gaze travelled over the surrounding scenery, a sharp eye of practiced and trained precision to detect the unfamiliar. Nothing was out of place, however. Except joy. Joy had steadily been sucked out of his father's lands year after year. But despite their current lack of elation, the lands were still sleeping from a restful night.

The morning sun, shrouded by clouds, had yet to make its appearance. He knew the depressed state would lift as soon as the sun's first rays filtered through the fog. Well, some of the depressed state. He sighed heavily as he turned to face the opposite direction. Nothing depressing about the land that faced him now. The Land of Unfading Beauty. That is what stood before him as he gazed through the glossy veil overhanging the boundary line from his realm and hers. The lush grass beckoning bare feet and long strolls, the dense forest with trees stretching to the highest heavens created a longing in his heart. Grass the color of emeralds, ponds so clear the sun sparkled upon them like glass. He watched as birds happily flew from one tree to another, deer lingered beneath the shade of a draping Willow. Perfection. He gently raised his hand and placed it closely to the fog that separated him from her and waited patiently as she did the same. He watched as the sunlight danced through the leaves, leaving a menagerie of reflections upon her silky blonde hair. If only he could touch her hand. If only he could cross the line without fear and reprimand. She smiled. Oh, how she had the most beautiful smile he had ever seen. He could get lost in her beauty. He wanted to get lost in her beauty. Her deep, sapphire eyes soulful and full of longing. Longing that matched his own.

"Edward"! He flinched at the young voice of his sister Elizabeth coming through the trees. He bowed to his lady on the other side as he began to turn and walk back towards his horse.

"Edward?" Elizabeth pulled the branches from her path and made her way towards the river's edge, the boundary line within sights, she treaded carefully along the tree line. "Edward! There you are!" Breathless she stared at her brother with her hands on her narrow hips. "Father has been looking for you." She cast him a pointed gaze of annoyance as she swatted away a fly.

"So he sent you?" Edward asked in disbelief and a small tilt to his lips.

A glower furrowed his younger sister's brow and made him smile at her stubbornness and pride. "No. But I knew where you would be, and I did not think you would want Father discovering your current place of interest."

"Indeed, sister. I thank you for intervening. I am leaving now and headed back to the castle. Did you come on foot or is your horse lurking about?"

"Of course my horse is out there. It is too far a walk on foot, Edward." Elizabeth replied ruefully. She turned and began stalking back towards her horse.

    Edward smiled at her retreating back and clicked the reins to his regal mare. Triton had been his trusted companion since his early teens. In fact, Edward could scarcely think of a memory that did not include his horse. He affectionately patted a roughened palm on Triton's neck as he shuffled through the tree line. Elizabeth leapt into her saddle with an ease and skill that spoke of the riding lessons

Edward had been giving her the last three years. He smiled at her accomplishment as she flicked her thick braid over her shoulder. "Race you back?" Elizabeth asked with a glint of mischief in her eyes. She quickly clicked her reins and Edward watched as her long, dark braid blew in the wind. He then kicked in his heels and set out after her.

Elizabeth leaned forward in her saddle as the wind whipped against her face and hair. She smelled the grass, the trees, the dirt, and of course, her horse, Lenora. She loved riding on the wind. Her gaze travelled over the vast landscape of the Northern Highlands, her father's kingdom. The rolling hills of lush green grass, the flowing river that sparkled in the sunlight… yes, she loved the kingdom. She loved riding through the meadows, fearless and free. Her sister would be appalled at her behavior at the moment, but Edward always encouraged her. Speaking of her older brother, she watched as he flew by on his white horse with an arrogant salute in her direction, his dark hair, same as her own, teased by the wind. She squinted in fierce determination, hunkered down against the wind and slapped her reins even harder as she entered through the main entry gate of the castle's exterior wall.

Edward tugged on his reins and halted his horse at the base of the looming castle steps, his attendant accepting the leather straps from his hand. Elizabeth trotted to a stop next to him with a scowl. "I almost had you."

Laughing heartily, Edward waited for his sister to dismount before he retorted. At eighteen years of age, his youngest sister had blossomed into a beautiful and independent woman. She stood with grace and elegance, her dark hair long and soft. Her high cheekbones and sharp blue gaze melted many hearts in the kingdom, but Elizabeth never seemed to notice. In fact, her desire for a mate in life had yet to surface. He knew she craved adventure beyond the castle walls, but her position and responsibilities held her rooted and captive within their father's realm.

He watched as she expertly dismounted and handed her reins to her attendant. "Thank you, Mary." She walked over to him on the steps and draped her arm around his shoulders. "One day, Edward. One day I will beat you."

"One day indeed, little sister. Until then, perhaps we should make less of an entrance next time. I feel the heated and disappointed gaze from our sister penetrating my very core."

Elizabeth giggled as she glanced up and noticed her older sister, Alayna, standing within the doorway, her arms folded in frustration and her usually stunning beauty marred by a deep scowl.

"I see you two have been out frolicking this morning." Her pursed lips and hard gaze caused Elizabeth to twitch in nervousness. She noticed Edward only stood straighter and firmer. She tried to mimic his resolute confidence, but Alayna's gaze pierced through her false bravado and melted it quickly.

"Elizabeth was just fetching me for Father, sister. She knew I was in a place of deep reflection and did not want the servants to interrupt me. I thank her for her generosity." Edward lightly hugged Elizabeth, his blue eyes twinkling at their little secret.

Shrugging, Alayna waved them inside. "Well, I suppose her reckless ride can be forgiven this once, then. But hurry, Father needs to speak with us all at once."

∞

Elizabeth lifted her leather riding skirts as she hurried up the stone steps after her sister's brisk retreating back to their father's chambers. Noting the concern in Alayna's face, she wondered what could possibly have her sister so vexed. Knocking swiftly on the heavy door to their father's chamber, his trusted servant Tomas answered the door to the three siblings. Bowing his overly lanky frame, Tomas ushered them inside the crowded room.

Elizabeth noted the surrounding men, captains in her father's army, standing behind his table as he signed a document in front of him. A sea of emerald green uniforms, the color of the Royal Guard, standing resolute behind their king. The intensity in the room left a weight upon her chest. The parchment her father penned contained regal handwriting in a language Elizabeth had never witnessed before; she leaned in closely as to grasp a name of its sender, but her father quickly folded the paper and poured a dollop of wax and with a wave of finality, pressed his signet ring into the red, molten liquid until his seal had been stamped. He then handed the letter to Tomas, who delicately placed it in the hands of one of the royal messengers, who bowed and made haste of his exit.

"Please, sit." Their father waved his hand at the three hand-carved, heavily set chairs in front of him, his sharp blue gaze traveling from one child to the next. "Leave us." He ordered politely to the surrounding officers and servants. He waited until the sliding of the door bolt told him they were alone. Elizabeth noticed the slight deflation of his shoulders when the room was emptied. The signs of her father's failing health hidden beneath the tough facade he wore as a mask. She could see the small effects of the illness. The lines of his face deepening, the pallor of his skin he attempted to hide beneath his thick, gray beard. She always thought her father a handsome man, an honorable king. Joyful, strong, and loyal. But the weakening of his health and his kingdom had begun to show signs of strain, not only on his face, but in his temperament as well.

He then smiled and relaxed in his chair as his gaze travelled over Elizabeth and her current attire. "I see you have gone for a ride this morning, Lizzy."

Elizabeth grinned and nodded. "Yes. I found the morning too beautiful to be locked inside."

He chuckled when he caught Alayna's disapproving gaze. "I see. And did you take your attendant?"

Elizabeth's smile slowly faded as she shook her head. "No sir."

"I see. Have I not told you to keep your attendant close when outside the castle walls?"

"Yes sir." A sense of dread filled the pit of her stomach. She recognized that shift in his tone.

"And yet, you continue to ignore my request. You are hereby restricted to the grounds for one week. No riding except within the royal carrier."

Elizabeth gasped. "But Father!"

He held up his hand. "No buts, Lizzy. You must learn that your safety is of utmost importance." Ending the line of debate with Elizabeth, his steel gaze then transferred to Edward. "And you, son. What sort of example are you setting for your sister when you do the same? I need you here, Edward. As the future leader of this kingdom and the realm, I need you here learning and participating in the ruling of your kingdom."

Edward sighed as if bored with the topic of conversation, his lean shoulders relaxed within the chair, though he openly accepted the lethal barbs of disapproval from his father. "Father, I do not wish to be king. You know this."

Elizabeth watched as her father's face turned from cream to crimson as his anger consumed him. "You do not have a choice my son! You are the crowned prince of the Highlands and the Realm. You will be king once I am gone, and you will respect the position!"

Edward stood abruptly, his chair slightly tilting from his quick departure. "I do not wish it, Father. I know who I am. And if you knew me well at all you would see I am not fit to be king in the first place. I am not like you, nor do I wish to be."

"Absurd!" Her father slammed his fist against the worn table causing Elizabeth and Alayna to jolt in their seats. He then shook his head in disappointment. "Do not think I do not know your whereabouts my son. You are flirting with a dangerous consequence."

"Perhaps so, Father, but that is my decision to make."

"It is a decision of death!" Her father warned, a subtle sadness in his tone. His eyes followed his handsome son as Edward paced in front of his desk. Edward, the prince. His only son. The unruly mass of black hair that framed a lean and chiseled face of creamy skin and piercing blue eyes that resembled his mother's, the late Queen Rebecca. King Granton shook his head of the sentimental thoughts of his late wife and focused his attention, and frustration, back on his son.

Elizabeth sat knowing her father, King Granton, spoke of Edward's interest in the Unfading Lands. Alayna seemed confused by the current turn in the conversation, but Elizabeth knew her father had found out her brother's secret. She was not sure how, but he did. And poor Edward— his heart torn between love for the woman on the other side and his duties here in the Realm. She knew his heart was here with his family and kingdom, but she also knew of his desire to confront Lancer, the leader of the Unfading Lands about a truce. Not that it would help. Everyone knew that if you crossed the boundary line between the Highlands and the Land of Unfading Beauty, you could never return. Many had tried crossing out of pure curiosity, but then found themselves forever displaced in the strange land.

"It is a land of selfishness and vanity!" Her father raised his voice again, and she jumped in her seat as she attempted to stay focused on the conversation.

"How do you know, Father? Have you ever crossed the boundary? No. You have not!" Edward exclaimed.

"Neither have you! You believe yourself to be in love with a young woman over there, but it is not true, Edward. The woman is a ploy. Lancer wants you to cross the boundary. Do you not see? He is tempting you to cross. He knows you are the next ruler of the Realm and therefore wants to weaken our kingdom by enticing you to cross. Do not give him the victory, or our lands will suffer the consequences."

"I do not wish to cross, Father. I wish to retrieve her and bring her here. Because you are right, I do love her. Cecilia is the one my heart belongs, and I wish her to be free from Lancer's power."

"Cecilia?!" King Granton boomed, "How do you know her name? No sound carries through the boundary."

"No sound, yes. But animals do. We converse through letters." Edward explained.

King Granton's face darkened to a deeper shade of red—*almost purple*, Elizabeth thought. "You are treading in dangerous waters, Edward. I forbid you to see the girl again. There will be consequences for both of you if anything were to happen. Your future has been decided upon. You will marry Princess Melody of the Western Kingdom and together you will rule the Realm."

"I will not give up, Father. I do not wish to marry the princess. I will bring Cecilia out of the Unfading Lands."

"You are a fool! No one is able to leave the Unfading Lands once they have crossed. That is their punishment! They choose to cross in order to remain young and beautiful and that is where they stay. Even if you succeeded, how do we know she will not die here? How old is she? How long has she been in the Lands? Would her age catch up to her even if she did cross? These are questions that must remain unanswered, Edward." King Granton looked to his two daughters with concern. "Dare I even ask if you two have a desire towards the Unfading Lands?"

Alayna firmly shook her head. Elizabeth tilted her head as she pondered the question. *Did she want to cross the boundary? Was she curious?* Noting the concern in her father's gaze, she finally shook her head. She really did not have a desire to cross the boundary. The underlying fear of never seeing her family or friends again being the main reason. She was a curious woman, but her curiosity had its limits.

"Good. You two may be excused. I will discuss my matters with each of you later. Your brother and I have more to discuss."

Elizabeth and Alayna stood and bowed to their father. Elizabeth lightly squeezed her brother's shoulder before exiting, hoping to encourage.

As she stepped through the doorway, her sister, Alayna, exhaled loudly, releasing the tension from the room from her lungs. "Can you believe Edward? Loving a woman across the boundary? Have you ever heard of such nonsense?"

"I think Edward has the right to love whomever he wishes." Elizabeth's simple reply caused Alayna to abruptly turn with wide brown eyes.

"You cannot be serious, Lizzy. Do you know how dangerous the people are over there?"

"Do you?" Elizabeth countered. No one knew how dangerous the people were, because no one had willingly crossed and come back successfully. So how could anyone know?

Alayna shook her blonde curls. "I'm surprised at you, Elizabeth. I know you and Edward are close, but to have him even thinking about the boundary— how can you remain so calm?"

"Alayna, Edward said he did not wish to cross. He wanted her to cross. They are trying to figure out a way she can. I think it is quite romantic really."

Alayna rolled her steady brown eyes. "Romantic? You? We are royals, we do not get the luxury of being romantic. Our fates and marriages are decided for us."

"But is that really fair? Have you not ever liked someone, Alayna? Or loved someone? Do you not wish to marry whom you please?" Elizabeth pleaded as if an ally was her only desire. "I know I wish to marry the man I want, otherwise I wish to not marry at all."

"Even if it means bringing peace to the kingdom?" Alayna watched as Elizabeth nodded.

"I think the people of our kingdom would want us to be happy."

Alayna laughed in disbelief. "You have much to learn, sister. Much to learn. Word has it that Father is already looking for a mate for you from the West."

Elizabeth stopped in her tracks and watched as her sister slowly turned with an amused smile on her face. "But I am only eighteen." Elizabeth defended. "You are older than I am. Should you not marry first?"

"Elizabeth we are both well past the marrying age. Besides, Father is looking for me to marry a man from the Eastern Kingdom. We must keep our allies in good relations, and marriages will be the seal of allegiance for all parties involved."

Elizabeth's mouth dropped open. "But I do not wish to marry right now."

"Then perhaps you should talk to Father about that." Alayna turned and continued on her way towards her wing of the castle, her pale, pink dress sashaying behind her.

Elizabeth sighed and began walking towards the kitchen. She needed one of Gretchen's sweet jam tarts to remove the sour taste in her mouth that lingered from her conversation. Marriage?! Yes, she had thought of marrying one day, but not right now. And certainly not to a complete stranger. When the time came, she wanted to marry for love. And like Edward, she would fight for that right.

∞

The nerve. How dare his father forbid him from seeing Cecilia?! Edward paced along the cool, stone floor of his bedchamber and realized he needed to see Cecilia and talk with her. He needed to see her soft, blonde curls and sky blue eyes, her easy smile and delicate features. He fiercely wanted to retrieve her from the Unfading Lands. They had tried for two years, testing different methods, passing tokens to and from one another, but to attempt her own passage— Perhaps they should try tonight. He needed to make haste considering his father's plans to pursue him a mate from the Western Kingdom had recently been the newest topic of discussion. Time was limited. Time was of the essence. In a matter of months, he and his two sisters would be married off to the prospective kingdoms, and his time with Cecilia would be gone. He gently rubbed his palm over his heart anticipating the heartache that would ensue. No. He could not let that happen. He would not.

He wanted Cecilia. Only Cecilia. He loved her. Edward paced towards the mahogany bureau across the room and snatched his leather satchel. Quickly packing a pair of trousers and a shirt, he grabbed his journal, and stuffed it into the small pocket inside his brocade coat. He opened his door quietly, the rusty hinges creaking in the still night air. He donned his emerald cape and retreated into the shadows. Knowing most everyone in the castle had retired for the night, he quickly made his way down the vast hallway to the back stairwell, careful to walk in the cover of darkness and away from the lanterns that shined light amongst the halls. No guards would stand at the foot of the stairwell, he knew, for he had made this same escape many times in the past. Cecilia would be at the boundary line waiting for him. He knew it. She seemed to always know when he would be there.

∞

Combing his way through the thickened tree line, the moonlight glistened off of the Rollings River, the smooth surface spotlighting the moon's beams. *No lantern needed*, he mused. He stepped onto the river's banks and walked down the shoreline to the boundary between his father's kingdom and the Unfading Lands. The river, divided perpendicularly in half by the boundary, rippled onward downstream, the sound fading into the distance. The cloudy haze of the boundary, more transparent at night, allowed a clearer view of Cecilia's face as it reflected the moonlight. She was there. He smiled as he spotted her. He spotted a small bunny hovering nearby in a clover patch and thistles. Stalking quietly over, he quickly reached into the shrub and snatched it. He eased onto the large boulder next to the river and tore a piece of paper from his journal and wrote to her eagerly, tying it to the back of the rabbit. He then placed the small creature on the ground at the base of the boundary line. The young rabbit sniffed the air and turned to run away, but Edward caught him, giving him a firm nudge to hop across the line. The rabbit stopped as soon as it crossed. Cecilia bent down to retrieve the letter, stroking the young rabbit and softly nuzzling her cheek against its downy fur in thanks. Hoping and waiting she agreed to attempt to cross, Edward waved her forward in love. She read the letter, her eyes widening in surprise.

When she gazed up at him, her radiant eyes filled with love. She visibly took a deep breath and stepped forward. She gently raised her hand and pushed it through the fog. A bolt of light, fierce, electrifying and bright, rippled along the boundary wall and Cecilia flew back with such force Edward prayed for no injury. She landed on her back several yards away, Edward's heart pounding in his chest as he waited for movement. She slowly stood up and cowered in pain. A tear slid down her cheek as she shook her head. She could not cross. The boundary was too strong. Edward paced. *What was he to do? He loved her.* He thought about his Father's harsh words and the unfortunate marriage he would be forced into for the sake of the kingdom. *Did no one care if he were happy?* He wanted to be with the woman he loved, not with a stranger. If his Father would help him find a way to break down the barrier instead of fearing it, then all kingdoms could unite, including the Unfading Lands. The people would be free of its curse! Perhaps if he crossed, his Father would then want to help. Then he could also work from inside the Lands against Lancer, overturn his rule and perhaps break down the boundary from the inside out. He could also see Cecilia every day and speak to her every day. Oh, how he longed to hear her voice. He looked into her sweet gaze and then pointed at himself and to the boundary line. Cecilia's face changed from love to horror. She vehemently shook her head and waved her hands "no."

But Edward would not be swayed. He pulled out his journal and began to write a letter to his sister, Elizabeth. He knew she would be the first to discover his absence, and she would also know just where to look for him. He would wait on the other side of the boundary for her in the morning, to watch her and make sure she retrieved it. She was the only one who knew where to find him. He would figure out how to restore the Unfading Lands, whether his father wanted to help him or not.

He tied the letter to the limb of a nearby tree and then stepped close to the boundary. Cecilia stood with her hands over her heart as she worried her bottom lip in anticipation and nervousness. His toes tingled the closer he stepped, the sensation seeping through his feet, up his calves and into his chest. A deep breath later, Prince Edward of the Northern Highlands Kingdom and of the Realm, crossed the boundary into the Land of Unfading Beauty.

FIVE YEARS LATER…

CHAPTER 1

Elizabeth sat warily, noting the discomfort that lingered about the table and the room at the sight of her father's empty chair. The elaborate dining table extending the length of the room always seemed a lonely place when not everyone feasted. She plucked the seam at the edge of her lace-cuffed sleeve and waited patiently for the attendants to finish delivering the dishes. She sat quietly by herself as dish after dish of food was brought before her to the table. The smell of the breakfast breads making her nauseous, she reached for her water goblet instead.

"What do you mean he is not in his chambers?" Alayna demanded as she walked into the room, her burgundy dress incessantly swishing and adding a flair of drama to her entrance. She sat in her seat at the end of the table, opposite the end her father would normally occupy. "Father should not be up and walking around. He is ill."

Tomas, their father's most loyal attendant bowed politely, his aged frame looking frail beneath his emerald, satin trimmed coat. "Yes, Princess Alayna. However, your father requested a stroll in the garden. He needed fresh air this morning."

"Tomas, you should not leave him unattended. Please see to the King and that he makes his way back inside the castle." Alayna ordered sternly without glancing up from unfolding her napkin and laying it delicately in her lap. Tomas bowed obediently and walked away.

"You should not be rude to Tomas, sister. He is only doing what Father asks of him. Plus, it is not going to hurt Father to retrieve some fresh air." Elizabeth stated softly to her sister. "If anything, I believe it will help."

"I appreciate your input, sister, but I politely reject it." Alayna replied with determination, her jaw set defiantly against the world. "Father must learn that he needs to stay indoors."

Elizabeth looked away from her sister and to her plate in frustration. She pushed the food around with her fork as she tried to muster up an appetite. The tender egg yolk burst and began to seep across her plate, the yellow puddle normally a temptation to dip her bread in, only reminded her of her childhood. Her father had introduced her to the delicious combination of bread in yolk. She took another sip of her water to wash away the sudden sadness that fluttered through her heart. Her father's health was failing. It had been since Edward's betrayal of crossing the border into the Unfading Lands. None of them had ever really been the same. Alayna attempted to fill the void of their brother by stepping into the role of successor to their father. But the transition placed tremendous pressure on her sister's shoulders, the result usually being an indignant attitude. Elizabeth's defiance to everything her sister recommended did not help matters either, she admitted to herself. Not that she did not believe her sister capable of the position of queen, but that accepting her sister as queen meant dismissing her father as king, and she could not bring herself to do so just yet.

Alayna cleared her throat and fluffed her skirts to sit comfortably in her chair. "So, we will have visitors coming in all week long and staying at the castle. Our friends from the Eastern and Western Kingdoms will be arriving starting tomorrow. Remember, Elizabeth," Alayna waited to continue until Elizabeth glanced her direction. "Remember we are attempting to establish a renewed alliance with both of these kingdoms, so it is important we remain open to the possibilities of a merger."

Elizabeth rolled her eyes. She escaped her father's ploys of marriage years earlier and had finally convinced him to refrain from the pursuit of a mate for her until she was ready. Her sister, since stepping into the leadership role, seemed to have Elizabeth's love life as her top priority.

"Don't roll your eyes at me, sister." Alayna chuckled as she spoke causing Elizabeth to relax. "I'm just saying I would like for you to keep your eyes open amongst all the gentlemen that will be here. You never know, perhaps one of them will catch your eye."

"And what of your eye, future Queen?" Elizabeth teased, her blue eyes dancing. "Does our kingdom not need a king before they do a prince?"

Alayna grimaced. "Yes, well, perhaps that is a just question; unfortunately, I believe my fate has been decided. Father seems to think it is in our best interest if I align with the Renaldi's of the South."

"The Renaldi's?!" Elizabeth choked on her sip of water, her attendant Mary stepping forward to aid in her recovery by lightly patting her on the back. Elizabeth waved her off and patted her chest to clear her airway and then gaped at her sister with eyes wide in shock and mixed with horror. "You cannot be serious? Why? They are horrid, barbaric, our enemies. Why would Father ever subject you to that kind of cruelty?"

Alayna's caramel gaze softened at Elizabeth's concern. "Yes, we know. However, think about it. The strength of the Unfading Lands has grown considerably in the last five years since Edward crossed. As Father weakens, Lancer strengthens. Think of how strong we could be if we not only renew allegiances with the East and West, but also become allies with the South. Lancer and the Lands would not be able to withstand that unification and shifting of power, and the Lands will weaken. We cannot afford for that boundary to keep moving over our lands. We have lost considerable ground the last few years as the boundary has pushed its way further up the river."

Elizabeth sat stunned, wracking her brain in an effort to wrap her mind around the idea of her sister marrying into the most despicable kingdom. "But the Renaldi's? There has to be another way. I want you to marry for love, not obligation."

"And I appreciate that, Lizzy." Alayna lightly squeezed her hand. "But I have come to terms with my fate. I know what I must do, and I will do it for the sake of the kingdom. It is the best decision for me."

"No. It is the best decision for the kingdom. Not for you." Elizabeth corrected with a tinge of annoyance in her voice.

They heard a shuffling noise filter through the room as footsteps neared the dining hall. Tomas walked back into the room, followed by their father. Elizabeth bolted from her seat to her father's side. "Father! It is so good to see you up and about this morning." She flashed him a warm smile, the small dimple in her left cheek emerging briefly before he lightly cupped her cheek. "It is good to see you as well, sweetheart."

He eased himself into his seat his cheeks flushed with the exertion from his walk. He flipped his napkin from its home on his plate to place it in his lap. He ate heartily, his appetite greatly improved from the previous days. Elizabeth sat back in her chair and began to eat with a heartier appetite as well, but her concern for her sister's future engagement twisted her heart. "Father, is it true you wish to align Alayna with a Renaldi?"

King Granton looked up from his plate from one daughter to the next. "It is."

"Why?"

"Elizabeth!" Alayna scolded. "It has been decided."

"Father—" Elizabeth continued as if Alayna's interruption meant nothing, "I must protest. The Renaldi's are a cruel family and the Southern Kingdom has been a nuisance for years. How could you ever desire one of your daughters to marry one of them?"

King Granton listened patiently, his tenderness towards his daughters evident in his light blue eyes. "My dear Elizabeth, Alayna and I have discussed multiple options, and we both feel her betrothal to a Renaldi could aid in our defense against the Unfading Lands."

"I understand that, but--"

King Granton held up his hand, warding off any further comments from Elizabeth and causing her to frown. "That matter is settled, Lizzy. Unless you would like to discuss alignment plans for yourself."

"No, thank you." She answered firmly, her temper rising within her chest and flushing her face.

"Very well then." King Granton sipped from his goblet as he watched his eldest daughter filter through some papers. "How goes the preparations for our guests, Alayna?"

"Going well, Father. I believe the Eastern Kingdom will be arriving tomorrow. King Eamon and two of his sons will be joining us. The following day, the Western Kingdom will be arriving with King Anthony along with his daughter and son as well. It seems we will have a full house. No word from the Renaldi's as of yet."

Her father grunted as he took a bite of oat cake. "It will be good to see Eamon. It has been too long since I last saw my dear friend."

"I believe he feels the same way, Father." Alayna smiled. "His letter was quite attentive and sweet. I will have Tomas bring it to your chambers after breakfast."

The King nodded as he continued eating his breakfast. "And what of you, Lizzy girl?" He asked tenderly as he gazed at his youngest daughter, forgiveness of her previous outburst evident in his voice. "Are you ready for some male companionship the next few weeks?"

Elizabeth felt her face heat as the blush colored her cheeks. "I do not see why I would have male companionship the next few weeks, Father. However, I do intend to help Alayna with whatever she needs."

King Granton chuckled at the defiant tone in his daughter's voice. "Allow me to clarify, Lizzy. King Eamon is bringing two of his sons... His two unmarried sons. King Anthony is bringing his unmarried son as well. I am sure they will all have intentions of courting you over the next couple of weeks. You'd best be prepared."

Elizabeth forcefully laid her hands on the table. "How many times do I need to repeat myself? I do not wish to be courted! Can I not enjoy my youth? Why do they not court Alayna? She is the eldest, after all."

"Your sister is potentially betrothed to another. We have already established that." King Granton replied with patience.

"*Potentially* being the key word, Father. The Renaldi's have not even replied to our invitation. Should that not give us some inclination to where we rank on their priority list? Besides, would you not rather have one of your daughters aligned with your dear friend King Eamon's kingdom?" Elizabeth's pleading gaze caused her father to smile.

"I wish that very much, Lizzy. I think a marriage between our kingdom and Eamon's would continue our hearty friendship and alliance to the greatest degree. But it is you that must be open to the possibility. Alayna is spoken for."

"Until the Renaldi's show up and sweep her off her feet, I refuse to believe we have aligned ourselves successfully." Elizabeth crossed her arms over her corset and exhaled in a deep sigh. "I'm going for a ride." She abruptly stood from her chair and quickly walked over to kiss her father's worn cheek. "I shall return later."

King Granton watched her retreating back in dismay and shook his head.

"She will come around, Father." Alayna eased.

"I hope you're right, Alayna. I hope you're right."

∞

Elizabeth hurried up the stairway to her bedchamber and slammed her door behind her. Renaldi's?! Marriage?! She quickly changed into her riding pants and braided her thick waves of dark hair. Feeling refreshed, she gazed in the floor length mirror beside the vanity table and giggled. She would never get used to seeing herself in trousers. However, they did make riding her horse much easier, as well as her lessons. She headed down the stairs again, passing through the dining hall. She heard her sister's loud gasp.

"Lizzy! What are you wearing?!"

Elizabeth froze and a slow smile spread across her lips as she stood proudly with her fists on her narrow hips. "They are trousers. Like them?"

"No." Alayna simply stated. "They are scandalous. Women do not wear trousers. What on Earth were you thinking?"

Elizabeth shrugged her shoulders. "I like them. They make riding more comfortable."

"You must change at once. No one must see you in those. Who made you those horrid pants?"

"I asked Mary to make them for me."

"Mary!" Alayna called loudly, her shrill voice making Elizabeth cringe. Elizabeth's attendant quickly made her way into the room and bowed.

"Yes, milady?"

"Did you create my sister's terrible trousers?"

Mary's face blanched and she nervously glanced at Elizabeth. "Yes, milady." She answered softly, her gaze shifting to her feet.

"Do not scold Mary for my request." Elizabeth interrupted adamantly. "She made them because I asked for them."

"Yes, well this is the last time I want to ever see those trousers. Go change into your riding dress, Elizabeth, and then you may leave." Alayna went back to her ledger as if the matter had been dropped.

"Come, Mary." Elizabeth motioned for her attendant to follow her out of the room and back upstairs.

Once inside her chamber again, Elizabeth whirled towards Mary with bright eyes full of mischief. Mary inwardly groaned. That look was never good. "So Alayna does not want me wearing trousers, but if she does not know I'm wearing them, then no harm done, right? I need you to sew me a skirt that ties around my waist and covers my trousers. I will wear it out of the castle, and once in the horse stall, I can take it off and ride in my trousers."

"I am not sure that is a wise decision, Princess Elizabeth. She seemed quite adamant about your apparel."

Mary watched as Elizabeth paced back and forth with her hand under her chin, deep in thought.

"Nevertheless, it is my request. My corset will remain the same as it is now, but to tie the skirt around my waist it will look like a normal riding dress. I think it will work. I need to be wearing these trousers for my lessons, Mary. Please?"

Mary nodded curtly and motioned for Elizabeth to choose one of her current dresses to make the changes to. Elizabeth grabbed a pale blue dress that had seen better days and handed it to Mary.

"For today, I will remain in my trousers, I will just use the back stairwell to make my way to the stalls. Thank you, Mary."

"But Elizabeth!" Mary called at her retreating back. "I am to go with you when you leave the castle."

Smiling sweetly, Elizabeth turned and winked before darting out her door and down the back stairwell.

CHAPTER 2

Elizabeth waved as she spotted her brother through the boundary fog. He grinned and laughed heartily as he pointed to her trousers. She spun in a small circle so he could see her wardrobe. She then reached into her saddlebag and withdrew her small bundle of parchment. She then began to write to him. As she penned her last sentence, she walked over to a small shrub and reached inside the heavy foliage. Withdrawing a small rabbit, she lightly snuggled it close and stroked its fur. "Hello there, Thatcher." She greeted the small animal as she tied her note to the string around its neck. She walked with Thatcher in her arms over to the boundary line and lightly nudged the rabbit to cross over. Once upon the other side, Edward untied her letter and read:

Hello Brother!

I'm sorry I was late, but Alayna caught sight of my trousers and sent me back to my chambers to change at once. However, I came via the same stairwell that brought you here. I am ready for training today. I hope you can see the targets I have created and hung on the trees. I hope to be the fearsome fighter needed for the battle against the Unfading Lands. Any news on your side? Has Lancer caught on to your scheme? How is Cecilia?

Edward withdrew from the line and began writing upon the parchment as Elizabeth began unholstering her sword. She practiced her footwork as he wrote. She swung her sword over her head and tapped the first wooden target. As it swung, she fought her invisible foe and ducked as the target swung over her head. Her movements smooth, quick, and fluid as she worked her way around her small arena with impeccable skill. When she finished jabbing the last target, she glanced over at the boundary line. Edward stood smiling proudly as Thatcher sat on her side of the line. As she walked forward, Edward withdrew his own sword and struck a defensive pose. He motioned to the straight and firm arm he held while holding his sword. Elizabeth nodded, knowing she needed to work on her defensive frame more. Her arms were not as strong as they needed to be to hold a firm stance for long. She untied his parchment from Thatcher's neck.

She sat and read:

Dearest Elizabeth,

Nice trousers! I bet those did give Alayna heart failure. How is Father's health? No news on my side in regard to Lancer. There is strong opposition towards him, but without the ability to flee his realm, there is little the people can do here. Cecilia is doing wonderfully. She sends her best regards to you.

Your swordsmanship has improved greatly this past week. I see your lessons have paid off, dear sister. Does Alayna or Father know of your lessons or skills? I have a strong inclination you withhold that information from them. Then again, that is probably a wise decision. Your markings have shifted the last couple of days. This can only mean that Father's realm is weakening. Lancer's strength remains powerful, people cross every day. Is Father doing anything to prevent the Lands from growing? I fear for you and Alayna. I pray you two will never have to cross the boundary line.

Elizabeth quickly glanced up as her brother brushed the coat of his horse and waited patiently for her to answer his letter. She quickly made haste:

Father is still weak, but I believe his stubbornness keeps him alive these days. I will not lie, it is one attribute I most admire in him, though I will never tell him for fear we will always tangle our antlers together. Neither Father nor Alayna know of my lessons with you. I find it best they not find out as well. Such behavior is unbecoming of a lady... or in Alayna's eyes it is. I did notice my markings have moved.

Elizabeth glanced to her left at the red markings she carved into the rich clay. Two notches, a foot length apart from one another now appeared on Edward's side of the boundary. The boundary line had swallowed more of her father's realm in less than a week.

I fear the Unfading Lands may swallow my training arena soon. Although, Alayna and Father are attempting to gain strength among the kingdoms. Tomorrow the Kings from the Eastern and Western kingdoms will be arriving to the castle, along with their sons. Father and Alayna hope for a merger between one of the Eastern and Western kingdoms through a marriage. Not for Alayna mind you, but for me. Father has promised Alayna to the Renaldi's. Can you believe that? The Rendali's, Edward?! Why can't Alayna not wed one of the princes from the East or West? Wouldn't we rather have a new King the people will respect? But what do I know of the matter? I fear for our sister's happiness and the conditions of our kingdom if she weds a Renaldi. I pray she falls in love with one of the princes coming tomorrow. Perhaps that will change her mind and Father's.

Elizabeth sent Thatcher across the boundary and picked up her sword again, continuing with her practice.

Edward sat on a large boulder as he read his sister's letter. He grinned at the thought of Elizabeth marrying. His little sister had so much spirit, it would take a strong man to keep up with her. Then again, he longed for her to find love. He also hoped Alayna would find love as well. The Renaldi's were not a family to be linked with no matter how desperate his father's realm seemed. *What must his father be thinking?*

Sounds to me you will have an exciting next few weeks, sister. Be on guard, I figure you will have several gentleman callers after you and your trousers. Should you be forced into a decision of courtship, I highly recommend a prince from the East. The Eastern Kingdom has been friends with our family for many years, and they are decent human beings. However, if you wish to remain a maiden Princess a little while longer, I say go for it, little sister! You are a brave young woman who has the world and many adventures ahead of you. I must go now. I hear the bugle. Lancer's guards will be making the rounds soon. I must not be seen conversing across the boundary line. I love you, and have fun this week.

Edward sent Thatcher across the line and then quickly mounted his horse. With a wave, he disappeared as quickly as he had come. Elizabeth read his letter then tucked it into her saddlebag. She mounted her horse, Lenora, and headed back towards the castle. She enjoyed her time with her brother. She came to their spot every day in hopes of finding him there. Unsure of his schedule or the precautions he must take, she was never upset if he did not make an appearance. He was always sure to leave her a letter on Thatcher if his absence spread more than three days. He knew she would otherwise worry about his safety.

∞

She dismounted Lenora in the stable and led her towards her stall. She then unbelted her saddle and slipped it off, carrying the heavy weight over to its stand. She grabbed the bristled brush and began to swipe it over Lenora's chestnut hide. The sleek horse snorted in pleasure. Elizabeth smiled as Lenora nuzzled her shoulder. "I know girl, you love having your hair done." Lenora whinnied softly, and Elizabeth giggled. Finished, she stowed her tools and quickly and stealthily made her way up the back stairwell. Once inside her chambers, she retrieved her letters from Edward and placed them in an intricately carved wooden box, that had once belonged to her mother, under her bed along with all their previous letters. A knock sounded on her door as she began slipping into a new dress.

"Come in."

"Princess Elizabeth," Mary entered and quickly stepped forward and laced Elizabeth's corset. "King Anthony has arrived early with his son and daughter. Your father and sister wish for you to join them downstairs to receive them."

Elizabeth quickly braided her wind-blown hair and pinched her cheeks. "Do I look like I have spent the morning outside?"

Mary lightly dabbed Elizabeth's throat with rose water and shook her head. "No, milady. You look beautiful as always."

Elizabeth smiled at the sweet compliment and then grabbed Mary's hand, pulling her towards the stairwell. Taking the stairs two at a time, Elizabeth hurried through the corridor leading to the main hall. She slid into place beside her sister, Alayna casting a look of approval at her punctuality just as the castle doors opened. A tall, lean man stepped forward, his white, neatly trimmed beard the only indication of his older age. His red tunic adorned with brass buttons and buckles and his cloak the white fur of a winter wolf, hung snugly around his trim frame. The coat of arms for the Western Kingdom, a lone white wolf encircled by a golden ring blazed with fire, stitched on the front of his tunic, sealed the man's identity as King Anthony. A young woman, petite and blonde headed, stepped closely behind him in an intricate red and same white furs as her father, followed by a tall, lean young man with dark hair and eyes dressed in his finest apparel.

Elizabeth's father stood from his throne and opened his arms. "Anthony! Dear friend! Good of you to come!"

King Anthony stepped forward, along with his children, and bowed humbly to King Granton. He then stood and walked forward embracing her father in a tight hug. "Good to see you, Granton. You are a sight for sore eyes."

"Allow me to present to you my son, Isaac, and my daughter, Melody." King Anthony motioned towards his children, who politely bowed and curtsied again.

"Of course!" King Granton beamed. "My have you two grown into a handsome man and beautiful young lady. I present to you my daughter, Alayna, future Queen of the Highlands and the Realm, and my daughter Elizabeth, Princess of the Highlands and the Realm."

Alayna and Elizabeth curtsied politely.

Prince Isaac's eyes never left Elizabeth as she stepped closer to her father. She squirmed under his scrutiny. *He's a handsome man*, she thought. But something in his eyes told her he was not a man to be trusted.

Her father, noticing the young man's attraction to his daughter, grinned and motioned towards Tomas. "Tomas, why don't you show our guests to their quarters. We will allow you some rest after your travels and will reconvene at dinner."

King Anthony and his children bowed and followed Tomas out of the room. Once the main hall doors closed, Alayna giggled. "Looks like Prince Isaac fancies you, Elizabeth."

Elizabeth shook her head in denial. "No. He does not."

King Granton chuckled at Elizabeth's adamant tone. "Well, remember Elizabeth, keep an open mind."

"Yes, Father." Though she intended to forget about Prince Isaac the moment she retired to her chambers.

∞

The next morning Elizabeth awoke to the sun shining through the heavy velvet drapes and dancing across her closed eyelids. She sighed, stretched, and slowly crawled from beneath her covers. A light knock sounded on her door and Mary stepped inside. "Good morning, Princess. Looks to be a beautiful day today."

"Indeed." Elizabeth groaned on a yawn. She slowly walked to her wardrobe and opened the doors. "I'm not quite sure what to wear today Mary, perhaps you will pick for me?"

Mary smiled and nodded, walking over and immediately withdrawing a pale green dress with cream corset and accents.

"Good choice, but it is awfully formal, don't you think?"

"No ma'am. With the King from the East arriving today, your sister asked that I have you dress for the occasion, formal cloaks and all. This green one always makes your eyes shine bright, and dare I say with a glint of mischief?"

Elizabeth laughed. "Oh, Mary. You know me too well sometimes. I would be honored to wear your choice today. My cloak will also look wonderful with this color." Elizabeth praised, as she gazed at her formal cloak that hung by her door. Emerald, the colors of her father's realm and the Northern Kingdom. She sighed as she traced the image of the crowned crest with her eyes. *Her father's kingdom. Soon to be Alayna's kingdom.* Mary pulled the strings to her corset, jerking Elizabeth back to attention. She placed a hand over her chest as Mary's diligent fingers made swift work of the ties.

The two women quickly worked to ready Elizabeth for the day. Mary brushed her hair and braided Elizabeth's dark mane, pulling loose strands to frame her face. Her braid draped over her left shoulder and her corset tied, Elizabeth stood and lightly dabbed rose water along her neck and wrists.

"Perfect. I feel so pretty today I may just skip my lessons for the day." Elizabeth twirled around in her dress and then opened her bedchamber door. Mary followed as she normally did, and the two made their way down the master stairway that led to the main hall.

When Elizabeth reached the bottom of the stairs she turned towards the dining hall. Her boot slipping on the newly waxed floor, she caught herself on the banister and sighed. "Did they wax the floors last night?"

Mary nodded. "Yes ma'am. Best be careful today."

Elizabeth stepped lightly as she made her way to the dining table. King Anthony sat beside her father, Alayna and Melody sat deep in conversation, and Isaac only stared at her as she entered the room.

"Princess Elizabeth." Mary announced, causing all heads to turn towards her.

"My goodness, someone must have been tired this morning." Her father chuckled as Elizabeth hastily made her way to her seat next to Prince Isaac.

"Good morning, all." Elizabeth greeted as Renee placed a silver platter in front of her with fluffy eggs, buttered toast, and a slice of ham.

"Your agenda for the day, sister." Always down to business, Alayna handed Elizabeth a piece of rolled parchment with a ribbon tied around it. Elizabeth's right eyebrow arched in curiosity. She reached to untie the ribbon, but Alayna cleared her throat. Elizabeth glanced up to see her sister shaking her head. Elizabeth placed the parchment in her lap and began eating her breakfast.

"So, Princess Elizabeth, what do you normally do on such a beautiful day as this?" Prince Isaac leaned close as he spoke, his dark brown eyes pouring into Elizabeth's. She blinked and went back to her plate, trying to think of evasive tactics.

"I have yet to decide what I shall do for today, Prince Isaac. Normally, however, I go for a ride on my horse." Elizabeth's quick and direct response had Alayna shooting her a warning gaze.

"I see. Perhaps we shall embark on a ride together later this afternoon?" Prince Isaac winked as Elizabeth's gaze snapped to his.

"Perhaps." Elizabeth answered politely, even though in her heart and mind she knew she would not be riding horses with Prince Isaac if she had a say in it.

She finished her meal and Renee retrieved her plate.

"Thank you, Renee. It was delicious, as always. Please give my compliments to Gretchen as well."

"You're welcome, milady, and I will." Renee blushed at the praise and quickly made haste back to the kitchen.

"You praise her too kindly, I'm afraid." Prince Isaac stated.

"Pardon?" Elizabeth asked in surprise. "Are you unhappy with your meal, Prince Isaac?"

"Not at all. Though eggs, ham, and toast are not difficult to cook."

"That may be, but I appreciate her cooking them nonetheless." Elizabeth responded. "If you will excuse me." She laid her burgundy napkin on the table and stood holding the parchment from her sister in her hands. "I will speak with you later, Alayna."

Alayna nodded her dismissal and watched as her sister and her attendant walked out of the dining hall. Poor Prince Isaac did not stand a chance with her sister, and Alayna found herself wondering if Elizabeth's dislike of the prince may be the wisest decision her little sister had currently made. Alayna mentally noted to keep her eye on Prince Isaac.

∞

"Can you believe that man?" Elizabeth asked in disgust as she walked through the castle gardens and clipped a yellow rose for a flower bouquet. She handed the rose to Mary who gently laid it in her basket.

"He meant no disrespect, ma'am." Mary answered.

"Yes, he did. Not to me, but to Renee and Gretchen."

"Of course, milady."

"Mary, how many times do I have to tell you? You do not always have to agree with me." Elizabeth chuckled as her attendant blushed. "My apologies, milady."

"For heaven's sake, don't apologize!" Elizabeth giggled and lightly tucked a rose behind Mary's ear before turning to the sound of hooves coming up the royal entrance. She spotted the pale blue and white striped flag of the Eastern Kingdom with its majestic stallion emblazoned across the middle, blowing in the wind.

She untied the string from her sister's parchment and handed it to Mary. "Looks like a schedule for the day. Will you please keep me on schedule for Alayna?"

Mary nodded and then pointed towards the gate of the garden where Prince Isaac stood watching Elizabeth.

"Come, Mary." Elizabeth stated loudly, avoiding the prince. She turned towards the castle entrance. "It looks like King Eamon and his sons are arriving. I mustn't be late."

Elizabeth heard the doors to the castle open and began to trot at a brisk pace. She lifted the ends of her skirts and hustled as fast as was polite. She wasn't going to make it in time if she didn't run. "Come Mary, we must hurry!" She began to run, her heavy skirts and cloaks restraining her usual speed. "Blasted dresses." She mumbled.

She entered the main hall just as King Eamon bowed before her father. She tried to slow her pace, but the waxed floor betrayed her. She squealed as she slid across the floor, her arms waving frantically through the air for balance. Several heads turned as Elizabeth skidded across the floor. Alayna watched in horror as Elizabeth slid and stumbled straight towards King Eamon's son. The man turned just in time.

Elizabeth slammed into the man's arms, his strong embrace catching her and setting her feet correctly. She gripped his forearms, feeling the muscles beneath his crisp tunic. Her heart racing from her near fall, she slowly stood and straightened her posture.

"And that would be my daughter, Princess Elizabeth." Her father's voice rang with amusement as he watched Elizabeth attempt to compose herself.

"I am terribly sorry, my Lord." Elizabeth reluctantly stepped away from the strong embrace and glanced up. She gasped as she stared into the greenest and kindest gaze she had ever seen. She blushed at her outburst and politely curtsied.

The man chuckled. "I could not ask for a better welcome." He bowed towards her. "I am Prince Clifton, my lady."

Elizabeth nodded and slid into position next to her father's throne. King Eamon chuckled and bowed to her as well.

"It is so very good to see you, my friend." King Eamon stepped towards her father and hugged him. "You have two very beautiful, and spirited, daughters."

"Yes, indeed." King Granton agreed with a chuckle.

"Princess Elizabeth, may I introduce my sons, Prince Ryle and Prince Clifton." King Eamon's sons bowed once again.

When Elizabeth caught the emerald gaze of Prince Clifton, she blushed under his scrutiny but did not glance away. His eyes danced in amusement as he stood awaiting further direction from his father. He stood taller than his father and brother by several inches, Elizabeth noted. His broad shoulders and lean frame accentuated his height quite nicely. His green eyes shone bright against his tan skin and golden blonde hair. Hair in much need of a trim, Elizabeth thought, but she found she liked the unruliness of his mane and the way it brushed his collar. His pale blue tunic, the colors of the Eastern Kingdom, shone calmly and he wore them well.

His brother, Prince Ryle, stood tall as well, only a complete contrast in appearance with onyx hair and sharp blue eyes. Eyes, she noticed, that lingered upon her sister.

King Granton motioned towards Tomas. "Please, allow Tomas to show you to your quarters. You three must be tired from your journey."

"Actually, King Granton," Prince Ryle stepped forward, "I don't feel in much need of rest at the moment, but I did notice your horse stables. I wonder if I might borrow your arena there for a few hours?"

Pleased with the young man's response, King Granton nodded. "Of course. Please feel free to help yourself to any of our amenities during your stay. Allow my daughter, Alayna, to show you the way. She has business to discuss with the stableman."

Prince Ryle bowed in thanks and then offered his arm to Alayna. Dressed in her pale pink surcoat with mauve skirts and cream corset, Alayna showcased an immaculate feminine beauty Elizabeth knew she could never obtain. Alayna politely took the offered arm of Prince Ryle not even noticing the Prince's pleased expression, and they made their way out of the main hall.

Elizabeth softly smiled as she watched her sister exit with the handsome prince, with good thoughts and wishes, she prayed her sister found his companionship more pleasing than her Renaldi proposal.

"Elizabeth?" Her father called, bringing her attention back to their audience. "I trust you read the parchment from your sister?"

"I gave it to Mary, Father. She has promised to keep me on schedule." Elizabeth motioned to Mary, who shyly stepped forward.

"What on Earth do you have in your hair, Mary?" King Granton asked, pointing towards the rose Elizabeth had placed there previously in the garden.

Mary jolted and quickly fumbled to remove the flower from her hair. Elizabeth, dropping all formality, darted towards her attendant and grabbed Mary's hand and draped her arm around Mary's shoulders. "I placed it there, Father. Doesn't it look lovely?

Mary has the most beautiful hair, and how perfect a beautiful rose fits in it."

"It is most lovely, Mary." King Granton replied in understanding and nodded towards Elizabeth in dismissal.

Prince Clifton and King Eamon smiled at the exchange. Clifton, pleased the Princess seemed to value her attendant, found he wanted to converse with her more. It was not every day that royalty respected and enjoyed the company of their attendants.

"Tomas, if you would, please show the King and Prince Clifton to their chambers."

Tomas stepped forward and motioned for the men to follow.

Prince Clifton stepped forward then, causing Elizabeth's father and his own father to stare at him with amusement. "My Lord," he bowed. "I wonder if I might borrow your spirited daughter to guide me in the direction of your gardens? I find resting outside more favorable on a day such as this."

King Granton's mouth twitched as he tried not to laugh at the young man's obvious attraction and excuse to be near Elizabeth.

"Elizabeth would be happy to show you the way." He motioned for Elizabeth to step forward. She did not move until Mary lightly nudged her from behind. Clifton offered his arm, and Elizabeth shyly and slowly slipped her arm in his as she continued to gaze in his emerald eyes.

She swallowed hard and prayed her voice did not betray her. "It is right this way, my Lord." She whispered as she began to walk towards the castle exit.

King Eamon and King Granton grinned at one another as they watched their children leave arm in arm.

"You are quite an accomplished rider." Alayna complimented as Prince Ryle halted his mare and expertly dismounted. Smiling he wrung his reins through his gloved hands. "Yes, well, years of practice and lessons must have paid off." He began leading his horse towards the stables and Alayna walked leisurely beside him, the wind lightly teasing the golden curls framing her face.

"Do you ride, Princess?"

Alayna shook her head. "I'm afraid not. My sister does, quite well actually, but it is a skill I unfortunately did not learn."

Prince Ryle surveyed the Princess's face as she sweetly ran her hand over his mare's mane. Longing hid in the liquid caramel depths and had him stepping forward.

"You just hold onto the saddle horn." He explained.

Alayna blinked, shaking her head from her thoughts. "I'm sorry, what?"

Before she could think, Prince Ryle lifted her off of her feet and placed her into the saddle. She gasped and fumbled for a grasp, gripping the saddle horn. "W-what are you doing?" She glanced around the stables for an attendant but none were about. Prince Ryle swung into the saddle, his arms lightly wrapped around her as he took the reins. "Just hold onto the saddle horn, Princess. We are going to take a stroll."

"I-I do not wish for a ride. Thank you." She challenged. "I-I'd like to get down. Immediately. Please," she added softly as she realized Prince Ryle had no intention of setting her down. She watched as the ground moved beneath them and as her nerves slowly ebbed away, she raised her head to gaze at the rolling hills of fresh green grass.

"It's quite a different perspective, isn't it?" She had almost forgotten the man behind her. She sat sidesaddle, her left shoulder grazing against Prince Ryle's chest. She smelled the light scent of masculinity as she brought her gaze to his and he smiled. He leaned forward slightly. "I won't let you fall, Princess." His blue eyes calm and kind, Alayna released a carefree smile. He led the horse around the stable yard and then back into the stalls. Alayna felt the slight flush to her cheeks from the wind. How invigorating it had been, riding on such a creature. Prince Ryle slipped from the saddle and reached up to grasp her small waist. He lifted her as if she weighed nothing and gently placed her on her feet. She brushed a hand down the front of her skirts. "Thank you, Prince Ryle, for the lovely ride."

Ryle grinned at the Princess. No doubt he had terrified her, but she had quickly regained her regal composure and he hoped, enjoyed herself. "You're welcome, Princess. Thank you for the lovely company." The compliment had her blushing until a throat cleared at the entrance of the stable. Prince Isaac stood firmly with his hand on the hilt of his sword. "Ah, there you are Princess. Your father sent me to find you. He wishes to speak with you."

Gone was the carefree spirit, gone was the beautiful blush to her cheeks, all replaced by a stony face of calm and expectation. Alayna bowed to Ryle and quickly exited leaving the two princes eyeing one another cautiously.

"Prince Ryle, of the Eastern Kingdom." Ryle bowed politely towards Isaac, knowing full well who the man was.

"Prince Isaac, of the Western Kingdom." Isaac stated and bowed in return. "I see you and the Princess had a brisk ride." Isaac strolled into the stables over to the stall that housed his own horse and gently patted the animal's nose.

"Yes. The Princess wished to experience a ride."

"Is that so?" Isaac eyed him with curiosity. "Funny, Princess Alayna does not seem the type to wish for such frivolities when her duty is to remain at her father's side."

"Yes, well, today she did." Ryle lowered the stall door's bolt and removed his gloves. "It was a pleasure, Prince Isaac. I'm sure we will be seeing much of each other the next few weeks."

"Aye." Isaac bowed and watched as the eldest Eastern prince exited the stables, his eyes shooting arrows in his back. If anyone were to win the hand of one of King Granton's daughters, it would be him, not some prince from the Eastern Kingdom.

∞

"So Princess Elizabeth, tell me, what do you love most about your garden?" Prince Clifton continued to hold her arm in his as they walked the pebbled path through the royal garden. Roses bloomed on every archway and along each path. The pinks, purples, yellows, and reds creating a menagerie of beauty that almost captivated Prince Clifton as much as the Princess on his arm.

Elizabeth tilted her head in consideration of his question and grinned. "I'm not sure I could choose just one thing. I love the feel of the sunshine on my face, the smells of the different flowers, the butterflies, the dirt. It's a number of things I love." He noted the small dimple in her left cheek when she smiled and found it quite charming.

Clifton listened intently to the princess, her confident voice strong and direct. She truly was a beautiful woman. Her dark hair braided neatly in a style he had not ever seen, hung over her shoulder. The sage green dress she wore made her blue eyes and creamy complexion stand out against what seemed, the rest of the world. He could not help but feel flattered it was his arms she stumbled into that morning. As he thought about her response, his brow furrowed. "Did you say dirt?"

A light chuckle escaped her lips. "Yes, I did. I know it must sound strange, but I love the outdoors and all the different smells that go with it. Including dirt."

Clifton smiled at her honesty and fresh outlook. "I see. I would have to agree with you, Princess. The outdoors possess a freshness about them that relaxes and inspires."

Elizabeth gazed up at Prince Clifton's strong face as he looked over the horizon. Sensing her gaze, he glanced down into her bright blue eyes. Something hung in the air between them, Clifton could feel it. He wondered if the Princess felt it as well.

"Oh!" Elizabeth startled, breaking the moment. "Mary!" She turned around quickly, removing her arm from Clifton's.

"Yes, milady." Mary rushed forward. "Are you alright?"

"Is everything okay?" Prince Clifton lightly touched her elbow in concern.

"Yes, I apologize for the alarm. I just forgot something terribly important. Mary, would you please write a letter to my instructor and let him know I will not be at my lessons today?" Elizabeth narrowed her gaze at Mary, hoping she understood the meaning behind her words. She wanted her to leave a letter for Edward that she would not be at the boundary line.

Mary nodded. "Of course, milady. But I am to stay with you. Whom would you like to deliver it?"

"It must be you Mary. Only you." Elizabeth stated. "I'm sure I can twist Prince Clifton's arm into walking the garden another turn until you return." Elizabeth glanced up at Prince Clifton, his smile making her heart do funny things. He nodded. "See? I will be in good hands. You must make haste." Elizabeth watched as her attendant hurried away.

"Lessons?" Prince Clifton asked as Elizabeth walked over to a yellow rose and snipped the bud away from the bush. She held it to her nose and then continued on her way.

"Yes."

Clifton chuckled at her refusal to tell him what lessons she spoke of. "You are full of secrets, Princess."

Elizabeth laughed. "Not so, Prince Clifton. I just prefer to remain mysterious."

"Mysterious?" His wide smile and chuckle had Elizabeth smiling up at him. "Perhaps if I guessed?"

Elizabeth shrugged. "I will give you three."

"Only three?" Clifton glanced up at the sky in thought. "Embroidery?" The small snarl of dislike that wrinkled her nose told him he was wrong. Laughing, he rubbed his chin. "Hmm… horseback riding?"

"No. I am quite an efficient rider."

Liking her confidence, he nodded in consideration. "Alright, one more guess." He studied her carefully as she clipped another rose and added it to the growing bouquet in her hands. "It must be an interesting talent if you wish for it to remain a secret. So, I am going to say… fencing?" He watched as her back slightly stiffened, but she quickly reset her shoulders and offered a smile. "No." She walked back over to him and slid her arm back into his without invitation. Clifton beamed.

"I fear you have used all your guesses, Prince Clifton." Her blue eyes held a small glint of mystery that he found fit her perfectly. *Mysterious, indeed*, he thought.

"Princess Elizabeth!"

Clifton heard Elizabeth groan softly as she began to turn. "I fear, Prince Clifton, that I must make another request of you if at all possible?" Clifton leaned down to listen as she whispered. He watched as a tall man with an even stride and wearing the colors of the Western Kingdom made his way through the garden towards them.

"Of course, Princess. I am at your will."

"I must not and will not be left alone with that man." Elizabeth stated firmly.

Clifton's back straightened at the Princess's comment and his smile faltered. "Does this man mean you harm?" He whispered.

"I'm not sure." Elizabeth answered softly and truthfully, her soft blue gaze hardening as the man drew near.

Prince Isaac stepped forward breathless from his pace. "Princess, I have been looking everywhere for you."

"You have found me." Elizabeth stated matter of factly, waiting patiently for Prince Isaac to respond.

"Yes, indeed. Your sister, Princess Alayna has asked to meet with you at once."

"My sister? Whatever for?"

"I do not know, Your Highness. I was just asked to bring you to her into the castle at once." Prince Isaac flashed a non-apologetic glance towards Clifton.

"I thank you for your messenger services, Prince Isaac. However, I feel my sister can wait, due to her currently being at the stables instead of the castle." Elizabeth firmly answered and then turned away from the man.

Clifton held back his smirk as he too, turned to leave.

Prince Isaac reached forward and grasped Elizabeth's arm forcefully, pulling her towards him. She gasped. "I must insist." Isaac stated and stepped forward, just as Clifton stepped into his path. Isaac's grip on her arm released immediately as Clifton looked down at him. At 6'4" Clifton held a good five inches on the man and with a practiced air, he stepped in front of Elizabeth. "I believe Princess Elizabeth has made her decision."

Prince Isaac stood straight and gently tugged the bottom of his red tunic. "And may I ask who your newest acquaintance is, Princess?"

"Oh, of course." Elizabeth smiled as she looked at Clifton. "Prince Isaac, I would like you to meet Prince Clifton of the Eastern Kingdom. Prince Clifton, this is Prince Isaac of the Western Kingdom." Clifton bowed politely and waited to rise until Isaac did the same. Slowly Isaac bowed and then stood.

"Well, I will see you back to the castle, Princess." Isaac stepped forward again but Elizabeth held tight to Clifton's arm.

"I do not wish to be indoors at the moment Prince Isaac, but as soon as I am, I will send for you." His firm gaze travelled over her face before he nodded and turned away at a brisk pace.

Clifton felt Elizabeth relax beside him and felt himself doing the same. "Prince Isaac of the Western Kingdom… it is nice to put a name with a face." Clifton stated. "My father has asked me to visit the King of the Western Kingdom and his children several times, but I have yet to make it out that direction."

"Perhaps now that you know Prince Isaac personally, it will make your journey there more pleasant." Elizabeth suggested.

"I highly doubt that."

Elizabeth looked to him in surprise as he chuckled. A small smile tugged at her lips as she turned away.

"I assure you Prince Isaac is a valiant man."

"Are you so sure?"

"No, but he has not given me full reason to think otherwise."

"Then why the fear of being alone with him, when you so freely walk the gardens with me?" Clifton asked, noting the soft flush that covered her cheeks.

"Well…" She nervously glanced at her arm linked in his, "I did not appreciate the way he looked at me upon his arrival."

"I see." Clifton's brow furrowed as he wondered about Elizabeth's explanation.

"And did I look at you any different?"

"Yes. You looked at me with respect… and surprise, considering I slammed into you and almost knocked you off your fee—" She cut off her words realizing she carried a less formal conversation. "I mean, yes. You looked at me with respect."

Clifton nodded. "Well I certainly respect you, Princess Elizabeth."

"Why?" Elizabeth wondered. *Yes, she was the daughter of the King, but why else would anyone respect her?*

Clifton halted his steps and turned towards her. "Why, you are the daughter of the King of the Realm, of course." He briefly caught the disappointed gaze she held before she turned towards the flowers next to them. He cleared his throat. He hoped he had not offended her. *Perhaps she wanted to be respected for her own merit,* he thought. "And of course, because you are a respectable woman, my Princess."

"And how would you know that? You just met me." Elizabeth shot a gaze of fire at him as she challenged his answer.

"For the very reason you asked not to be alone with Prince Isaac. You suspected his actions were not honorable, and you used your knowledge of your first encounter wisely. You wish to maintain your honor by not being alone with him. I find that quite respectable." Clifton watched as she let his words sink in and then a slow smile blossomed on her face.

"Good answer, Prince Clifton." He laughed as she snipped another rose, his face immediately sobering as he saw Princess Alayna, followed by his brother, walking towards them quickly.

"Princess?"

"Hmmm?" Elizabeth asked as she sniffed a rose.

"We have company." Clifton answered softly.

Elizabeth turned and spotted her sister. "Oh… this should be good. Brace yourself, Prince Clifton, my sister is normally quite fearsome when she walks like that." Chuckling, he allowed Princess Elizabeth to link her arm in his again.

"Elizabeth!" Alayna called. "Why are you still out here in the gardens when I summoned you earlier?"

"Summoned?" Elizabeth challenged, a warning tone in her voice at her sister's demanding attitude.

"Yes. I sent Prince Isaac to fetch you. Why did you not come?" Alayna demanded.

Prince Ryle stood silently behind her as he watched his younger brother. Clifton found his brother's eye and nodded a greeting.

"I did not believe him. I thought you and Prince Ryle were at the stables."

Alayna gasped. "You insulted the Prince? What did you say? You must tell me everything." She grabbed Elizabeth's arm, causing her to drop her flowers, and pulled her away from Clifton and marched back towards the castle. Elizabeth cast an apologetic glance over her shoulder at Clifton who stooped to retrieve her blossoms.

"You would not have anything to do with her refusal, would you brother?" Prince Ryle asked with a smirk.

Clifton smelled one of the rose buds and thought of Princess Elizabeth doing the same. Her small petite nose sniffing the blooms and her tanzanite eyes shining with pleasure. "I did not. She requested I not allow him to take her with him. It seems our Princess distrusts the Prince from the Western Kingdom."

"Is that so? Now that is intriguing."

"Indeed. I must say I question his character a bit as well after our brief meeting." Clifton began walking alongside his brother as they followed the sisters back into the castle.

"Be sure to express your concerns with Father later." Prince Ryle stated softly as they entered the main hall. They froze in the doorway as they heard Elizabeth's raised voice.

CHAPTER 3

"I WILL NOT!" She stated firmly and loudly. "How dare you make an arrangement without first consulting me!"

"I did consult you. I wrote of the agreement in the parchment I gave you this morning. A parchment that clearly, you did not read." Alayna answered.

"I gave it to Mary because it looked like a schedule." Elizabeth explained.

"And where is Mary? She was not in the garden with you and Prince Clifton as she should have been."

"I sent her to complete a task for me."

"And what task was that?"

"A task." Elizabeth answered firmly.

Clifton listened as Elizabeth evaded her sister's question much like she had his own question of her lessons in the garden.

Alayna sighed. "Well the request is the same. Prince Isaac has requested the honor of remaining close to you for the next few weeks, and Father and I have granted his request."

"Funny thing sister… a request to remain close to *me*, and *you* granted the request. Do you not see anything wrong with that picture? I should be the one to determine whether or not I want to be close to the royal pin cushion, not you!"

"Elizabeth!" Alayna scolded.

"I have told you and Father countless times that I do not wish to be courted or married! You fail to listen!"

"We are aware of your feelings Elizabeth. Unfortunately, the Realm is not strong right now, and a way to strengthen it is with a marriage to one of the outlying kingdoms. You know this."

"I understand the reasoning, but I reject the proposal." Elizabeth crossed her arms as she paced.

Prince Ryle and Prince Clifton stood in the shadows, hoping the sisters did not discover their conversation was no longer private. However, neither brother wanted to leave due to their unbridled curiosity. Clifton smiled at Elizabeth's refusal. The woman definitely had spirit, and he liked it. Her obvious disgust with courtship seemed intriguing as well. He wondered what her reasons would be for the rejection of such proposals.

"The situation is perfect, Elizabeth. Prince Isaac has taken an interest in you. Isn't that what you have always wanted… love? You will marry for love, and that is a great thing." Alayna implored.

"No, Alayna. Clearly you and I have very different outlooks on love. Prince Isaac may fall in love with me one day, but I am not in love with him, nor intend to fall in love with him. The request is unfair. It is much like your betrothal to the Renaldi's."

"Do not bring my affairs into the picture. This is about you. Besides, they are completely different scenarios."

"No, they are not." Elizabeth replied, her face flushed. "You are forced into a marriage you do not want, and yet you are doing the same to me. I do not want to be courted by Prince Isaac, and that is my final response. You can either tell him, have Father tell him, or I will tell him myself. But I reject the proposal of courtship." Elizabeth began to storm away.

"And what if the proposal came from Prince Clifton? Would you reject the proposal from him?" Alayna asked, causing Elizabeth to turn back around.

"Why would you ask such a thing?"

"You two seemed quite comfortable in the garden earlier, and Prince Isaac made it very clear Prince Clifton was interfering with the agreed upon proposal." Alayna tilted her head as she waited for Elizabeth's answer. The blush to her sister's cheeks told Alayna what she needed to know, but she also wanted to hear it from her sister's lips.

"Prince Clifton is a good man, and he remained close to me because I requested him to do so. Besides, when was it formally announced that Prince Isaac and I are courting? Never." Elizabeth answered firmly. "I find pleasure in Prince Clifton's company, but that does not mean I want to marry the man! Can't a woman just walk in her garden anymore?"

"With a handsome prince?" Alayna teased, her new, light-hearted tone catching Elizabeth by surprise.

Elizabeth uncrossed her arms and placed her hands on her hips and rolled her eyes at her sister. "I suppose it is much like wandering the horse stables with a handsome prince. You would know all about that."

Alayna's mouth dropped open in shock and she stammered. "T-that was different."

"Was it?" Elizabeth jested as she escaped her sister's attempt to grab her. Alayna attempted again, and Elizabeth jerked away. Alayna's eyes narrowed as she stepped forward again and into a run as Elizabeth tried to escape. Elizabeth squealed as her boots slipped along the floor, regaining her balance she swiftly darted out of Alayna's grasp yet again. Alayna laughed and squealed as Elizabeth watched her sister begin to lose her balance on the slick floor as well, her golden curls bouncing as she struggled to gain her balance.

Ryle and Clifton chuckled softly as they stepped into the room.

Alayna abruptly stopped in place as Elizabeth slid into the back of her causing her to stumble forward into Prince Ryle. Elizabeth laughed as Prince Ryle caught her sister much like Clifton had caught her that morning.

"My Lord, my apologies." Alayna stood and slipped again, her hand sliding down the front of Prince Ryle's chest. Her sister's face turned crimson. "My goodness, yes, I apologize. The floor is…. mighty slippery." Prince Ryle chuckled as Alayna found her footing again and adjusted her skirts in nervousness.

Elizabeth draped her arm across Alayna's shoulders. Alayna shrugged the informal gesture off and cleared her throat. "Well, I must be going." Elizabeth looked to her sister in surprise. "I need to speak with Father… immediately." Alayna stated conspiratorially to Elizabeth as she winked at her younger sister and lightly nodded towards Prince Clifton. Elizabeth smiled and curtsied.

"I must say, you brothers have a knack for being in the proper place at the perfect time." Elizabeth grinned as they chuckled.

"It is our pleasure, Princess Elizabeth." Prince Ryle bowed as he made his exit.

Prince Clifton remained, and they stood staring at one another. Neither knowing, but wondering, the other's thoughts. "Oh, I brought your flowers. You dropped them on your way out of the garden."

Elizabeth smiled as she took them, her fingers brushing his hands and sending a rush through her veins. "Thank you, Prince Clifton.

How very thoughtful." Her voice was a hushed whisper as she sniffed her flowers and peered over the top of them.

"Milady!" Mary's voice drifted through the main hall as she trotted towards Elizabeth waving a piece of parchment.

"You must read the bottom of your sister's parchment! I did not see it until I was on my way back from—" she trailed off noting Clifton's presence. "My Lord." She curtsied and then thrust the parchment into Elizabeth's hands. "You must read it."

"It is alright, Mary." She placed a comforting hand on Mary's shoulder. "Alayna and I have already discussed what is written in her parchment. Were you able to deliver the letter?"

Mary nodded.

"Was there any news for me?"

Mary shook her head.

Elizabeth smiled but disappointment laced her voice. "I see. Well, perhaps tomorrow then."

"Ah! There's my boy!" King Eamon's voice travelled through the main hall causing Clifton to stand up straighter. Elizabeth turned and curtsied as the King approached.

"Princess." King Eamon greeted, bowing to Elizabeth.

"Cliff, I wondered if you would like to travel through the village this afternoon? It is much too pretty of a day to be indoors."

Elizabeth smiled at the tender and affectionate way the king addressed his son. "Of course, Father. I would be happy to. Shall I find Ryle as well?"

King Eamon shook his head. "No, your brother is meeting with King Granton over military strategies. It will just be the two of us, unless Princess Elizabeth would like to join us."

They looked to Elizabeth and she nodded. "I would like that very much. Please allow me to inform my sister of my whereabouts."

"Of course." The king bowed as she walked away.

"Do I sense something between you and the Princess?" King Eamon asked Clifton as they watched Elizabeth disappear around the corner.

"I am not sure, Father. I am most intrigued by her, I will admit. However, she does not seem to be a mouse that can be caught."

Laughing heartily, King Eamon slapped Clifton's back. "Son, the best ones usually are the hardest to catch."

Elizabeth came back with her outdoor cloak on and Mary carrying her parasol. "I am ready when you are, gentlemen."

"Oh, my dear, you do not have to walk in the hot sun, please allow us the pleasure of letting you use our carriage." The king offered nodding towards Elizabeth's parasol.

"Actually, King Eamon, I much prefer walking, if you do not mind. There is just something refreshing about the wind in your hair and sun upon your face, wouldn't you agree?"

The king exchanged smiles with Clifton and then nodded. "Very much so, Princess. My, how you are so much like your mother."

Elizabeth's smile faded. "My mother? You knew her? I mean, of course you knew her. You have been Father's good friend for years. What was she like? Was she beautiful? Was she—" Mary gently placed her hand on Elizabeth to stop her rambling. Elizabeth straightened and cleared her throat. "My apologies, my Lord. I know my father and our family are grateful you have had such a long-standing friendship with us."

"No apologies my dear. It is quite normal for you to be curious. Your mother was a delightful woman, and very beautiful, like yourself."

Elizabeth blushed under his scrutiny.

"Please, allow me." Clifton stepped forward and offered his arm to Elizabeth. She slid her arm in his, smiling up at him with pleasure. Mary handed Elizabeth her parasol and walked a comfortable distance behind the young couple, the King to the right of Elizabeth, as Clifton escorted her out of the castle on the left.

∞

Reining in his mare, Edward hopped from his saddle over to Thatcher, the small brown bunny waiting on his side of the boundary line. A small letter tied to his neck, Thatcher waited patiently as Edward removed it. He scanned the scrawly handwriting of what could only be from Mary, Elizabeth's attendant. Elizabeth would not be coming for lessons today and possibly for a few days due to their visitors at the castle. He tucked her letter into his trouser pocket and then pulled out his journal. He began composing his own letter that perhaps she would find in a few days and understand the reason for his possible absence as well.

My Dearest Sister,

I am glad Father has reached out to the Eastern and Western Kingdoms. It is about time. I must say, my efforts in the Lands have been fruitful as of late. There is a strong resistance. I have a meeting with Lancer later this afternoon. Word has come to me that he wishes to recruit me to his personal guard. This could be a step in the right direction for my work here. He trusts my crossing of the boundary was indeed meant to betray our father. He feels that the current strength in the Lands stems only from my connection. The higher I move in his ranks, the stronger he will be, or so he believes. This puts me at a considerable advantage for us, sister.

I do not wish to scare you Elizabeth, but there are dark forces over here. Dark forces intent on harming Father's realm. I have yet to find the power that feeds Lancer his strength, but I do know it is dark.

Now, do not worry about me, however. Cecilia and I are well looked after here. We have a small band of fellow Uniters, as we call ourselves. Those who wish to destroy the Unfading Lands and reunite the Realm. We are few in number, but strong in heart. Given time, I believe our numbers will grow. And the stronger Father's kingdom becomes, the better. Any word on his latest efforts?

I fear it is going to take more than a marriage amongst the kingdoms to strengthen the Realm against what Lancer has in store.

I hope and pray for your continued safety through it all. And Lizzy... have a bit of fun with your guests. Princes aren't ALL bad.

He smiled as he folded the letter and tied it to Thatcher and sent him across the boundary. The small bunny scurried beneath the protection of his clover cubby. He would check back in a few days. Until then, he would continue to gather Uniters and do what he set out to do.

∞

"I understand, my King." Prince Ryle stated in understanding. "But the fact remains that the latest devastation on the edges of the Eastern Kingdom's lands has been caused by the Renaldi's of the South. They are not open to merging with the rest of the Realm."

King Granton rubbed a hand over his worn face as he looked to the young man seated across from him. *Young*, he thought. He would be around Edward's age— if Edward were still around. Yet something about Prince Ryle spoke of wisdom beyond his years. Perhaps the many years of combat training, military education, and battles along his borderlines had turned the young man into a seasoned general earlier than was usual. He watched as Ryle's piercing blue gaze roamed over the charted maps of the Realm. He pointed a finger to the Eastern Kingdom. "If we take the King's Guard and move them to the Eastern Border, then Renaldi's forces dare not test their strength. The Eastern armies are not strong enough to fight the Southern Kingdom alone. We need help, my King."

"I see." King Granton stated. "Mosiah?" King Granton called to the Captain of his Royal Guard. "Can we spare a few men to investigate the borderlines of the Eastern Kingdom?"

"No, my King. All of our extra forces have been stationed along the boundary line of the Unfading Lands to prevent crossings, sir."

King Granton rubbed a hand over his beard as his eyes searched the maps before him. "Anthony?"

King Anthony nodded in acknowledgment. "Does the Western Kingdom have guards to spare at the moment?"

"Perhaps a few. However, we too have been guarding our Southern lines tightly. The Renaldi's cannot be trusted. I fear if we move our own guards to the Eastern Kingdom, then the Western Kingdom will be at risk, Your Grace."

King Granton harrumphed. "I see."

"Has the King not finalized the marriage plans of Princess Alayna and Prince Eric of the Renaldi's in the South? Perhaps attacks along our borders will cease once their marriage has taken place." King Anthony suggested, noting the apparent dislike written on Prince Ryle's face.

"The Renaldi's have yet to accept the betrothal request. I fear we may need to find other alternatives." King Granton suggested.

"Alternatives?" King Anthony interrupted. "Alternatives do not grow on trees, Granton. You have but two daughters. It only makes sense that one be aligned with our wavering kingdom in the Realm. The Southern Kingdom needs to be aligned in order for us to withstand the Unfading Lands."

Ryle watched as King Granton's face turned into an unhealthy shade of red. "Do not speak of my daughters as pawns in a chess match, Anthony. The decision of Alayna's fate is in my hands, her *father's* hands. I have issued a message to the Renaldi's. Their lack of acceptance to attend this week is a confirmed disregard for the request. Alayna is not to wed into the Southern Kingdom." He took a deep breath.

Ryle breathed a sigh of relief that he mustered beneath the fist he rested underneath his chin.

"That being said," King Granton continued. "I do have hopes that a reestablished allegiance between our three kingdoms will be enough strength to suffice for now, until we can build up our armies to fight off Lancer on our own."

"And if that does not work?" Anthony challenged.

"Then we reach out to neighboring realms. The Unfading Lands may not be a threat to them now, but if we fall, the Lands will only spread."

"How do you wish to align our kingdoms then, since the proposed marriage of Prince Edward and my Melody fell through with his betrayal?" King Anthony straightened in his chair. "And the blatant refusal on Princess Elizabeth's part in regard to my Isaac. What say you of that?"

King Granton's shoulders slouched in his chair. Ryle could tell the king was tiring, yet the current discussions needed to take place.

"Elizabeth has a strong will." King Granton explained. "She wishes to make her decisions freely."

"But you are the king!" Anthony demanded. "If our realm's fate is left to the emotions of a woman, then we are doomed to fail."

Ryle noted the spark in the king's eyes and the fury he restrained. Ryle cleared his throat and waved a hand to gain the elderly men's attention. "If I may, my King?"

"Oh, I see. You want to step in and recommend the Eastern Kingdom as the aligning kingdom, is that it?" Anthony barked.

"No." Ryle stated simply. "I was going to suggest that perhaps we should focus our attention on military strength before alignments. Our kingdoms are united now. Yes, a reestablished agreement may strengthen us, but only a few feet. We need more than a few feet to defeat Lancer. Our strength is in the guard. We need to focus our efforts on building our armies. We need a force that is threatening, and as of right now, we do not have one."

"Prince Ryle is right." King Granton confirmed and glanced around the room at his generals and his captain. "We need to build our protective forces. Mosiah, I want you and Prince Ryle to discuss protective measures for the Eastern Border. Anthony, I wish for your army to spare as many guards as possible without sacrificing your kingdom's protection." He stood from his chair, all the other men standing in respect as he exited. "We are finished for now." He stated and walked out.

∞

Walking in the market place energized Elizabeth, the hustle and bustle of the merchants making it all the more exciting. She watched as children ran and weaved between tents and carts giggling as they chased one another. She loved the variety. The crafts, the spices, the breads, the dresses, she could find anything she needed here at the market. Though she rarely ventured out of the castle the past few months, she enjoyed the time when she could walk amongst their people. The merchants took time to show her their latest products or crafts, so pleased they were with a member of the royal family gracing them with their presence.

"Princess Elizabeth, it is an honor." An older man bowed humbly before her and motioned towards his cart of pelts. "The latest furs, milady." Elizabeth smiled as King Eamon stepped forward and began sorting through some of the pelts.

"These are quite nice." King Eamon held up a pelt for Clifton to survey.

The older man straightened in pride at the compliment. "I only catch the finest animals, sir."

Elizabeth smiled at the man's eagerness to make a sale and the pride he took in his merchandise. "Dear Sir," She began, "Allow me to introduce you to King Eamon and Prince Clifton of the Eastern Kingdom."

The man's eyes widened in surprise. He bowed to the gentlemen and placed his hand on his heart. "It is an honor, my Lord." King Eamon smiled as the man, energized by the presence of royalty, began showing him his finest pelts.

A small girl wandered over and tugged on Elizabeth's skirt. "Oh, hello there." She greeted. The mother of the child rushed over. "Terribly sorry, Princess." She grabbed her daughter's hand and began to tug her away. Elizabeth knelt and pulled one of her roses out of her bouquet and handed it to the little girl. "A beautiful rose for a beautiful little girl." Elizabeth lightly tapped the little girl's nose and stood. The little girl beamed and raised the pale pink rose in the air for her mother to see. The woman smiled graciously. "Thank you, your Highness."

Elizabeth nodded and then turned back to King Eamon's shopping. The King and Clifton stared at her in surprise. "Did you find anything you could not live without?"

The King laughed. "Indeed. I purchased two fine pelts." The merchantman bowed and waved his thanks as they walked away.

"I believe you just made that little girl feel like a princess." Clifton smiled down at her as she grinned.

"She was a sweet girl. Most children are just curious when they see us walking about. People tend to place us on a pedestal and forget that we are actually people too. I think the children see us through untainted eyes full of wonder. They do not see the politics of our position. They see it as magical." Elizabeth grinned as the little girl brought one of her friends up to her. She pulled a yellow rose from her bouquet and handed it to the little girl. Smiling and comparing roses, the two little girls ran off.

"You are gracious to take the time to acknowledge the little ones." Clifton continued. "Most royals do not do such things."

"Which is a pity." Elizabeth added. "Do you take the time, Prince Clifton?"

He tilted his head at her question. He could not lie to the beautiful princess. "Not as often as I should." He answered truthfully looking into her eyes for acceptance.

"Then here." She handed him several roses. "You can hand roses out as well." King Eamon watched as his son willingly took a bundle of roses.

Clifton chuckled as several children walked up to them. He knelt beside Elizabeth as she lowered herself to eye level with the children. She then took the time of placing each flower with a certain child. Several of the young boys showed Prince Clifton their sling shots, rocks, or whatever they found in their trouser pockets. The prince kindly took notice of each item and even cast a few stones playfully at his father making the young boys giggle in excitement.

"And what is your name, sweet girl?"

"Annabelle."

"Annabelle, that is a lovely name. Did you know, Annabelle, that you have the prettiest eyes I have ever seen? Don't you agree, Prince Clifton?" The little girl looked shyly towards Prince Clifton. With a warm smile, he lightly tilted her chin up so he could see her eyes. "I must say they are a beautiful blue. Much like yours, Princess." He winked at the little girl. She smiled a toothy grin, two of her bottom teeth missing, creating an adorable absence in her mouth. "I think this flower would look lovely in your hair." Elizabeth snapped off the stem and placed the flower behind the girl's ear. The little girl lunged forward and hugged Elizabeth around the neck. Taking Elizabeth off guard, she fell backwards into the dirt, her right arm catching her fall and Clifton's strong arm quickly sliding around her waist as well. "Oh my." She giggled and patted the young girl's back. Mary rushed forward and helped Elizabeth to her feet and lightly beat the dirt off of her dress. "It is fine, Mary." Elizabeth stated, lightly brushing her attendant's hands away. She did not move from Prince Clifton's light embrace, but instead continued walking.

King Eamon watched as the princess finished handing out her roses and helped his son hand them out as well. The woman was a gem. The people loved her and she seemed to equally love them. She would make a great asset to the Eastern Kingdom. Since the passing of his wife, the Eastern Kingdom had lacked a strong female presence, especially one that loved the people. He watched as his son doted on her as well. Yes, there was definitely something brewing between the two young ones. The long looks, the restrained touches, and the nervous chuckles gave their hearts away as he watched. He smiled to himself. He would have to discuss the possibilities of a merger with Granton.

∞

"What do you mean the king has revoked my request of courtship?" Prince Isaac asked as he stormed through their guest chambers. He removed his outer cloak and tossed it across the chaise his sister Melody currently occupied.

"Just that." King Anthony interjected. "It seems Princess Elizabeth does not wish for a courtship from you or anyone at the moment. The king has granted her request."

"That is absurd!"

"Isaac." Melody's calm voice filtered through the room to her brother.

"Do not shush me, Melody." Isaac warned. "We would not be in this mess if you had agreed to marry Edward earlier. Then he would not have been able to cross the boundary."

Melody dropped her eyes to her lap and nervously wringed her hands.

"Do not blame your sister for your current situation." King Anthony stated. "It seems King Granton wishes to drop the matter of marriage being a unification tool for the Realm. His attention has now shifted to military strength. Prince Ryle and I have been working closely with Mosiah, the Captain of the Royal Guard, to establish ways to prevent Lancer's strength from expanding."

"Prince Ryle." Isaac snarled. He paced holding his chin in his hand. "What of Princess Alayna and the alignment with the South?"

"Failed. Princess Alayna is no longer betrothed."

"So why not establish a courtship with her? Yes, I had preferred Elizabeth, but Alayna will suffice."

"This is not an auction, son." King Anthony eased into a chair near Melody and lightly nudged her chin with his thumb and smiled tenderly at his daughter.

Isaac finally sat and ran his hand through his dark hair. "Then what do you suggest?"

"My suggestion, Isaac, is that perhaps you attempt to woo the princess while also aiding in the guardianship of our lands. The Eastern Kingdom needs our help against the South."

"And which princess should I woo, Father?" Isaac asked with a bitter chuckle.

"Whichever strikes your fancy, son. Just remember they are to be respected."

"Always." Isaac replied with forced cheerfulness. "Perhaps Melody could distract the princes of the East while I attempt to establish a merger?" Isaac looked to his sister and winked. A light blush stained her cheeks and she shook her head.

"Your shyness is a hindrance, Melody." Isaac explained. "How do you plan to marry one day when you refuse to put yourself on display?"

"Stop badgering your sister, Isaac. She is a lady. Besides, Melody is still within the marrying age. She has plenty of time." King Anthony affectionately glanced at his daughter and then back to his son.

"Well I will do my best to win over the princess." Isaac announced. "If the Eastern Kingdom continues to have issues along their borders, perhaps my princely competition will have all the distraction they need, and I will have more time with the princess in their absence."

King Anthony sighed and stood. "Well, perhaps you can seem slightly interested in the protection of our lands and follow me to a meeting with the King and your *princely competition*." Isaac smirked as he followed his father out of their chambers and through the castle halls.

∞

Edward dismounted his white horse and handed his reins to the fully armed guard at the base of the castle steps. His gaze travelled up the marble steps to the wide wooden doorway that would lead him to Lancer. He took a deep breath and surveyed the surrounding guards. None glanced his direction. He walked up the steps and the doors opened freely. He stepped inside, greeted with a wide array of brightly colored glass in the windows, ornate chandeliers hanging from vaulted ceilings, and a grand staircase that encircled the main hall. He spotted a single chair, ornately carved and ordained with gold, centered at the end of the room. Standing on either side of the chair were two guards, relaxed in stature, but gracing the sides of the chair that housed a man.

"Ah, welcome Prince Edward." The man stood. Tall. Elegant. Strong. Edward stopped several paces away from the figure. "Or should I just call you Edward?" The man smirked at his own joke and then extended his hand. Edward gripped the man's hand and shook it. Smiling, the man's dark eyes gleamed with pleasure. "Glad you agreed to come." The man began to walk towards a doorway to the left. "Follow me."

Edward surveyed the room. Smaller than the previous room, it held a warmth much like his own personal chamber back in the Northern Kingdom. An intimate space meant to entertain friends or family, he thought. The man turned and gestured to a comfortable chaise and took a seat on the matching one opposite it. "I am Lancer. Although I am sure you have heard of me by now. I am pleased to have you on our side of the boundary. I understand you crossed to be with the woman you love and to oppose your father, King Granton?"

Edward cleared his throat. "Yes."

"Just like that?"

"It would seem." Edward replied.

Lancer grinned. He lightly ran a hand through his dark hair, the close-cropped cut accentuating his slashing cheekbones and sharp gaze. He wore a golden yellow tunic with golden buckles and a red sash across his chest. Edward noted his lack of weapon and thought it curious. "You may be wondering why I asked you here today." Lancer continued, his gaze measuring Edward much like he had him. "I must admit my curiosity has been piqued for quite some time, but your whereabouts have been quite elusive."

"I find it hard to stay in one place for too long." Edward admitted, not wanting to give the man any information about his usual locations, especially his spot where he conversed with Elizabeth.

"That is one of the reasons I wished to speak with you. I find your previous status on the other side quite valuable, as well as your nomadic ways on this side. I would like to recruit you, Edward, to my personal guard."

Edward inhaled deeply. He felt a slight twitch in his left eye, but attempted to halt the movement as he stared at Lancer. There wasn't anything powerful about the man's appearance, Edward thought. *What was it about him that stirred souls to leave their families? What had people flocking to follow him with abandon?*

"Is this a position you would be interested in?" Lancer continued.

Edward shook his head and fostered a smile. "Yes, of course. My apologies. I am just surprised— and honored."

Lancer laughed. "Oh no, Edward. It is I who am honored. I feel your insight into the Realm will be of great use to the Lands. Word has it your father's health is fading. We have gained considerable ground the last few months. I feel it will not be long before we breach the Northern Kingdom's inner villages."

Edward's brow rose in surprise at the man's confidence. "So quickly?"

"Well, I am hopeful. We have seen an increase in defense along the boundary line. It seems your father has guards posted to prevent people from crossing. But with help from the Southern Kingdom, we have still gained a considerable amount of strength."

"The Southern Kingdom? Are they allies?"

"Not per se." Lancer replied nonchalantly, snapping his fingers and signaling a servant to enter carrying a tray with two glasses of amber colored liquid, the scent causing Edward's stomach to roll. "My sources say the Southern Kingdom wishes to be independent of the Realm but lacks the strength to rebel. They seek help elsewhere. Some have crossed into our lands seeking aid and found out the cost of their crossing." Lancer waved his hand as he spoke as if someone crossing were of no consequence to them or him. "Failure in the attempt to cross back over the boundary line opened their eyes a bit." He chuckled and took a sip of his drink. He nodded towards the glass in Edward's hand. Edward took a slow sip, the amber liquid hot as it slid down his throat, leaving a bitter taste in his mouth.

"The Southern Kingdom wishes to be free of the Realm and now— the Lands." Lancer set his glass to the side and brushed a hand over the front of his chest. He patted his heart softly. "The Southern Kingdom has always been quite savage, haven't they?"

"Yes. My father could never quite control them."

"He and I have that in common. At least now, however, they recognize my threat."

"So why not extend your reach to the Southern Kingdom first?" Edward asked.

"Because they are child's play." Lancer replied as if bored with the topic. "They do not have ties with the rest of the Realm. Who would care if they disappeared? No one. But the Northern Kingdom... The seat of the throne of the Realm... now that... that would cause the Realm to crumble."

Edward's heart rate kicked into overdrive as he listened to Lancer's plans to overthrow his father's kingdom. Elizabeth. Alayna. His father. No. He had to convince Lancer of another path.

"Alright." Edward stated confidently. "I will join your guard."

A slow smile spread across Lancer's lips and he toasted his glass towards Edward. "I was hoping you would say that, my prince."

Edward clinked his glass and took another 'celebratory' sip as Lancer beamed across from him. Now, thought Edward, now his plan to save his father's kingdom had officially begun.

∞

The next afternoon Elizabeth saddled her horse, Lenora, and swung herself into the saddle, the new riding skirt Mary had made tucked into her saddle bag as she shifted in her trousers. She snapped the reins and Lenora took to a quick gallop. She had to talk to Edward today. It had been a couple of days since she last went to the boundary line, and she had so much to share with him. She galloped out of the stable yard and across the picturesque pasture.

Prince Clifton watched as a chestnut mare darted out of the stables and a black braid blew in the wind. Princess Elizabeth. He watched as she hovered low in her saddle to face the fierce wind, her slim frame only accentuated by— *were those trousers?* He chuckled to himself as he watched the beautiful princess ride over the top of the hill, promising himself a glimpse of her upon her return.

Elizabeth slid from her saddle and tied Lenora's reins to a tree and waved excitedly to her brother on the other side. Edward beamed as his sister eased his letter off of Thatcher's neck. He watched as her brows lifted in surprise of his news. She then sat on the large boulder to write her own letter. She tapped her finger to her chin as she thought of a response and then eagerly began to write.

Edward eased onto a tree stump and waited patiently until he saw Elizabeth slide a letter onto Thatcher and send the young rabbit across the line. He snatched the rabbit and read eagerly.

Brother,

Sorry I have been absent the last couple of days. It has been busy up at the castle. Our visitors have arrived, all but the Renaldi's. Prince Isaac requested to be my escort during his stay... Thankfully that agreement did not work out. I will say I am surprised at the friendship from the East. Prince Eamon and his sons Ryle and Clifton have proved to be upstanding men, with a kindness I have rarely seen. Prince Eamon claims I have a mirror temperament of our mother. I wish I remembered her enough to know. I guess you and Alayna would be a better judge of that. However, I must admit I have enjoyed their company.

I cannot believe Lancer requests for you to join his guard. You must tell me everything, brother. Do you feel it wise? What is he like in person? Does he know of our meetings?

Elizabeth walked to the edge of the river and lightly washed her hands of the mud that covered Thatcher's fur. She then began her practice with her targets, her sword swift, accurate, and strong. Edward wrote back, his attention switching from his letter to Elizabeth and then back to the letter.

She felt a quiver in her forearm as her muscle strained against the weight of the blade as she held her sword straight at her assailing target. Never wavering, stance firm. Then she bolted forward in another round of target practice through her small arena. When she had finished, she walked breathlessly over to her brother's smiling face as he released Thatcher to her side. She untied the letter.

"Good to see you, sister. You look bright and fresh. Glad to hear King Eamon and his sons have brought good humor to the castle, especially for Father's sake."

Elizabeth glanced up as Cecilia joined Edward on the other side, along with several other new faces. Edward pointed to the letter in her hands and she continued to read.

While you bring in friends from the Realm, I wanted you to see some of our friends on this side of the line. Cecilia and I have reached out to many people here who hope for a change. If you haven't noticed yet, your red markings have emerged on your side of the line again... well, a couple of them. Four remain on my side. But at least we see some strength emerging in the Realm. Perhaps your current visitors are to thank for that.

Your swordsmanship has only improved. You are quick as a cat, sister. I fear I cannot explain my visit with Lancer at the moment. For so much detail requires a longer letter, of which I currently do not have the time to write. The bugle will sound in a few minutes. I promise to prepare a letter for you. I will fill you in on my current status. Do not lose hope. Things are looking up. I hope to see you again tomorrow, but I understand if that is not possible with the current hustle and bustle at the castle. Take care, my sweet sister."

She glanced up as her brother and his friends bowed to her once more before stepping away from the boundary line. She waved in return and then hid her letter in her saddle bag and tucked her sword under her saddle blankets. She swung onto Lenora's back and headed back to the castle. Her lessons needed to be short the next few weeks so as not to draw suspicion amongst their new guests or even her sister. It was easier to get lost in a castle of only three royals, but with the current population lurking about, her presence, or lack thereof, would be noticed. She reached the stables and unsaddled Lenora. Tying her riding skirt back in place around her waist, she brushed Lenora's coat.

"You ride alone?" Elizabeth's back tightened as Prince Clifton walked into the stables, but her strokes only briefly wavered.

"Do you not have a stable boy for that?" Clifton asked.

"Aye, we do. But I find it is relaxing as well as a chance to bond with my horse." Elizabeth nervously continued her task as Prince Clifton stepped forward and cupped Lenora's cheeks in his hands. "A fine horse, indeed. She has spirit. I see it in her eyes."

Elizabeth relaxed and lightly patted Lenora's side. "Yes, she does. I like to think that is why we get along so well."

"Kindred Spirits." Clifton provided on a chuckle. "Indeed." Elizabeth and Clifton stared at one another. "Does she also encourage you to ride in trousers?" He asked with amusement.

Her eyes widened and a blush crept up her cheeks. "I... um..." She stuttered not knowing what to say. *He had witnessed her trousers! What was she thinking wearing something so ghastly when they had company at the castle?!*

His warm green gaze never left her face and made her heart flutter in warmth. She cleared her throat. "I'm not quite sure what you are talking about, my Lord." She smirked as he laughed and lightly trailed his fingers over the sloppily tied ribbon at her waist.

"Of course. I must have been mistaken." He winked.

"So, what brings you to the stables, my Lord?"

Clifton nervously glanced away, realizing his gaze had lingered beyond what was polite. "I wish to do the same. Ride alone for a bit, that is. Your father is kind enough to let my horse stay in your stables."

"I see. Well, enjoy the day then. It is bright and beautiful."

"Thank you, Princess, as are you." He complimented as he playfully tugged the corner of her riding skirt. He bowed before walking towards the end of the row and took his reins from the young stable boy who had readied his stallion for him. Clifton swung into the saddle effortlessly and his long legs rested comfortably down the sides to his stirrups. Elizabeth's heart raced at the sight of him. Tall, regal, handsome. Gorgeous. He gave her one last wave before clicking the reins and heading out.

Elizabeth watched until his blonde hair disappeared over the horizon, her eyes dreamy as she imagined what it would feel like to be Prince Clifton's lady. Lenora snorted, bringing her attention back to the mare. "Oh, alright." Elizabeth grumbled as she handed the horse an apple and walked her back to her stall.

CHAPTER 4

Clifton sat atop his black horse and looked out over the Northern Kingdom's lands. The surrounding villages were completely unaware of the trouble brewing in their lands and beyond. He could see the sheer fog of the boundary hidden behind the tree line that ran parallel with the river. He had never seen the boundary line in person, but the sight of it now had his insides tightening. What was it about the Unfading Lands that had people abandoning their loved ones to cross over the line? What power did Lancer hold? His sharp green gaze flashed over to a movement lurking within the trees. There it was again. He shifted in his saddle as he narrowed his gaze. "Move again." He mumbled softly. "Let me see you." He saw a head pop out from behind a tree and then back again. Someone was hiding from him. He clicked the reins of his horse and slowly galloped towards the tree line. As he neared, he caught a glimpse of a retreating black tunic. The Renaldi's? It couldn't be!

Clifton slapped his reins and set out after the man. The man sprinted, and as Clifton reached his side to snatch his collar, the figure dove to the ground. Clifton pulled back on the reins and dismounted quickly, sprinting after the man as he climbed to his feet.

He dove into the tall grass, snatching the man by the ankles. Crawling up the man's legs, Clifton deflected the punch to his jaw and landed a fist in the man's face. The man guarded his head with his arms and pleaded. "No, please! Please, do not hurt me!"

Clifton froze but continued to straddle the man's chest and pinned down his arms. "Who are you and what are you doing here?" Clifton demanded on a breath. "Speak!"

The man lowered his hands and his young gaze roamed over Clifton's face and his eyes widened in panic. "Prince Clifton of the Eastern Kingdom?"

"Aye."

The young man closed his eyes and leaned his head back in regret.

"If I rise, you will not run." Clifton stated, slowly rising up off of the boy. He quickly unsheathed his sword and held it to the boy's neck. "Tell me why you are spying on the Northern Kingdom."

The boy held his hands up in surrender. "I-I am only doing what I am told, my Lord."

"Who sent you?"

"My father, the king of the Southern Kingdom."

"You're Prince Eric?"

The young boy shook his head. "No. I am his brother, Samuel."

"Why did your father send you here, and why were you hiding from me?"

Samuel shifted nervously on his feet. Clifton, feeling pity for the young man, lowered his sword. Visibly relaxing, Prince Samuel slowly inhaled a deep breath. "I cannot tell you why I am here."

Clifton narrowed his eyes and surveyed the boy closely. Fear. Fear of him, but mostly fear of his own father lurked behind his dark gaze. "You will tell me." Clifton replied firmly. "For if you do not, I will take you with me to the castle. If you tell me, perhaps I will let you return to your father."

The boy's gaze darted around the horizon. He wrung his hands nervously in front of him.

"Do not think of running. I will catch you." Clifton stated, recognizing the signs of imminent flight.

Finally, the boy's shoulders slumped. "I was sent to survey the boundary line, my Lord. My father wished to know how much of King Granton's lands had been taken by Lancer."

"Why?"

"I cannot say, sir."

"You will."

"I cannot because I know not, sir. My father has not shared with me his reasonings."

Clifton crossed his arms over his chest and towered over the boy. "Does your father communicate with Lancer?"

"I am not sure, my Lord. He is concerned about the boundary line and that King Granton has done nothing to stop it from moving."

"Has your father not read his letters? The king sent letters to all kingdoms requesting us to come here to discuss the matter. Your father did not reply or attend."

"All I know is what my father has told me, my Lord. He does not share with me like he does my older brother."

"Perhaps you should come with me to the castle." Clifton waved him forward. Terror lit in the young boy's eyes.

"It is quite alright. I assure you nothing will happen to you."

"I'm sorry, Prince Clifton. I cannot. I am to return at a specific time or my father will consider my task a failure. I must not fail him, my Lord."

"Is there anything else you wish to tell me before you leave then? Anything?" Clifton waited as he saw the turmoil in the boy's eyes. Clearly he knew something he did not want to share. His honest conscience eventually won out. "I fear, my Lord, that the boundary line and Lancer's lands offer a sanctuary for evil men."

"Evil men? What do you mean?"

The boy took a step back. "We have lost troops, your Grace. Guards have crossed, only they cannot return once they have done so."

"Yes, that is common knowledge. Everyone knows you cannot cross the boundary and return."

"We did not, but now we do. We lost guards to the boundary line. Many guards. My father is concerned that the only way to defeat the Lands is to join them. I was sent to survey the strength of the Northern Kingdom. He was curious as to how much land had been taken by Lancer. King Granton's lands are not safe, my Lord."

"You are saying your father plans to unite with Lancer and attack the Northern Kingdom?"

"I do not say anything." The boy stated forcefully.

"Of course." Clifton lowered his arms and rubbed his chin. The boy offered invaluable information. He could not scare him. "So why has your father been attacking the Eastern Kingdom's borders?"

"To test their strength. He wishes to claim all the lands of the Realm so that when he joins with Lancer, he will share the rule of the Unfading Lands."

Clifton's face blanched. "The Southern Kingdom wishes to annihilate the Northern, Eastern, and Western Kingdoms?"

The young boy nodded. "I am sorry, my Lord. I do not wish you harm or Princess Elizabeth."

"Princess Elizabeth? What does she have to do with this?" Clifton stepped forward in defense and the boy shrank back. "I-I mean no harm. I see her at the river and the boundary line. I mean her no harm. I do not wish for anyone to be hurt. I am just a messenger."

"What do Princess Elizabeth's whereabouts have to do with your messaging?" Clifton asked.

"My brother, my Lord. My brother wishes to obtain Princess Elizabeth as his wife. He wishes to take her to the Unfading Lands with him."

Clifton's back stiffened and his gaze turned into a storm. "Over my dead body." He muttered.

"That is his plan." The boy's breathing wavered as he took a shaky breath of fear. His eyes flashed to the sword in Clifton's hand.

"And where do your allegiances lie, Prince Samuel?"

"With King Granton, my Lord."

"How can I be sure?"

"Because I mean you no harm. I have answered your questions." He looked nervously towards the tree line. "And because the boundary line is not to be trusted. There is darkness over there, my Lord. Darkness." The boy's eyes grew weary as he glanced back to Clifton.

"Say I believe you, young prince." Clifton stated. "You said evil men find sanctuary in the Unfading Lands. What did you mean by that?"

"Several of our top warriors and guards have been wounded in the battles with the East, but the Lands provide healing. When you cross, you are healed. My father sends his wounded guards across the boundary, so they will not die. They regain their strength and plan to establish my father's band of military leaders in the Lands."

"What use are they there if the Lands are but losing their claim on the Realm? As we strengthen, they weaken."

"They are not weak, my Lord. They are just resting." The fear in the boy's gaze had Clifton's insides jump. Something was afoot with the Southern Kingdom and Lancer, he could feel it. Not only would the Realm be fighting against the invisible foe of the boundary line, but a brewing storm behind it. The Realm was destined for a battle either way. There had to be a way to reach within the Lands and unite those who wished to overthrow Lancer. Surely there were people who regretted their decision of crossing the boundary—

"My Lord?" The young man studied Clifton carefully. Clifton straightened his shoulders and cleared his throat. "Aye. I trust what you say, Samuel. I will take this news to King Granton. Should you find yourself needing an escape, please accept my offer of the Northern or Eastern Kingdom. I now recognize that not all of the Renaldi's are of bad character."

The young boy offered a relieved smile and bowed towards Clifton. "I thank you, Prince Clifton. Your kindness extends much farther than your kingdom. I would not have believed it if I had not encountered you myself. I must go."

"Take care, Samuel. And be safe."

The young boy darted away quickly, slipping in and out of the trees until Clifton no longer saw his dark hair bobbing through the thicket. Clifton hopped back into his saddle and studied the boundary line. Elizabeth frequented the boundary line, according to Samuel. He wondered why. He readjusted his grip on the reins and then clicked his tongue to his horse. "Come Henry, we must make haste." He slapped the reins and Henry sped towards the castle.

THE UNFADING LANDS

∞

"Are you saying that the Southern Kingdom wishes to attack us?" Prince Ryle paced as Clifton relayed his conversation with Prince Samuel to his brother and father.

"That is exactly what I am saying. Prince Samuel was quite clear and quite afraid."

"You should have brought him here." Ryle stated with annoyance.

"And what? Have his father thinking we kidnapped him?" Clifton challenged. "Something tells me that would have encouraged even more hostility. The boy meant no harm. He was just doing his bidding."

"We need to speak to the King." King Eamon stated. "This is dreadful news."

"That's not even the half of it." Clifton mumbled, crossing his arms over his chest as he brooded into the fire. He watched the flames beneath the mantle lick over the wood logs and dance in colors of red, orange, and radiant blue.

"What do you mean?" Prince Ryle asked. "What else is there?"

Clifton diverted his gaze to his father and brother. "I mean, Prince Samuel also shared that Prince Eric's refusal of Princess Alayna was because he wants Princess Elizabeth instead."

"Princess Elizabeth?" Ryle asked curiously. "Why, that could solve our problems. King Granton thought the Renaldi's refused the betrothal request because of their lack of unity with the Realm. In reality, Prince Eric was just unhappy with the Princess. He wants Elizabeth, not Alayna. If we convince the King to reoffer the betrothal but with Elizabeth as the bride, then perhaps all of this can be avoided."

"I think not!" Clifton stood quickly, not catching the light tilt to his father's lips at his son's refusal.

"Cliff, think of it!" Ryle stated. "I understand you are sweet on Elizabeth, but think of the bigger picture here. We can avoid a war."

"No. We cannot. Prince Samuel was adamant that the betrothal meant nothing. Prince Eric wishes to take Elizabeth across the boundary line to wed her. He does not wish to take her to the Southern Kingdom." Clifton explained with distaste. "And it sounded as if Prince Eric would take Princess Elizabeth whether a betrothal was offered or not. It does not sit well with me." Clifton held up a hand to ward off his brother's next comment. Prince Ryle closed his opened mouth. "And I'm not just saying that because I value the Princess. I'm saying that as a guard in your army, brother."

Ryle nodded.

"It would seem, boys," King Eamon stood from his seat on the sofa and lightly patted Clifton on the back. "It would seem we have new topics to discuss with Granton and Anthony. Perhaps you two can find Prince Isaac and meet me at the Council Room?"

Clifton and Ryle nodded and watched as their father left.

"I do not have a good feeling, Ryle. My gut tells me we are in for a devastating blow soon."

"Aye, mine has been telling me the same thing. I am sorry to offer up Princess Elizabeth the way I did. I was voicing options without thinking of your feelings."

Clifton smirked. "Yes, well I cannot blame you. Perhaps we can make it through everything without having to offer up either one of our Princesses, brother."

Ryle chuckled. "Our Princesses? My, you are confident aren't you, little brother?"

Clifton shrugged. "Whether or not anything becomes of Elizabeth and me, I fear she will always be my Princess regardless."

Ryle's face sobered and he nodded. His clear blue eyes, much like their father's, weighed his next words cautiously. "I know exactly what you mean, Cliff."

"In the meantime, perhaps we can annoy a certain prince from the West?"

Laughing, Ryle slapped Clifton on the back as he draped his arm over his shoulders. "I like the way you think, Cliff."

The brothers rounded the corner of the stairwell and stopped in their tracks as they witnessed Prince Isaac assaulting the lips of a maiden. The woman giggled as the prince's hands roamed over the front of her corset and he kissed her willing lips.

"We hate to interrupt." Ryle's rich baritone echoed down the stairwell and had the prince and the maid jumping apart.

"My Lords." Prince Isaac cleared his throat and straightened the front of his tunic. His dark hair tousled and his skin flushed. "I was just… discussing my requests for new linens with—" He turned towards the young woman and she nervously nibbled her bottom lip. "This maiden." He rubbed a hand over his stubbled jaw and glanced at the brothers' disapproving glares.

"Yes, well we are to find you, Prince Isaac, for a meeting with our fathers and King Granton, immediately." Ryle explained. "Please feel free to join us when you are finished… discussing." The brothers passed by him and the maid without a second glance and headed towards the King's Council Room.

"Can you believe the buggar?" Clifton murmured. "One minute he's requesting a courtship with the Princess and then he is caught red-handed with a maid?!"

"Calm yourself, Cliff. That matter will need to be handled later. We have more important matters to discuss at the present." Ryle patted his brother on the back as they entered the room where the kings awaited.

"Ah, boys, glad you joined us. Prince Isaac?"

Clifton began to report the status of the slimy prince, but Ryle stepped in front of him. "On his way, King Granton." Prince Ryle smiled politely and bowed briefly as he took a seat next to his father. Clifton eased into a chair by King Granton and offered the man a polite smile, though his heart was heavily burdened over the topic of Lancer and of his Elizabeth. *His Elizabeth?* He asked himself. He rubbed his chin and pondered the thought and settled himself on the matter. *Yes, his Elizabeth.*

The doors opened and Prince Isaac stepped inside the room, avoiding the sharp gaze of Clifton and slyly slipping into a seat next to his father.

"Now, we are called here because Eamon would like to discuss a few things with us." King Granton waved for Eamon to begin.

"Yes, thank you Granton. I actually want to bring your attention to what happened to Cliff earlier on his ride. He stumbled upon a Renaldi near the river."

"What?!" Granton and Anthony asked at the same time, both rising from their seats and looking at Clifton. Isaac's brow rose in surprise as well as he watched the heavy scrutiny thrust upon the Eastern prince.

"Yes, it is true." Clifton stated evenly. "Prince Samuel, to be exact."

"Samuel?" Granton asked. "But he is young, barely fifteen."

"Yes. He was quite young."

"Tell us everything." King Granton stated, easing back into his seat.

Clifton relayed his encounter and conversation and watched as each king sat quietly listening. Three men, different in stature, but all possessing a quiet air of leadership. Clifton finished and glanced towards King Granton. "I fear, my King, that we will feel our first threat soon enough."

"This is devastating news indeed." Granton looked to Anthony and Eamon. "What are your thoughts, Anthony?"

King Anthony exhaled loudly on a sigh. "I must admit, the news is troubling. How are we to compete with an invincible army, Granton? If the Lands and the Southern Kingdom unite, we will not be able to withstand their forces."

"I agree." Eamon stated. "Our only way of prevention is to possibly move the Royal Guard to the Southern Boundary. Perhaps if we prevent them from crossing, then we could postpone the—"

"The what? The inevitable?" King Anthony finished. "What is the point in postponing what we all know will happen? I say we cut them off at the knees. We found out about their treachery, we force the Southern Kingdom to submit to the Realm or we assault their kingdom."

"An assault? But we are not ready for that sort of engagement, are we?" Eamon looked to King Granton.

The King's gaze travelled to each of the princes' quiet demeanors. "And what do you say, Prince Isaac?"

Isaac straightened in his chair. "I have to say I agree with my father, my King. We cut the threat off early."

"And you, Prince Ryle?" Granton asked.

Ryle took a deep breath. "I hate to say it, but the plan makes sense, my Lord. Perhaps it will at least show the Southern Kingdom we still have our strength and that their unification with the Realm is the only safe choice for them."

Clifton shook his head in disagreement and King Granton glanced to him. "And you, Prince Clifton. What are your thoughts? I see you disagree."

"Yes, with respect, I do disagree. Yes, that option makes sense on a tactical scale. But are you all forgetting that the Southern Kingdom is already a part of the Realm? They are still a part of *our* Realm. If we start attacking our own people, I do not see that as strengthening us, it would weaken us. Perhaps that is Lancer's plan, to turn us against one another. It seems to already be working."

"But if we do not do anything and the Renaldi's join with Lancer, then where will we be?" Prince Isaac challenged. "I say we kill them and find a new leader for the Southern Kingdom. It is the only way."

"Are you mad?" Clifton took a deep breath to calm his temper. "You can't just kill people. There has to be another way."

"Perhaps if we give them Princess Elizabeth." Prince Isaac recommended.

Ryle watched as King Granton and Clifton's faces both turned red with frustration.

"I do not think that will solve the issues at hand." Granton stated. "It sounds as if the Renaldi's plan to join forces with Lancer regardless of their ties with the Realm."

"What do we know of Lancer?" Clifton interrupted. King Eamon put his hand on his son's arm but Clifton shrugged it off. "No, Father. I wish to speak." Clifton stood and paced around the room. "Forgive me, King Granton, but what makes us think that Lancer will even tolerate the Renaldi's once they have crossed? What do we know of him? Not enough. We know nothing of Lancer's character except that he is powerful and holds a dark hand of power over the Unfading Lands. Something tells me he will not want to share his power with anyone else."

"He brings up a good point." King Eamon acknowledged. "We have yet to hear of Lancer accepting any help or sharing his authority with anyone else, why would he now?"

"We still have to do something." King Anthony chimed in. "We can't let them keep destroying and attacking the Realm."

"That is true too," King Eamon continued. "We have had two villages burned by the Southern Kingdom over the last year. Our guard is stretched thin. We need a solution that buys us more time until we can figure out a way to diminish the Lands."

A knock sounded on the door and Elizabeth poked her head inside. She grimaced. "Oh, my apologies, my Lords. I was not aware my father had company."

Clifton straightened in his seat and smiled. Granton exchanged a smirk with Eamon over the boy's reaction and then smiled towards his daughter. "Did you need something, my dear?"

"Oh, it is of no consequence, Father. I will just discuss the matter with you later."

He nodded for her dismissal and she turned to leave. When she reached the door, Clifton stood. "Princess!" Elizabeth froze and turned back around nervous that the prince would address her in front of their fathers. Clifton walked slowly towards her and lightly reached a hand towards her face. It slid behind her neck and his fingers lightly feathered against her skin. Her heart raced, and her gaze found his as he pulled his hand in front of her. Housed between his fingers was a large brown spider. Elizabeth gasped and jumped back as the gentlemen chuckled. She placed a hand over her heart. "Thank you, Prince Clifton. I… um, yes… a spider… in my hair." Her face grew pale as she swallowed her nerves.

Clifton tossed the now dead spider into a wastebasket and wiped his fingers on a handkerchief Ryle handed him. He then bowed and sent her a small wink before turning back towards his seat.

"Thank you, Prince Clifton." Granton chuckled as his daughter nodded briskly and quickly exited.

"A hero in our midst." Ryle jested as the other men laughed. Isaac rolled his eyes and grinned. "A bit of a spider scares the Princess, whom I thought feared nothing."

"Yes, Lizzy has always hated the creatures. Your rescue is much appreciated Clifton."

Clifton nodded.

"Now, where were we?" Granton asked. "Ah, back to the topic of our current circumstances. What if we extended extra guard along the Southern Boundary line to the Unfading Lands and make our presence known? We push the Western Kingdom guards over to aid the Eastern Kingdom, maintaining a tight perimeter around the Western lines as well. I feel a strong military presence might ward off any thoughts of future attacks and will give us ample time to come up with a solution for any potential threats from the Lands."

All the men nodded.

"I still think we should just wipe them clean." Isaac stated.

"For now, we wait, Prince Isaac. I feel much like Prince Clifton on the matter of killing our own people. We should prevent it at all costs. If it comes to that later down the road, we will decide then. I appreciate you gentlemen bringing this to my attention. Prince Clifton, if you encounter Prince Samuel again, I wish for you to extend the invitation for his protection here." Clifton nodded as the King stood. "Now, if you will excuse me, I must meet with Mosiah over the matters we have discussed."

∞

Elizabeth waltzed in a circle with Mary in the garden. "See, you just count, Mary. One, two, three. One, two, three. And turn, two, three." She lightly turned Mary beneath her arm and back to the main frame, Elizabeth leading her attendant.

"Elizabeth, what are you doing?" Alayna's voice carried over in amusement.

Mary pulled quickly away from Elizabeth's grasp, her cheeks stained red. Elizabeth turned to her sister and smiled. "I was taking Mary on a waltz through the roses."

Alayna, Prince Ryle, and Prince Clifton stood watching with smiles on their faces.

"Mary does not know how to dance, and so I offered to teach her." Elizabeth then grabbed Mary again and forced the attendant to comply. "Don't be shy, Mary. Let's show them what you have learned." She then began counting softly as she led Mary around the cobblestone.

Clifton watched as Elizabeth beamed in pride and the shy Mary watched Elizabeth intently, her gaze drifting from Elizabeth's proud gaze and back to her feet for counting. Without thinking, Clifton stepped forward and tapped Mary on the shoulder. The women stopped dancing. Clifton bowed, as was custom, to Mary and then Elizabeth. "I wonder, Princess, if I may cut in for one minute."

Mary began to back away, but Clifton caught her hand. Elizabeth curtsied and smiled. "Why of course, Prince Clifton." She stepped to the side as Clifton began leading Mary around the cobblestone path in the garden. Elizabeth began humming a tune for them to dance with as she watched Clifton in admiration.

Alayna and Ryle watched in surprise at the three, and then Prince Ryle stuck out his hand. "May I have this dance, Princess?" Alayna's face flushed but she nodded as Prince Ryle swung her into his arms and began waltzing.

Elizabeth's humming wavered in excitement and she began tapping a stick to the rhythm. "You all look beautiful!" She continued to hum and walk around smelling the rose blossoms. She picked two, and snuck behind Alayna, sticking the bloom behind her sister's ear. She kissed her sister's cheek as she danced with the handsome Prince Ryle. She then walked to Mary and did the same. Clifton watched as Elizabeth waltzed to her steady hum as well around the garden with an invisible partner.

Prince Isaac emerged in the garden and followed the hum of a melodic voice. He froze as he watched the small dance circle. He smiled and walked over to Elizabeth as she tapped her stick. He bowed and offered her his hand. She grinned and politely accepted, allowing him to lead her around the garden with the others. She continued to hum and slowed her pace as the song came to an end.

She stepped back from Prince Isaac and curtsied. "Thank you, Prince Isaac, for joining us."

"How could I not? Your song floated clear across the garden, and seeing how you did not have a partner, I could not call myself a gentleman if I did not step in to guide you." He winked at her. Elizabeth flushed at the flirtatious gesture and turned towards Mary. "Mary, why don't we go down to the pond?"

"Of course, milady."

Mary began to walk away, but Clifton grabbed her hand. "Lady Mary, I thank you for the wonderful dance." He bowed and lightly kissed her hand. Mary blushed and quickly curtsied before darting towards Elizabeth. Elizabeth smiled tenderly at the exchange. Clifton caught the Princess's eye and bowed to her as well. Instead of her formal curtsy in return, she waved and draped her arm over Mary's shoulder as they walked towards the pond.

"Your sister has such a fondness for her attendant." Clifton turned towards Alayna as he spoke.

"Yes, it is most abnormal." Isaac added, causing all to drop their smiles and glower at him.

"Elizabeth appreciates Mary. Mary has been with her most of her life, I dare say she considers her a friend more than an attendant. I also believe it is not abnormal to have a friend in close company." Alayna responded forcefully. "It was a very sweet act you did, Prince Clifton, dancing with Mary. I am sure it meant much to her, and equally as much to my sister."

Clifton bowed as Alayna stormed passed Prince Isaac to walk back inside the castle. She then turned abruptly. "Oh yes. Prince Ryle, thank you for the dance." She curtsied in her lilac colored dress and quickly turned to her retreat again.

"Princess Alayna, huh brother?" Clifton smirked at his older brother catching a brief glimmer of a spark in his eye.

"Indeed, I provided her a partner." Prince Ryle's posture never wavered. He nodded his head in the direction of Prince Isaac who stared across the garden at Elizabeth as she stood by the pond with Mary.

Clifton nodded as well and walked up next to him, crossing his arms as he stood. "A pretty sight, is she not?"

Prince Isaac acknowledged Clifton's presence with a low grunt. "Indeed. Please note, Prince Clifton, that my first offer of courtship with the princess was denied, but that I will continue my pursuit. I must ask you not to interfere."

"I will respectfully not agree."

Prince Isaac, expecting the friendly prince to comply, turned in surprise, unfolding his arms and narrowing his gaze.

Clifton continued, "As I am aware, the courtship proposal was declined by King Granton and the floor is open. It has also been brought to my attention that our dear Princess Elizabeth has no intention of marrying anyone."

Prince Isaac scoffed. "That is absurd! She is a woman well beyond the marrying age, she should marry as quickly as possible. It is not acceptable for a woman to be single past the age of seventeen."

"Both Princesses are well past that age, and they do not seem to mind not being married." Prince Ryle stepped forward as well.

Isaac looked at the two brothers. "Yes, well, if our Realm is to strengthen, Elizabeth must become my bride before the Renaldi's snatch her. You two can hash out the details on which of you would like the future queen. My fate has been decided. I will wed the Princess."

"Your fate has been decided?" Clifton asked tightly. "And how do you feel of your fate?"

"I am neither disappointed nor pleased. I do not like a woman who freely roams and dictates life how she pleases. I figure once Elizabeth is my bride, those attributes can easily be contained. She is an attractive sort, so there is pleasure in that. We shall see if there is anything more pleasurable once I have bedded her as my wife."

Prince Clifton clinched his fists and sharply turned. His brother catching his arm before he threatened Prince Isaac.

"Do not speak of the Princess in such a disrespectful manner in front of me."

Prince Isaac smirked and lightly slapped Clifton on the back. "Yes, well, I see the way you look at her, Prince Clifton. It must be frustrating knowing another man will receive her. Good day, gentlemen." Prince Isaac whistled a happy tune as he exited the gardens, no doubt knowing he had set Clifton's blood to boiling.

"There is no way I am going to let that man marry Princess Elizabeth. Especially after he was caught red-handed with a maid in the stairwell."

"Calm down, brother," Prince Ryle placed a calming hand on Clifton's shoulder. "Something tells me Princess Elizabeth will refuse to be caught anyhow. And we both know Prince Isaac will not win over the Princess. Let us pray he loses complete favor in King Granton's eyes in the next few days to protect the Princess from another courtship offer from him. You, however, must tread lightly."

Clifton exhaled slowly and loudly, his obvious anger at Prince Isaac's words haunting his thoughts. "I agree, and I will… try. It seems I will not only be protecting Elizabeth from the Renaldi's, but I will also be protecting her from Prince Isaac if the need should arise."

"Careful, Cliff. We already have one kingdom attacking our borders. Tread carefully that we do not have another." Ryle warned softly as he left his brother.

Clifton watched as Elizabeth skipped a rock across the pond. She and Mary cheered when a successful four hops ensued. He smiled and found himself walking down to the pond's edge as well. "Impressive, Your Highness."

Elizabeth jumped and then recovered with a welcoming smile. "Why thank you, Prince Clifton. It is a skill I have worked on mastering for quite some time."

"Ah, *lessons* perhaps?" He teased as she giggled and shook her head. "No, and no more guesses." She bantered playfully as she handed him a smooth gray stone. "Dare you challenge me?"

Her right brow arched in contest and had him lightly tracing his finger over it, catching them both by surprise. He lowered his hand quickly and took a step back. Gripping the rock in his hand he held it up to survey it. "How do I know you handed me a proper rock?"

Fisting her hands on her hips, Elizabeth laughed. "Feel free to choose one of your liking, Prince, but I assure you that *that* particular rock only aids in your success."

"Is that so?" He gripped the rock in his fingers and then flicked his wrist. The rock skipped three solid times across the smooth water and then sunk leaving small ripples.

"Three. Not bad." Elizabeth complimented with a smirk as she took her stance on the edge of the pond.

"Mary?" Clifton asked, Elizabeth's attendant jumping to attention.

"Yes, my Lord?"

"What is Princess Elizabeth's record for rock skipping?"

Elizabeth turned to her attendant and nodded with a smile.

"Six, my Lord."

"Six?" He asked and then looked to Elizabeth with wonder. "I dare say that is quite a record."

"Yes. It is." Elizabeth stated confidently. "Do not feel intimidated," she grinned with a fire in her blue eyes that had his feet stepping towards her. She stepped back in a happy retreat and flicked her wrist. They watched as her rock skipped four times. "Four!" She jumped and clapped her hands cheerfully. "I win!"

Clifton threw his head back and laughed. "If I had known I only had one turn I would have stepped up my game, milady."

"You should always treat your first time as your only time, Prince Clifton." Elizabeth stated as she bundled up the bottom of her skirts in her left arm and lightly stepped into the shallow water. He then noticed her bare feet.

"Wisdom, Princess Elizabeth, which I will cherish always." He replied watching as she stepped slowly through the water. "May I ask where you are headed?" He chuckled as she teetered for balance on the slippery rocks.

"I wish to acquire a rock from the small pile over there." She pointed to a small rise in the water where several rocks rested along with cattails and clovers.

"I see. None of the other rocks will do?" He waved his hand to the vastly populated pebbled terrain surrounding his feet.

"Nope. Sometimes the best ones are the farthest to reach." Elizabeth stated as she reached her destination and fingered several different stones.

"You have no idea." Clifton mumbled under his breath. He heard a small snicker from Mary and flashed her a small smile.

Elizabeth held up a rock in success. "Aha! Found it."

"The perfect rock?" Clifton asked in disbelief.

"Yes. For your demise."

"My demise?" He laughed. "Perhaps I should traipse around the entire kingdom to find my perfect rock to use in our friendly competition."

She waved him off. "Suit yourself, Prince Clifton, but I assure you it will be to no avail."

"Confident, isn't she Mary?" He teased, glancing at Elizabeth's sweet attendant. Mary giggled and nodded. "Always, my Lord."

Elizabeth landed on the bank beside him and dropped the hem of her skirts. She handed him the rock for his perusal. Clifton smoothed his thumb over the white stone. "I must say, it is quite good. Perhaps if I just—" He acted as if he were going to flick the rock into the water and Elizabeth leapt at his hand. She attempted to grab the rock and laughed. Playfully swatting his arm, she smiled up at him. She felt his hand at the small of her back as he stepped closer to her. She lowered her gaze and stared at the brass buttons that clasped his sky blue tunic across his broad chest. She lifted her gaze slowly, having to glance up at him as he stood more than eight inches above her. She found his meadow green gaze and grinned at the spark she saw hidden in their depths.

A throat cleared and Elizabeth took a quick step away from him as Princess Melody waved shyly from the edge of the garden. "Princess Elizabeth, your sister said I could find you out here. If I am interrupting, I can just—"

"Oh, no interruption, Princess Melody, I would be delighted for your company. Prince Clifton was just…" She trailed off as she glanced at the handsome prince again. He did not smile, but his face held a kindness nonetheless. Disappointment shined in his gaze, but he bowed. "I was just leaving. Perhaps I will let you beat me at rock skipping another day, Princess." He handed her the smooth white pebble and gently folded her fingers over the top of it. "I enjoyed our time together, milady." He bowed again and then turned to Mary as well, bowing. "Good day, Mary. Always a pleasure."

Mary curtsied, and all the women watched as he glided across the garden and into the castle.

∞

Edward stood at attention as Lancer waved his hand in dismissal. "Get him out of my sight." His voice dripped with disdain as one of Lancer's guards yanked the Southern Kingdom guard to his feet and forced him to walk in front with a sword grazing his lower back. Edward watched as guard after guard from the Southern Kingdom was brought into the great hall and before Lancer. Lancer listened with patience to the pleas, the begging, or the offers each of the men proposed. When pleased, he would look to Edward for a nod of approval. If he disapproved, he would simply wave his hand and they would be taken away. Edward wasn't quite sure where they were being taken, but he assumed it was not a good alternative. Edward listened to the man in front of them. "I assure you, my Lord, that the Southern Kingdom is a strong ally for you."

Lancer smirked at Edward. "What makes you think I need allies?" He asked with a deep chuckle. "Edward?" He turned towards Edward, "Is this how the Realm sees me?" He asked in mock concern. "That I am just a weak man with no possible strength?"

Edward did not respond, knowing the question was rhetorical. The man's gaze glanced over at Edward and his eyes widened. "Y-you're Prince Edward." He pointed to him. "You crossed?!"

Edward continued standing at attention next to Lancer. Lancer smiled at his obedience and then pointed to the guard standing next to the man. "This one has promise. Take him." The guard helped the man to his feet and took him the opposite direction of the last man.

"I trust, Edward, that you will be able to guide that man and the others I have selected."

Edward turned towards him, his newly pressed golden tunic's collar stiff and rubbing against his neck. "I'm sorry, my Lord?"

"I am building you an army." Lancer whispered quietly and with a small smirk. "I would like you to train them for me. I figure of all the men in the Realm and the Lands, you would be my best choice for the position of Captain in my ranks. Do I assume incorrectly?"

Edward swallowed slowly. He felt his palms sweat. How could he train an army that was meant to destroy his father's kingdom? "I am honored, my Lord, but I must admit I'm quite perplexed as to the reasoning behind an army. We cannot cross the boundary, and minus the willing, the Realm does not plan to cross over here. I do not see how a war between forces would be possible."

Lancer chuckled, the sound low and menacing. "Oh, dear Edward, there are ways. They have yet to discover, but there are ways."

Edward's heart beat rapidly in his chest. "What ways are there?"

Lancer tilted his head and studied Edward. "Can you not tell me that your father contemplated at one time or another to invade the Lands?"

"He's thought about it many times, my Lord, but the consequence of crossing the boundary withheld him from pursuit."

"I have a feeling, a strong feeling, my dear prince, that once our strength envelopes most of the Northern Kingdom, we will face a military advance of some sort."

"But how? They cannot cross back if they come here. I do not see them risking that."

"Nevertheless, it is what I see, therefore I request your skill in training my men. Is this task acceptable to you?"

"Of course. I did not mean to seem ungrateful, sir. I am just adjusting to the idea of an attack."

"Do not worry, Edward. I am glad you speak freely. It is important for you and me to discuss such matters openly. It is one of the reasons I selected you."

Smiling, Lancer waved to the guard at the door. A flood of sunlight entered the room as another man, dressed in black dress representing the Southern Kingdom, stepped through the door begging for his life.

CHAPTER 5

"Did you see the way Prince Clifton danced with Mary?" Elizabeth turned to her sister with a wide smile. "I believe he may be the sweetest man I've ever met."

Alayna laughed at her sister as Elizabeth readjusted the pin in her hair, attempting to tame the thick black mass. She pinned back the silky curl and glanced up at her sister. "And you, dancing with Prince Ryle. I must say the two of you make a handsome couple."

"Don't get any ideas, Lizzy." Alayna warned.

"What?" Elizabeth challenged innocently. "Your betrothal with the Southern Kingdom fell through, thank God." she mumbled softly before continuing. "You are a free woman now. Free to love whom you please."

"Who said anything about loving?" Alayna baited. "I have a kingdom to run and with the new developments with the Southern Kingdom, it is best my full attention be focused upon that instead of a handsome prince."

"Yes, well, excuse me if I choose to focus upon both." Elizabeth stated. "I find the condition of the Realm depresses my spirits. Talk of war and battle make my heart ache. I wish we could just advance upon the Lands and get it over with." She swiped her hand through the air in finality.

"If only it were that easy." Alayna said wishfully as she flipped through several stacks of parchment.

"Your face will freeze that way if you continue to frown." Elizabeth warned softly as she sat across from her sister and looked over the parchments. She lightly tapped her finger on her sister's furrowed brow. "Tell me what you would like to see, Alayna."

"What do you mean?"

"I mean, how do you think Father should handle the threat of the Southern Kingdom and the Lands?"

Alayna sighed heavily and leaned back in her chair. "It's a delicate situation, Lizzy."

"I know, but that does not mean you have not thought about it."

"Father's strength fades every day." Alayna stated softly, her eyes reflective as she studied the hem of her sleeve. She lightly tugged the silk fabric until it covered her wrist. Glancing at Elizabeth, she smiled softly. "I know it sounds awful, but I wish Father would just step down as King and grant me the position now. The stress and worry of the Realm weighs heavily upon him and I fear his health cannot take much more. Why not step down now and enjoy the last few months or year of his life without having to confront those stressful issues? I could relieve that burden from him."

Elizabeth listened to her sister's passionate speech and her heart leapt in her chest. If Alayna were so willing to take upon the stress of potential war then perhaps she would understand Elizabeth's desire to aid in the fight. She sat up eagerly, straightening in her chair. "Have you discussed this move with Father?"

"Not yet. I do not wish to upset him."

"It will never happen unless you ask, Alayna. And I think you are more than ready to take the role as Queen."

"Thank you for the confidence, sister, but I still am not sure our father feels the same way."

"Why do we not discuss the matter with him?"

Alayna glanced up, her caramel eyes full of nerves. "You would address him with me?"

"Of course I would." Elizabeth agreed. She smiled confidently and extended her hand to her sister. "Come. Let's do it now."

"Now?" Alayna asked nervously.

"Yes, now." Elizabeth tugged her sister out the door and towards her father's chambers. "If we do not discuss it now, it will never happen."

Elizabeth knocked on the heavy doors. Hearing their father's voice carry though the wood, she opened the door. "Hello, Father."

King Granton glanced up from his table. Seeing both his daughters made him smile. His glance carried to Alayna's worried face and had his left brow rising. "To what do I owe this visit?"

Elizabeth nudged Alayna into one of the chairs and then took the one next to her. "Father, Alayna and I have an important matter to discuss with you."

"Is that so?" He smirked at his youngest daughter as she confidently spoke.

"Yes. We fear the matter may be a delicate one, but we wish to speak with you all the same."

"Does this pertain to the current military strategies?" He glanced to Alayna. She shook her head.

"Partially." Elizabeth interrupted and corrected.

"I see." King Granton rubbed his chin and set his papers to the side. Clasping his hands in front of him, he waited. "Proceed."

Elizabeth looked to Alayna. Alayna sat quietly, her nerves betraying her and her silence deafening. Elizabeth cleared her throat, but her sister continued staring at their father's hands.

"Father," Elizabeth began. "How have you been feeling lately?"

"Feeling?"

"Yes, your health? How is your health?"

"Oh, my dear Lizzy, you do not need to worry about me. I am fine."

"Are you sure?"

The King's face relaxed and he smiled. "Of course, dear."

"Well then I fear our conversation is for naught." Elizabeth stated, slapping her hands on her thighs and then standing.

The King leaned back in his chair in surprise at her abrupt dismissal. "Now wait a minute. What is this about?"

Elizabeth turned back around and eased back in her chair. The King looked to Alayna and she nervously cast her eyes elsewhere. Elizabeth looked up at the ceiling and prayed her sister would muster the courage to speak to their Father.

"Elizabeth?" Her father asked.

Sighing, she folded her hands in her lap. "Okay, I'm just going to come right out with it then."

"That would be best." King Granton stated on a chuckle.

"Father, we were wondering if you had given any thought to a timeline for Alayna's coronation."

Her father's eyes briefly widened in surprise. Clearly not the topic he had been expecting. "Coronation?"

"Yes, as Queen." Elizabeth stated. "We fear the stress of the current conditions in the Realm and with the Unfading Lands may be harming your health."

His gaze softened upon his daughters. "Ah. I see. You two are worried about me, is that it?"

Alayna finally glanced up and nodded with her sister.

"I assure you I am doing fine. Yes, these times are difficult and stressful, but my health remains intact."

"Father, be honest with us, please." Elizabeth challenged. "We know you have struggled the last few weeks. I hate to admit it as much as you do." Elizabeth heard her sister's quick intake of breath at her words.

King Granton listened patiently, his eyes steady.

"It's not that I wish you to not be king anymore, Father. I know the Realm loves you almost as much as we do. But perhaps you could step back and let Alayna take over the Realm, that way you can rest. You've spent over 40 years as king. I think you deserve some rest, especially with your health the way it is." Elizabeth finished, her courage slightly fading as her father sat in silence.

"Is this what you wish as well, Alayna?" He asked.

Alayna nodded. "I only wish for what you want, Father, but I want you to know I am willing if need be."

"I see." King Granton steepled his fingers in front of his lips and lightly tapped them against his chin. "Perhaps it is a fair matter to discuss."

Both sisters looked to one another in shock. "It is?" They both asked.

He chuckled. "Yes, my princesses, it is. I have been thinking quite hard on the subject matter. In fact, I have discussed it quite openly with Mosiah."

Elizabeth smiled. "Really?"

"Yes, Lizzy."

"Father, I want you to know that I will accept the position as Queen only when you are ready." Alayna stated.

He reached across the table and both girls offered a hand for him to hold. "You two are my life." He smiled, his eyes becoming glassy. "I wish to remain in the Council of the throne once I step down. I will be a guide, Alayna."

"Of course. I would not make a decision without first discussing the matter with you."

"Good." He squeezed her hand and then looked to Elizabeth. "And you Lizzy… what of you? What is it you wish during this transition?"

Elizabeth took a deep breath. "I wish to be a part of the Council as well, Father, especially in regard to the guard."

His brow rose. "The guard? And what interest do you have in the guard, my dear?"

Elizabeth squirmed. "I feel I could be quite an asset to military strategy."

He chuckled. "Lizzy, war is no place for a lady. Military strategy is best left to the Captain and the generals."

"With Alayna as Queen, war will become a place for a lady. She will be making decisions on behalf of the kingdom. If she can make military decisions, then certainly I can supply some insight." Elizabeth stated forcefully, her passion and frustration surprising the king and her sister.

King Granton leaned back in his chair. "Perhaps we will give it a try then."

A relieved smile washed over her face as she raced around the table and hugged her father. "Thank you, Father."

Patting her back he looked to Alayna. "I am glad you came and spoke with me. The Council and I will convene in two days' time in the Council Room. I wish to start incorporating your inputs. Please be punctual."

"Yes, Father. Of course."

Elizabeth smiled and nodded.

"Very well. The matter is settled." King Granton stood from his chair and hugged each of his daughters closely. "Things within the Realm will be hard soon, I hope you girls know how much I love you and wish for things to be different."

"We do, Father." Elizabeth assured him. "We do."

He released them and waved them on. "Now go, leave me to my work."

The sisters curtsied and then left their father's chamber.

∞

Elizabeth wrote vigorously as she tried to recount the previous days' activities for her brother. She tied her letter to Thatcher and nudged him across the boundary line. Edward scooped him up and tilted his head at his sister's obvious excitement. He grinned as he opened the letter.

Edward, you would not believe what happened yesterday! I enjoyed the most amazing day with Mary. Mary has never learned to dance, can you believe that? All the balls we have hosted at the castle, and she has never learned to dance. Naturally, I had to teach her. So there we were, in the garden, and I kept count, just as you taught me. I taught her a basic waltz. We were interrupted by

Alayna, Prince Ryle, and Prince Clifton. Instead, of Alayna being upset, she allowed me to continue. However, I was interrupted by Prince Clifton. He requested to dance with Mary, like a true gentleman, bowing before us. I willingly obliged because I could see how excited Mary was at the prospect. I then began to hum the tune Mother used to sing to us, and not only did Prince Clifton dance with Mary, but Prince Ryle danced with Alayna. It was magical. Truly magical, Edward. Prince Isaac showed up and danced with me... Oh how I wish Prince Clifton had interrupted our dance to step in. His dance with Mary was much more important however, and I am glad he did not relinquish her as his partner.

Also, discussions are under way for Alayna's coronation. Yes, Father is open to the prospect. Alayna and I will join in on our first Council meeting tomorrow evening. I cannot wait. My opportunity, Edward! My opportunity to display my military skills. Yes, my lessons will remain secret, and yes, they must not know I know how to fight just yet, but to have input?! I am excited for the opportunity.

How are things on your end, brother? I see you now wear the colors of the Unfading Lands. Should I be worried?

Elizabeth watched her brother read and bounced in place with anticipation of his response. He finally looked up and grinned. She clasped her hands over her heart and twirled in a circle laughing. Edward began waltzing in place and they danced together. Separated by a thin veil, but they danced together. Elizabeth's heart was full of joy as she watched her brother continue reading. His head then snapped up quickly. He glanced around and waved her away from the boundary line. Elizabeth ducked behind one of the trees near the river and watched as a guard in Southern Kingdom colors emerged from behind a Willow. Edward and the man exchanged words and Edward patted the man on his shoulder and sent him on his way. He waited a few beats and then waved her forward. She smiled as he fished in his pocket and retrieved a letter tied with a piece of rope that he had prewritten for their meeting. He slipped it on Thatcher and then waved to his sister. She blew him a kiss that he pretended to catch and held his fist next to his heart. He eased Thatcher across the boundary, mounted his horse and then was gone.

Elizabeth slipped the letter from Thatcher's neck and sat on the boulder near her arena. She glanced at the markings in the clay and noticed one of her markings had moved back to the side of the Lands. Strength was growing, she thought in dismay. She untied Edward's letter and read eagerly.

My Dearest Lizzy,

So much has happened over here, I fear I cannot put it all into words. I'm sure you will have noticed my new tunic. I now wear the colors of The Unfading Lands because I am now officially Lancer's Captain of the Guard. Please, do not be troubled by this news. We both knew it as a possibility. This can work in our favor, sister. I am not quite sure how just yet, but I am working on it. I have built a small band of Uniters amongst the ranks as well, but our meetings are in secret. My position is crucial for any future success of the Realm.

I must maintain my position close to Lancer in order for the Realm to stand a chance, Lizzy. Lancer has every intention of swallowing up the Realm. He has me preparing an army for him, because he believes Father will send troops across the boundary out of desperation. Most of Lancer's guards are now coming from the Southern Kingdom. I fear the Realm will have attacks coming from both the Lands and the South now. Please, be prepared and provide Mosiah with some insight. I know you can persuade him to listen. I have grown close to Lancer, or at least he takes me into his company quite often. Yet there is a portion of his life that remains private. There is a room inside his castle that no one enters but himself. I feel this must be where he seeks refuge to meditate on his strategies. I also believe there is something inside that room, something... powerful. I have yet to venture to it. However, I aim to discover its secrets.

Cecilia has been working vigorously at gaining followers. She walks the boundary line every day to encounter new crossers before they have had time to acclimate to Lancer's rule. We will defeat him Lizzy. We will.

What are Father and the other kings doing to protect the Realm? I must admit I feel disheartened by what I have seen here. The Southern Kingdom's rebellion against Father has caused me extreme worry. Are you continuing your lessons in my absence? I do hope so, sister. Though I wish for you to never have to raise a sword, I would feel much better knowing you could if the need arises.

I will do my best to meet with you, but I fear my new schedule is tightly woven. I also find it hard to be alone these days. Fellow guards, Cecilia, or even Lancer tend to consume my time. I promise to continue with letters, Elizabeth, but my physical presence may be quite scarce in the next few weeks. Take care, Lizzy, and be watchful.

Elizabeth folded the letter and tucked it into her saddle bag. She unsheathed her sword and turned towards her hanging targets. Edward wanted her to be ready, she would be ready. She heard a rustle within the trees and turned swiftly. Narrowing her gaze she surveyed the thicket for movement, but saw nothing. Watchful eyes were upon her, she could feel them. She tucked her sword away and climbed into her saddle. Clicking the reins, she sent Lenora into a fast gallop back to the castle. Something was stirring, she thought. A slow rain began to drip as she topped the horizon, the wind and rain pelting against her face as she drove Lenora faster. Her trousers drenched, she heaved a sigh of relief once inside the stables. She dismounted and snatched her skirt from her saddle bag and tied it around her waist. She then set about removing her saddle and brushing down Lenora's wet coat.

The rain sounded on the rooftops and Elizabeth found her gaze drawn to the horizon and the tree line that shadowed the river and the boundary line. *Who was out there?* Lost in thought, she did not hear footsteps emerging from a stall two doors down.

"Princess Elizabeth."

Elizabeth snatched her sword and whirled, pinning a wide eyed Prince Isaac with his back against the stall. He held his hands up in surrender as her blade pointed directly at his Adam's apple. He swallowed deeply. She heaved a breath of relief and dropped her stance. "Prince Isaac, you scared me."

"I am sorry, Princess. If it is any consolation, you scared me too." He tilted his head towards the sword still gripped in her fist.

"Yes, well… it is best to always be on guard."

"Aye. I find it interesting you prefer to carry a sword instead of being accompanied by a guard." Prince Isaac stated.

"I like to be alone with my thoughts, and a guard would simply be in the way." Elizabeth explained as she tucked her sword away.

"You are an interesting woman, Princess." Isaac grinned as he studied her wet hair and dry skirt. *Curious*, he thought.

"I take that as a compliment, Prince Isaac."

He shrugged as if he did not quite care how she accepted the comment.

"So, what brings you to the stables?"

He rubbed a hand over a small smirk that had briefly travelled over his face. "I… I wished to check on my horse. He's the scared sort when it comes to storms."

Elizabeth placed a hand over her heart in pity. "Poor thing. How sweet of you to check on him."

Isaac's eyes gleamed with pleasure at her reaction. "Yes, well he is important to me."

Smiling, Elizabeth linked her arm through his. "Shall we make our way back to the castle? I fear the rains will only become worse and we do not want to be stranded out here in the stables."

She grimaced playfully as Isaac chuckled. "Indeed, milady. Lead the way."

He allowed Elizabeth to escort him through the stables. Turning before exiting, he shot a sharp eye to his stall where he housed his horse and saw the young maid run out. Smirking, he turned back to face the rain. Yes, the Princess had interrupted him and the maid, but the Princess did not hear or know of her interruption. He listened half-heartedly as Elizabeth carried on a conversation as they walked through the portico that led to the back of the castle. Perhaps the stables were a brazen choice for a rendezvous location, however the Eastern princes had discovered him in the stairwell. Perhaps he needed to venture to other areas of the castle and discover secret places. His chest warmed at the thought and also at the thought that Elizabeth actually thought he was extending a generous gesture to his horse. He did not care whether his horse slept in the rain much less in a stable listening to the rain. But if it pleased the Princess to think him sensitive to his creature's needs, then so be it. After all, he had his kingdom to think of, and the Western Kingdom *would be* the aligning kingdom to the throne if he had a say in it.

∞

Elizabeth and Alayna stepped towards the looming doors of the Council Room and both took a deep breath. *This was it*, thought Elizabeth. Her chance to prove she could contribute to military strategy. A chance for Alayna to prove she was ready to be queen. Alayna gripped the brass handle and heaved the door open. As they stepped inside, all heads turned towards them.

"Ah, and here they are now." King Granton announced, waving his daughters into the room.

Elizabeth's gaze flashed from one man to the next. Mosiah, the Captain of the Guard, King Eamon, King Anthony, Prince Isaac, Prince Ryle and Prince Clifton. All glanced at the two princesses as if they had sprouted extra heads. She rolled back her shoulders and tilted her chin and proudly walked to the available seat between

Prince Clifton and King Eamon. Alayna slipped into a chair next to Mosiah and Prince Anthony.

"I have asked the two princesses to join us today because there are matters we need to discuss that involve them."

Prince Isaac straightened thinking that perhaps his courtship may be reinstated.

"I have asked Princess Alayna to join in on the discussions because, as future queen, her opinions and decisions will be guiding the Realm in the near future. It is her authority to make the final decision on all matters brought to the Council." King Granton glanced around the room at the surprised faces of the men, but none vocalized their thoughts.

"I asked Princess Elizabeth to come today, because my daughter wishes to be amongst the Council for strategic military planning with the guard."

Prince Isaac scoffed loudly, causing all to glance his direction.

"Isaac…" His father warned softly.

"Forgive me, my King." Isaac smirked at King Granton. "But a woman? Aiding the guard?"

"Yes." King Granton and Elizabeth stated at the same time. Elizabeth shot her father a fierce gaze and then turned her attention towards Prince Isaac. "Is it so hard to believe, Prince Isaac, that a woman may have a level head for such matters?"

"A level head?" Prince Isaac repeated. "Forgive me, my Princess, but it takes more than a level head to enforce the guard."

"I do not wish to enforce anything." Elizabeth challenged bravely. "I wish to supply insight. I am quite confident in my abilities. I know more about military strategy than you know."

"I find that hard to believe." Prince Isaac baited, leaning across the table and winking at her.

Elizabeth's cheeks flushed with fury as she leaned forward as well. "I held you at the tip of my sword, did I not?" Her eyes narrowed as everyone else's in the room widened at that announcement.

Clifton wondered why the Princess had pulled a sword on Prince Isaac. By the look in the other prince's eyes, the current announcement had infuriated him. Elizabeth leaned back in her seat with a triumphant smugness set in her jaw and a nod towards her father's direction for him to continue. King Granton cleared his throat. "Alright, if there is no other debate, shall we continue?" His crystal eyes scanned the room, and no one objected. "Very well. Mosiah, please tell us the latest from the guards."

Mosiah sat straight in his chair and spread out the maps on the table. "My Lords… and ladies," he added, "I spread before you the current lands of the Realm. This line here marking the boundary of the Unfading Lands." He waved a finger over a thin red line. "Since Prince Clifton's encounter with Prince Samuel of the Southern Kingdom and the announcement of the South's potential threat, we have moved the guards from the Northern boundary lines down to the South. We also began placing guards along the Eastern and Western borders as well. Since the arrival of our guards, the Southern Kingdom has retreated within their city gates. We have extended friendship to the king, but no word has been returned, and neither has our guard. We suspect he has been imprisoned."

"Imprisoned?" Elizabeth questioned with shock.

All the men glanced at her. "And what are we doing to get him back?" She asked.

"Nothing as of right now, milady." Mosiah continued and turned back to the king.

"And why not?" Elizabeth asked, causing Isaac to roll his eyes and for Mosiah to turn towards her again in surprise for her questioning.

"We feel the matter to be an unstable one, Princess. We do not want to risk advancing on the kingdom for one guard. It may spur a series of conflicts resulting in the loss of more guards." Mosiah patiently awaited her response.

"So we leave him at the mercy of our enemies?" Elizabeth's brow furrowed. "This is unacceptable. Father, please say you have a solution."

King Granton held up his hand. "Elizabeth, please let Mosiah continue and then we will discuss the details."

Elizabeth nodded and sat back in her chair. She felt a light squeeze of her left hand underneath the table. She slightly jumped in her seat until she realized it was Prince Clifton giving her a reassuring squeeze. She turned towards him and smiled graciously. He removed his hand and she immediately missed his strength.

"It is hard for us to determine the amount of guards the Southern Kingdom has behind closed gates." Mosiah continued. "If we could somehow get a man inside, or perhaps appeal to Prince Samuel for more information, we may have a better idea of the threat we are facing."

"Why not send Princess Elizabeth?" Isaac invited the notion sarcastically. "She is eagerly anticipating action."

Clifton stiffened in his seat and began to rise before Elizabeth laid a hand on his arm. "The Princess will not be taken to the Southern Kingdom." Clifton growled.

"Think of it." Isaac stated. "It's what Prince Eric wants, right? He wants Elizabeth."

"What?" Elizabeth asked in confusion. "When did this come about?" She turned anxiously to her father, who continued watching Isaac.

"Let's just say we offer her up as an… option." Isaac raised his hands in an innocent gesture. "If Prince Eric wants her as badly as Prince Samuel says he does, he'll take the bait. Then we will have someone on the inside to feed us the information we need."

"At what cost?" Alayna interrupted. "At the risk of my sister marrying a prince set upon ruining her kingdom? This solution is preposterous. Please continue Mosiah." Alayna caught the grateful gaze of Elizabeth before turning back towards the Captain.

"Yes, as I was saying, we must find a way to gain more insight into the Southern Kingdom and their relations with the Unfading Lands." Mosiah explained.

"I can do it." Clifton stated.

Elizabeth turned to him in surprise and lightly placed a hand on his arm. He gently placed his hand atop hers and continued, "We know Prince Samuel has been sent to spy on the Northern Kingdom, and from what he told me, it was not the first time. He will be back. I know where he will go. I will wait for him and then propose the idea of him feeding me knowledge."

"How do you know where he will be?" Elizabeth asked, her blue eyes shining.

"The same place he always goes." Clifton replied vaguely and turned towards her father. "Look, I know I can persuade Samuel. Give me a few days. If I do not encounter him or he fails to agree, we can try a different route."

King Granton looked to Alayna. "Alayna, what say you of this plan?"

Prince Ryle studied Alayna's soft features and the hard look her father cast her way. Her confidence did not waver as she sat straight in her chair, her hands neatly folded in her lap. "I feel it is the best route to take as of now. I do not want us to cause unnecessary turmoil with the South. A rescue mission for the guard should be arranged, but not until we know the forces we are up against."

King Granton nodded in approval and then glanced around the room. "It is decided then. We meet in three days' time. Prince Clifton, please notify me the instant you learn something."

Clifton nodded. "Yes, my King."

"Any other matters?" King Granton asked.

"Yes, my King." Clifton stated again. "I wish to consult with Princess Elizabeth over matters regarding Prince Samuel and his usual whereabouts, if possible."

Knowing the young prince had been sent to spy on Elizabeth and the kingdom, King Granton obliged. He knew Clifton would look after his daughter while also receiving information from the young prince. "I think that a wise decision. You may meet with her following the Council."

Clifton nodded obediently.

"Any other matters?"

No one answered. "Dismissed." King Granton waved his hand and everyone stood.

Elizabeth exited quietly with her sister. In the hall, Elizabeth linked her arm with Alayna's as they began walking down the main stairwell towards the grand hall.

"You did well, future Queen." Elizabeth complimented softly.

"As did you." Alayna stated. "I must admit, Elizabeth, I was quite impressed with your outspokenness. I think I will value having you on the Council when I am queen."

"Really?" Elizabeth asked with pleasure.

"Yes." Alayna smiled softly. "I feel there is more than what you are telling me, but the fact you can hold a prince at the tip of a sword and make him squirm in his seat gives me a strong feeling you could quite possibly do the same to an entire army."

Elizabeth giggled softly and lightly swatted at her sister's arm. "Yes, well I appreciate you backing me up on the fact we need to save the guard that is being held captive. I agree we must wait until we hear of the risks involved, but a rescue must be made."

"Indeed." Alayna agreed. "I feel there is more information we have missed by not being involved in past meetings, but maybe Prince Clifton will enlighten you once you two discuss matters about Prince Samuel."

"Yes," Elizabeth's brow furrowed. "I must admit I was quite perplexed as to why Prince Isaac believes Prince Eric has his sights set on me."

"Me as well. Find that out, will you?" Alayna's gaze carried over the grand hall as she spotted Prince Clifton waiting patiently at the base of the stairs. "Your prince awaits, little sister." She softly squeezed Elizabeth's hand and then released her as she turned to head the opposite direction of Elizabeth. Elizabeth smiled as Clifton bowed. "Princess."

"Prince Clifton." She curtsied in return.

"I wonder if I might steal you away for a stroll around the grounds?"

"Of course, I would be delighted." She linked her arm in his as he guided her towards the doors. Mary followed obediently behind.

"You look lovely today, by the way." He complimented as they stepped into the fresh sunshine.

"Thank you." Elizabeth's gaze fell upon the horizon and towards the tree line. She wondered if Edward had left her another letter.

"I'm sorry Prince Isaac was…" He trailed off as if not knowing what to say.

"Insensitive?" She supplied.

"Ah, yes. I guess for lack of a better word, and a kinder one, that one will work."

"No need to apologize, Prince Clifton. I take everything he says with a grain of salt."

"As is wise."

"I sense you dislike Prince Isaac?" She asked curiously.

"Not dislike completely, just wary."

"As is wise." She mimicked his previous statement making him smirk and softly chuckle at her retort. She glanced up at his sea green eyes and smiled. Worry lurked in their depths, she could tell. She could also see the grim set to his lips that spoke of regret for their future conversation.

"Something is on your mind, Prince. You wished to speak with me in the Council room. Care to share with me your thoughts?"

Clifton sighed deeply and led her towards the stables. "Will you take a ride with me?"

Surprised at the turn in conversation, Elizabeth nodded. "Of course." She turned to Mary. "Mary, I am going for a ride with Prince Clifton. Please let Alayna know of my whereabouts. We will return shortly."

Mary curtsied and wandered off quickly.

"Mary is always attentive." Clifton complimented.

"Yes, she is. I value her greatly." Elizabeth watched her attendant disappear into the castle.

∞

Reaching the stables, the stable boys readied their horses and Elizabeth hoisted herself into her saddle. She watched Clifton swing himself up on Henry and then fall into step beside her. "I want to take you somewhere." Clifton stated as he headed to the top of the hill overlooking the kingdom. Tugging on his reins he drew to a stop and waited for Elizabeth and her horse to settle in beside him.

"It's a beautiful view of the kingdom." He stated as his green eyes reflected the sunshine. Elizabeth studied him quietly.

"It is." She agreed softly. He finally turned and caught her eye, the light tilt to her brow telling him he better share what he needed to before she lost interest in their ride.

"May I share something with you, Princess?"

Elizabeth's heart pounded in her chest. What would Prince Clifton need to share with her in private? Her mind wandered through various scenarios, all of which ended in a passionate confession of love. She silenced her heart as she watched the green depths of his eyes darken in turmoil. "Please, feel free to share whatever you wish." She waved a hand before them, trying to outwardly appear nonchalant, yet inwardly chastising her racing pulse.

"I must admit I am glad you have joined the Council." He began.

Good start, she thought.

"However, I must also tell you that what you heard today is just the tip of the iceberg, I'm afraid."

"How so?"

He shifted in his saddle and then pointed to a tree quite a distance ahead of them. "It was that tree that I found Prince Samuel of the Southern Kingdom lurking behind a few days ago."

Elizabeth nodded for him to continue.

"My conversation with the young man, though disturbing, was quite insightful. Most of the conversation you know by now, but I sensed your confusion over the topic of you and Prince Eric."

"Yes, I was not quite sure why Prince Isaac would offer me up so freely and how he would know the desires of Prince Eric."

"Because Samuel told me. Samuel stated that Prince Eric wished to claim you as his bride and take you across the boundary line into the Unfading Lands."

Elizabeth gasped. "W-what? No. Wait. Did my father agree to this? Is this why you brought me here?" Panic rose in her throat and her gaze darted around the meadow. She gripped her reins tightly and adjusted her feet in her stirrups. She would run away before she would succumb to a marriage with a Renaldi. How could her father do this to her? How could Alayna? Tears threatened her eyes as she took a deep breath. Clinching her thighs against Lenora's back, Elizabeth raised her hands to click her reins. Before she could complete the task, however, Prince Clifton placed a firm and steady hand over hers.

"No, Princess. Do not run in the midst of our conversation. There is more."

Elizabeth relaxed once her eyes settled upon his calm and kind gaze. "Your father did not agree to the arrangement. In fact, none of the Council did, minus Prince Isaac."

She exhaled loudly. "Oh. That is encouraging news." The corner of his mouth tilted into a small grin as he continued. "The conversation with Samuel was eye opening for me as well as the other members of the Council. Samuel was sent by his father, the king, to spy on the Northern Kingdom, but he was also specifically told to spy on you for his brother. He knows your whereabouts, Princess. Which means, I now know your whereabouts." He cornered her with a steady, but firm gaze and waited to see if she confessed anything. She didn't move but waited for him to speak.

"I must ask you, Princess, what your interest may be in the boundary line. Samuel says he finds you there quite often."

Elizabeth felt the air leave her lungs. How could she reveal her lessons with Edward? Her conversations with Edward? Her private oasis of escape?

"It is complicated, I'm afraid." She stated softly. "Do the other members know of my interest in the boundary?"

"No, milady. I left that part out. I just made it known you were being watched."

Grateful, Elizabeth reached over and squeezed his hand in thanks. "Thank you, Prince Clifton."

"Do not thank me yet, Princess." He cleared his throat and glanced down at her hand on his and then back to the horizon. His gaze travelled to the tree line. "I wish for you to tell me."

Elizabeth followed his gaze towards the river and nodded. He needed to know. He had already proven to her he was an honorable man. He did not share with the rest of the Council of her interest at the boundary line. Perhaps he could help her and Edward.

"I can do better than that, Prince Clifton. I will show you." She raised her chin confidently as she clicked her reins. "Follow me."

Clifton inwardly sighed in relief. He was afraid his request would insult or upset Elizabeth, but it seemed, he believed, that she was quite relieved. Henry followed behind Lenora as they made their way to the edge of the tree line. Elizabeth swung down from her saddle and tied her reins to a low-lying limb. He did the same. She watched him carefully, her blue eyes weighing his every move. She stepped close to him and looked up, the sun casting a sparkle in her bright blue eyes.

"May I ask for your discretion?"

"For now." He replied.

She lowered and shook her head. "I'm sorry, Prince, but I need more affirmation than that."

"Princess, it is all I can offer you. If there is something beyond the trees that wishes to harm you, I will raise every flag in the kingdom to draw attention to it." He spoke fiercely and had her smiling. His brow furrowed in confusion.

She reached for his hand and squeezed. "Nothing harmful is awaiting us, Prince Clifton. I can assure you of that. But I thank you for looking out for me. I wish for you to keep this location secret from the rest of the Council."

"May I at least see what it is you are wanting to hide before I make a decision?" He asked.

"No. That would not be very fair for me, now would it?"

He rubbed his chin in his hand and studied her beautiful face. Her eyes pleaded for his agreement.

"Alright. You have my word."

A wide smile spread over her face, her dimple flashing. She kissed him on the cheek and pulled him towards the tree line. "Thank you, Prince Clifton. Now just follow me in here." She grunted as a twig snagged against her dress skirts, but she fought through the brambles into a small clearing. The river rushed by them, a mere thirty feet from the tree line.

Clifton turned to see Elizabeth walking towards the boundary line. A man stood on the other side with a large smile at her presence. Did she have a love living on the other side? *It all made sense,* he thought. She refused to marry, denied betrothals, because this man held her heart. He watched as she stooped to lift a small rabbit from beneath some clover. She turned to him and waved him forward. The other man's eyes widened in surprise. Elizabeth handed Clifton the small rabbit and removed a piece of parchment from around its neck. "This is my oasis, Prince Clifton. I come here daily, if possible, to escape the confines of the castle. It is my personal place of reflection."

Clifton stood silently. Words failed him as his gaze darted from one thing to the next. He caught sight of the small arena, the deep red marks in the earth near the boundary line, the river. He struggled to comprehend what he was actually being introduced to.

She placed her hands on either side of his face until he glanced down at her. She smiled warmly. "Calm yourself, Prince. I promise it is safe here. Allow me to show you around." She nodded waiting for him to nod in agreement. He held the small rabbit in the crook of his arm as she lightly guided him towards the arena. "This is where I have my lessons." She winked at him as understanding dawned on his face.

"You are studying swordsmanship?"

"Indeed. You were close when you guessed fencing." She smirked at his dumbfounded face. Turning him towards the marks in the ground she pointed to them. "These marks— I carved these over five years ago. They help me gauge the strength of the kingdom."

"How so?" He asked curiously, bending down to rub his hand over them.

"As the Unfading Lands strengthen, the boundary line consumes some of the marks on our side. If the Realm strengthens, the boundary line gains marks and pushes over those on Lancer's side. You would be surprised at how little, every day events can change a kingdom's overall strength."

He looked at her in wonder as she sat upon a large boulder.

"This is why you wish to be a part of the Council, isn't it? You study the transfer of strength and weakness."

"Partly." She admitted. She glanced to the man behind the boundary who wore the colors of the Unfading Lands, his arms crossed over his chest, and his stance unwelcoming. She gave him a small wave and then reached for a piece of parchment she kept in her skirt pocket. She wrote quickly and then tied the letter to the rabbit. She grabbed the rabbit and placed it near the boundary line and nudged it across.

Clifton's eyes widened at the sight. "I...." He walked briskly over to the spot and waved his hand as if testing for a gap in the fog.

Elizabeth grabbed his hand quickly. "You must not touch the boundary line." He turned to her in surprise.

"I have never seen the boundary line this close before. I— it amazes me that animals can pass so freely." He watched as the man across from the boundary lifted the note off the rabbit and unfolded it to read. As soon as he had, his head popped up and an excited smile spread over his face and he waved.

Clifton, completely amazed at the fact he was conversing with someone across the boundary, felt his left hand rise and give a small wave in return. Edward pointed to Elizabeth and she nodded as he pointed back to Clifton. Edward wished for her to share his identity with Clifton now that she had explained Clifton's identity to him.

"What is he telling you?" Clifton asked quietly on a whisper as if his words could be heard across the line.

She giggled, which caused him to look at her in surprise.

"You do not have to whisper, my Prince. No sound carries across the boundary, and there is no one who knows of this place but me. Well, and Mary, Samuel, and now you. It is quite safe." She lifted her face to his and smiled. "He wants me to introduce you. I have told him who you are and he wished for you to know him."

"Is this man…" Clifton paused, the words hard for him to say as his heart twisted in his chest. "Are you in love with this man?"

Her nose scrunched in distaste and she laughed as she shook her head. "No, not at all. Well, I love him, just not in the way you are thinking."

Relief flooded through him as he watched her gaze lovingly at the man across the line. "Prince Clifton," She turned to him and then gestured towards the other man, "I would like you to meet my brother, Prince Edward."

Clifton's jaw dropped. He could not help it. He stood in awe at the sight of the lost prince. Healthy, young, probably around Ryle's age, he thought. He was... alive.

She nodded to Edward and Edward bowed towards Clifton. Clifton bowed in return. He placed a hand over his heart as he attempted to comprehend everything he had just experienced. "I must sit." He announced and had Elizabeth nervously linking her arm in his as he eased himself onto the boulder. "Are you alright? You have gone pale, my Lord."

He held up a hand to ward off her words. "I just need a second to... comprehend this, Princess." He sat silently as she shrugged towards Edward. Edward paced nervously as he waited to see the Prince's reaction. From what Elizabeth had told him, Prince Clifton was an honorable man. He prayed his sister's trust in the man did not ruin their chance at meeting one another. "You come here every day?" Clifton asked.

Elizabeth nodded. "Mostly."

"And this is where you come for your lessons?" He quoted her words.

"Yes, Edward is my teacher."

Clifton gaped at her. She wound her hands nervously in front of her and nibbled her bottom lip as she awaited his reaction.

"How long have you been conversing across the boundary line with your brother?"

"Since he left." She answered simply.

"Five years?" He asked in bewilderment.

"Yes. Five years. Five long years."

"And he has not aged?"

"No. He is the same age now as he was then. I will pass him in a few years." She softly chuckled at the baffling thought.

"He wears Lancer's colors. Is he part of the Lands' guard?"

"Yes. He has recently been placed as Captain of Lancer's Royal Guard."

Clifton stood swiftly. "Captain? So, he plans to take over his father's kingdom?!" Anger flushed Clifton's face red as he stormed towards the boundary line. He wished to pummel the traitorous prince right in the face. Elizabeth snagged his arm and pulled. "No, no, no. You cannot lose yourself just yet. Listen to me." He turned towards her and lost himself in her soft eyes of pure hope. Hope for an ally. "He and I have been conversing for five years, my Lord. We have wished for this day many times. Don't you see? Having Edward on the inside can only help the Realm. He knows Lancer's plans. He controls Lancer's guards."

Understanding hit Clifton and his eyes widened. "He joins Lancer's guard. You join the Realm's Council. You two have been strategizing on how to overcome the Unfading Lands all these years?"

She nodded. "Yes."

Overwhelmed by what Elizabeth was saying, overwhelmed with her bravery, intelligence, and beauty, he cupped her face in his hands and kissed her soundly on the mouth. He released her as quickly as it happened and turned towards the boundary line with exuberance. "This is brilliant, Princess!"

Elizabeth lightly traced her fingers over her mouth, her lips still humming from the contact. She had never been kissed before, much less by a prince. He turned and spotted her, realization of his previous action hitting him full force. His smile faded, and he reached for her hands. "I apologize Princess. I meant no disrespect. I…" He trailed off. *How could he be so stupid?* He inwardly kicked himself and lightly brushed a curl out of her eyes and tucked it behind her ear. "I am truly sorry, milady. I lost myself in the wonder of the moment."

Elizabeth shook her head to clear her thoughts. She tilted her head up towards his. "No apology necessary, my Lord. I understand how something like this," she waved her hand around the area, "could be quite shocking."

He flashed a quick grin before he began to pace around the clearing. "And you have told no one of your interaction with Prince Edward?"

"No. Only you."

"Only me." He repeated and gazed at her in amazement. "I am honored you would trust me with such a secret, Princess."

"*Can* I trust you with my secret?" She challenged, their conversation outside the tree line finally making sense to him.

"Yes. Most definitely." He heartily agreed.

Elizabeth flung herself into his arms and hugged him tightly in relief. "Thank you, thank you, thank you, Prince Clifton."

He peered over her shoulder at Edward as he laughed. He nodded towards Clifton and then mounted his horse. He saluted towards Clifton and rode away. All the while, he held Elizabeth tightly in his arms. She felt perfect. She felt right. She eased out of his embrace and smiled. "I should hope to include you in my conversations with Edward and our strategizing from now and in the future."

"I am honored, my Princess."

Elizabeth nodded in approval. "Wait here."

She walked through the tree line and then led both their horses into the clearing and retied them to a branch. "I normally bring Lenora inside the tree line so as not to draw attention to my location." She explained. Clifton stepped towards her and was quickly taken aback as she spun around unsheathing a sword and penning him towards a tree. The blade held steady and strong with capable hands, and he felt his heart in his throat. Was she meaning to harm him? Was he to die here on the banks of the boundary for learning her secrets? Then he saw it. A small flash of a devilish grin as she backed away slowly. "Arm yourself, Prince. For you are about to find yourself in a duel."

She struck a pose of defense as he reached to the hilt of his sword and brought forth his blade. He mimicked her pose and they studied one another a moment. Elizabeth's heart raced at the sight of him. *A warrior, indeed,* she thought. His green eyes flashed with power and strength, and a little amusement at their current circumstance.

She lunged forward and the sound of blade on blade echoed in the clearing. Parrying back and forth, Elizabeth's footwork and quickness matched his own. She lunged in response and had him beat attacking her with which she expertly countered in a circle parry, regaining her control. He nodded his head in acknowledgment of her skill and smiled.

He attacked again and this time overpowered her and disarmed her, her sword flying towards the edge of the river. He held his blade firm as he backed her up towards the same tree she had held him. She panted breathlessly as she studied his gaze. "You are quite good." He complimented, his blade lightly flicking her braid off of her shoulder. She did not flinch at the movement earning another level of his respect. "I practice every day, what did you expect?" She challenged, the slight tilt to her stubborn chin making his heart turn and his face to break into a smile. He dropped his sword and swooped in, cupping her face in his hands and claiming her mouth with his. He kissed her deeply, relishing the taste of her and the feel of her soft lips. He felt her fingertips nervously brush along his jaw as her lips glided over his. He then pulled away slowly, studying her carefully. He leaned his forehead against hers and placed his hands against the tree on either side of her. Both breathless, neither of them spoke.

Finally, he raised his head and met her gaze. "You bewitch me, Princess Elizabeth." A smile spread over his handsome face, his blonde unruly hair disheveled from their duel and from his nervous hand as it swiped through the golden locks. He lightly ran a hand over his face and smile as if trying to erase it, but it remained. Elizabeth found herself smiling in much the same way. She reached into her skirt pocket and pulled out the smooth white stone from the pond in the garden a few days prior and tossed it to him. "For the victor. You win this round, Prince Clifton."

He laughed heartily and rubbed his thumb over the stone before slipping it into his tunic pocket. He bowed and she curtsied.

"Shall we head back to the castle?" She asked.

He nodded. "Aye, I believe we should." He walked up to her and saw her sharp intake of breath as if bracing for another kiss they both wished would happen. Instead, he offered his arm. She slipped hers in it and laughed as he led her to her horse.

"Race you back?" She asked with a slight glint in her eye."

"I was counting on it." He replied quickly as he hopped into the saddle and slapped his reins, leaving her behind. Elizabeth gawked at his dismissal and then shook her head with a smug smile as she slapped her reins and raced after him.

CHAPTER 6

Edward whistled as he brushed the coat of his horse. Prince Clifton and Elizabeth. He shook his head and smiled. His sister was blind if she did not see the love the prince had for her. He ran his fingers through Triton's white mane and removed the small blades of grass that hid beneath them. With Prince Clifton on their side, new ground could be covered. His heart burned with excitement at the possibility of overthrowing the Lands.

"My Lord?"

Edward jerked to attention as one of his guards stepped into the stable area and bowed. "Lord Lancer wishes to speak with you."

"Ah, very well then." Edward tossed the man his brush. "Finish up for me, will you? I shall return to check your work."

"Yes, my Lord."

Edward bounded up the castle steps and slipped through the heavy doors. There Lancer sat in the single chair at the end of the grand hall. He beamed when he saw Edward.

"Ah, Edward!" He stood and clapped his hands together before embracing him. Edward's brow furrowed as Lancer pulled back and looked him in the eye.

"Exciting news, Edward."

"Oh?" Edward asked curiously. He watched as Lancer's dark eyes danced and he grinned.

"Yes, oh yes, Edward. The Southern Kingdom prince has made contact with me."

"When?"

"Not a half hour ago."

"And?"

"And he wants to unite forces."

"But I thought you wished to remain independent from allies." Edward stated.

"I do."

"Forgive me, my Lord, but I am slightly confused."

Lancer laughed heartily and slapped him on the back leading him into his personal chamber. "Oh Edward, I love you for a laugh. I am excited to discuss the news with you. I have had the guards looking for you all day. Where did you run off to?" Lancer waved his hand. "Never mind, I don't want to know. Have a seat." He gestured towards the plush sofas and sat across from Edward. He snapped his fingers and a servant stepped forward. Lancer pointed to the fireplace. The servant diligently began preparing a fresh fire. Once finished, Lancer merely waved him away.

"Now, where were we? Oh yes, the South. I was in my reflection chamber," Lancer began, mentioning the room no one was allowed to enter, "and I had a sudden urge to ride along the boundaries of the Lands."

Edward's heart sank; he prayed Lancer did not see his interaction with Clifton or Elizabeth.

"I immediately arose and called for my horse. I searched for you as well, but you were away doing whatever it is you do, and so I decided to set out on my own. I was told to go along the boundary line."

"Who told you?" Edward asked, hoping the ruler would divulge some information of the source of his knowledge.

"I told you, I was in my reflection chamber." Lancer replied with slight annoyance at the thought of Edward not paying attention.

"Of course." Edward replied. "Please continue."

Lancer shrugged and poured himself a drink. "As I neared the boundary line of the Northern Kingdom, I saw an increased number of Realm royal guards, except along the river. All that was happening there was a young couple sneaking kisses in the trees by the river, however, I continued on and came to the Southern boundary."

Edward sighed. He had not seen him. How did Lancer not see him? And the young couple kissing in the trees near the river? His mind stopped. Elizabeth. Prince Clifton. Kissing? It would seem Lancer rode past their meeting place after he had already left. Thank goodness for timing. And Elizabeth… kissing? He smirked at that news but trained his mind to concentrate on Lancer's words. His sister's heart would need to be contemplated later.

"When I reached the Southern Boundary line, Prince Eric had just shoved one of his guards through the boundary line and into the Lands. The man was wounded, and his wounds began to heal instantly due to the Lands' healing nature. Don't you see, Edward? Prince Eric is using my lands for his own gain!" A storm brewed in Lancer's eyes.

"We knew they were crossing, my Lord. Half of our army are Southern Guards now."

"Yes, but I did not realize he was sending me his weaklings!" Lancer boomed. He slammed his glass down on the small wooden table and began to pace. "How dare he send me his cast offs. I was so angered by the sight, I dismounted and walked to the boundary line with my sword. Every man that came over the line I killed. Fatal blows so no healing could take place. Every. Last. One." Lancer's voice grew dark and his eyes flashed with fury.

"So, what is your exciting news, my Lord? I thought you said you met with the prince?"

"Ah, indeed. To his horror, I stepped from the shadows and revealed myself. I then crossed the boundary and held my sword to his throat. Most exciting. The shock on his face."

"You crossed? Into the Realm? But how?"

"I told you there were ways, Edward."

"Yes, but… I did not know anyone still could."

"I can." Lancer corrected. "I told the prince that if he sends me one more cast off guard then I would personally cross back over and annihilate him completely. He then pleaded with me for his life and also for a position of power here in the Lands. Ha! Can you believe he dare ask me to share my power with him?! I think not."

Edward's head spun. Lancer could cross the boundary! He had to tell Elizabeth and Clifton about this sudden news. There was a way. Lancer said there were ways, but how? Who could cross and how?!

"The prince then begins spilling his guts about his ideas of conquest over the Northern Kingdom. He wishes to kidnap your youngest sister and bring her here to the Lands to be his bride. I assured him that she was not his prize to gain him access into my inner courts. It would take more than a princess of the North to share my power. It would take—" He paused and caught himself. "Never mind that." He added. "The point of this meeting, Edward, is that I want you to gather up all the guards that have come from the Southern Kingdom. We will rid ourselves of them tonight."

Edward's eyes widened. "Rid ourselves? But they are our army, my Lord."

"We will train others. I do not wish to fight with a mediocre army. Kill them all." Lancer drained the rest of his drink and then waved Edward away.

Edward stood obediently and bowed before exiting. He jogged to his chambers and immediately set about writing a letter to Elizabeth telling her of the news. He then found himself walking to the armory and arena where his guards awaited him for training. *Kill them all*, he reminded himself. *Kill them all.*

∞

Alayna swiftly made her way down the main stairwell and into the main hall of the castle. Her father had felt weak this afternoon and asked her to fill in for the open doors. A concept her father had created to allow people of the kingdom to appeal to the throne for needs that may arise. She eased into the large, sturdy seat. The carvings ornate and detailed, she traced her fingertips over the wings of a dove. The room was empty, minus the guards at the door and she felt small. Her chest felt heavy as she took a deep breath and tried to calm her nerves.

"May I stand guard for you, my Princess?"

Alayna jolted to attention at the sound of Prince Ryle's voice as he eased into step next to the throne. "Mosiah is with King Anthony and my father discussing matters for the Eastern Borders. I volunteered to fill his position, if the matter is approved by you." Ryle awaited and watched as Alayna surveyed him closely. She nodded and then placed her hands in her lap.

"Princess?" He whispered softly.

She glanced up, her brown eyes soft and fearful.

"Are you nervous?"

Alayna took a deep breath and nodded. "I apologize, my Lord." She stated shakily. "This is the first time for me to sit in my father's chair. I must admit, I do not feel adequate."

Ryle smiled softly. "Well this is my first time to play Captain of the Guard, so how about we learn together?"

A relieved smile washed over her face as she set her shoulders and nodded towards the guards at the doors. When they opened, a long line of people stood in hopes of speaking with the king. The first man stepped forward and bowed. "My Princess," he began, "It is an honor. I thank you for letting me speak with you today."

"You are welcome, sir. Please, state your request." Alayna's voice strengthened as she spoke and Ryle watched as she comfortably settled into the role.

"I hear your request, dear sir," she stated. Ryle focused upon the man's face as he listened intently. "I will have our guards look into the matter today. Thank you for bringing it to our attention." She turned her head to Prince Ryle, "Prince Ryle, will you retrieve two guards for me please?"

Ryle nodded and swiftly walked to an open corridor and grabbed the first guards he saw, they followed him obediently and bowed before Alayna. "Please go with this man and check the forest behind his house. He believes two thieves have been stealing from his sheep herd. If you should find said thieves, please bring them to the castle for disciplinary action immediately." The guards bowed again and the man bowed towards Alayna and exited.

Ryle resumed his position next to her throne as a woman stepped forward carrying a small baby wrapped in a ragged piece of cloth.

"Milady," the woman began, "I must beg you for help."

Alayna took a deep breath and nodded. "Please, state your request."

"My lad is only but a few days old and he will not eat."

"Have you visited with the village healers?"

"Yes, milady. They gave me a tonic, but he has yet to respond to it. I fear he will die." Surprising the woman and Prince Ryle, Alayna extended her arms for the baby. The woman stepped forward and placed the baby in Alayna's arms. She held the baby close and glanced down into its innocent face. She lightly rubbed a hand over its head and kissed its nose. She then handed the baby back to the woman. "Prince Ryle, please have a guard escort this woman and her beautiful son to the castle medical wing."

Ryle bowed and gestured for the woman to follow him to the corridor on the right. He then explained to the guard his duty and left the woman in his care to be escorted through the castle. He returned to Alayna's side swiftly. She glanced up at him and smiled. He winked at her as she awaited the next guest.

A sudden pounding of hooves flooded to her ears as several in the line whispered in excitement. Alayna could not see past the sea of people to catch the reasoning for such a stir until she spotted her sister's dark hair dismounting from a horse.

Elizabeth and Prince Clifton walked through the entryway both with wind flushed cheeks and radiant smiles. Elizabeth stopped to greet people as she went and then caught sight of her sister sitting in her father's chair. She froze in shock and then a slow smile spread over her lips. She walked forward, followed closely by Prince Clifton. As she approached the throne, she curtsied. "My sister." She greeted warmly and then curtsied towards Prince Ryle. "I must say you two make a most welcoming sight."

Alayna smiled and then reached for Elizabeth's hand. Elizabeth could feel her sister's nerves and sweetly kissed her cheek. "Father wasn't feeling well." Alayna explained.

Elizabeth's face blanched. "Is he alright?"

"Yes, yes he is quite alright. Tomas is looking after him. He just asked me to step in for the day."

"I find it quite fitting." Elizabeth stated confidently.

"And where have you two been off to?" Alayna asked, glancing from one smile to another. Elizabeth looked adoringly over at Clifton and linked her arm in his. "We went for a wonderful ride through the meadows of the kingdom."

"Lovely." Alayna replied.

"Do you wish for me to stay with you?"

"Actually, I would like that very much." Alayna replied warmly. "You as well, Prince Clifton, if you do not mind."

Clifton bowed politely. "I would be honored, my future queen." Elizabeth beamed at his response as she stepped into place beside her sister and Clifton stood next to her. The four of them, united, welcomed the remaining petitioners.

King Eamon, King Anthony, and Mosiah walked into the main hall astounded at the large crowd that lingered in line to speak with King Granton. King Eamon smiled as he spotted his two sons next to the throne and it spread even further when he realized Alayna occupied the throne instead of Granton. Granton was not lying when he said he wished to extend some of his duties to his daughter. She sat regally, her emerald dress showcasing her beautiful blonde hair and fair skin. His sons stood proudly, and Ryle expertly attended each matter she requested.

"I feel as if I am gazing upon the next generation of rulers." Mosiah stated.

"Aye." King Anthony responded, inwardly upset with his children for not being present, but grateful that Alayna seemed in control of the room. As he expected, he caught sight of Isaac down the opposite corridor pulling a red-headed maiden into one of the rooms. He cleared his throat and diverted his gaze. "If you two gentlemen will excuse me, I believe I need to seek out my children."

King Eamon and Mosiah nodded as they watched King Anthony stalk over to a room across the hall.

"I see our future queen has made use of the throne." King Eamon complimented as he bowed before Alayna. Mosiah bowed as well. Alayna's cheeks flushed. "You make a glorious sight, my dear." Eamon complimented. "Boys." He nodded at his two sons in greeting and then smiled at Elizabeth. "Princess Elizabeth."

Elizabeth curtsied in response.

"How long has the queen been responding to petitions?" King Eamon asked as he stepped out of the way and stood next to Ryle.

"Two hours." Ryle explained.

"Two hours?!" Mosiah and Eamon asked at the same time.

"My sweet Princess," King Eamon stepped forward. "You must not tire yourself dear. Normally petitions last half an hour at most."

"A half hour?" Alayna asked.

He nodded.

She waved her hand at the line of people in front of her. "But what about those in line?"

"They are to wait until the following week, my Lady."

"That hardly seems fair." Elizabeth stated.

"Elizabeth." Alayna scolded. "If King Eamon believes we are finished then we are finished."

"Oh no, Princess, if you wish to continue that is up to you. I just do not want you to tire out."

"I was unaware of the proper protocol on this matter, King Eamon. I did not realize it was a short-timed event. Thank you for letting me know."

"Do you wish to stop, my Princess?" Ryle asked.

Alayna shook her head. "No, I shall visit with a couple more."

He smiled and nodded, waving the next person forward.

King Eamon stepped out of the way and stood next to Clifton. "And you Cliff, where have you been off to?"

"I was beating Princess Elizabeth in a horse race."

"Now wait a minute," Elizabeth interrupted quietly and with a slight swat to Clifton's arm. "That is untrue, my Lord. Your son cheated."

King Eamon's brow rose as he glanced playfully at his son. "Is that so?"

Clifton shifted on his feet under his father's scrutiny. He heard Elizabeth giggle softly and caught her smug smile. King Eamon chuckled as well at the young couple's interaction and lightly patted his son on the shoulder. He smiled at Elizabeth and then saw that Clifton held her gaze. The two young ones held a secret, he could tell. Of what, he did not know, nor did he care. He smiled as he made a mental note to address Granton about a proposal and a note to address his son about his feelings.

  King Granton stood on the second landing overlooking the grand hall watching as his daughter took his role in front of the petitioners. She handled them with love and grace and he smiled proudly. He watched as Prince Ryle did her bidding and protected her with ease. The young man would be a fine Captain if he were not in line to take his father's throne, Granton thought. His gaze then travelled to Elizabeth and Clifton, their backs to him as they stood side by side. He noticed several small glances bouncing back and forth between the two. His Lizzy. His heart warmed at the thought of her finding a connection with one of Eamon's sons. He knew Prince

Isaac would not be suitable. He had heard the rumors of the boy's cavalier ways and thanked the stars for Elizabeth's refusal of him. And as his thoughts travelled to the Western prince, Granton spotted the boy sneaking out of a doorway down the hall followed by a castle maid. He shook his head in disappointment. The lad would learn soon enough, he thought. Princess Melody kept to herself mostly within the chambers of King Anthony's quarters. She rarely ventured out and only for meals or group activities. The young princess took after her mother, shy and timid. Granton knew her sweet spirit balanced out her brother's pretentious one. Edward would have been good for Melody. His son had always been outgoing and courteous. Yet, part of him knew deep down that she would not have been good for Edward. Why had he fought him so? Why had he pushed his son's desires away? He knew he was to blame for Edward's crossing of the border. That is one reason he granted Elizabeth's request for more time before she married so eagerly. He could not bear it if she crossed the boundary. He would give her all the time she needed, let her marry whomever she pleased… just as long as she stayed in the Realm. It took Edward's crossing to teach him that. His children's happiness mattered, as much to them, as to him. His gaze fell upon Alayna as she finally stood and the villagers were being escorted out of the castle. She immediately sought Prince Ryle's arm as he escorted her away from the throne. A match they would make, yet he was not quite sure Alayna had her heart set upon romance or that Ryle had his sights set on being King, whether of his father's kingdom or the Realm. Neither of his daughters sought out suitors like many women did. He loved that about them. They were strong, opinionated, and fierce when need be. He was pleased with their appearances at the Council meeting. He witnessed a new side to each of them. Sides that pleased him greatly.

Elizabeth turned and spotted him at the top of the landing upon her exit. She waved and smiled. He returned it. Prince Clifton leaned towards her and whispered in her ear, causing his daughter to laugh and nod as she linked her arm with his. Yes, he would do anything for his sweet daughters. Anything.

∞

The next morning was dreary and wet. Elizabeth watched the rain pour against the stained-glass windows of her bedchamber as she waited for Mary to finish braiding her hair. She loved rain, but not when it trapped her indoors. She had hoped to write Edward a letter and see if he had written one for her. She had so much to tell him. She leaned forward resting her elbow on her vanity with her chin in her hand. Mary lightly tugged her hair to pull her back to a proper sitting position so she could continue braiding.

"You do not seem like yourself this morning, my Lady." Mary commented as she weaved strands of hair in and out.

Sighing, Elizabeth caught Mary's worried gaze in the mirror. A small smile of gratefulness tugged at her lips as she watched her precious attendant style her hair. "I am fine Mary. I am just trying not to allow the weather to dampen my spirits. I guess I am failing."

"It must rain for the grass to stay green and the trees so pristine," Elizabeth joined her as they recited the small poem together. They ended on a smile as Elizabeth sighed again thinking of riding through the green meadows of the Realm with Clifton.

"Ah, see a smile." Mary pointed out with a satisfied grin.

Elizabeth rolled her eyes playfully and then spun around on her stool. Mary gasped, her fingers slipping from the braid and part of it unraveling. "Miss Elizabeth, I was not finished."

"Mary." Elizabeth stated completely ignoring Mary's concern. "May I tell you a secret?"

Mary's eyes widened in surprise. "You may tell me anything, my Princess."

"I know, and I need to tell someone." Elizabeth squealed in delight as she grabbed Mary's hands. "I showed Prince Clifton my meeting place with Edward."

Mary's jaw dropped, and she remained speechless as Elizabeth continued.

"He met Edward. He saw my arena. We even battled blades for a bit. And then…" Her voice trailed off as her blue eyes became dreamy and her smile widened. "He kissed me."

Mary's shock broke into a fresh smile. "You trust him with these secrets? With your heart?"

"Yes, the funny thing is, I do." Elizabeth added and turned back around so Mary could repair her braid. She continued watching Mary as she spoke. "It took him a few minutes to understand, but he came around." Elizabeth explained. "Oh Mary, he is such an amazing man."

"Have you spoken to Princess Alayna of this matter?"

"No. Only you. I'm not sure what Alayna would say to be honest, and I fear her disappointment. I'm so happy about it I do not wish for someone else not to be. I believe that might just crush my spirit."

"Does Prince Edward approve of Prince Clifton knowing?" Mary asked.

"Yes, in fact we all three find it extremely helpful in planning our strategies against the Lands. I now have an ally, Mary. An ally with influence. Prince Clifton can take the news from Edward and place it on the Council table with more authority than I." Mary tied the end of Elizabeth's braid with a small white ribbon and then helped her stand, her pale, yellow dress making her dark hair and blue eyes shine. "Do I look alright?" Elizabeth smoothed her hands over the front of her dress and fingered a hand over her braid.

"You look beautiful, milady. As always. Now come, let's take you to breakfast. Perhaps there will be an open seat next to Prince Clifton." Elizabeth smiled as she exited and made her way to the dining hall. Mary announced her, and she rounded the corner to find only King Eamon at the table.

"Ah, good morning Princess. It would seem the weather has infiltrated the castle and set everyone's moods to brooding, except for you and me." He waved a hand at the chair across from him. She sat and flashed him a polite smile. The man was kind and she found herself searching every inch of his face to see what parts of him he shared with his son.

"Good morning, King Eamon. I trust you slept well?"

"Yes indeed. I find storms relax me." He grinned as he took a sip of his water. "And you, Princess? You look absolutely stunning this morning."

She blushed. "Thank you, my Lord. I did sleep well." She unfolded her napkin and placed it in her lap as Renee brought her a plate of food. "I apologize for my father and sister not joining us." Elizabeth stated.

King Eamon waved the apology away swiftly. "Granton needs his rest and your sister and Ryle set out a half hour ago."

Elizabeth's eyes widened in surprise. "Where did they go?"

"Your sister wished to accompany a woman and her child back to the village. Apparently, the castle has been housing the sick child. Ryle went as her guard."

Elizabeth smiled. Yes, she bet Ryle would not pass up the chance to be near her sister.

"Did I say something amusing?" King Eamon asked as he studied her.

"Oh, no my Lord. I was just thinking of how kind it is that Prince Ryle accompanied my sister."

"Yes, he seems to be quite attentive to your sister."

"You think so too?" Elizabeth blurted out in pleasure.

The king chuckled. "Oh, my dear, of course he is. She is the future Queen of the Realm."

Deflated, Elizabeth shrank back in her chair. She had hoped Ryle was attentive due to feelings of a more amorous nature, not duty.

"You seem upset." King Eamon stated as he took a bite of bread.

"Not at all, my Lord. I guess I am allowing the weather to affect my mood as well."

"It is hard not to sometimes." He added.

"Has Prince Clifton eaten breakfast yet?" Elizabeth asked.

The king could not hide his smile at her question. "No, he has not. I'm afraid Cliff woke up with a sort of headache this morning. He remains in our chambers."

"Oh, I am sorry to hear that. Please give him my best."

"I will, Princess. I will. You and Cliff seem to be good friends." Eamon fished for a reaction and was pleased when a slight tinge of pink stained the young Princess' cheeks.

"I guess you could say we are. Your son is a good man, my Lord. Both of your sons are good men."

Eamon sat up proudly. "I believe so too. They continually make me proud. Their mother would be proud too."

"I am sorry to hear of the queen's death, my Lord. Though I never met her, my father spoke very highly of her."

"Aye, she was wonderful. Full of spark that one. She had Cliff's green eyes and Ryle's dark hair, a beauty. She won my heart immediately."

Elizabeth grinned as she listened to the love in the king's voice. "She sounds most lovely." Elizabeth added.

"Aye, she was indeed. I hope one day my sons will find the same happiness." He hinted, noting the way Elizabeth's eyes avoided his. He watched her carefully as she sliced the ham upon her plate. "I have been meaning to tell you that your appearance at the Council meeting was quite refreshing."

That had her blue eyes popping up from her plate. He smiled. "Thank you, King Eamon."

"I find your 'level head' quite an asset, as well as your outspokenness."

Elizabeth simply stared at him in surprise making him chuckle.

"I see that my comment surprises you."

Elizabeth nodded. "Yes, I must say it does. I feared my presence was unwelcome and my opinions—"

"Unwarranted?" He finished for her.

"Why yes, that is exactly the way I felt, at the beginning. It was not until after the meeting my sister and I discussed the matter more thoroughly."

"Ah, Princess Alayna will be a wonderful queen."

"Agreed." Elizabeth faithfully responded.

Eamon relaxed against the back of his chair and folded his napkin onto his plate. Renee swiftly cleared it and refilled his water goblet. "Please do not feel the need to stay with me, my Lord." Elizabeth granted. "I am accustomed to breakfast alone, it will not hurt my feelings."

He tilted his head at that response and shook his head. "It is no bother, Princess. I find your company quite invigorating on a morning such as this. Plus, I wish to enquire more of you."

"Oh?" Elizabeth's brows rose, and she waved a hand for him to continue.

"Well, since we are speaking so freely I wish to ask you your thoughts on the guard. Your father said you wished to be more involved. I wondered what made you wish to be informed?"

Elizabeth finished her meal and politely placed her napkin on the table. She glanced at King Eamon's soft gaze and kind face. Smiling, she softly sighed. "May I speak freely?"

"Of course." He invited.

"I have always been drawn to the guard, my Lord, ever since I was a little girl. My brother used to take me to the armory and explain every weapon and every piece of armor in detail." A small smile tugged at her lips at the memories of Edward and her sneaking into the armory. "Edward and I were inseparable. Alayna never joined us for fear of the consequences from our father, but Edward and I could not help ourselves. We found it all fascinating and exciting. Knights and guards— Captain Mosiah patiently tolerated us following him around like leeches."

King Eamon chuckled and then took a sip of his water.

Elizabeth continued. "I loved watching the guards practice in the arena. The swift flash of a blade, the sound it makes slicing through the air. The power in a single stroke captivated me. I often thought, what would it be like to hold that power in your hands? To feel brave and courageous?"

"Not all men that fight are brave, milady." King Eamon replied softly.

"Yes, I know that now." Elizabeth countered. "But my feelings are the same. I feel brave when I clasp my sword. I feel invincible when I strike a blow."

"When *you* strike a blow?" Eamon's eyebrows rose in curiosity at the Princess's candid slip of her hidden talent.

Flushing, Elizabeth realized honesty would be her best tactic with the king. "Yes. I am no stranger to a sword, my Lord. Though my father and sister do not know, I am quite a practiced swordsman."

"Interesting." He rubbed his bearded chin as she continued.

"I tell you this in confidence, though I don't quite care if you share it with my father at this point. Your son, Prince Clifton, knows of my talent. In fact, he has been helping me fine tune it."

"Has he now?" King Eamon asked with a small tilt to his lips.

She nodded. "He is a good teacher, my Lord."

"He has been taught well. Cliff has always loved the sword, not as much as Ryle, but he loves it all the same."

They heard a shuffle and Prince Clifton emerged at the edge of the dining hall. "Morning." He greeted as he slipped into the seat next to his father. Elizabeth softly smiled at him as she noted the light shadow of a beard forming along his jaw.

"Morning, Cliff." His father affectionately wrapped an arm over his shoulders and squeezed him in a hug before allowing him to eat. "Headache gone?"

"Yes, thankfully. I feared having to stay locked in the chambers all day."

"Yes, you most certainly would have been a bear if that had happened." His father teased as his son took a sip of water.

"You are looking lovely this morning, Princess Elizabeth." Clifton complimented stiffly in front of his father making the older gentleman laugh heartily. Clifton blushed and turned to his father with a fierce gaze.

"Don't look at me like that, Cliff. Miss Elizabeth and I were just discussing you."

"Is that so?" Clifton turned to Elizabeth as his father continued.

"Yes. She tells me you have been teaching her the sword."

Clifton's eyes widened as he looked to her again. She nodded and shrugged her shoulders.

"Just one lesson thus far."

"Ah. I see." Eamon replied. "I trust you to be careful when teaching the Princess."

"Yes, Father."

"Well, now that you have risen to greet the day, I think I will go make myself busy." King Eamon stood and then bowed towards Elizabeth. "My dear Princess, it was an extreme pleasure speaking with you this morning."

"And you as well, my Lord."

He smiled and patted Clifton's shoulder affectionately before exiting.

They sat in silence for a moment.

"Your father is a great man." Elizabeth complimented.

Clifton smiled at the thought of his father. "Yes, he is. I'm glad you like him."

"Do you have any other brothers or sisters?"

"At one time. We had a younger sister, but she did not live past infancy." Clifton replied.

Elizabeth placed her hand on her heart. "I am sorry to hear that."

Clifton sighed and leaned back in his chair. "It is not uncommon."

"But still sad." Elizabeth replied kindly.

"Indeed. But Ryle and I gave my parents enough to worry about and fill their time on our own."

Elizabeth grinned. "I imagine you did. Two boys so close in age. I imagine you two were quite a handful."

"Is that so?" Clifton smirked. "I guess we were." He admitted. "What of you and your siblings, Princess?"

"Alayna has always been the tame child in the bunch, I'm afraid. Edward and I tended to test the boundaries of our father's patience." She chuckled softly. "I think I still do now and again."

"I find your adventurous personality quite intriguing." Clifton stated, causing a slight flush to rise to her cheeks.

"Thank you."

"May I find you later? Perhaps we can continue your lessons?" Clifton stood straightening the edges of his pale blue tunic.

"It is raining, my Lord. My lessons may have to wait for another day."

He glanced out the floor to ceiling windows and surveyed the steady rain. "I suppose you are right. Then may I escort you somewhere, Princess?"

Elizabeth stood and nodded to Mary across the room. Mary followed obediently behind. "I wish to make a visit to the stables, my Lord, but you do not have to escort me there. I know the way."

Needing time alone with her thoughts, Elizabeth hoped her request did not sound too harsh. Instead of being insulted, Prince Clifton beamed. "How about I escort you to the portico and then leave you in the capable hands of Mary?" Sensing the Princess needed her space, he did not wish to hover.

"That would be lovely, thank you." Elizabeth replied with relief. They reached the edge of the hall and the imposing bolted doors. Clifton gestured for the guards to open them. Granting his bid, the two guards pushed open the doors, the scent of rain and wet earth seeping into the castle. "Give Henry a hello for me?" Clifton asked for his horse as he released her arm and bowed before her.

"Of course." She smiled and blushed when he lightly kissed the back of her gloved hand. She watched as he made his way back down the hall and turned around the corner.

∞

Edward stood before the guards, each wearing the colors of the Unfading Lands. A sea of golden tunics covered the armory. Edward glanced to the guards at the doors, Lancer's faithful followers. "Thank you gentlemen, but I believe I can take it from here."

The guards nodded and exited. Edward faced the men before him and took a deep breath. "Grab your weapons men, we are going for a ride." Without waiting for them to obey, Edward exited the room and hopped into the saddle on an awaiting Triton. A few minutes later, he led the men deep into the trees of the Unfading Lands. "Kill them, Edward. Kill them all." Lancer's words echoed in his mind as he led the lambs to their slaughter. The Southern Kingdom guards had trained well, and he considered them a strength for the Lands. Lancer's request was rash, Edward thought. But as he pulled his reins and stopped in the shadowed clearing, he waited patiently for the other men to dismount and face him.

"You have been relieved of your duties in The Land of Unfading Beauty. Lancer has released you of your duties to the Guard. From this moment on, you have two options: Death or Life."

He watched as shock spread over the faces before him… and fury. He held his hand up indicating for no one to speak. "You have been brought here for slaughter." Edward explained, noting the panic rising in their eyes. "UNLESS!" He yelled to be heard over the murmurs. He finally had the attention of all the men. "Unless you join me. We all know Lancer's power is great, but the Realm strengthens day by day. I offer you a choice, gentlemen." Edward pulled his sword to attention. "You can join me, Prince Edward of the Northern Highlands and of the Realm, and fight for the Realm of King Granton, or you can stay members of Lancer's guard and die. He has ordered me to kill you. I lead a band of Uniters who wish to overthrow Lancer's power and reunite the Realm. If you join us, you not only live, but you will have served King Granton and the Realm faithfully and your service will be rewarded. Now make your decisions. Those who wish to die remain here. Those who wish to live and fight for the Realm, follow me." Edward turned his horse towards the river and men began to follow. All of the men followed. He led them to the clearing near the river, not far from his meeting spot with Elizabeth. He turned around and noticed the men lining up and awaiting instruction.

Edward dismounted and handed his reins to one of his fellow Uniters. He glanced over the small army and breathed a sigh of relief that he did not have to kill anyone. "You now live in secret. These woods are your sanctuary. We train, we prepare, and we wait for our opportunity. We have communication across the boundary with the Royal Guard of King Granton. Success is ours if we wait patiently for the right moment."

The guards watched as more and more Uniters stepped forward from the forest and stood guard around the clearing. "Should you betray me, your fate is left to that which Lancer has ordered for you, death." Edward stated firmly. He turned to one of his guards. "Continue their training." Edward caught Cecilia's gaze through the trees and smiled at her as he mounted his horse. He slapped his reins and road back to Lancer's castle.

As he walked through the main doors of the castle, Lancer's chair was empty. Edward glanced around and saw no one. He walked over to Lancer's personal quarters and knocked. Nothing. His eyes then travelled to Lancer's room of reflection. He had to be in there, Edward thought. He walked to the door and raised his knuckles to knock when a maid rounded the corner of the hallway.

"No, my Lord!" She shouted and hurried over. "You must not interrupt him."

"What does he do in there?" Edward asked her, hoping someone in the castle knew of the room's contents.

"I do not know, my Lord, but no one dares enter the room. The last few that went inside never came out."

Edward's brows rose at that news and he narrowed his gaze at the door. "Thank you for the warning."

"Aye, my Lord." She curtsied and hurried away.

Edward glanced at the door once more. He would wait until Lancer emerged and then he would sneak into the room. It was time he found out what lie behind that door. Until then, he would write Elizabeth a letter and update her on the current news of his growing army. He darted out of the castle once more and headed to his spot near the river. He noticed the rain on the side of the Realm and realized Elizabeth would not be riding out to meet him whilst it poured. He sat on the boulder and began to write.

Elizabeth,

So much has happened I feel I have put you at a great misfortune for not writing you until now.

I must assure you that I am well and so is Cecilia. I also must say it was quite an extraordinary day to meet your Prince Clifton and to know he is helping us in our quest. I sense his attention towards you is more than his duty, however. I believe the prince may have feelings towards you, little sister. Be careful with his heart and yours. I know that look. I see it when I gaze upon Cecilia. The man would do anything for you, sister. It lessens my worry knowing he is looking out for your safety.

Aside from that, I wish to report the Uniters band has grown rapidly the last few days. Many Southern Kingdom guards have joined our forces. Lancer came across the Southern Kingdom sending their wounded guards across the line for healing. Lancer informed me he witnessed the act with his own eyes and spotted Prince Eric as the enforcer. Lancer crossed the boundary and threatened the prince. I hope you read that sentence again, sister.

Yes, Lancer can cross the boundary. It was news to me as well. He had told me there were ways, but I did not know he could willingly cross back and forth. I'm afraid that provides a heightened since of danger to the Realm. He has yet to tell me how he is able to cross, but I aim to find out. So many questions whirl in my mind now. Who can cross? Just him? How does he cross? Please inform Prince Clifton of this news as well. Perhaps if we all three think on the subject a solution will arise. Meanwhile, I will continue recruiting these Southern guards. Have you received any threats from the Southern Kingdom?

Also, please fill me in on the latest military talks from the Council Room. I hope your first meeting went well and that the other kings and guards took your presence seriously. How great an asset you are, Lizzy. If only they knew...

I hope you stressed the importance of our meetings to Prince Clifton. He seemed quite taken aback by the whole matter, but I sensed his trust. I pray he becomes an asset for us as well.

I must go now. I am to meet with my guards for training in a few minutes.

Take care, sister.

Edward tied his letter to Thatcher and sent the small rabbit across the boundary from sunshine into rain. The rabbit quickly scurried into his burrow beneath the brambles to await Elizabeth. Satisfied, Edward mounted Triton and disappeared into the woods.

∞

A knock sounded on the door. King Granton and Princess Alayna glanced up as King Eamon slipped inside the Council Room. The two sat alone, despite the room normally being the crowded place of generals and guards of the Realm's military.

"Ah, Eamon, do come in." King Granton sat in the oversized mahogany chair and began sorting through different parchments as Princess Alayna sat across from him doing the same.

"Afternoon, Granton. Princess." He bowed. "I wonder if I might have a word."

"Of course." Granton replied. "Do you wish for the Princess to leave?"

"Fantastic, and no, that will not be necessary. What I have to mention can be heard by the both of you. Perhaps she can provide insight into the matter."

"Please, sit." Granton motioned to another chair and then pushed his papers to the side. "You seem— excited, Eamon."

King Eamon beamed. "Yes. Quite so. I wanted to speak to you on the topic of a merger."

Alayna's eyes widened as she sat quietly, curious as to what the king would propose.

"A merger?" King Granton asked curiously, his left brow rising and disappearing into his gray hair.

"Yes, my Lord. It has come to my attention that our two youngest, Clifton and Elizabeth, have been spending quite some time together and, well, they seem to enjoy each other's company. I have yet to speak with Cliff on the matter, but it would seem the two are headed in the direction of courtship, my Lord. I thought it best to bring the matter to you now in case something does derive from their interactions."

King Granton stroked his beard and glanced at his other daughter. Alayna sat primly and properly as she listened to the king. He noted the softening in her gaze at the mention of Elizabeth and Clifton. "What say you of this, Alayna? Do you have any inclinations of Elizabeth's feelings for Prince Clifton?"

"No Father. I mean— well, she has mentioned him once or twice and I have questioned her intentions. But she has yet to admit to any personal feelings beyond friendship, Father."

"Do you think her feelings towards the prince are advancing towards courtship?" Granton asked, pleased to note Elizabeth had mentioned the prince to Alayna and that Alayna seemed pleased with the current conversation.

Sighing, Alayna briefly glanced down at her hands in her lap. Should she advocate a relationship for her sister knowing Elizabeth wished to make those decisions by herself?

"Alayna?" Granton prodded.

"Yes." She stated simply. "Yes, I believe there is potential for courtship." She answered curtly. If Elizabeth wished not to be courted, she would make her feelings known, but until then, Alayna felt, she could help the plan set in motion for Elizabeth to marry into the Eastern Kingdom.

"Wonderful!" Eamon exclaimed as he clapped his hands.

King Granton held up his hand to halt his friend's celebration. Eamon sobered and waited his response. "Eamon, we need to ask Clifton and Elizabeth if this suits them before we allow our excitement to overcome us."

"Of course, my King. I celebrate prematurely. I assure you Cliff will agree to your terms. I have hope that Princess Elizabeth will as well."

"Alayna, seek out your sister and find out the conditions of her heart and wishes. Eamon, please send Prince Clifton to me when he has a moment." Alayna and Eamon stood, bowing as they exited. Once outside the doors, Eamon turned to Alayna. "Was my request too bold, Princess? Do you think your sister will be insulted I spoke to your father on her behalf?"

Alayna smiled at the sweet king. "No, my Lord. Elizabeth has a mind of her own, of which is no secret, but when someone as kind as you is trying to offer her a chance at happiness, I do not see how this would upset her."

Relaxing, Eamon nodded. "Thank you, Princess, for that reassurance. I best seek out Cliff now." Bowing, he walked down the hall towards his chambers.

Alayna took a deep breath. Elizabeth. Married. She giggled softly as she rounded the corner and slammed into Prince Isaac. Gasping, Alayna straightened her dress and hair as if the small encounter had tousled her appearance. "My Lord, I am terribly sorry. I did not see you."

Isaac bowed. "No, milady, it was my fault. I am terribly sorry. May I ask what has you in such a rush?"

"I seek out my sister." Alayna replied. "Do you know where she may be perhaps?"

Isaac glanced out the large window and smiled. "What little I know of the princess, I imagine she is with her horse on a day like this."

Alayna's brown gaze warmed. "You know, Prince Isaac, you are right. I imagine she is. Thank you for your insight." She curtsied and bustled away.

Isaac's deep brown gaze followed the future queen as she exited out the doors and into the portico and then shot towards the large tapestry hanging on the wall opposite him. He leaned back against the stone wall and surveyed the wall hanging. A tapestry of the royal family. King Granton, Queen Rebecca, Prince Edward, Princess Alayna, and Princess Elizabeth. He rolled his eyes as they fell upon Edward. The man gave up his right to the throne of the Realm just to be with a woman. He snickered as his gaze then followed one of the maids of the castle as she bustled by carrying a handful of linens from King Granton's chambers. There were plenty of women to keep a man occupied, why settle for just one? Especially one that required relinquishing your rights to the throne. He shook his head and studied the prince's face. Why would he risk everything to cross? There had to be more to his story, Isaac thought. No man in his right mind would give up his rule to live as a simpleton, no matter how stout of heart. He heard footsteps coming from the main stairwell, but he continued his brooding hoping to unmask Prince Edward's secrets.

"Prince Isaac." Prince Ryle and Prince Clifton emerged at the top of the stairs and followed his gaze to the tapestry.

"Princes." He greeted smugly. "I hope you two are enjoying your rainy day."

"We are." Ryle stated. "You?"

"Somewhat, yes."

"Admiring the tapestry?" Clifton asked as his gaze fell upon the elaborate stitching of Elizabeth's face.

"Indeed. I was just pondering over Prince Edward."

Clifton's back straightened as he surveyed the prince.

"Oh?" Prince Ryle asked.

"What sort of man gives up his right to his father's throne just to be with a woman?" Isaac asked the two men. His gaze bounced between the two brothers and then he pushed himself off the wall and crossed his arms.

"I imagine there is more to the story." Ryle stated, making Clifton's pulse race. What did his brother know of Prince Edward?

Shrugging, Prince Isaac sighed. "I don't know. I just don't understand it. I cannot imagine giving up my claim to my father's throne."

"Even if it were for the good of the kingdom?" Clifton asked curiously.

Isaac's eyes narrowed. "And why would my giving up my right be good for the kingdom?"

Clifton held up his hands in peace. "I did not say that for you specifically. I think maybe our Prince Edward may have felt that way at the time of his crossing. Yes, he would be with the woman he loved, but perhaps he felt it was the best decision for the kingdom as well."

Relaxing a bit, Isaac tilted his head in consideration. "No, I think he was just being selfish." He concluded with confidence. "I will be seeing you, princes." He bowed as he nonchalantly strolled in the direction of the maid he saw prior.

The brothers watched him leave and then both turned to face the tapestry. "You believe Prince Edward crossed for other reasons than for his girl?" Ryle asked Clifton quietly.

"Yes, I do."

"What other reasons would he have had?"

"Plenty, I would think." Clifton provided. "You tend to feel weighted by the responsibility of filling in our father's shoes one day and you would just be ruling the Eastern Kingdom. Imagine having to rule the entire Realm. I imagine that looming responsibility could be quite intimidating. Perhaps he sensed an unforeseen threat from the Lands and felt his crossing could help matters."

"How could crossing ever help matters?" Ryle asked dumbfounded his brother would even suggest such a ludicrous notion.

Clifton studied his brother closely. "I think, brother, that in time, that question will turn into our only option to defeat the Lands."

Ryle's brow furrowed as he met the calm, steady green of his brother's gaze. "I hope you are wrong, Cliff. I hope you are wrong."

"Me too, Brother. Me too."

CHAPTER 7

Clifton sat on the edge of the hill watching the horizon for any sign of Samuel. The slight breeze teased his unkempt hair and one rogue curl grazed across his forehead. He absentmindedly swished it out of the way. The landscape smelled of fresh rain and rejuvenation and he found the overall scents calming. He caught movement near the tree line but nothing substantial enough to send him into a trot. He patted Henry's neck and waited. He was good at waiting. He found patience to be one of his strongest attributes. He just hoped that in the instance of Samuel, his patience would pay off, as well as, in the case of Princess Elizabeth, he selfishly admitted.

There. He saw it. The slight dance of a head along the reeds. He studied it carefully until it moved again. He then clicked his reins. Within a few yards, he dismounted. "Samuel?" He called. "Samuel, I mean you no harm."

The young prince emerged from behind a tree and cautiously stepped out. He eyed Clifton closely taking relief that the prince had not drawn his sword. "Hello, Samuel." Clifton greeted warmly.

"Prince Clifton."

"I have been wanting to speak with you."

"Me? Whatever for, my Lord?"

Clifton held out a hand and waved him over to a small rock outcrop and took a seat on a large boulder. The young prince sat opposite him on the very edge of his rock in preparation for flight. Clifton made a conscious effort to appear even more relaxed to encourage the boy to do the same.

"Samuel, I wanted to speak to you about your father's kingdom."

"Yes, my Lord."

"I shared my last encounter with you to King Granton."

The boy's eyes widened in fear. Clifton held up a hand, hoping the boy didn't bolt. "I assure you he means you no harm, Samuel. In fact, he has offered you sanctuary if you ever need it." The boy sat speechless. "However, discussing our previous conversation with him, he has concerns about your father's kingdom, especially the royal guard your father and brother are holding captive. He wishes to retrieve the guard but has reservations."

"He should not attempt a rescue, my Lord. My brother's army can be quite vicious."

"I see. And how many guards does your brother's army contain?"

"I do not know, my Lord."

Clifton sighed. "You do not have any idea?"

"No, my Lord. A week ago I would have told you hundreds, but we have lost many to the boundary line."

"Do you think you could find out for me? Perhaps you can give me some insight into your brother's army and what they are planning?"

Samuel shifted uncomfortably and lightly ran a hand over his worried face. Yes, the decision was a big one, traitorous in the eyes of his father and brother, but the young boy studied the prince from the East carefully. He seemed kind. And good. He turned swiftly as the sound of approaching hooves bombarding the quiet. Prince Clifton turned and a slow smile spread over his face as Princess Elizabeth slid from her horse to the ground. She wore a riding skirt of pale blue that Clifton recognized as the one that hid her trousers. Grinning, he turned to Prince Samuel.

Winded from her brisk ride, Elizabeth smiled as she spotted Clifton speaking with who could only be Prince Samuel. She waved as she approached. "My apologies, my Lords." She curtsied to both of them. "I did not realize this area of the meadow would be taken." She smiled at Clifton and then turned her bright blue eyes towards Samuel. "You must be Prince Samuel of the Southern Kingdom. I am Princess Elizabeth." The boy nodded shyly. She grinned and lightly squeezed his shoulder. "It is so nice to meet you. Prince Clifton has told me of your bravery and insight. On behalf of the Northern Kingdom and the Realm, I wish to thank you."

A blush fluttered over the boy's face as he stared adoringly at the princess. "Well I will leave you two gentlemen to your discussions. Prince Clifton you know where to find me when you are finished?" She mounted upon Lenora and flipped her braid behind her as she looked to him for an answer. "Yes, milady." She nodded at his response and flicked her reins and continued upon her journey towards her break in the tree line that led to her arena near the river. Clifton watched until she was out of sight and then glanced back to Samuel.

"I will help you." The boy stated firmly as if sight of Princess Elizabeth had swayed him. "But I must be careful, my Lord. If my brother or father were to find out, I would be banished or killed."

"Yes, I understand your risk, and I appreciate your loyalty to King Granton. Your help will not go unrewarded."

"Prince Clifton, I must tell you that my brother is aware of Princess Elizabeth's hiding place."

"Yes, you told me this before."

"Yes, but I feel he will act soon. Lancer has angered him recently and my brother wishes to show Lancer how powerful he is. He feels by obtaining the princess Lancer will recognize his strength and rejection of the Realm. She must not be alone, my Lord." Samuel rose quickly.

"You wish to follow the Princess?"

"Yes, my Lord."

Clifton waved him onward and walked with him, guiding Henry behind him. They reached the clearing and Clifton ducked under branches and emerged in the small clearing just as Elizabeth jolted from her seated position in surprise and raised a sword in defense. When her gaze landed on the two princes, she lowered her sword and sighed. "You two scared me. Did your mothers never teach you not to sneak up on people?" She teased lightly as she sheathed her sword and tucked the letter in her hands into her saddle bag.

"Sorry, Princess, but Prince Samuel was concerned of your safety, so we ventured over immediately." Clifton explained.

Elizabeth glanced to the young prince and smiled in thanks. "That is most thoughtful, but I assure you I am alone as of right now, except for you two."

"Yes, for now you are." Prince Samuel stated. His tone relaying that her peace in the clearing may soon disappear in the coming days. "You must be cautious, Princess. You must not come here alone."

She tilted her head and narrowed her eyes. "And why is that?"

"For your protection, my Lady." Prince Samuel stated, his gaze traveled over the small area searching for signs of disturbance.

Clifton nodded towards Elizabeth's trousers. "I see you have changed into your lesson's wardrobe."

She blushed but waved his comment away. "If I am to be a master swordsman, Prince Clifton, I must look the part, don't you think?"

"Indeed." He snuck a wink at Samuel, the boy smiling at the friendly princess.

"Samuel, perhaps you and I can meet every other day here at the clearing?" Prince Clifton asked.

Samuel nodded. "Of course, my Lord."

"If you hear of anything on your end that may prevent our meetings or disrupt the princess' lessons," Clifton hinted to Samuel, not wanting to frighten Elizabeth with talks of kidnapping, "I request you find me at the castle immediately."

The boy nodded. "Yes, my Lord. I will find the information you seek in regard to my brother's army as well. It may take a few days, but I believe I know where to begin my search. I will send your regards to your captured guard. I believe he will find hope in the fact he is being thought of."

"Please do." Clifton admonished and nodded to the boy. Samuel turned to make his exit and paused at Clifton's voice. "And Samuel?"

Samuel turned. "Be careful." The boy nodded with a small smile of thanks and wandered off.

Clifton turned to find Elizabeth studying him carefully, her arms folded across her chest. "You care for him." She stated simply.

"Yes, I do. He risks much."

"As do you." She replied.

He shrugged in response.

"Well I hate to add to your worry, but we have bigger problems now than that of the Southern Kingdom." Elizabeth stated on a sigh as she reached in her saddle bag and grabbed Edward's letter.

"What do you mean?" Clifton took the letter from her hands and unfolded it, her brother's regal handwriting filling the page. He froze, and his stormy gaze met hers. "Lancer can cross?!"

"I'm afraid so."

"How?! When?!" Clifton paced back and forth as Elizabeth sat patiently waiting for him to continue. "This is grave news, Elizabeth, very grave news. We must tell our fathers."

Elizabeth shook her head and jumped to her feet. "No, we cannot. If we tell them, this place will become known. My father would put a stop with my time with Edward." Elizabeth frantically ran a smooth hand over her braid and worried her fingers over the ribbon tied end.

"We have to Elizabeth." Clifton stated firmly disregarding formality. "This changes everything."

Nervously releasing her breath, she nodded. "At the next Council Meeting I will reveal the news and.— my letters with Edward. Until then, I will write Edward a letter letting him know of our decision. It is my news to tell, Clifton." She stressed his name to emphasize her notice of his lack of formality when addressing her earlier and to emphasize her dislike of the situation. She cast a hard glance his direction. It was not his fault and she knew what he said was the right thing to do. But she did not have to like it. She huffed a breath of air out and then drew her sword. "Are we going to practice now, or shall I submit to an afternoon of dawdling elsewhere?"

Clifton smirked at her aggravated attitude. He liked that the Princess was able to push aside her personal feelings for the sake of the kingdom, yet he also liked that she was not too hesitant on showing her true feelings on the matter. Clifton drew his sword and lightly tapped hers. "You? Dawdle? Why I don't believe it for a second." He taunted as she lashed her frustration out on him by combating with a swift lunge and attack. Elizabeth brought her sword in a round parry and kicked out, her foot planting firmly in Clifton's chest as she pushed him back a few steps. He effortlessly blocked her blows and even managed to strike out against her with a few surprise swishes of his blade. She blocked him well. *She was stronger,* he thought. He lunged and swiped his blade close to her side and she blocked him, locking blades. She then rotated, turning her back on him in a spin that not only unlocked his blade but had him dropping it at their feet. Her eyes narrowed as she pushed him towards a tree, her blade at his throat. Panting and out of breath a small smile tilted the corners of her lips. She held him there a few minutes, her blue eyes blazing with fury. Not at him, he realized, but at the thought of Lancer's threat. She was fighting Lancer, not him. She lowered her sword and took a deep breath, sheathing it at her side. Breathless, Clifton ran a hand through his hair and chuckled softly. "Not bad, Princess. I would say your anger makes you a master swordsman." He reached into the front pocket of his blue tunic and pulled out the small white pebble and tossed it to her. "You are the victor this round, Princess."

She caught it midair, unsmiling, as she tucked it into her trouser pocket. "We should head back to the castle. I wish to prepare my letter for Edward in my chambers." She tied her riding skirt around her waist to cover her pants and then hopped into her saddle. Without waiting for him, she clicked her reins and slipped through the brambles.

∞

Elizabeth entered the castle in a brisk wave of emotions and outdoors. Alayna awaited her in her chambers. Elizabeth whisked through her doors and slammed them behind her, huffing a frustrated breath. The idea of sharing her secret location with everyone had her heart twisted into a tight knot of worry and angst. Would her father understand? Would anyone understand why she kept her time with Edward secret? She ran a hand through her hair and worried it over her face, lightly nibbling her nails.

"Is this a bad time?" Alayna's voice cut through her thoughts and had her jumping back a couple of paces. She placed a hand on her heart as she gasped.

"Alayna." Breathless, Elizabeth attempted to relax and appear normal. "I did not realize you were in here."

"Apparently."

"To what do I owe the pleasure of having the future queen in my chambers?" Elizabeth teased lightly as Alayna continued to regally sit at her vanity table. She lightly trailed her fingers over Elizabeth's silver hairbrush and the soft bristles.

"Alayna?" Elizabeth prodded, her brow furrowing as she studied her sister.

"Oh, yes, I am here to discuss something with you sister. Please, have a seat." She waved her hand to a small wooden chair across from her and watched as Elizabeth eyed her with suspicion and slowly eased into the seat.

"I want to ask you something, Elizabeth, sister to sister."

"Alright." Elizabeth dragging out the word as if she were unsure of Alayna's motive.

"Prince Clifton," Alayna began.

"He told you?!" Elizabeth bounded out of her seat, her face flushed with fury at the thought of Clifton betraying her trust and telling her sister of her meetings with Edward.

"Whoa, whoa, whoa sister." Alayna waved her hands to calm Elizabeth's pacing. "Told me what? He hasn't told me anything. I am here to discuss him with you."

Elizabeth froze. "Oh." Her cheeks tinted a light shade of pink in embarrassment at her outburst and she slid nervously back to her chair. "Please, continue."

Alayna chuckled softly at her sister's awkwardness. "Um, yes. Well, I was wondering if you had feelings for the prince. As in, do you care for him?"

"Yes. I care for him very much. I care for all of them very much."

"That's not what I meant." Alayna stated.

"I know." Elizabeth countered.

"Then why do you evade the question when we both know you truly have feelings for him?"

Elizabeth blew a frustrated breath, her feathered bangs lifting lightly off her forehead. "I do not wish to leave the kingdom right now, sister."

"What? Why would you have to leave?"

"If Father establishes a courtship between Prince Clifton and me, an engagement will soon follow. I will be married by month's end."

"And this is not a good thing?" Alayna asked in confusion.

"Yes and no. I would be honored to be married to Prince Clifton, but as soon as I am, I will be leaving to go live in the Eastern Kingdom."

Understanding dawned on Alayna's face at her sister's concern.

"I cannot leave the Northern Kingdom right now. Not when interactions with the South and the Lands are so volatile. We need to be here to help. I need to be here to help."

"I see. So, you are not opposed to a courtship with the prince?"

"Did you not just hear what I said?" Elizabeth asked in annoyance.

"I did. And I understand your concerns Lizzy. But those are small matters. Your exit of the Northern Kingdom is flexible. You can stay as long as you wish. I feel Prince Clifton will not be willing to leave so soon either. I do not find that prospect a deal breaker at the moment."

"Oh." Elizabeth replied softly and sat in defeat, her shoulders slumping.

"You seem disappointed. Were you wanting me to put up a fight over the matter?" Alayna asked curiously, her steady brown gaze weighing her sister's emotions.

"No." Elizabeth sighed. "I just have a lot on my mind at the moment, and I feel the turmoil is stealing away the joy of the day."

"Care to share with me? I'm a good listener you know."

"Yes, I know you are Alayna. I just… I have to sort some things out first."

"Well is everything alright?"

"Yes."

"Do you wish for me to inform Father and King Eamon of your acceptance of a potential proposal of courtship from Prince Clifton?"

"Do as you wish. I honestly cannot think of myself at the moment."

Alayna's brow wrinkled as she worried over her sister's aloof attitude to a possible courtship. Normally her spritely sister quite vocally expressed her opinion of such matters, especially when they regarded her. She watched Elizabeth carefully as she unraveled her long braid and brushed out her dark hair. Her normally bright blue eyes were serious and clouded. Yes, something weighed heavily upon her sister's mind.

"Well, I will leave you to your day. Father just wished for me to ask the conditions of your heart because King Eamon wishes to establish a courtship if Prince Clifton agrees as well."

"They haven't even asked him yet?" Elizabeth's eyes widened in surprise. "Please do not say anything until King Eamon discusses Clifton's wishes. I do not wish to appear too eager."

Alayna grinned and lightly patted her sister's hand as she stood. "Now sister, you think I would hand your heart over so easily?" She winked as she made her way to the door, her deep emerald cape trailing behind her.

"Thank you, Alayna, for speaking to me before making the arrangement."

Alayna turned and smiled. "Of course. See you at the Council Meeting."

Elizabeth nodded as Alayna exited. She motioned for Mary to step forward and braid her hair as she continued to ponder different ways to introduce the subject of Edward's involvement and her interactions across the boundary line at the Council Meeting.

∞

Clifton whistled as he made his way back into the castle from the horse stables, thoughts of Elizabeth's fiery response to their duel and his suggestion of mentioning their news of Lancer at the next Council Meeting floated through his mind. He smiled to himself at the thought of her vibrant blue eyes and the sparks that flew as she sliced her sword through the air. A warrior princess, indeed, he thought. Chuckling to himself, he opened the doors to his chambers and found King Granton, his father, and his brother all awaiting him. His whistling stopped on a shrill note as he quizzically glanced from one face to another. "Is this an intervention?" He asked curiously, his right brow slightly rising. His father smiled and waved him inside. "No, my dear boy, please come in and have a seat. We wish to have a word with you."

Clifton stepped forward and accepted the chair next to his brother as King Eamon grinned towards Granton.

"Son, we wish to discuss with you the potential courtship between you and Princess Elizabeth."

Clifton's brows rose in surprise as he glanced at his brother. Ryle smirked and then squared his shoulders and acted as if the conversation were meant to be more serious. Clifton's gaze nervously flashed towards King Granton, who sat with a grim line set to his mouth. He felt his pulse quicken at being placed on the hot seat.

He cleared his throat. "I see. Please continue."

His father chuckled and then eased his leg upon the top of the table as he sat on the edge. "Well, do you wish for there to be a courtship or not?" King Eamon asked pointedly.

Clifton shifted uncomfortably under King Granton's weighted gaze. He lightly pulled at the collar tightening around his neck. "I, um— well..." He trailed off and cleared his throat again.

"Oh, come Cliff, do you have feelings for the Princess or not?" Eamon countered pointedly, his gaze narrowing at his son.

Taking a deep breath, Clifton turned towards King Granton. "I do, yes. But I also know the Princess does not wish for decisions of courtship to be decided upon without her consent. I am a patient man, my Lord. If she does not wish for a courtship right now, I will wait." He eased back into his chair as if his small speech somehow zapped him of all confidence.

A slow smile spread over King Granton's face. "It is settled then. Should Elizabeth be open to a courtship, we shall make the announcement."

He extended his hand toward Clifton. Clifton firmly clasped the king's hand, noting the cold clamminess of his skin. He studied the king's face, the pale blue eyes full of warmth at the subject of courtship but clouded with a sickness he wished to hide.

"You will find my Elizabeth a worthy bride, Prince Clifton. I see the way you interact with her and am most confident you are a great match." King Granton stated warmly.

Honored by the king's confidence, Clifton placed a hand over his heart. "I am most grateful, my Lord. And I assure you she will be loved and looked after for all of her days. That is… if she agrees."

Chuckling, King Granton patted Clifton's shoulder and rose to his feet. He stumbled slightly, King Eamon stepping forward to help his friend regain his balance. Concern etched along Clifton's father's brow as he escorted King Granton out of the room.

Ryle then gave a celebratory clap on Clifton's shoulder. "Well how does it feel?"

"How does what feel? Elizabeth has not agreed just yet."

"She will." Ryle stated confidently.

"I'm glad one of us is confident. I must admit that I may not be her favorite person today. Perhaps they should talk to her tomorrow."

Ryle laughed and pinned his brother with a wide grin. "Brother, Princess Elizabeth will agree to the courtship. If anything just to escape the clutches of Prince Eric of the South."

"Gee, thanks." Clifton replied. "Nice to know I'm a better alternative."

"I did not mean it like that. I was just teasing. We all see the way you two look at one another. Trust me, she will agree."

"I hope you're right. I think the Council Meeting will confirm her decision."

"Why the Council Meeting?" Ryle asked.

"You will see, brother." Clifton exhaled loudly as he rolled his shoulders and tilted his head from side to side to relieve the tension from his back and neck. He nervously wiped his palms on his pant legs. What if Elizabeth wished to remain a maiden? What if she rejected his proposal of courtship? Yes, he felt she cared for him, but enough to marry him? He ran his hand over his jaw and grimaced at his rough appearance. His mind wandered to the subject of

Elizabeth's letter to her brother. Perhaps they should write one together, each placing questions to the prince. Clifton knew Ryle would certainly have questions in regard to the guard. Should he have told the kings and his brother of the matter before the meeting? No. Elizabeth said she would share the subject at the next Council Meeting. He would trust that she would. If she did not, he would. Simple solution. He thought of Samuel as well, the young prince, risking everything to supply them with information. He would meet him tomorrow at the clearing, receive his information and present it at the Council Meeting tomorrow evening. Clifton nodded to himself decisively. Yes, this meeting would certainly prove important, perhaps changing their tactics against the Lands forever.

∞

King Anthony paced around his chambers. His long stride covering much distance very quickly. Princess Melody studied her father closely, noting the strain around his eyes as he continued to run his hand over his chin in thought. Her brother, the man her father wished to speak with, emerged in the doorway.

"Well it is about time." King Anthony barked. "Where have you been?"

Isaac halted his steps at the altercation and slowly shut the door. "I was walking about the castle."

"I'm sure you were. Sit." King Anthony ordered pointing at a seat on the sofa next to Melody. He slowly eased next to his sister trying to read her face for any inclination as to why their father seemed irate. He read nothing. "I am going to speak frankly to both of you, though I have much to say to you, Isaac." King Anthony began. He stopped pacing long enough to face them with a disappointed glare. "We are in a tumultuous situation within the Realm. Unity is important. Our actions are important. Our *presence* is important." He pinned a sharp gaze on each of his children and began pacing again, casting them glances every now and then. He stopped again, peered into the fireplace and tried to formulate his words. "It is of utmost importance that you two attempt to form bonds with the other princes and princesses. Melody," he turned to face his daughter and his gaze slightly softened. "I know you are shy, my lovely, but you must leave these chambers. Can you do that for me?" She nodded quietly, and her gaze fell to her hands nervously wound in her lap. His gaze then switched to Isaac and the hardness returned. "And you son—" he shook his head in dismay. "I walk into the main hall to find Princess Alayna seated on the throne taking kingdom requests, Prince Ryle by her side serving faithfully, Prince Clifton flanking the other side and standing with Princess Elizabeth. A united front, and where should I see you, son? I see you scurrying in the shadows with a chamber maid! Hiding behind pillars and in secret rooms up to no good! You are the future king of the Western Kingdom! I do not wish for the kingdom to fall into the hands of a floundering scoundrel!" His father's face reddened as he yelled. Isaac saw Melody flinch out of the corner of his eye. "Your lack of propriety stops here, Isaac." Anthony continued. "You will serve your kingdom and the Realm by recognizing your responsibilities as future king of the West."

Isaac shifted in his seat, his own temper flaring within him, but he also recognized the gravity of the situation. His father was a man of his word. Of all things King Anthony stood for, it was honesty. The man never shied from the truth. His threats of withholding the throne and kingship of the West were real, and Isaac knew his father would always do right by the kingdom. If he wished to pass the kingdom to Melody, King Anthony would, if he felt it best. And Isaac wanted to be king. He'd wanted it his whole life, dreamed of it even. If setting aside his affairs and distractions regained his father's faith in him, he would do it. Temporarily, but he would do it.

"I understand Father." He stated calmly. "I do not wish to be a disappointment."

"It is not just that, Isaac," King Anthony exhaled loudly as if his tirade had finally left his system. He sat across from his children and leaned forward to state his point. "The Realm will fall if we do not stand up against the Lands united. All of us are in this together. We cannot afford to be distracted or aloof. Your aloofness is what worries me. Both of you." His gaze travelled to Melody yet again. "We are not here to vacation from our kingdom. We are here to formulate a plan to stop Lancer's power and strength from spreading. Now may I have your word that you will do better at being present?" He looked from one child to another and they both nodded.

"Good." He patted his hands on his knees as he rose to his feet. "The Council Meeting is tomorrow evening. Isaac, you will be punctual. In the meantime, Princess Elizabeth's safety is at risk with the Prince of the South wanting to claim her. Though she is not your betrothed, you will aid in protecting the Princess. That is an order."

Isaac stood and nodded. "Of course, Father."

"Melody I wish for you to befriend the Princesses as well. They are older than you and I feel you could learn a great deal from them." King Anthony stated.

Melody nodded in agreement.

King Anthony straightened his scarlet tunic and readjusted his sleeves. "Now, if you will excuse me, I am to meet with King Granton and King Eamon over other matters. Please heed my warnings and my words." He exited swiftly, the heavy wooden doors clattering at his exit.

Isaac and Melody sat quietly a few moments before Melody spoke. "I worry for you Isaac." She stated softly.

He turned to her in surprise. "Whatever for?"

"Father is not idle in his threats. You are to be king, you must act like one."

Isaac sat stunned by his sister's abruptness, yet equally impressed by her candor.

"I do not wish to run the kingdom," she began, "please do not leave me that responsibility whether purposefully or not."

"You are a princess, Melody. You will be marrying a prince and possibly one day being a queen somewhere. You will be running a kingdom."

"Not today at least, and I will be supporting my prince or king when that time comes, not ruling for him." She clarified firmly.

"We will see." Isaac gently tugged on one of her curls. "You are eighteen Melody, you should be married by now. Father's softness towards you has held a proposal back for too long. He should be looking at outside realms for a suitor."

Her eyes widened at that revelation and she shook her head. "No, I belong in this Realm."

"And who do you suggest you marry then? Prince Ryle? Prince Clifton?" Isaac scoffed. "Those two have removed themselves from the market. It is clear Prince Clifton has wishes for Princess Elizabeth, and Prince Ryle attends the future queen too faithfully not to be in love."

"Perhaps the South then." Melody stated.

"Prince Eric?" Isaac's smirk faded. "No. Even I would not relinquish you to him."

She shrugged her shoulders. "Time will tell. I am willing to marry or do whatever needs to be done to protect the Realm."

"Spoken like a true queen." Isaac complimented tenderly as he began walking to the door. "I cherish you, sister. I hope, despite my actions and words of late, that you always remember that."

"I do, and I will, brother." Melody smiled at his retreating back and silently hoped her brother took their father seriously.

∞

Walking along the stark hallway, Edward noted the flames of the sconces and the ethereal glow they cast about his steps. He neared Lancer's chambers and raised his hand to knock just as the man stepped out. Lancer's eyes widened in surprise until he realized Edward's identity. A large smile spread over his face. "Ah, Edward! Perfect timing. I was just about to send for you."

"Is that so?" Edward asked.

"Indeed. I must say I am impressed by our mental connection Edward. It's one of the reasons I was to send for you." Lancer winked and began walking down the hall. Edward fell into step beside him. He seemed cheerful, Edward thought, as if no weight pressed upon his shoulders. As if nothing could tamper his joy. How could a man so dark feel so light? Lancer turned when Edward began to lag behind. "Did you hear what I was saying, Edward?"

"Oh, my apologies, my Lord. My thoughts drifted for a moment."

His smile never faltering, Lancer waved him off. "Oh, it is no bother. I have satisfied myself in the fact that you are a dreamer, Edward. Dreamers need to drift off every now and then." Lancer stopped in front of the door to his reflection chamber. "I wish to bring you with me today." He turned towards Edward and studied him closely.

"Inside your chamber?" Edward asked, a slight jump in his pulse and a sinking in his stomach warned him of the consequences should he enter.

"Yes."

Edward's mind swirled with possibilities. The maid had said everyone who went inside never came out. Perhaps Lancer was on to him? Perhaps he knew Edward was planning a rebellion? Edward's palms began to sweat, and he nervously wiped them on his tunic as he linked his hands behind his back.

"I would be honored, my Lord." He replied, taking a deep breath to calm his nerves when Lancer turned back towards the door. He opened the door and stepped inside. Edward followed. The room was dark. No light, no windows, no sound except for the drumming of his heart in his ears. "Follow me." Lancer stated in a hushed whisper as he lightly grabbed Edward's sleeve to pull him forward. He felt a cold blade against his palm and the quick slice of pain and skin. He hissed.

"Blood must be paid for entering, Edward." Lancer stated, his voice hollow and low. "It all began with blood." Edward heard another slice and Lancer's own hiss. Thereafter, the lanterns around the room lit in unison and the flames fired towards the ceilings. Lancer held his arms open as he stood in the middle of the room, head tilted back as if awaiting an epiphany. Edward searched the room for signs of life, but no one else was present. Lancer's head snapped back up and he glanced at Edward, his eyes darker and pupils fully dilated. "It is time, Edward." He waved Edward forward.

Making his way towards Lancer, Edward felt his breathing hitch. He took a deep breath as he stood before the man. And that's what he was, Edward thought, just a man. Why was he scared of a man? He continued to remind himself of that fact as Lancer's voice changed to a low growl and he spread his arms out as a dark cloud of fog crept into the room and around their feet. A deep cold filtered into Edward's skin so far he swore he felt it in his very bones. His hand ached. His mind whirled. And he watched as Lancer's smile widened as the darkness crept up their legs.

"You have to be open to it, Edward." He grinned mischievously as he stretched out his arms again. "You have to let it overcome your senses."

Edward watched as the blackened smoke climbed over Lancer's body like a disease flooding his veins. Blackened veins of darkness roping themselves around his arms, his neck, his legs. Edward glanced down and realized very little fog remained around him. It all had drawn towards Lancer. Lancer hissed in pain as a cloud of black burst forth from the wound on his hand.

"It all began with blood, Edward. You must give in order to receive." Lancer glanced over at him and realized he stood enveloped in black and Edward stood in silent shock at what he was witnessing. He chuckled. "Come Edward, be brave. Embrace it."

Edward didn't budge. He had never seen anything like this before. What was this darkness? A spirit? A demon? He had heard such stories growing up, but no one had ever truly witnessed such... evil. He placed his hand over his heart to make sure he was still alive. He felt a solid thump in his chest and breathed a small sigh of relief. Lancer clapped his hands and the darkness disappeared. The flames reduced to a normal flicker and he shook his head and laughed. "Too soon wasn't it?"

Edward blinked in shock at Lancer's reaction which had the man bellowing in laughter even harder. He slapped Edward on the back. "In time you will join me again, Edward, and we will both embrace the power and knowledge that is given to us. Did you feel the power at all?"

Edward shook his head. "No, my Lord. I— I do not understand."

"Ah. Perhaps it was just too soon, or perhaps our blood must be mixed. We will figure it out. Until then, you must speak of this room to no one, and you must not enter without me."

"Of course, my Lord." Edward replied and stepped back into the hallway with Lancer.

Lancer took a deep breath and sighed. "Well, I guess we should go about with our business of the day now, my friend."

"My Lord," Edward began, "May I ask you a question?"

"Of course, but not here. Let's go into my chambers first." He led Edward into his personal chamber and sat on one of his sofas. "Go ahead."

"That... smoke in the other room. What is that?"

Lancer's gaze narrowed as he studied Edward.

"Oh Edward, I do not believe it is a secret that I have a source of power besides myself. How else could I erect an invisible boundary and remain young forever?"

"Is it magic?" Edward asked, sounding foolish to his own ears at the words.

Lancer laughed and shook his head. "No. It is power, Edward."

"But where does it come from?"

Lancer shrugged. "Who knows? All that matters is that it is here, and I am its vessel, Edward. Don't you see the gift? We have the power to create a world all our own and never die. A place we can rule in complete freedom."

"But how, my Lord? I just don't understand how this power chose… you." Edward prayed Lancer did not take offense to his words.

Lancer sighed. "Because I was willing to be its vessel, Edward. Don't you see? You were not ready to surrender yourself to the power, therefore it did not enter you. Speak to you. Change you." Lancer explained. "It all begins with blood, Edward. That is why I sliced your hand. You must give of yourself in order to accept the gift that is given."

"So, you give your blood each time you enter the room?" Edward asked curiously.

"I give my blood, and I gave my life." Lancer replied. "I gave everything, and my reward is the Lands and all the power I desire."

Edward rubbed a hand over his jaw as he sat and listened. Confused did not even explain the thoughts rolling around in his head. How could this man be so willing to surrender his life to nothing? He gave his soul to darkness in order to live forever? Edward cringed at the thought. Must he do the same in order to cross the boundary line? He feared the thought.

"I see you have much to consider." Lancer stated warmly. "Please, take your time and should you have any more questions, I will be here. I wish to bring you into the fold, Edward, so I will be patient."

"Yes, my Lord. I thank you for your faith in me."

Smiling, Lancer nodded. "Of course. Now go, see to that hand." He waved Edward out of his chambers and shut the door.

Edward rushed to the stables and mounted Triton. He had much to write to Elizabeth. He still had not made sense of what he had just encountered, but his eyes had never seen anything so bewitching or evil. The Realm was up against more than just a man now. Darkness, all-consuming darkness wished to infiltrate the Realm, and Edward prayed he could stop it.

Edward slipped the letter from Thatcher's neck as Elizabeth swung her sword against her targets. Mary sat on a rock and watched as Elizabeth ducked and rotated to attack another one. He eased onto a stump and read:

Brother,

I am sorry for the slight delay in my writing to you. It has been quite eventful around here as of late. I trust you are doing well and that Cecilia is as well. I wish to write to you inquiries of happy matters, but we both know the time has passed for such things. I need news of Lancer, brother. The Council meets tomorrow evening, and Prince Clifton and I will be sharing our communication with you and the grave news of Lancer you just shared. Father will be finding out about our meetings the last five years. I suspect he will be quite angry with me at first... but we both know he will forgive in time. However, I wish to supply the Council with much needed assurance from your end. How many troops do you now have fighting alongside you? Have you found out how Lancer can cross? What are his plans? Does he plan an attack?

As you can see, I have many questions. Pray, please answer them if you can.

I must also tell you of other news. Alayna has approached me about a courtship with Prince Clifton. I will be accepting his proposal should it arise. I will find out in a day or two. I will let you know of the decision. I feel this will be a wonderful union for the Realm as well as for me. I do care for him, Edward. He is an honest and kind man. His heart is pure, and he serves the Realm with all he has. I must say he takes after his father, a man I have also come to greatly admire.

We have strength in bonds on this side of the line, I hope you do as well. Tread carefully on the other side, brother. I feel a heaviness to the air. Something is brewing beneath the senses and we shall all find out soon enough what it is.

Edward lifted his gaze to find his sister standing exhausted from her efforts and taking a sip of water from the leather pouch Mary supplied. He grabbed his parchment and began to reply to her letter. He filled her in on his experience in Lancer's reflection chamber and his theory of the darkness being the reason Lancer was able to cross the boundary line. Edward ran a hand through his dark hair as he sat pondering how best to convey his fears. As prepared as his army may be, it could not withstand what he just witnessed. Lancer seemed invincible now. Edward penned his letter and placed it upon Thatcher and sent the rabbit across the line. Elizabeth swooped over and untied it, tucking it into her trouser pocket. Edward blew her a kiss and disappeared within the trees.

Elizabeth looked to Mary. "He looked worried, Mary."

"I supposed he did." Mary agreed.

"Do you think he is okay?"

Mary smiled at the princess. "Of course, he is, milady. He wrote you a long note did he not? I am sure he just has much on his mind like you do."

Sighing in resignation, Elizabeth agreed. "I suppose you're right. We best make it back to the castle Mary. I need to prepare for the Council meeting tomorrow."

"Yes, milady."

Elizabeth and Mary rode through the trees, their horses appearing just on the edge of the horizon. Prince Isaac squinted to make out the two figures and a small smirk tilted his lips when he noticed the princess. He trotted forward at a lazy pace until he neared the female riders. "Out for a ride today, Princess Elizabeth?"

Elizabeth forced a smile. "Yes, my Lord. It was a glorious day for it."

"Did your father not warn you of riding alone when your safety is at risk?"

She glowered, making his smile widen. One thing the princess did have that he respected was her gumption.

"Forgive me, Prince Isaac, but when did you last become my guardian?"

"Oh, it comes from the goodness of my heart, milady. I do not wish to see you harmed."

She scoffed in disbelief as her horse fell into step beside his.

"Does Prince Clifton know your whereabouts?"

Elizabeth turned to him sharply. "Why would he need to know?"

Isaac shrugged as he threaded his reins through his fingers. "He seems quite interested in all things related to you." Isaac stated bluntly. He caught the slight blush to the princess's cheeks and chuckled. "Ah. I see that pleases you."

"I did not say anything."

"You didn't have to." Isaac stated with a warm tone to his voice. "As much as I would like to admit my dislike for the prince, I must say he is an honorable man, and a lucky man, should he win your heart."

Surprise lit Elizabeth's blue eyes. "I am surprised to hear you say such words, Prince Isaac."

He laughed. "Honestly, so am I." He admitted with a small blush to his neck. He cleared his throat. "Moving on." He continued.

"I know your father wishes to keep a watchful eye on you, Princess. We all feel the pressure of the South and the Lands."

"I appreciate your concern." She took a deep breath and surveyed the castle before them. Her father's castle. The place she was born and the place she had lived her entire life. Once married, it would no longer be her home. A sadness filled her heart to think of leaving her father while his health continued to fail.

"It's a lovely view, is it not?" Isaac asked as he studied the castle as well. "Reminds me of the Eastern Kingdom a bit with the portico and arches." He pointed as if to show her what he spotted.

"You've been to the Eastern Kingdom?" Elizabeth asked curiously.

"Yes, when I was a boy. I remember it vividly though. The queen was beautiful. I remember her smile most of all. She had bright green eyes and hair the color of a raven. She doted upon me greatly during my visit."

"King Eamon spoke highly of her at breakfast the other day. Seems he cherished his wife dearly." Elizabeth added. She studied the prince closely as a softness held in his gaze at his recollection. She had never seen this side of Prince Isaac, and though she felt camaraderie within the moment, an underlying sense of distrust still tainted her thoughts.

"Yes, he did. I remember the day we were to leave, the queen was saddened by our departure, and King Eamon simply plucked a yellow rose and handed it to her." He chuckled at the memory. "At the time I thought that must be the way to a girl's heart, a flower." He turned and winked at Elizabeth making her laugh in return. "I'm sure there was a hidden meaning in the exchange that my young eyes did not know, but I took what I saw and used the method several times to impress the women of the court in my youth."

"I see. And did you have any luck using King Eamon's method?"

"Not at all." He replied, and they both laughed. "I quickly found out it takes much more than a flower."

"Indeed." Elizabeth agreed amicably.

They reached the stables and she dismounted, quickly tying her skirt around her waist to cover her trousers. Isaac's brow rose, but he did not inquire after her attire. Instead, he waved his hand outward towards the path traipsing to the castle. Elizabeth fell into step beside him and for the first time, enjoyed his company.

∞

"There you are Granton, nice and easy my friend." King Eamon eased the king onto the edge of his bed and gently grabbed his ankles and helped Granton swing his feet onto the bed. Anthony and Mosiah stood to the side with somber faces as Eamon situated the pillows and propped Granton up. Granton coughed vigorously, the quakes sending his frail frame into a fit of shakes. Tomas rushed into the room followed by two maids as he quickly took over caring for the king. Granton's coughs ceased and he looked from one face to another. "Don't look at me like that." He grumbled as he leaned his head back in exhaustion.

"You aren't doing well, Granton." King Eamon stated kindly. "We hate to see you like this."

Granton sighed as he looked to his closest friends and allies. "I do not like being like this, either. However, the truth is, my time is limited. I do not wish my daughters to see me like this. Please make sure they stay away from my chambers today, Tomas." His faithful servant nodded as he forced a sip of cider down his throat.

"Granton," King Anthony began, unsure of what to say, shifted on his feet. "Have you spoken to Alayna about the status of your… condition?"

"No." Granton coughed into his fist a couple of times, Eamon stepping forward and lightly fluffing his pillows behind him as he did. "Alayna is aware I wish to pass off some of my duties to her, but she does not know the gravity of my health."

"Should this be kept secret?" Anthony continued with concern.

"I do not wish to overwhelm her with responsibility. If Alayna knew the true condition of my health, she would throw every ounce of her being into becoming queen. I want her to enjoy what little time she has left in her role as Princess. Ruling is a great responsibility, a heavy one. I do not wish that upon her shoulders as of yet. I do not want to hand over the Realm when our lands are being threatened."

"You may have no choice." Mosiah stated. "I apologize, my Lord, for speaking so plainly, but Princess Alayna must be aware that she will be making decisions on her own soon."

"And what of Elizabeth?" King Eamon asked. "Does she know your condition?"

Granton shook his head. "No, but she suspects. Elizabeth is an observant one. She senses I am not being truthful when she asks me of my health. I know she realizes I am slowly fading."

"Is there nothing that can be done?" Eamon asked. "Perhaps if we sent for my healer in the East. He is well known for his miracles from his former realm."

Granton held up his hand. "No, Eamon. Thank you, but no. There is nothing that can be done."

A light knock sounded on the door and all the men turned as Elizabeth poked her head into the room. Her brow immediately furrowed and she rushed inside to her father's bedside. "Father! Are you alright? What has happened?"

Granton forced a smile and eased into a sitting position. "Lizzy dear, nothing to be worried about, my love. I was napping for a bit and my fellow kings needed me."

Elizabeth's gaze narrowed as she studied her father and then looked at the sober faces of the other kings. When she caught King Eamon's gaze, she knew her father was lying. The kind king of the East cast her a sympathetic gaze before glancing back to her father.

"I will pretend to believe you." She stated firmly and sat by his side. "Is there anything I can get for you?"

"No, my dear. Tomas has me well looked after. Are you wandering about by yourself? I assumed Prince Clifton would be by your side this afternoon."

Elizabeth's cheeks flushed before she could muster her annoyance. "Father, I am perfectly capable of finding my way around my own castle."

He chuckled but began a fit of coughing once again. Tomas gently shifted Elizabeth away from the bedside as he tended to her father. She felt a strong arm drape over her shoulders and turned to find King Eamon's worried gaze. "Why don't you come with me, dear?" He caught Granton's grateful nod before he turned and escorted Elizabeth out of the room.

"He is not doing well." Elizabeth stated as soon as they exited.

"No, my dear, I am afraid he is not." Elizabeth turned in surprise at the king's honesty. "I fear, Princess Elizabeth, that your father will not be with us much longer. I do not mean to sound morbid, it's just—" King Eamon looked away and out the window as his mind wandered elsewhere. "I've seen this illness before." He finished softly. His eyes took on a sadness and Elizabeth realized the Eastern King had lost his queen to what ailed her father. She lightly hugged him around the waist and brought his sad smile back towards her. He lightly kissed the top of her head. "But enough sadness for today. Your father is a strong man and will fight for as long as he is able. You mustn't worry too much, Princess."

"How can I not worry, my Lord? My sister and I spoke with my father but a few days ago about his condition and he attempted to convince us he was fine. I knew he was not, but Alayna still imagines him guiding her when she is queen. Should he not step down now? Should Alayna not be crowned now? That way she has some comfort with the position before events in the Realm grow harder?"

"You are a wise woman, Princess." Eamon complimented. "I must admit I agree with you. I feel it wise for your father to step down, but Granton is…"

"Stubborn." They both stated at the same time. Smiling softly, Eamon squeezed her hand. "I will talk to him, dear. In the meantime, perhaps you can track down my sons for me?"

Elizabeth nodded but her expression remained worried.

King Eamon studied the young woman for a moment. Sensing her hesitancy, he shifted his stance and crossed his arms. "Was there anything else, Princess?"

Elizabeth's sad blue eyes looked up at him. "Now would not be the time for me to address it, my Lord."

"But I see something is weighing heavily on your mind." He pointed out gently.

Sighing, Elizabeth stepped towards the railing of the balcony that overlooked the main hall. She spotted Alayna ordering an attendant around and smiled softly. *Her sister was always bossy,* she thought. She spotted Prince Clifton and Prince Ryle seated in the conservatory studying charts and maps of the Realm no doubt. King Eamon clasped the railing next to her and waited patiently for her to speak.

"Alayna approached me about a courtship with your son, my Lord."

"Yes, I knew she would." He studied her delicate features and the softening in her gaze as she stared in the direction of his son. "Was the matter settled?"

"I am not sure. At the time she and I spoke, Prince Clifton had yet to be asked as well. I wished not to agree until I knew the true conditions of his heart."

"Ah, I see. Would it ease your mind to know he has already spoken with your father on the matter?"

Elizabeth turned in surprise, her dark brows rising. "He has?"

"Yes, my dear. He spoke with Granton and me this afternoon."

"And?" Elizabeth's breath caught on the word as hope lit her gaze, and a flutter in her chest tightened in anticipation of the king's response.

"Well, he wishes to court you, should you accept." Eamon explained.

"I see." Elizabeth tried to sound calm, though her insides erupted into joy.

"Does that suit you, Elizabeth?"

Elizabeth turned and faced the king and placed her hand on her hip. She tilted her head and studied him, her gaze narrowing and chin slightly jutting out in stubbornness. Granton's daughter, indeed, King Eamon thought.

"I have conditions, my Lord."

His brows slightly rose. He waved his hand for her to continue.

"First, I do not wish to leave my father until his condition either improves or… well, you know. Second, I wish not to leave until I am sure Alayna is well looked after. I do not wish to leave her alone here, my Lord. She must not be expected to face her new destiny alone. And third, I wish to continue to be a part of the Council of the Realm, though my title will be changing from Princess of the North to that of the East."

A slow smile graced the king's face. "I find those conditions quite agreeable, Princess."

"Then I accept. The courtship proposal, that is."

"Splendid." King Eamon opened his arms for a hug that Elizabeth sweetly accepted. She could not ask for a better marriage. "I shall inform your father and my son, Princess. Both will be extremely pleased. In fact, I believe Cliff may seek you out once he hears the wonderful news."

Elizabeth smiled as she gazed back down towards the two Eastern princes. "He is a good man, my Lord. I count myself very fortunate to be his betrothed."

King Eamon beamed. "It is we who are blessed to have you join our family, Elizabeth. Truly." He bowed and then left her to her thoughts. She leaned her chin in her hands as she rested her elbow on the banister. Princess Elizabeth of the Eastern Kingdom. It would take some getting used to, but she found she liked the sound of it. As if sensing her gaze, Clifton glanced up and spotted her. She saw the flash of his teeth as he smiled up at her. He gave a small wave as if unsure if she were still aggravated with him. She waved in return and then slid from the banister and headed towards her chambers. She needed to prepare her notes for the Council meeting tomorrow night, and she needed to prepare her heart for the courtship acceptance that would be announced tomorrow afternoon to the kingdom as well. She took a shaky breath of uncertainty as she walked past her father's chambers. Tears stung the back of her eyes as she thought of how frail he looked earlier. Shaking away the thought, she turned down the side hallway towards her personal quarters and sought out the comfort of her bed when she entered.

CHAPTER 8

"We will need music," Alayna stated excitedly. "And dancing. Ah! The grand banquet hall will be perfect!" Her sister wrote down a note on her parchment. "And yes, of course, we will have the tailors begin work on your dress. It shall be the beautiful blue of the Eastern Kingdom. You will look stunning. And then—"

"Can we please slow down a minute?" Elizabeth waved her hands to stop her sister's planning. "Allow me to catch my breath, sister. I just accepted the request. Don't you think it is a bit quick to be planning my wedding ball?"

"Not at all. You said it yourself. You will be married by month's end. There is much to be done before then." Alayna pointed out.

"Yes, you are right." Elizabeth challenged. "Things like battling the Unfading Lands and securing the boundaries of the South."

Alayna huffed in frustration. "Elizabeth, we are handling those things."

"Not quick enough."

"Well, what do you suggest then? We have the Council Meeting tomorrow. Do you wish for it to be tonight?"

Elizabeth glanced out the window at the bustling castle grounds. The market square was teaming with carts and trade. She smiled as she caught sight of a small boy shooting a little girl with a rock out of his slingshot. Youthful innocence, she thought. No worries of the world around them. Just a world of fun and freedom.

"Elizabeth?" Alayna's voice interrupted her train of thought and brought her back to their discussion. "I just feel that my marriage can wait when there are bigger issues to deal with at the moment."

"True." Alayna stated. "But I think what this Realm needs is a bit of good news. Everything has been so dark and foreboding lately, it will be nice to celebrate something. I think the people will be excited of the union."

"I hope the Eastern Kingdom people are equally as excited." Elizabeth worried.

"How could they not be? There is no greater honor than to marry a Princess of the North." Brushing a hand over the pleats in her skirt, Alayna resituated her bustle in her chair.

"When do we make the announcement?" Elizabeth stated.

"At high noon, in the market square. You and Prince Clifton will stand on either side of Father as he presents the engagement to the people. Which reminds me, Mary should be dressing you in your dress robes." Alayna clucked over to the doorway and called for Mary. Elizabeth tensed at the loud call, and Mary rushed into the room.

"Yes, milady?"

"Mary, we need to dress Elizabeth in her dress robes for the noon announcement of her betrothal. Please see that she is punctual."

"Yes, milady."

Alayna stood and smiled at her sister. "I am excited for you, Elizabeth. Prince Clifton is a most suitable partner for you." Elizabeth smiled softly, her usual spark not quite reaching her eyes as she worried over future events that lurked on the horizon.

Alayna slipped out the door of Elizabeth's chambers and made her way towards the Council room for her meeting with her Father. Glancing up from her parchments she spotted Prince Ryle making his way to the room as well. He stopped and flashed a charming smile. "Princess Alayna, good to see you."

"And you, Prince Ryle. You wish to council with the king?" She asked, pointing at the doors they both wished to enter.

"Actually, I was wishing to council with the Queen."

Alayna straightened, and her eyes sparkled with pleasure at his consideration.

"Shall we?" She motioned for him to open the door.

Stepping into the dark room, King Granton sat in the chair Alayna normally occupied. She froze for a brief second before raising her chin and walking purposefully around the room to the head of the table. She stopped briefly by the window and pulled back the heavy velvet drapes in one large swoosh, flooding the room in bright sunlight. Several of the men squinted against the bright assault before adjusting to the change. Alayna sat and crossed her hands upon the tabletop.

"Morning, Father."

"Good morning dear. I trust things are in order for the announcement?"

"Yes. I have Mary dressing Elizabeth now. Prince Ryle, is your brother ready?"

"He will be, your Grace. I believe Cliff is as nervous as a cat in a room full of rocking chairs at the moment."

King Granton burst into a bellow of laughter causing Ryle and Alayna to do the same.

"The poor boy." Granton stated. "I remember those feelings. Nerves, excitement, and complete and total loss of my head. Love does funny things to us."

"Indeed." Ryle agreed with a smile.

"Are you up for making the announcement, Father?" Alayna asked, a slight discomfort filling the air.

"Yes. I would like to make the announcement very much."

Alayna nodded. "Very well then. I have requested Elizabeth and Clifton to be at the front entrance at a few minutes before high noon. We will make the announcement on the front parapet overlooking the market square."

"Sounds lovely, dear." Granton complimented. "I trust plans for the wedding have commenced."

"Yes, well, what little I can get Elizabeth to agree upon. Her mind is elsewhere at the moment." Granton's smile slightly faltered, knowing his health, among other things, weighed heavily upon his youngest daughter. Ryle studied him carefully and he realized the young prince read through his thoughts easily, much like his father, Granton thought. "I am sure she is just slightly overwhelmed with all the happenings." Granton assured Alayna.

Nodding, Alayna turned to Prince Ryle. "That is all of my news, but Prince Ryle had wished to speak to me as well. What is it you wish to discuss, Prince?"

Ryle straightened in his chair and he looked from one royal face to the other. "I wish to speak on a more somber matter, unfortunately. My king…" He looked to Granton with humility. "Mosiah and I have been in great discussions as of late over the upcoming battles against the Lands and possibly the South. I— he—

we were discussing the possibility of a change in ranks soon, amongst the Realm's Royal Guard."

"A change?" King Granton studied the man carefully. Alayna leaned forward intently as she listened to the prince.

"Yes, my Lord. It is my wish to serve as Captain of the Royal Guard, your Grace."

Alayna's eyes widened, and she leaned back in her chair just as her father did with the shock of Prince Ryle's announcement.

"Have you voiced this desire to anyone else?" Granton asked.

"No, my King. I fear my request may ripple into an argument amongst my father and myself. I have not discussed my wishes with him as of yet. I wanted to gauge the possibility of the change before making my wishes known to him."

"This is a serious matter indeed, Prince Ryle. You realize that by taking the position of Captain of the Guard of the Realm that you relinquish your rights to the throne of the East?" Granton pointed out.

"Yes, my Lord."

"You do not have a desire to be king?" Alayna questioned.

Ryle's gaze found hers and he shook his head. "If that is to be my role, I will accept it and serve wholeheartedly. However, my true desire has and always will be to serve the crown of the Realm." His eyes narrowed as if he were trying to send a silent signal to Alayna. Granton caught the undertones of the prince's heart towards his daughter and cleared his throat.

"You wish to serve the Realm's crown of authority by giving away your rights to your father's throne, by laying your life at the hands of the Realm?" Granton stressed the importance of the prince's request. Prince Ryle nodded.

"It is a decision I have been quite patiently pursuing. My feelings have only been confirmed since coming to the Northern Kingdom, my Lord. I have always wanted to obtain a military status of Captain, but my role as successor to the throne has always prevented such a move. With the threat of the Land of Unfading Beauty and quite possibly Prince Eric of the South, I feel my role as a military man far surpasses that of my role as future king."

"You would give up your kingdom for—" Alayna trailed off as she realized Prince Ryle would replace Mosiah and would be her personal guard and most trusted aid to her throne. The thought had her heart betraying her. She fixed a calm expression upon her beautiful features though her pulse raced beneath her wrists.

"I would not be giving it up, my Lady. My brother, Prince Clifton, would easily slip into the role as future king. With Princess Elizabeth as his queen, I know the East will remain in good hands and I can serve here. Mosiah has spoken of his stepping down once the throne is bestowed upon Princess Alayna, my Lord. He has served you faithfully for many years, I wish to do the same for the future queen." Ryle shifted in his seat, his long legs stretching out briefly to ease the tension in his knees. He turned towards the king. "Is this a possible move, my Lord? Or should I consider the matter closed?"

Granton rubbed a hand over his beard as he studied Ryle. He would be a gifted and protective Captain for his daughter, but he hated the thought of the young man relinquishing his rights of kingship, even if they would pass to his brother. And Eamon. Eamon had trained the boy from infancy to take his role as king. How would his good friend take the news?

"I think it is a matter worth further discussion." Granton stated.

Alayna's brown gaze grew hard. "Father!" She gasped. "You cannot be serious?" She turned towards Ryle and held a hand up to prevent any interruption. "Forgive me, Prince Ryle. Though I am grateful for your servant's heart, I do not see the forfeiture of your kingship a wise decision. We will need strong allies in the East. And though your brother, Prince Clifton, is more than suitable for the position, I do not wish for us to make such a change in haste."

"I understand, my Lady." Ryle stated calmly.

"We will consider his request, Alayna." Granton stated firmly, causing Alayna's gaze to snap towards him. "I will speak with Mosiah of his wishes and his thoughts, Prince Ryle. We are both pleased and honored you wish to serve the Realm so faithfully."

Ryle bowed his head humbly and then his sharp blue gaze found Alayna. She sat dumbfounded, her mouth slightly ajar as if she were shocked out of her senses. She nodded as if she did not trust her words.

Ryle stood. "I thank you for the audience, your Graces." He bowed regally and turned to exit. When he reached the door, he turned to find Alayna still studying him. He bowed once more and left.

"A most interesting request." Granton softly eyed his daughter.

"An absurd request." She replied. "King Eamon would be devastated, Father."

"I am not sure about that. I think the fact the kingdom would continue to pass to a son would be a comfort for Eamon. Has he expected it to pass to Ryle? Yes. But I do not find the passage to Clifton a bad alternative."

"But… it just seems unheard of, Father. Has this ever happened?"

"No. But the man wishes to serve you Alayna. I have watched him the last few weeks and he is protective of you and your sister. He would be a fine Captain."

"But…" Alayna trailed off, no more arguments found her lips as she studied the doorway. "I just am not sure what to say."

"Be grateful you have a faithful servant, my dear. His loyalty and service will be of great importance soon. It eases my mind that whether he takes his reign as king or whether he becomes our Captain, he will serve the Realm faithfully."

"Yes, he is most admirable." Alayna agreed. She shifted the parchments of Elizabeth's wedding plans aside and stood. "Well, it is almost time for the announcement, Father. I will see you at the front entrance shortly. I need to grab my formal robes."

"Yes, dear." Granton watched her gracefully leave. He would speak to Eamon about Ryle's request. As a father, and a king, he approved of the prince for the position. He knew Mosiah had discussed stepping down when Alayna was crowned. It was only a matter of time for guards to step forward to nominate themselves for the position of Captain. But to have a Prince claim the position, a prince he knew had the best training and skills, yes, Ryle would be a perfect choice. And Granton thought, Ryle cared for Alayna. He sensed the boy's attraction to his daughter, but the formality of his position and her future one as queen prevented him from pursuing her. As king of the East he would not be able to marry Alayna. As Captain of the Guard, there could be a possibility. He shook his head and chuckled. Brushing a hand over his smile his eyes clouded as he thought of having to leave his daughters behind. *Death was a part of life,* he thought. There was no fear in the inevitable, but he prayed he had a chance to see his daughters cared for before he departed this world. As this thought surfaced, he stood to make his way to the front entrance. If he knew one thing about his daughter, it was that Alayna despised a hitch in her schedule. He best be on time.

∞

"Your ambitions are far too great, son. Our numbers have greatly decreased due to your advanced lessons. We do not have the numbers to take on the North." King Titus watched the blood rush to his eldest son's face as he stripped off his cape and tossed it onto one of the straight-backed chairs.

"You underestimate our strength, Father." Prince Eric countered. "The North is weak. King Granton is ill and his failing health has weakened his influence. His Royal Guard is weak. The Captain of the Royal Guard is past his prime and believes their armies invincible. They are wrong. And so are you. We can take the North, the throne of the Realm. Father, this is what we have wanted!" Eric stepped forward, his hands outstretched in front of him as he pleaded for his father's blessing.

"It is not I who wishes to overcome the throne of the Realm, son. I wish to be a vessel for Lancer to do that, so that when the Unfading Lands take over the Realm, he will remember our service and perhaps let us remain as we are." King Titus watched as his son paced back and forth, his boots clicking on the marble floor and echoing through the great hall.

Samuel leaned his head around one of the marble pillars and listened. He watched as his brother's anger bloomed inside of him and his father studied him. Dark eyes found Samuel and he ducked behind the pillar. When he peaked around again, his father continued to stare at him. A small smile tilted the corners of his lips at the sight of his youngest son.

"I think you are outdated in your thinking, Father." Eric continued. "Lancer only understands power. If we show him our force, our strength, by overtaking the other kingdoms, then he will allow us to share his power within the Lands."

"And what of the other kingdoms? The East and West? How do you suppose we overcome them?" Titus asked patiently.

Samuel strained to hear his brother's words. He had to know his brother's plans in order to report back to Prince Clifton.

"We storm their villages. Both kingdoms' rulers are currently residing in the North. They are distracted. I have had Samuel studying their actions."

"The Eastern and Western Kingdoms are stronger than you think, son."

"No. They are preoccupied at the moment. King Granton has moved his Royal Guards to the boundary line. The West has supplied some additional forces to aid the East against our small attacks, but they have no idea the forces we possess. If we pushed a quarter of our forces into the East, the North will send their troops to aide in the fight. That leaves the North wide open, Father." Eric ran a hand through his dark hair and sighed. "It will work, Father."

Samuel watched as his father shook his head. "No, I do not grant permission for these advances. I order that we stand down. No more attacks on the other kingdoms, Eric. Time will come when Lancer will make his move, and when he does we will aide him."

Eric stared at his father in disgust. "You are weak, Father, and a fool!" He barked.

King Titus stood quickly to his feet, his large frame, once intimidating to his son, now seemed old and wasted. "You dare insult your king?!" His face flushed, and his breaths deepened as he stepped towards Eric. "I have ordered your submission to my request! If you so much as breathe in the direction of one of the other kingdoms I will restrict you to the castle grounds!" Titus waved his hand in the air flourishing his last threat. Samuel's eyes widened at the sight of his father's anger and the defiant attitude of his brother. Did his brother not see the importance of the Realm staying united and strong? The only chance for defeat against Lancer would be to remain united. Talk of uniting with the Lands or talk of demolishing the other kingdoms were both future failures. His father and brother were both wrong. His eyes darted across the room to the door that led to the prison chambers. The Northern Guard was still down there. Samuel had snuck in the room yesterday to talk with him and give him hope. The man was kind and appreciative. Everyone he had met from the other kingdoms was kind, he thought. He heard a loud crash and saw his father leaning heavily on the tabletop as the pewter dishes crashed to the floor. Samuel narrowed his eyes and watched closely. King Titus pulled his hand away from his side and glanced at it in horror. Blood stained his hand and dripped down his wrist as he gazed at his eldest son in terror. Prince Eric stood over his father's hunched figure gripping a bloodied dagger in his hand. He lunged forward again, stabbing King Titus in the stomach. Samuel rushed into the room towards his father. Prince Eric turned in surprise and pierced a stern gaze upon Samuel. Samuel gripped his father's shoulders and tried to pull him up off the table for escape.

"Choose wisely, Samuel." Eric stated in a dark tone. He watched callously as his father's breath became ragged and Samuel struggled to carry the weight of his father.

"Help! Help! Somebody help!" Samuel screamed, his eyes watering as his father's footsteps became sluggish. He spotted two attendants rushing down the hall as he eased his father into the great chair at the front of the room. He knelt beside him, his hand providing pressure to his wound. Titus grabbed Samuel's hand and squeezed. "Run." He whispered on a breath as the dagger flew across the room and landed in his heart. Eric stood tall and unsheathed his sword as the servants rushed towards his father's side. He sliced his blade through the air sending them both to the ground. Samuel jumped to his feet as his brother's gaze fell upon him. "You have made your choice, brother? You wish to follow in the steps of our cowardly father? Or do you wish to join me?"

"I will never be like you." Samuel stood firm, fists clenched as he watched his brother's ambition blind him with a darkness that Samuel feared would take his life. His father drew a loud and shuddered breath. Eric's eyes glowered at the older man and he swung his blade in a swoosh over his head to drive it into his father. Samuel held up his arm to block the blow. "No!" He felt the slice and yelled as his brother brought his other fist down and hammered it into the side of Samuel's skull. Blackness took him.

∞

Princess Melody lightly squeezed Elizabeth's hand in support as Elizabeth anxiously glanced out the front windows at the crowd of people beginning to group together in the market square. The emerald flags hung in banners lightly blowing in the wind. The royal guards lined up and down the front steps, the signal of an announcement from the king, had people whispering in anticipation and excitement. Elizabeth smiled graciously at Melody as she paced back and forth. So, lost in her thoughts, she did not hear the arrival of Prince Clifton and his family.

Clifton noted the worried expression on Elizabeth's face and doubt swarmed in his mind. Was she second-guessing her decision? Mary lightly tapped Elizabeth's shoulder and the princess turned, freezing as she spotted him. He met her nervous gaze and offered a nervous smile of his own. He watched as the worry melted away from her face and she stepped towards him. Before she reached him, Prince Isaac slipped between them. "Ah ah ah. You two will get to see one another after the announcement." He winked at the annoyed Prince Clifton and offered his arm to Elizabeth. "Your sister has requested that I escort you out, Princess… to show unity amongst the kingdoms."

Elizabeth reluctantly slipped her hand through Isaac's elbow and began walking away. She cast one last look over her shoulder at Clifton before the doors opened. The sunlight swept into the castle as the crowd began to cheer at the sight of Princess Elizabeth on the arm of Prince Isaac. "The crowd loves me." Isaac stated and laughed at his own attempt at humor as Elizabeth lightly rolled her eyes. He escorted her to her position and bowed before sliding to position several steps down. Princess Melody and King Anthony followed, staggering themselves on the steps facing the parapet where Elizabeth waited patiently. Prince Ryle and King Eamon emerged next and the people cheered happily. They took their places on the steps as Prince Clifton emerged in the doorway. Elizabeth's breath caught at the sight of him. He stood tall and trim and absolutely perfect, she thought. The sun glistened off his golden hair and the crisp blue tunic stood radiant against the dark walls behind him. He turned without glancing her direction and took his place on the opposite side of the parapet from her. Alayna and King Granton stepped through the doors arm in arm as they made their way to the center of the parapet and stopped. King Granton smiled and waved as Alayna did the same. He then signaled the trumpeter to sound. The crowd quieted.

"Dearest people of the North and of the Realm!" His voice boomed over the crowd and he surveyed the eyes glancing up at him. "It is with great pleasure and honor that I announce the engagement of my daughter!" Several cheers erupted, silenced by the lift of his hand and his small chuckle. "Princess Elizabeth of the Northern Kingdom and of the Realm has accepted the hand of Prince Clifton of the Eastern Kingdom!" Applause erupted and Elizabeth noted several small children waving at her as she stood. She winked at them and smiled.

Alayna stepped to the side and motioned for Elizabeth to approach her father. She slowly stepped towards him and stood by his side. Granton turned to Clifton and waved him forward. Clifton held his breath as he flanked the king. King Granton stepped back and grasped each of their hands and placed Elizabeth's small hand in Clifton's. He then held them up in front of him. "Blessings on this union!"

Cheers and applause echoed through the market as flower petals were thrown in the air surrounding them and music began to play. Elizabeth could not help but smile at the joy that radiated within the gates. She turned and found Clifton beaming as well. She met his bright green gaze and giggled at the commotion. He stepped towards her and stopped abruptly as his gaze fell upon a dark uniform lurking behind a market tent— a Southern Kingdom uniform, but not Samuel. He met Elizabeth's concerned gaze, and tried to mask his worry. He smiled again and lifted her hand to his lips. More cheers erupted. They both waved to the people as the royal families began to ascend back up the stairs and into the castle. She and Prince Clifton were to stand outside alone for several minutes waving and showcasing their announcement. As they stepped closer to one another, Elizabeth smiled but mumbled through her teeth. "Something worries you, my Prince."

Clifton acted as if she had stated something funny and chuckled lightheartedly as he mumbled in return. "I spotted a Southern Kingdom tunic amongst the crowd."

"Where?" She turned and waved as Clifton slightly pointed and waved in the direction of the market tent. Her gaze followed, and she saw nothing. "Samuel?"

"No. Not sure who it was. Keep smiling." He told her as her brow furrowed. She erased the lines immediately and smiled openly.

"My cheeks are beginning to hurt." She stated and held a hand to her face.

Clifton laughed, genuinely, as he lightly placed his hand at the small of her back. They both bowed to the people and began making their exit. Once inside the castle and the doors closed, Elizabeth and Clifton both exhaled loudly and then laughed.

"We did it." She stated in relief.

"We did it." He repeated softly as he lightly brushed his thumb over her knuckles.

He jolted at the thunderous slap on his back as Ryle stepped forward and draped his arm over his shoulders. "Are you sure you want this rogue of a man, Princess?" Ryle teased his younger brother as he playfully strong-armed Clifton.

Elizabeth grinned at the brotherly affection and nodded. "I suppose I do, although I'm not sure about his family." She jested in return. Ryle froze in surprise and then threw back his head and laughed. "Aye, a great fit you are indeed, Princess."

Alayna watched longingly at the small celebration. Prince Isaac slid beside her and sighed. "We are both happy, yet disappointed, are we not?"

Alayna turned to him in annoyance. "I do not know what you mean, Prince Isaac."

"Sure you do." He replied flippantly and lightly placed his hand on her shoulder. "You wish to be the center of a celebratory ceremony as much as I do."

Alayna gasped softly at his nerve.

"Don't get frustrated, future queen. I am just stating the facts."

"Well considering I have a Realm to run, I find my celebration will only come once the Unfading Lands have been defeated. I believe I can wait until then."

"And what of your heart, Princess? Do you not wish to marry?"

"No. Not at the moment." Alayna replied truthfully. Though she longed for the relationships and interactions her sister was experiencing, she also knew her time would come when it was meant to. It was her time to be queen. She caught Elizabeth's happy stare and smiled. She watched as Prince Ryle pulled Elizabeth under his other arm and squeezed her in a hug before kissing her cheek playfully.

King Eamon stepped forward with his arms wide and enveloped all three of the smiling faces in a large hug. He laughed heartily as his gaze met Granton's. "She will be in good care, Granton."

Elizabeth's father beamed and nodded. "I have no doubts, Eamon."

King Anthony stepped next to his son and Alayna. "It is a joyous occasion to celebrate. The Realm needs a lift in spirits right now." He caught Alayna's worried gaze and nodded. She smiled at the king and noticed Isaac shift uncomfortably on his feet. "Isaac, have you given your regards to the Prince and Princess?" Anthony asked pointedly.

"I have to the princess, Father. I have yet the opportunity to speak to Prince Clifton, but I will."

"Good." Anthony nodded in approval as he walked towards King Granton.

Princess Melody walked over to Elizabeth and offered a warm hug. "So happy for you, Princess Elizabeth."

"Thank you, Melody." Elizabeth genuinely smiled and rubbed the young princess' shoulder. "I am so pleased you were able to join in the festivities."

Melody nodded and curtsied. Prince Clifton stepped forward and lightly placed a hand at the small of Elizabeth's back, the gesture sending a thrill of excitement up her spine. "Princess." He bowed towards Melody.

"Prince Clifton, I wish to offer my congratulations."

"Why, thank you. I must say I am quite pleased by Princess Elizabeth's pursuit."

Elizabeth's mouth dropped open in shock and she turned with a fire in her eyes. He laughed as she playfully swatted him when she realized he teased. "Excuse him Princess Melody, my prince does not realize he is not a humorous man." Clifton grinned and winked at her as he suppressed another laugh.

Melody smiled shyly and walked over towards her brother and Princess Alayna.

"Well my friends, I believe a celebration is in order." King Granton announced. "How about we enjoy some dinner and drinks in the dining hall?" He led the way. Elizabeth lightly tugged on Clifton's hand before he walked away. He turned, and his smile slowly faded at the seriousness on her face. "Something wrong, my love?"

Her cheeks warmed at the endearment, but she whispered softly. "You and I need to speak to one another before the Council Meeting tonight, prince. I received a letter from Edward earlier that is most disturbing. I thought perhaps we could plan our words together for tonight."

"A letter? What did it say?"

Elizabeth's gaze glossed over as tears stung the back of her eyes. "I fear it is terrible news, my Lord. Lancer has an unspeakable power. I cannot tell you right now, and I am sorry to lay this upon you at this time of celebration, but I wanted you to know my wishes of sharing it with you before we meet for the Council."

Clifton lightly trailed his fingers softly down her silky cheek. "I appreciate you letting me know."

Her blue eyes searched his for reassurance. "It will be okay, Elizabeth. We will figure this out, alright? There has to be a way for us to defeat Lancer. We just have to find it. Don't fret on it, love." His voice was quiet as servants wandered to and fro delivering food. Elizabeth nodded and accepted the arm he offered and allowed Clifton to lead her into the dining hall.

She sat in her usual seat, nearest her father, and Clifton occupied the seat on her right. She smiled and laughed at the boisterous conversations around the table, but inside her head she worried over the context of Edward's letter. Her brain tried to wrap around the mental picture of what Edward described. Swirling black smoke, bloodshed, and darkness. She feared for her brother's safety. She felt Clifton squeeze her hand under the table and smiled up at him softly. She saw the same worry echoed in his eyes as well.

King Granton studied the two lovebirds closely. Something lurked behind their gazes as they stared at one another. He prayed he had not forced Elizabeth into a union she was not happy about. Studying her closely, he noticed their entwined hands in her lap and his fears subsided. Something else worried the two, but certainly not their feelings for one another. "Elizabeth," he quietly leaned towards her. She turned and smiled at her father, reaching for his hand and squeezing it. "Is everything alright, dear?"

"Yes, Father. Clifton and I just have much to discuss before the Council Meeting this evening. We are hoping we have time later."

"Ah, I see. Well whenever you feel the need to excuse yourselves, it is perfectly alright."

"Thank you, Father." She smiled lovingly at him as she turned back to Clifton.

"Should we wait a while longer?" Clifton asked as he placed his napkin on his empty plate.

"I am ready now, if you are." Elizabeth stated.

Clifton rose, the conversation at the table silencing as Elizabeth stood with him.

"On behalf of my future bride and myself, we wish to thank all of you for the love and support." Clifton stepped away from the table and Elizabeth followed. "If you will excuse us, I wish to escort my lovely princess to the gardens for a walk." They both bowed and curtsied as everyone smiled at their retreating backs.

Elizabeth snagged Mary by the arm as they stepped out into the gardens. She whispered in Mary's ear and Mary immediately made haste back into the castle.

Clifton turned and faced her and clapped his hands. He walked towards her and lifted her around the waist and spun her around before setting her back on her feet. Elizabeth laughed at his excitement. He beamed at her as he plucked a rose and handed it to her. She smiled at the sweet gesture and thought of the story Isaac had told her of King Eamon bringing his queen a rose. Perhaps Clifton learned a few tips from his father as well. "I am quite happy, my Princess."

"I am glad." Elizabeth stated as she walked with him to a small bench by the pond. "I am quite happy too."

"Are you?" He asked with a wriggle to his eyebrows. She nudged him with her shoulder. "You are quite obnoxious when you wish to be."

Clifton laughed in surprise at her comment. "And you are quite fiery when you wish to be."

She grinned and nodded, the wind brushing her black hair away from her face.

"Now," Clifton began. "Let's discuss our game plan for this evening. Tell me of this letter. Do you have it with you?"

As he asked, Mary emerged carrying the small wooden box Elizabeth kept that housed all her letters from Edward. She handed it to Elizabeth and she placed it in her lap. "This was my mother's." Elizabeth explained softly as her hand gently brushed over the intricately carved crown on the lid. She flipped it open and the mounds of letters began to spill forth. She placed a hand on top to hold them inside. She plucked the letter nearest the top and handed it to him. He opened it carefully and read Edward's words. She saw as he reached the part of Lancer's possession. His eyes darkened, his brow furrowed, and his mouth set into a grim line. He eased the letter down and stared out over the water. She didn't push for his thoughts because she knew he was trying to comprehend what he had read. He looked at the letter again and he took a deep breath. "This certainly changes matters, doesn't it?"

"I find it almost hard to believe. If Edward were not as confused by it as I, well, I may not believe it. However, I trust what he says." Elizabeth stated.

"I trust him too." Clifton replied. He ran a nervous hand over his face. "How can we defeat this?" He asked rhetorically. "How can we beat such... evil?"

"I have no idea." Elizabeth answered. "All I know is that now, more than ever, we must figure out a way to help Edward on the inside. What we do out here is of no consequence. What matters is what can be done inside the Lands."

"You are suggesting we send guards over the line?" Clifton asked curiously.

"Not yet. I just think that Edward needs support. Should he find a way for people to cross back and forth, I think we may have our opportunity to supply him with the army he needs to overrun Lancer."

"Smart in theory, but that plan all depends on if he finds out how Lancer crosses back and forth. We cannot send troops over the line if they are not able to return."

"I agree." She sighed heavily and took the letter from his hands and placed it back in her box. "No word from Samuel on the South?"

He shook his head. "I rode out this morning, but he was not at the clearing. Something doesn't sit right with me. I feel the air is off."

"I feel the same." Elizabeth admitted. Clifton turned to her and lightly kissed her forehead. "I am pleased you will be my wife, Elizabeth. I know we have yet to discuss details of the matter, but I want to make my wishes known."

"Of course, my Lord." He cringed at her formality but continued.

"I do not wish to leave your father's kingdom until we have settled matters with the South and quite possibly the Lands. I know we may have to venture back and forth to the East, but for the time being, I wish for our residency to remain here in the North. I know it is not quite the normal structure of things, but I hate to leave on the eve of something like... this." He motioned towards her box of letters. Elizabeth felt the smile split across her face as she lunged at him and enveloped him in a tight hug. Clifton patted her arm and chuckled at her enthusiasm. "Thank you, thank you, thank you." She pulled away and smiled. "I do not wish to leave either, well not soon anyways. With my father in his condition, with this new knowledge of the Lands, everything just seems to be brewing to a massive eruption, and I do not feel it wise to leave on such a note."

"Then we agree." Clifton nodded as if the conversation were settled. "I am glad. I was struggling with a defense if you had wished differently."

Elizabeth chuckled. "I would have accepted your decision regardless of your choice, Prince Clifton."

He tilted his head at her statement and nodded with pleasure. "Thank you."

She stood. "Shall we find our way to the Council Room? I feel the meeting will be underway shortly."

"Yes, I believe we should. I want you to know that whatever you say in the meeting, I will support you."

Elizabeth's blue eyes flashed with admiration. "And I you."

She could tell his thoughts were wandering then, as his gaze hardened and his jaw set. They were both about to unleash a world of chaos upon the Realm, and she feared they might just deflate the joy of the day.

∞

The room was brighter, Clifton noted, as he stepped through the heavily guarded doors of the Council Room. The normally closed curtains were pulled back and the scenery of the Northern Highlands appeared in the vast window. Rolling hills and small villages speckled the skyline. He waited until Elizabeth sat before taking his own seat next to her. She guarded her wooden box carefully in her lap. King Granton and Princess Alayna occupied seats side by side at the head of the table. King Granton waved his hand as Tomas exited and shut the doors quietly behind him. Mosiah sat at attention to the right of the king and waited for him to speak.

"I wish to first open the floor to myself." King Granton spoke calmly his eyes roaming from face to face around the room. "As you may notice, Princess Alayna sits beside me at the head of the table this evening." He motioned to his daughter. She sat tall, shoulders back and confident in position. Pride swelled in Elizabeth's heart at the sight of her sister. "I wish to announce that a coronation date has been set for Princess Alayna to step forward as Queen of the Realm by week's end."

Everyone's eyes widened in surprise, including Alayna's. She turned towards her father and he lightly patted her hand. "It is time I step down as active King and the next generation take command. Does anyone have objections?" No one made a sound. "Then it is settled. Arrangements will be underway starting tomorrow. Now, I know Princess Elizabeth and Prince Clifton wished to share something this evening."

Elizabeth took a deep breath. She faced Clifton and he nodded for her to go ahead. "Father," she began nervously, her hands slightly shaking as she placed the box on top of the table. "And fellow kings and princes... I..." she froze and took a deep breath, her heart pounding and vision slightly blurring as she feared the outcome of what she was about to speak. "I fear I have some encouraging news as well as some grave news."

King Granton leaned forward in his seat and studied the turmoil in his daughter's gaze. "Go ahead, Elizabeth."

She turned glassy eyes upon her father. "Father, I must first beg you of your forgiveness." Granton's left brow rose in surprise as well as everyone else's in the room. "I do not wish for you to be upset with me Father, but I fear you will be. And I wish to say that I understand if you choose to be, but request that you please hear everything I have to say until the very end."

Granton waved her onward as he leaned back into his chair. Her gaze bounced from person to person until it rested on the calm gaze of King Eamon. He smiled encouragingly.

She slid her box towards her father. "Prince Clifton has graciously agreed to let me share the news of which he stumbled upon several days ago. He did not share everything pertaining to Prince Samuel of the Southern Kingdom."

"What else is there?" Granton interrupted with a fierce gaze towards Clifton.

Elizabeth held up her hand. "Please Father, please listen to me first." She waited until she saw her father take a calming breath. "Prince Clifton shared with you that Prince Samuel was sent to spy on me for his older brother, but what he did not mention was *where* Samuel spied on me." She took a deep breath and let it out shakily. "He saw me at the boundary line."

Her father's gaze hardened, and his cheeks flamed red and he opened his mouth to speak.

"No!" Elizabeth stood quickly, her chair rocking back on its legs as she forcefully shoved the box towards her father and pointed to it. "No Father. Wait. Before you lash out, you must listen to me." She held up a calming hand.

Granton reached for the box. "I have never attempted to cross the boundary, Father. I told you I had no desire, and that sentiment remains to be true. But I did not stop visiting the boundary line. I have a secret place I escape to daily, if possible."

Granton shook his head in disappointment as shock continued to flutter across the faces around the room.

"I understand you are angry, now I am asking you to push that anger aside and listen to me, Father." She gripped the back of her chair as she stood. "I go to the boundary line, because I communicate with a man on the other side."

"Elizabeth!" Alayna gasped at the scandalous announcement.

"Shhuushhh." Elizabeth breathed out in frustration her fists clenched at her side. "Please Alayna, let me speak." She glanced at Clifton and he nodded for her to continue. He felt Alayna's sympathetic gaze towards him, no doubt thinking her sister was about to admit to a love on the other side of the boundary.

"I converse with Edward." As soon as the words left her mouth, her sister and father both turned in shock. "Edward?!" They asked in unison.

"Yes. Edward and I have been conversing through letters since a week after he crossed the boundary line."

Everyone shifted in his or her seats. Ryle leaned forward as he studied the princess closely, eager to learn more.

"Edward... is alive?" King Granton asked on a shaky breath. A soft smile tilted the corners of Elizabeth's lips. "Yes Father, very much so."

"W-why did you keep this from me? Why are you telling us this now?" Granton demanded.

Elizabeth eased back into her chair and gently cupped her father's hand. "The reason I wished to be a part of the Council is to share what news Edward provides me in regard to Lancer."

Hushed whispers filtered through the room at the mention of Lancer's name.

"Lancer?" Granton asked. "What do you know of Lancer, Lizzy? Please tell me you have not encountered the man."

"No, Father, I have not." She saw her father breathe a sigh of relief.

"But Edward has." She saw his back tighten once again and his steel blue eyes met hers.

"Edward is the Captain of Lancer's Royal Guard." She stated.

Betrayal flashed across her father's face.

"Traitor." Mosiah stated as he shifted in his seat.

"No." Elizabeth stated forcefully and glowered at the Captain. "He is not. I assure you Father, Edward is no traitor. When he spoke of crossing in order to be with Cecilia, he did not lie. When he spoke of crossing to aid the Realm, he did not lie. For the last five years, Edward has worked his way up in the ranks to become close to Lancer in order to feed us insight into the Lands. He has provided me with insight, Father. These letters," She flipped the lid off the box and Granton stared down at the multitude of parchment that fluttered to the table. "These letters are his responses to me, Father. I have asked questions, and he provides me with every detail he knows. He actively seeks to find answers. He risks his life daily to find answers for the Realm."

"This is overwhelming news," Princess Alayna stated. "How could you keep this secret, Lizzy?"

Elizabeth shrugged in defeat. "I did not wish for my meetings with Edward to be stopped. I feared that I would be forbidden to see him again. And it has not been until recently that our letters have been centered upon combat and strategy."

"I wish to know more of what your brother says of Lancer." King Anthony stated curiously.

"That is what I fear will be grave, King Anthony. You see, Prince Samuel told Prince Clifton of my whereabouts and Prince Clifton confronted me. He discovered my hiding place and my interactions with Edward. He has also conversed with Edward recently."

Eamon's eyes flashed to his son in surprise.

"He has convinced me to step forward with my news so that we may share the latest information that Edward has provided. You see, the Southern Kingdom, Prince Eric I should say, has been sending his wounded soldiers across the boundary line so that they might use the Lands' power to heal. He wishes to provide Lancer with these same guards so that he may cross and join forces with him. Lancer discovered this and confronted the prince about his actions."

"How?"

Prince Ryle asked.

Elizabeth took a deep breath. "He crossed to our side of the boundary line."

"What?!" Everyone began asking questions and talking over one another. Panic seared through the room and Elizabeth quickly swiped a tear from her eye as it slipped down her cheek. She caught Prince Ryle's studious eye as she dropped her gaze to her hands. Prince Ryle banged his hand on the table and everyone quieted. "I want to hear the rest." He stated. "Please continue Princess Elizabeth."

Elizabeth inhaled deeply. "Edward explains that Lancer can cross the boundary line willingly, but only he can. Up to that point,

Lancer had requested Edward to train all the Southern guards that had ventured over to be a part of the Land's Guard. When he noticed Prince Eric sending him the injured ones, the weaker fighters, he ordered Edward to kill them all."

Granton studied Elizabeth closely. Her voice had gained strength as she continued. "Instead of killing them, Edward offered them an alternative. If they joined with him in opposing Lancer, he would grant them their life. If they did not, they would be killed. Edward has been building an army to rise up against Lancer, Father. They call themselves the Uniters. For they wish to unite back with the Realm. They want to see the boundary line vanish and Lancer overpowered. Your son wishes to fight for you, Father."

Granton rubbed a hand over his brow and released his hold on one of the letters.

"And you knew of this?" He pointed Clifton with a firm gaze.

"Yes, my Lord. I have recently been introduced to your son and I vouch for the truth to Ms. Elizabeth's and his statements." Clifton replied respectfully.

"Cliff." Eamon shook his head in dismay at what he was hearing.

"I do not see this as grave news, Father." Clifton stated abruptly. "This is actually the encouraging news. We have an armed guard awaiting our instruction on the other side of the boundary. An army willing to sacrifice their lives to serve this Realm. We have a prince leading an effort of rebellion against our number one enemy. This is encouraging. However, I fear there is also worsening news."

"By all means, please continue with that." Prince Isaac stated dryly, waving his hand.

"I received a letter from Edward today." Elizabeth explained. "It seems Lancer has complete trust in him. For Lancer took Edward into his personal room of reflection and Edward learned the source of Lancer's power."

The kings all gaped at one another.

"And?" Granton pushed.

"Well, Edward isn't sure what it is. His description is quite detailed, yet other than a darkness, he does not know what it is. All he mentions is that Lancer explained it all started by giving his blood and that he is the vessel of this… force. It is all in that letter, Father." She pointed to the one King Granton held. The king opened it and he caught a sob in his throat at the sight of his son's handwriting. He felt Alayna's comforting hand upon his arm as he briefly read through the letter.

"Again, I am sorry I have kept secrets from you, all of you. But I am sharing them now and for good reason. We have an opportunity, gentlemen. Edward is an asset. His army is an asset. Yes, Lancer has a power none of us understand, but at least we have someone who is actively seeking to figure the matter out for us. Edward is also trying to find out how Lancer is able to cross. If he can, then we have our answer. We will be able to bring troops back and forth within the Lands and defeat him."

Elizabeth eased into her seat and exhaled loudly. She watched as Prince Ryle continued to study her. He then cleared his throat. "This is all grave news indeed, Princess." He shifted in his chair and glanced to King Granton. "My Lord, if I may?"

Granton waved for him to continue.

Ryle inhaled a deep breath and glanced to Elizabeth. "What did your brother mean by "it all began with blood???"

"I am not sure. He is not even sure. He said Lancer slit both of their hands before entering the room, because the darkness has to flow through them. They must sacrifice of themselves. Edward did not embrace the power, therefore the darkness did not enter into him, but it did Lancer. Edward witnessed this."

"So, it did not work for Edward?"

"No. But Lancer believes that either Edward does not fully believe in the power or that they would need to mix their blood somehow."

"So, it all stems from Lancer's blood?" Ryle asked again. Elizabeth could see the wheels turning in the prince's head. She knew if all the men in the room put their heads together they could possibly figure out how Lancer can cross and what the blood sacrifice meant.

"There is something in that statement that holds the answer." Ryle stated confidently. "I will think on it. Princess Elizabeth, do I have permission to read your letters?"

Knowing her and Edward spoke of intimate subjects, she flushed, but nodded. There was no time for embarrassment, she thought.

"We will all read them." King Anthony stated. "We must all know what the prince has witnessed these last few years. Anything could hold the answer."

Granton slipped the lid on top of the box. "No one reads these letters until after I read them." Her father's face brooked no argument as his sad gaze fluttered back to her. "Is there anything else you wish to share, Elizabeth?"

She shook her head.

"Ah, forgive me, my Lords," Prince Isaac interrupted. His father tapping him on the arm to straighten his slouching demeanor. Isaac waved his father's hand away. "I do not wish to add kindling to this..." He waved his hand around, "fire of news that Princess Elizabeth has shared, but, does Prince Edward share any clues on how to defeat an invincible army? I mean, the Lands offer healing. How do we kill men who can just heal within minutes of being stabbed?"

"He offers a good point." Ryle stated on a mumble.

Elizabeth straightened in her seat. "Edward speaks of Lancer killing the guards as they cross by... chopping off their heads." She dropped her gaze to her hands before continuing. "A fatal blow that no man can dare survive."

"So, short of beheadings, there is no way of killing the Lands' army?" Isaac asked with doubt in his voice.

Elizabeth nodded solemnly.

The air thickened in the room at the gravity of the situation. Not only did they need to find a way to cross the boundary willingly back and forth, not only did they need to understand Lancer's power, they also had to find a way to strike deadly blows with every swing of the sword if they wished to achieve success. The hope in the room dwindled.

King Granton cleared his throat. "Prince Clifton, you wished to add something else?"

"Actually, yes. I did not receive word back from Samuel, my Lord. The boy was to find out the numbers of his brother's army for me, but he did not arrive at our meeting place today. I fear something has happened to him."

"That poor boy." Alayna stated quietly.

"I fear, gentlemen," King Granton began, "that our meeting has now commenced in earnest. Mosiah, I need to hear the status of our guard."

∞

Princess Melody walked down the grand stairwell and into the main hall. She brushed her hand over the smooth marble banister as she went and relished in the quietness of the castle. She wondered what was discussed behind the Council Room doors, but knew her place. She did not expect an invitation into the room, nor did she desire one. She spotted Mary, Princess Elizabeth's attendant and smiled at her. "Hello, Mary."

"Hello, Princess Melody." Mary curtsied in response.

"Has anyone exited the Council yet?"

"No, milady. I am afraid not."

"I see." Melody reached the base of the stairs and smiled. A loud shuffle and scuffle sounded on the other side of the castle doors and had her turning just as the doors burst open and the smell of sweat and blood assaulted her nostrils. She gasped as a young man lunged at her, stumbling over his feet and gripping her elbows as he righted himself. He panted as he struggled to find words. Blood dripped from his temple and into his left eye as his gaze pleaded with her.

"P-Prince Clifton." He stated. Melody glanced to Mary in panic. Mary stepped forward and noticed the boy's face. "Prince Samuel?"

He nodded and recognized her instantly. "Urgent. Please!"

Mary waved him forward. "Come! Princess Melody, come!" Melody lifted her skirts as they all made haste up the stairwell to the second landing and towards the Council Room.

Tomas and two guards stood outside the door and all took a defensive stance when catching sight of a Southern Kingdom uniform. Samuel slid to a halt his hands held up in surrender. Mary ordered the guards to drop their weapons, but Tomas ordered them to stand.

"He must speak with Prince Clifton, immediately." Mary explained, and felt herself being escorted away by another guard. She struggled to pull away. Her pleas vanishing around the corner. Two guards began to walk towards Samuel, spears drawn. Melody watched in a blur. She lifted the edges of her skirts and stomped her foot and sliced her arms through the air with a wave of finality and screamed. "Enough!" Everyone froze and stared at her in shock. "This is Prince Samuel and he is here to speak to the Council. NOW!" She pointed to the doors and Tomas hesitated. "I said NOW!" She yelled again. He reluctantly obeyed.

CHAPTER 9

The doors to the Council Room flew open and everyone turned as Prince Samuel stumbled forward, followed by a flushed Princess Melody.

"Melody, what is the meaning of this?" Anthony asked reaching for his sword.

Samuel found Clifton and rushed forward only to be halted by a sword at his throat by Mosiah.

"Mosiah, please." Clifton stood and held up his hand. "This is Samuel."

Mosiah slowly lowered his sword as Samuel held up his hands in innocence.

"Speak boy!" Anthony barked.

Samuel, still breathless, looked to Clifton. "I- I am sorry, my Lord. I…"

A growl escaped King Anthony as he stepped towards the young prince and grabbed the collar of his tunic and slammed him against the wall.

"My King!" Clifton yelled. "No, please. He is a friend to us."

"Then he best prove it." Anthony replied, his gaze hard.

King Granton stood all eyes gravitating towards him. "Let him speak, Anthony."

King Anthony released his grip on Samuel, the young prince smoothing a nervous hand down the front of his black tunic. Elizabeth handed him a goblet of water which he gulped earnestly. He took a deep breath and looked to Clifton again. "I am sorry to not have met you today my Lord, but my brother discovered my sleuthing. I fear news of your engagement to Princess Elizabeth reached my brother today. He is enraged my Lord. I..." Samuel nervously glanced at King Granton and back to Clifton. A tear fell down the boy's cheek as he nervously swiped it away. It was then others noticed the deep gash on his arm.

"What is it, Samuel?" Clifton asked kindly, gently placing a hand on the boy's shoulder.

"My brother marches towards the Eastern Kingdom, my Lord. He and his army."

Murmurs filtered through the room and King Eamon's eyes widened in shock. Prince Ryle stood and began barking orders to several guards.

"When Samuel? When did he leave?"

"Not but a few hours ago, my Lord. I came as quick as I could, but I was… detained. I am sorry, my Lord. My brother has lost his head. He—" The boy's lips trembled. "He killed our father, my Lord."

Granton stepped forward and placed a hand on the boy's shoulder as well. "Ryle, Mosiah, round up the guard."

The two men ran out of the room and Granton eased Samuel into a chair. "Samuel," he began, the young man's eyes, amazed at the sight of the king, poured into Granton's. "You are safe here. Please tell us what else you know."

∞

Ryle rushed around the armory as he hurriedly buckled his breast plate over his broad chest, the bold stallion emblazoned over his heart. He spotted his father rushing down the steps into the armory followed by King Granton and Anthony. His brother and Prince Isaac brought up the rear with all three princesses.

Clifton grabbed his armor and began to suit up as well. "What are you doing?" Ryle asked as he watched his father do the same.

"You are not going, Ryle." Eamon stated.

"What?!"

"You are to stay here. That is an order." King Eamon barked.

Ryle fumed. "No Father, I am going."

"No. You are the future King of the East. Your place is here. Cliff and I are going. Should anything happen to us you are safe."

Ryle turned a gaze to King Granton. Obviously, the king had yet to speak to his father of his wishes.

"Father, I must insist!" Ryle stepped forward towards his saddle and his father blocked his path. "No, son. Your place is here. Guard the crown."

Elizabeth rushed around the king and prince to Clifton's side and helped him with his armor buckles. They made quick work and he lightly trailed his fingertips over her cheek. "I shall return for you, my love."

A watery smile flashed over her face as she quickly leaned forward and pressed her lips to his. He roamed his gaze over her face one more time before leaping into his saddle. "We will send word!" King Eamon yelled as he kicked his heels into his horse's flanks and darted out. Clifton did the same. Ryle watched in defeat as he unbuckled his chest plate. Alayna studied the anger on his face and lightly touched his arm. He turned with a snarl that softened when he caught her understanding gaze.

"They will return, Ryle." King Granton stated. "Until then, you serve the throne with Mosiah."

Ryle huffed under his breath as he ripped the chest plate over the top of his head and tossed it into the corner with extra force. "Where is Samuel?"

He avoided Granton's sympathetic gaze and stormed back up the steps into the castle to seek out the young prince.

"Back inside." Granton stated to all the princesses. Elizabeth felt Prince Isaac lightly nudge her elbow as he escorted her back inside the castle. King Anthony brought up the rear with Granton. "Should we send reinforcements?"

"No." Granton stated. "The Eastern guard is strong. I feel this may just be a distraction. We need to send word to the West. We need your army to begin making their way here, Anthony. Keep enough to protect your kingdom, but all extra must come." Anthony nodded and quickly made his way to his royal messenger.

Elizabeth listened to her father behind her. She caught the tension in Prince Isaac's demeanor as well. They exchanged a knowing glance. "Don't get any ideas, Princess." Isaac warned under his breath. "You have to stay put for a bit. It isn't safe. You can send word to your brother later." Elizabeth ignored him and continued into the castle.

∞

Alayna rushed towards the Council Room and stumbled inside as Samuel sat with his head in his hands and Ryle stood above him.

"What is happening in here?" She requested.

"I am asking Prince Samuel for more information on his brother's plans."

"I told you, my Lord, I do not know his plans. All I know is what I have stated." Samuel pleaded and turned to Alayna in hopes for support.

"Prince Ryle, I wish to speak with you. Outside." Ryle stood still.

"It's an order." She stated in a low voice that had the prince obeying immediately to his queen.

"So, because you are upset you are not leading your army, you decide to bully an innocent young man?" Alayna searched Ryle's gaze intently.

Ryle ran a hand through his dark hair and his piercing blue eyes shot through her. "Cliff should not be leading this fight. It should be me."

"Whether you like it or not, Prince Ryle, you are currently the future King of the East. Yes, my father has yet to speak to King Eamon, so your status remains the same. Yet you need to brush aside those feelings of annoyance. Your place is here in this castle. With me," she added. "Whether it is where you wish to be or not. This is where you are meant to be at this very moment." Ryle studied her calm brown gaze. She cupped his face in her hands and narrowed her eyes. "Protect the Realm. As my future Captain of the Guard, your place is here. Now do as your queen commands and set a barricade around the castle gates." She ordered confidently. His eyes flashed to her lips before she released his face and turned and stormed away.

Ryle faced Samuel and nodded before darting down the hall and towards the front entrance. Alayna was right; he wanted to protect the Realm. He wanted to be Captain of the Royal Guard, and he was exactly where he needed to be to do just that. His brother and father could fend for themselves; it was his job to protect those who could not.

He slipped his thumb and forefinger into his mouth and whistled loudly as he emerged at the base of the steps. His horse was ready and waiting as he jumped into the saddle. He spotted Mosiah on the horizon and rode out to assess the protection of the gates.

∞

Samuel sat quietly as Princess Melody tended to the abrasions on his face. She delicately brushed the damp cloth over a scrape and he winced.

"My apologies, my Lord." She stated quietly.

The young prince studied her carefully. She was a few years older than him, he noted, but not quite the age of the princesses of the North. Her blonde hair framed a heart shaped face that held a softness of youth, and he found he liked the look of it.

"Thank you for helping me earlier… and now." He softly spoke.

"You are welcome." Melody replied as she rubbed a salve over the gash on his arm. "It was very brave what you did, risking your life to come here."

"I do not wish to see the Realm fall into the hands of Lancer. Or my brother." He admitted truthfully.

"I imagine not." She agreed.

"How come I've never seen you before?" Samuel asked curiously.

Melody found his dark gaze and smiled softly. "I do not venture beyond the castle walls much, my Lord."

"Even in your own kingdom?"

"Yes."

"Why?" He countered.

Melody lightly wrapped a bandage around his cut and tucked the fabric neatly until it held in place. "I am just the quiet sort."

"Me too." Samuel stated. "Well, until recently." He shrugged his shoulders.

Melody smiled softly. "Yes, well, when times of bravery are upon us, even the softest voice finds its strength."

"Yes, I suppose you are right." Samuel agreed. "Your brother, Prince Isaac, is he as reserved as you?"

A laugh escaped her lips as she shook her head. "Quite the opposite actually. My brother's mouth knows no bounds at times."

"He seems quite attentive to Princess Elizabeth." Samuel observed.

"Yes, he is. We all are." Melody added. "We are all close to one another."

"Yes, I noticed that too. I must say, I feel like an outsider here, yet I feel safer than I ever have in my own kingdom."

Wiping her hands on a damp cloth, Princess Melody stood. "Well you are welcome here, Prince Samuel. You are a part of this Realm and as such we welcome you with open arms."

"Well said." Princess Alayna complimented as she walked forward.

Princess Melody dropped her gaze and hoped the future queen did not feel she spoke on her behalf.

"Princess Melody, I wish to thank you for aiding Prince Samuel in his quest for Prince Clifton earlier."

"Yes, my Lady." Melody curtsied, and Alayna noted how Samuel watched Melody with admiration in his eyes. Smirking at the small crush, Alayna nodded her head towards him. "Prince Ryle will wish to speak with you, Prince Samuel, as soon as he returns from the gates."

"Yes, my Lady." He bowed and Melody and he both watched as Alayna gracefully made her way to her father's side.

∞

Elizabeth climbed the back stairwell to her chambers, Mary followed close behind carrying the edges of her formal cape. She reached her chambers and untied the robe and Mary made swift work of hanging it in her wardrobe. Elizabeth sat in the stiff-backed chair at her desk and quickly began writing a letter to Edward. So much to tell him and the urgency had her hand aching.

She heard Mary rustling around her room tending to chores, but Elizabeth blocked everything else around her out of her mind. Her heart hammered in her chest as she wrote of Samuel's interruption and Clifton's departure. She sighed as her mind wandered to thoughts of Clifton and King Eamon on the front lines. She worried her bottom lip as she thought of something terrible happening to either of the men, especially Clifton. Her heart ached at the thought.

A light knock sounded on the door and Mary answered. Prince Isaac stepped inside the threshold but did not venture further for propriety's sake. Elizabeth did not glance up.

He cleared his throat and Elizabeth turned. "Prince Isaac?"

He bowed as he rested his hand on the hilt of his sword. "Princess."

"What can I do for you?"

He shifted on his feet as his gaze travelled around the room and its ornate furnishings. The silk canopied bed, the heavy velvet drapes, all in shades of mauves and maroons. *Feminine*, he thought, *extremely feminine*. A light scent of rose carried over to him, the scent of the princess he had come to distinguish her by. His brown gaze met Elizabeth's inquisitive stare.

"Ah, yes," he began. "I— I wanted to check on you, Elizabeth. I did not see you retire."

Her eyes narrowed, and her chin tilted up. "You mean you were coming to make sure I did not rush to the boundary line."

"Guilty." He admitted unashamedly.

"Well I assure you, Prince Isaac, that I am indeed in my chambers, so you may rest your worried mind." Her irritated tone had him smirking.

"I can see that." He stated. "Well, should you decide to depart from your chambers, I will be just outside the door."

She turned and gaped at him. "I beg your pardon?"

"I have been asked to keep an eye on you, Princess. For safety's sake."

"You?" She asked in disbelief and had him tilting his head back and forth as if to work out a pain in his neck. A pop sounded through the air and he sighed. "Yes, me."

"I see. I'm so glad my father trusts me." A slight bitterness traced her voice as she turned back to her desk and continued writing.

"I do not think it is a matter of trust, Elizabeth. I think he just worries for your safety. Besides, it is not your father that requested me to keep watch over you, but Prince Ryle."

"Ryle?" Elizabeth's head snapped up again and she stood, her parchment fluttering to the floor. "That man." She grumbled as she lifted her skirts and made a quick exit to the back stairwell. On a mission, Isaac followed her with an amused tilt to his lips. Elizabeth barreled through the door at the bottom of the stairs and turned towards the main hall. "Is he back from the gates?" She asked Isaac.

"I am not sure, Princess."

She rounded the corner and found the room empty. She rushed to the front entrance and opened the doors to a bright sun and busy market, but no Prince Ryle. Growling in frustration she heaved the doors closed.

"Princess, if I may?" Isaac began.

"No, you may not." She declared forcefully shooting a glare of pure ice his direction. "This is absurd. Am I under house arrest? Am I restricted to the grounds of the castle?"

Isaac shrugged with indifference. "I think the Prince just wishes to keep you safe for his brother."

"Well I can assist with protecting the kingdom as well." Elizabeth defended. "I know this kingdom better than Ryle, I should be out there helping him. But instead, he has me barricaded indoors with a-a" she waved her hand in irritation, "a caretaker." She huffed sending her black bangs whishing into the air and back to her forehead. She stood with her hands on her hips as Isaac leaned against the stair banister in indifference.

"And you," Elizabeth turned towards him shaking her finger. "Of all people to keep an eye on me, why you?"

Isaac rested his chin in his hand as if bored. "Trust me, you think I like this... conundrum any more than you do? I am just following my father's orders."

"Your father? What does he have to do with this?"

"He wishes for me to put forth more effort in my inter-realm relations. Therefore, I am serving where needed."

Elizabeth rolled her eyes. "Well in that case, come with me. If I cannot go anywhere without you as my shadow, then you will come with me. Mary!" She yelled up the stairs until Mary appeared at the top. "Grab my parchment and meet me in the stables." Mary nodded and wandered away.

"The stables?" Isaac asked, his right brow lifting in curiosity.

"Yes. I wish to send Edward a letter. And you will escort me there." Her blue eyes held firm as she waited to combat any defense he proposed.

"Very well. Though I must state, for future reference when your father is displeased, that I strongly advised you against leaving the confines of the castle. That I had no choice but to follow you because you were irresponsible with your own safety, and that my duty as a prince and gentleman would not allow me to let you leave unguarded."

"Oh, shush up and let's go." Elizabeth grabbed his arm and pulled him in the direction of the stables. She heard the clatter of armor and swords as they passed the armory. She shot a gaze inside and did not see Prince Ryle. Continuing down the walkway she emerged in the stables as Mary directed the stable boy on where to tie Lenora. Mary handed Elizabeth the letter and she tucked it into her dress skirt. Still wearing her formal gowns from the engagement announcement, Elizabeth sighed in frustration. The heavy skirts and dress weighed her down and she turned to Prince Isaac's amused glare. He stood leaning on his left leg, arms crossed in sheer pleasure at her frustration. "Well are you just going to stand there, or are you going to help me into my saddle?"

He laughed as he hoisted her around the waist up onto her horse. The poufy dresses swallowing his face as she pulled them over the back of the horse to drape down both sides. He swatted away the fabric and sputtered as he pushed off the horse's side to escape the tangled mess. His hair was disheveled from his fight and he quickly swung into his own saddle.

Elizabeth had already slapped her reins and Isaac kicked in his heels to catch up to her. "You are reckless Princess Elizabeth." He called from his horse as she hunkered down against the wind.

She reached her clearing and waited for Isaac to help her down from her saddle. As soon as her feet touched the earth, Elizabeth darted through the trees. Isaac helped her combat the brambles and branches as they stomped into the clearing. Isaac's eyes widened as his gaze fluttered around the area and the arena and boundary line were in clear view.

"This is where you practice the sword?" He asked.

She grabbed his hand and pulled him towards the boundary line, Isaac digging in his heels.

"Another time for explanations, Isaac." Elizabeth dropped her gaze to the ground and began searching for Thatcher. She spotted him in a clover patch near the river and quickly snatched him.

∞

Edward glanced up as Lancer emerged at the entrance of his chambers and clapped his hands loudly in applause. He laughed heartily as he smiled. "Edward, I have great news!"

Edward stood from his chair and accepted the hearty slap on his shoulder as Lancer made himself at home on one of the sofas.

"The South is marching on the Eastern Kingdom." Lancer grinned widely, his dark eyes sparkling as he waited for Edward's reaction.

"My Lord?"

Lancer laughed at Edward's dumbfounded expression. "The. South. Marches. On. The. East." Lancer dragged out each word and syllable, the action grating on Edward's nerves. He kept his calm and then widened his eyes to offer the reaction he knew Lancer longed for.

"When?"

"Several hours ago. I just got word."

"How did I not hear of this?" Edward asked, jumping to his feet.

"You have been in here working. I was out walking the boundary line again and happened across a guard."

Edward froze. Lancer walked the boundary line again. He sent up a silent plea that Lancer did not discover any of the Uniters.

"What guard did you stumble upon?"

"Oh, I forget their names, Edward." Lancer waved his hand nonchalantly as he crossed his right ankle over his left knee.

Sighing in relief, Edward turned back around. "What do you wish to do, my Lord?"

"Do?"

"Yes…" Edward began," I am assuming you came to tell me this news so that we might create a strategy of sorts."

"Ah. I have no plans at the moment. If the Realm wants to attack itself, then I do not see the need for my intervention. Actually, this works quite well in our favor. The Southern Kingdom can obliterate anyone it wishes, especially the Eastern Kingdom. King Eamon needs humbling."

Edward's eyes slightly narrowed at that announcement. *What did Lancer know of King Eamon?* He wondered.

"Then after the South wipes out the strength of the East, I am curious to see where they head next. Their path of destruction only helps weaken the Realm for me. The Renaldi's always were an unstable bunch." Lancer smiled as he studied Edward's stark chambers. "You know you should really get some color in here Edward."

"Yes, my Lord."

"Oh, King Granton is probably beside himself with anger at the uprising in the South. I can only imagine the look on your old father's face." Lancer rubbed his hands in excitement. "Can you imagine, Edward? Don't you wish to see his face?"

"Yes, I do." Edward stated honestly, though his desires were not for the same reasons as Lancer's. "I think I will patrol the boundaries, my Lord, and see what other news I may learn." Edward straightened his tunic and watched as Lancer rose to his feet as well.

"Excellent idea! If you hear any other exciting news, rush to tell me. For I am jubilant today!" Lancer whirled in a circle of celebration on his way to the door. "Perhaps this evening you and I can immerse ourselves in the reflection chamber and see what powers emerge." He rubbed his hands in anticipation as he invited on his way out. Edward waited until Lancer rounded the corner at the end of the hall before he shut the door to his chambers. He then quickly scrambled around his room and packed his journal and satchel to make way for the boundary. He needed to see Elizabeth.

∞

"Arrows away!" King Eamon yelled as he hoisted his sword towards the sky. A cloud of arrows rained down from the first parapet above the castle gates in the Eastern Kingdom. Clifton watched as several Southern guards fell from injury and he redirected his horse through the cobble stone market grounds. Guards lined up along every entrance to the castle grounds and Clifton watched as panicked faces rushed into houses and under protection. He heard a whiz fly by his ear and spotted an arrow that landed in the plank of a market canopy beside him. He kicked his heels into Henry and moved. "Hold firm!" He yelled as he watched the Southern guards rampage through the small village outside the castle walls. He turned to see his father commanding the line of archers. Eamon looked down at him.

Clifton nodded at him as he turned his horse to the western exit. He and his troops would head out on foot. The village would be demolished if they did not. He lined up his guards and the gates opened. On horseback, they rushed through the ranks swinging swords and axes as Southern guards attempted to slice through their saddle straps. Clifton's sword met flesh as he speared the heart of one of his assailants. He grunted as he pulled his sword from the man's body and quickly sliced it through the air to block the blade of another black tunic. Groans and yells swallowed the air as the smell of sweat, horse, and blood filled his nostrils. His muscles ached at the assault of misuse and the affliction of repeated lunges of force. His blade found its home beneath the breastplate of another guard, the man's lifeless eyes haunting Clifton as he withdrew his blade. *Killing the Realm's own men.* He shook his head of the depressing thought and pulled his reins towards the valley. Was this not the fear he alluded to in the Council Meeting? The Realm had officially turned on itself.

∞

Prince Eric straddled his horse and watched as his army swarmed over the Eastern Kingdom. Swift and quick, they made hasty work of reaching the castle walls. It would not be long before they reached the inner courts and market of the kingdom. His dark horse shifted underneath him as if he too were ready for battle. He squinted as he caught sight of the prince wielding his blade through the air. "Prince Clifton," he mumbled softly. "Now isn't that interesting."

"Aye, my Lord?" His Captain sat regally beside him as they watched their army sweep across the land.

"Prince Clifton has come to fight for his kingdom." Prince Eric stated.

"And?" His Captain asked with a slight annoyance to his tone at the obvious statement.

"And that means he left Princess Elizabeth behind."

The guard's eyes turned towards his prince. "You plan to turn back?"

"Aye. There is no better time than the present. I know just where I will find her at a time like this." Prince Eric stated. "Missing her betrothed, she will go to the one place she can be alone... the boundary line. I will find her there."

"I am sure she has protection, your Grace. By now they must sense your threat. Besides, I did not realize you still aimed to obtain the princess."

"Indeed, but she will not take a guard to her secret place. It is her place of escape. And I wish to obtain everything I desire." Eric's jaw ticked as he set his teeth in a firm scowl.

"I must insist you take guards with you, my Lord, just in case you find resistance."

Prince Eric nodded. "You feel you can take care of this for me?" He waved his hand over the ferocious fight waging in front of them as if he were discussing the weather.

"Aye, my Lord. I will make sure the Eastern Kingdom suffers."

"Good. Oh, and kill Prince Clifton too. I do not need him getting in the way." Slapping his reins, Prince Eric turned his horse in the opposite direction and left the fight in the East for his own conquest in the North.

∞

Clifton felt the sharp sting of an arrow as it pierced just below his right shoulder blade. Slipping from his saddle to the ground, he thrashed his sword in a parry with two men before reclaiming time to breathe. He reached up and yanked the arrow from his shoulder and winced at the slight bite of pain. He surveyed the progress of his guards. The South had released their final rows of ranks and was just beginning to reach the castle walls. His father had to release the next wave of soldiers soon. The Eastern army still had two waves left; they could win this. Clifton turned at the sound of a sword slicing through the air. The Captain of the Southern Army stood before him with a menacing gleam in his eye. Clifton hoisted his sword, the weight of it slamming his shoulder with pain. He blocked the first lunge and felt the scream erupt from his chest as he shoved all his strength into the effort.

King Eamon spotted his son battling the Captain. He realized then the South had fully immersed their forces into the battle. No reserve guards awaited beyond the hills. Prince Eric's full force had been released. He waved his sword at his Captain who then rushed out of the Eastern gates with a second wave of soldiers on horseback. Eyes widened at the sight of the mighty wave of blue tunics that flooded the fields. Black tunics began to retreat quickly, realizing they were outnumbered.

Clifton landed a hard kick into the Captain's stomach as he pushed off and away from his attacker. He felt a blow to the face, a strong fist cracking his nose. His vision blurred, and he felt his steps falter as blood poured out of his nose and into his mouth. The lead taste of his blood sobered his wishful thoughts of victory. He fell to his knees as every ache and pain radiated through his body. He caught the menacing glare of the Southern Guard's Captain and braced himself for the pain. He watched the sun glisten off the blade and the air stilled. All he could hear was the drumming of his own heart and the ragged breaths that struggled to escape his bruised lungs.

"It has been a pleasure, Prince Clifton." The Captain sneered as he brought down his blade.

King Eamon raced forward; his horse leapt over bodies strayed amidst the landscape. Hooves pounded in the earth dampened by blood. Eamon carried his sword firmly in his right hand as he held the reins in his left. He stood in his stirrups as he brought back his arm. He would not lose his son, he thought. He would not. Screaming at his horse to move faster, he readjusted his grip on his sword.

The Captain turned in just enough time to meet the fury behind King Eamon's blue eyes as his sword swiped through the air and decapitated the man where he stood. The body lingered erect a few seconds before the extremities fell to the ground in the wake of Eamon's wrath. He dismounted quickly running and sliding to his knees before Clifton, the mud and blood surrounding them staining his uniform. He hoisted his son's arms over his shoulders and lifted him to drape over his horse. He pressed two fingers to his son's neck and felt a steady pulse and sighed in relief as his son's blood stained his fingers. He watched as the remaining black tunics were driven back into retreat. He mounted into his saddle and quickly galloped within the castle gates.

"See to my son!" He ordered. Attendants lowered Clifton carefully and carried him by the shoulders and feet into the castle. Eamon swiped a hand over his grimy face as he surveyed his unconscious son and the wake of destruction that scattered around his kingdom.

"My Lord," his captain stepped through the main entrance. "All have retreated, your Grace. The South has fallen back. The Renaldi's failed."

"Good." King Eamon stated, his gaze not leaving his son's beaten body. "We must regroup quickly. Leave one wave of guards here to protect the kingdom from a second assault should the South attempt. The rest leave with us as soon as the prince awakens. We travel to the North immediately."

"Yes, my Lord." The captain bowed and quickly exited.

A slow groan emerged from the room to his right and he walked in to find Clifton sitting up and holding a damp cloth to his nose. His gaze lifted at his father's entrance and relief flooded Clifton's heart. Eamon smiled and rushed forward to hug him. "You had me scared, Cliff."

"Aye… sorry Father. I could not see anything but stars after his last blow."

"Aye, well you are safe now. Unfortunately, we must ride north. You able to ride?"

"Yes." Clifton answered. He then began to hoist himself off the table grimacing when he pressed weight upon his right arm.

"You are hurt, Cliff?" Eamon asked and swiftly ran his fingers over his son's shoulder. Clifton groaned when his father's fingers found the wound from the arrow.

"This is not good, Cliff. You cannot fight with this."

"Yes, I can." Clifton stated firmly as he continued slipping to his feet. "We go north."

"Cliff-"

"We go north!" He bellowed as he waved for an attendant to find his horse. "I will not let Prince Eric take Elizabeth, Father. I will not." Eamon caught the stormy green eyes of his son and the fears lurking behind them and nodded.

"Then we ride."

Nodding in agreement, the two men hurried outside, Eamon keeping a close eye on his son as he continued to struggle to find his footing. Once their horses arrived, Clifton mounted easily and waited for his father to do the same.

Clifton held the reins in his left hand to ease the strain on his injured right arm and kicked in his heels. The sound of hooves carried him onward as he thought of Elizabeth and the Southern Kingdom advancing upon the North. Sending up a silent plea, he hurried to the North's aide.

∞

Alayna rushed through the castle. Swinging the door open to Elizabeth's chamber, she searched her room. Blowing an exasperated breath, she turned to rush back down the stairwell. Samuel met her at the bottom eagerly wishing to help. "May I aide in your search, Princess? Do you seek someone?"

"My sister, Prince Samuel. Have you seen her?"

"No, my lady, but I saw her attendant in the conservatory with Princess Melody."

"Ah, perfect. Thank you. Come with me, I may have a task for you shortly."

"Yes, my lady.'

Alayna rushed into the conservatory and found Mary bustling around with Renee and Gretchen in preparations of the nightly meal. "Mary, where is my sister?" Her voice rang out as she swished into the room. Melody's head snapped up at her entrance and all eyes gazed upon Alayna's fierce stance.

"My lady?" Mary asked.

"Princess Elizabeth. Where is she?"

"Oh." Mary's eyes dropped, and Alayna immediately knew. "She left didn't she?!"

Melody hopped to her feet. "Your Grace, my brother is with her. He has been asked to stay close to the princess. You can trust she will be safe."

Alayna took a deep breath as her cheeks darkened. "Prince Samuel, find me Prince Ryle immediately."

"Yes, my lady." Samuel rushed out of the room. "Mary, I am disappointed in you for allowing Elizabeth to leave. You knew the requests of my father and Prince Ryle. She was to stay within the castle."

Mary's eyes clouded with unshed tears at the scolding and nodded.

"I must share this news with my father now." Alayna mumbled as she turned to leave. She worried her hand over her brow as she walked up the stairwell towards her father's chambers. She heard a loud bang as the front doors of the castle flew open and hit the stone wall in their wake and Prince Ryle stepped inside, his eyes immediately seeking her out. He made his way to her in haste, Samuel following obediently behind him.

"My Queen," he began, "Samuel tells me the princess is missing." He stood at the ready, hand on the hilt of his sword, feet posed on the steps to dart either direction at any moment. He took heavy breaths as he tried to regain his breath after such a brisk pace to find her. Alayna nodded solemnly. "I fear, Prince Ryle, that my sister has coerced Prince Isaac to take her to the boundary line."

"I will find her. Samuel will show me." He looked to the boy for confirmation and Samuel nodded emphatically.

Alayna's gaze dropped for a brief moment and she glanced out the open doors.

"My Lady? Is something wrong?" Ryle asked quietly, lightly reaching for her hand.

She withdrew it quickly and rolled her shoulders back. "No. I am... I am just frustrated, my Lord. Your place is here at the castle and I now have to shift guards around all because my defiant little sister has disobeyed my father's orders." A sadness held in her eyes, but her words were forceful.

"I will make swift work of recovering the princess, Alayna," he stated quietly so his lack of formality did not drift to the attendants. "I will make sure she and Prince Isaac return so that we can fortify the grounds. There is movement in the East and I fear we will have our hands full come nightfall."

Alayna nodded soberly. "Then go, find my sister and Prince Isaac. I will share the news with my father."

Ryle nodded and turned Samuel's shoulder to walk with him as he left. Alayna watched him cover the stairs and the main entrance in long, confident strides. She heard him yelling orders as soon as he stepped foot outside and she smiled at his efficiency. *He would be a fine Captain of the Guard*, she thought. As she reached the top of the stairs, King Granton stood on the landing overlooking the main hall.

"Father, I did not realize you were up and about."

King Granton leaned heavily on the banister, his mobility sluggish and his shoulders slumped. "Father? Are you feeling okay?" Alayna placed a comforting hand on his shoulder.

"I heard your conversation with Ryle. I am disappointed in Elizabeth, but at the same time..." his voice trailed off as Alayna saw a deep sadness in his pale blue eyes. His hand clutched a piece of parchment. "Father?" Alayna surveyed him closely, concern etching her brow as she began escorting him back towards his chambers.

Once inside, she eased him into a comfortable chair and propped his feet upon a stool. "Tomas, please fetch some water for the king." Tomas bowed and whisked quietly away.

"I was such a fool, Alayna." Granton mumbled.

"I'm sorry?" She asked, unsure if she had heard her father correctly.

"A fool. Your brother. Edward." He shook his head in dismay. "My boy."

"Father, I am afraid I am not following you."

Sighing, Granton reached for Elizabeth's wooden box and held up a handful of letters. "Edward's letters to Elizabeth. I've been reading them."

"Father, perhaps you should set those aside for the time being and not think on matters that might upset you." Alayna recommended as she brought a blanket over his legs.

"No, I must read them. Your brother is a good man. Selfless, loyal, and brave. I was a fool to push him away like I did."

"You did not push him away, Father. Edward made his own choice to cross the boundary."

"Imagine if he were here with us now, Alayna. What a leader he would be."

Alayna's eyes slightly clouded at the small blow. She knew her father had not meant the comment to hurt her feelings or undermine her role as future queen, but she feared of disappointing him. She wanted to measure up to the expectations he had set long ago for Edward.

"Father, Edward is where he needs to be. If he were not in the Land of Unfading Beauty, we would not have the insight we do right now. Every choice, every action has led us to this moment."

"Spoken like a true queen." Granton stated softly and proudly. He lightly squeezed her hand. "Do not be mad at your sister for fleeing to the boundary."

"She disobeyed your orders, Father." Alayna stated with confusion.

"Yes, but for good reason. I would have done the same thing." He admitted with a half laugh. "Remember, Alayna, that Elizabeth has a strong will. Remember that."

"How could I forget?" Alayna remarked. "She reminds me every day."

Chuckling, Granton leaned his head back against the chair and closed his eyes as his chest wheezed with each breath he took. "Never fault her for who she is." Granton continued. "Her willfulness will be of use soon, I'm afraid."

"Father, you are talking in riddles to annoy me." Reaching for the blanket's corners, she adjusted the fabric over her father's tired figure.

"I do not intend to, dear. Just let her be who she is, and you be who you are."

"And who might that be?" Alayna asked with a cynical laugh in regard to her own personal frustration.

"A queen." Granton responded. "You have always been meant for the role, even before Edward left. You are so much like your mother,

Alayna. So strong." He turned and offered a weak smile. "You and Elizabeth have grown into strong women. I am proud."

Alayna glanced at her hands in her lap. "I'm thankful for your confidence Father, but I fear I somewhat question my strength, especially in times like these."

"It's times like these that determine your strength, Alayna. You will handle it well, I know you will. The kingdom trusts you. The Realm trusts your judgment as well. You are supported in whatever decisions you make."

"You mean decisions *we* make." She corrected him and saw him softly shake his head.

Tears began to threaten her eyes as she slid to the floor on her knees beside her father. She grabbed his hands in hers and rested her cheek against them. "Do not give in now, Father. Please." She begged quietly. She felt him rub his hand over her hair.

"You think I will give in so easily?" She heard the smile in his voice as he spoke. "No, my dear. I still have a little time, but it is your turn to take the lead. Trust your friends. Anthony, Eamon, Ryle, Mosiah. Trust their advice. Lean on their support. Elizabeth, Clifton, Isaac, Melody. Rely on their strengths when needed. You have support, my dear."

A tear slipped down her cheek and landed on his hands and he lightly patted her hair again. "Now, my queen," he stated and lightly nudged her chin for her to raise her face. "Go. See to your kingdom, and when your sister returns, please bring her to me."

"Yes, Father." Alayna forced a watery smile as she leaned forward and kissed his cold cheek. She flashed a cautionary glance towards Tomas as she exited. Her father's faithful servant nodded in understanding.

"Ah, Princess, I hate to be a ninny here, but we should wrap this— whatever it is you are doing— we should wrap it up and head back to the castle. It is not safe." Prince Isaac watched as Elizabeth nudged the small rabbit across the line, his brow rising as the small creature made its way to a small hollowed log and rested comfortably. Elizabeth brushed her hands together with a satisfied smile. "I had to leave a letter for Edward, prince. He must know the latest news."

Elizabeth watched as Prince Isaac's eyes widened and he pointed behind her. She turned to see her brother swiftly dismount off of his horse and walk straight towards them, halting within inches of the boundary. Elizabeth smiled in relief and pointed to the log Thatcher slept inside. Edward snatched the letter off the rabbit and held it up and slipped it into the pocket of his tunic. He nodded in the direction of Isaac, and Elizabeth nudged Isaac forward. "He wants to meet you."

"I really don't think there is time for formalities, Princess. We must head back. I have a bad sensation working its way up my spine."

She pointed at Isaac and then made a symbol with her hands representing the West. Edward nodded and bowed to Isaac.

"Okay, okay, nice to meet you." Isaac waved a dismissal hand and then turned to walk away. "Let's move."

Elizabeth cast Edward an apologetic glance before turning to find Prince Isaac standing with his hands held up in surrender as a blade pointed directly at his throat. Gasping, Elizabeth froze as black tunics began to filter through the trees.

"Ah, Princess Elizabeth." The tall man with broadened shoulders and dark eyes slipped off of his black horse and stepped towards her. She watched Isaac's back stiffen as a guard continued to hold him at the tip of the sword.

"W-who are you?" She asked, her eyes never leaving Isaac.

The man chuckled, the sound creeping up her spine and making the hair on the back of her neck stand up. "I'm surprised you do not recognize a Renaldi when you see one, Princess. I am Prince Eric." He bowed regally and then laughed at her stunned expression. "I know you have heard of me." He added. "Most people have." Elizabeth stepped lightly as he walked towards her, making her way towards Isaac. She reached his side and felt him tense.

"I see you are keeping company with the West's very own disappointment." Prince Eric pointed towards Isaac. "I'm afraid the pompous prince cannot help you, Princess. That would require him thinking of someone other than himself."

Elizabeth shot Isaac a quick glance and noted the embarrassment from Prince Eric's words in his flushed cheeks. Elizabeth reached a slow and steady hand towards Isaac and rested it on the crook of his arm.

"Sympathy is for the weak, Princess. He will die. There is no point in trying to comfort him. You, on the other hand, well… let's just say I have great plans for you. How is your brother?" Eric asked, pointing across the boundary line at Edward's infuriated figure. Elizabeth caught her brother's stormy expression and he narrowed his gaze at her and nodded towards Isaac. Elizabeth nodded. She knew what she had to do to give them a chance of escape or even a chance to fight.

"You will see your brother soon enough, Princess, when I take you with me across the boundary line." Eric grinned as he walked circles around her and looked her up and down. "Yes, you will do nicely." He complimented. "It's a shame Prince Clifton died earlier today. I hear you two were to be wed. Pity." His last word dripped with disdain, and Elizabeth's heart shattered at the news of Clifton's death. Her lip quivered, and she fought for control over her emotions. There was no time for tears, she thought. Eric nodded over her shoulder to one of his guards and Elizabeth heard one of the men dismount and begin walking her direction. "I wish to keep you safe from harm, Princess, as we invade your father's kingdom."

Elizabeth took a deep breath and slipped her hand from Isaac's arm to the hilt of his sword. In the blink of an eye, she unsheathed the blade and made quick work of a spin and stab to the guard holding Isaac hostage. The man dropped his arm and Isaac quickly snatched the wounded guard's sword as other guards began dismounting and pulling their swords. Prince Eric laughed at their attempt but did not draw his own sword. Elizabeth battled blades with the next assailant as Isaac did the same. They stood back to back as they worked in circle formation to combat all angles. Elizabeth lunged forward, her heavy dress skirts tangling around her ankles. She groaned under her breath at the added weight and the hindrance to her usual speed and agility. She caught sight of Edward on the other side of the boundary line, sword drawn and ready for battle. Her brows lifted as an idea came to her. "Push them towards the boundary line." She muttered to Isaac. She heard him grunt as he locked blades and pushed off the man's chest. "Working on it." He gritted his teeth as he thrust his fist into the jaw of the soldier. The man stumbled, and Isaac planted a kick in his chest sending him through the foggy veil of the boundary. Prince Eric watched as his guard stumbled for balance. Prince Edward grabbed the man's collar and pulled him towards him, driving his sword through the man's stomach. Edward withdrew his sword, the blood tarnishing the blade and he met the surprised gaze of Prince Eric with a smirk.

Elizabeth felt a blade strip the side of her dress and briefly thanked the stars for the annoying skirts, but she felt the fabric strip away. Lighter, she assaulted the next guard and ducked under his swipe, meeting his blade on the other side of his circle parry. She caught Prince Eric's amused gaze and thrust all her strength into shoving the guard in his direction. She watched annoyance flash across his face as he reached for his own sword.

∞

King Eamon brought his horse to a halt as he watched black tunics surround the Northern Kingdom's outer village. He barked orders for his captain to take a third of their troops to the opposite side of the kingdom to bring strength to the offside. He turned to Clifton. Face pale with pain, his son looked ready to faint, but the fire in his green eyes told Eamon he would not back down.

"I'm going to the boundary line." Clifton stated. "My ranks will assault from the South."

"Move in when my troops have reached the citadel." Eamon ordered. "Be careful, Cliff."

"Aye, you too." Clifton clicked his reins and branched off with another third of the Eastern army as King Eamon rallied his troops onward.

Clifton made his way along the tree line and the low valley south of the castle. He dismounted and turned to his guard. "We infiltrate on foot. There is a small clearing on the other side of the tree line that backs up to the Rollings River. Be on guard. I fear we will encounter the Prince of the South. Be cautious of the boundary line. If you should cross, you serve Prince Edward of the North. Understand?" The guard nodded and addressed the troops as Clifton slipped a dagger into his waist belt and repositioned his sword. The pain in his right shoulder reminded him to take caution. He listened closely and heard the clash of blades from Elizabeth's arena. He prayed they weren't too late.

∞

Samuel rushed into the main hall and found Alayna sitting in her father's throne and Princess Melody seated next to her. Alayna took calming breaths, and approached every question or concern from guards, servants, attendants, and maids with ease. Everyone's nerves and fears blossoming forth as the South began attacking the outer villages. She spotted Samuel as he rushed into the room. His eyes landed upon Melody first and then moved to her. "My queen." He rushed forward out of breath and pointed over his shoulder. "King Eamon and Prince Clifton have arrived from the battle in the East with victory. Prince Ryle has asked that I report to you that the King charges full force towards the citadel at this very moment. The

Southern guards are being assaulted from both sides, my Lady." He stated excitedly.

"And what of Prince Clifton?" Alayna asked, worried for her younger sister's betrothed and Elizabeth's safety.

"He plans to bring Eastern troops from the Southern point of the kingdom."

Nearest the boundary line, Alayna thought. Clifton was going to save her sister as if he knew exactly where she would be. Her respect for the man grew and she sighed in relief.

"And where is Prince Ryle?"

"He has made his way towards the clearing, my Lady. I showed him Princess Elizabeth's whereabouts. His troops are entering on foot, my Lady. I have their horses reserved in the valley."

"Good." Alayna stated. "Any word from King Anthony?"

"No, my Lady. There has been no sign of troops from the West as of yet."

Alayna stilled the panic rising in her chest. Anthony had to provide aide or they could not withstand the attack from the South. She lightly swiped a hand over her lap brushing away a piece of lint as her mind worried.

"Thank you, Prince Samuel. You are serving well."

"Yes, my Queen." He bowed. "I will go. I am assisting Mosiah in protection of the village. I will send word should more news arrive." He turned towards Melody and bowed, holding her gaze for a brave moment. Alayna caught the slight flush to the quiet princess' cheeks and hid her pleased smile.

"Be safe, Samuel." Alayna called to him as he exited.

CHAPTER 10

"I want ten soldiers on point." Ryle whispered as he motioned for his troops to immerse themselves in the trees. He paused and held up a hand to halt their movements as he caught sight of his brother appearing over the hill. He smirked and held up a hand for his troops to stay put. He then slinked towards the edge of the valley to await his brother, knowing full well, Cliff would come to the clearing for his princess.

Clifton stalked the tree line and his troops spread along the veil of trees and the river. He took a deep breath and waited for the sounds of blades again. He heard a snap behind him and whirled his sword at the ready only to find his brother creeping towards him. Both brothers grinned in relief and gripped each other's shoulders in embrace. "You hear what I hear?" Ryle asked. Clifton nodded. "We go in quietly. I feel Prince Eric awaits on the other side."

They heard a loud pitched scream, female, Elizabeth. Clifton jerked to his feet from his crouched position. Ryle grabbed his shoulder and pulled him back down to the cover of brambles. "Patience, brother." He whispered. He signaled his troops to move in and released Clifton's shoulder so they could move together.

THE UNFADING LANDS

∞

Elizabeth cringed as she felt the blade pierce through her arm and screamed. Isaac briefly turned and stepped towards her only to be brandished by two more guards. Elizabeth recovered quickly and forced herself to continue. She watched as Prince Eric stepped forward and waved his sword in several rotations of flourish as he watched Isaac and Elizabeth battle his guards. "There is no use, Princess. You might as well give up. You are mine now." He taunted.

Isaac shoved one of the guards in Eric's direction, the man slipping and stumbling across the boundary line. Edward immediately cut the man under the knee bringing him to a kneeling position and then decapitated the guard. Ryle's eyes widened at the brutality as he and Clifton cowered behind the trees near the boundary line. "Edward." Clifton whispered, knowing his brother's curiosity. Ryle nodded. "We move now." Ryle stated. He waved his hand and his guards filtered through the trees.

Isaac ducked and pulled Elizabeth's injured arm to pull her down with him as the blade of another guard swiped over both of their heads. He heard her grunt at the pain, but she never wavered. If he were not fighting for his life, he might take the time to be impressed by her skill, he thought. She had saved him earlier with her spontaneous attack. He threw a punch and received an answering one in his ribs. He dodged another one and landed his knuckles in the man's temple. He heard a loud clash, as he spotted the pale blue tunics filtering through the trees. The East had returned. He heard Elizabeth snarl in annoyance as she pulled a hand on her skirts. "You're stepping on me." She mumbled as she twirled to avoid another blow. Isaac grinned despite himself and quickly ducked and snatched his dagger from his waist. He slid to his knees behind Elizabeth and blocked a sword thrust to her back. He swiped his blade over the bustle of her dress and pulled, the heavy skirts ripped away and left her standing in her cream underskirts and emerald corset. He heard her sigh as he tossed her skirts in the faces of two guards who battled the obnoxious load of fabric.

"Thanks!" She yelled breathlessly as she ducked another blow and moved faster than she had previously been able. She heard it then, the loud thunder of footsteps coming from the trees. She turned to brace herself for more Southern guards, but instead caught sight of Prince Ryle as he barreled through the trees a dagger flying from his hand and landing in the chest of the guard behind Elizabeth. Relief washed over her face at the sight of him. He headed straight for her, removed his dagger from the dead body behind her and flanked her side as guards attacked again.

Elizabeth felt a grip on her arm and turned swiftly, sword raised bringing the blade down upon the man's wrist and slicing through. The man screamed as his hand and sword fell to the ground. Isaac made swift work of shoving the man across the boundary line and Edward finished him off.

Clifton emerged from the tree line shoving a guard over the boundary line. His eyes met Edward's and the Northern prince nodded in welcome as he drove his sword into the black tunic at his disposal. Clifton then rushed into the clearing to find bodies scattered and blood streaking the surface of the rocks and trees. He then saw Elizabeth as she whirled on a guard and saved his brother from an attack from behind. She pushed passed two more guards, heading in the direction of Prince Eric who battled an Eastern guard. Isaac spotted him and tossed him the sword of a Southern guard that had fallen at his feet. Clifton caught the hilt midair and brought the blade down quickly upon the arm of another guard and then plunged it within the man's side. Withdrawing his blade, he glanced up just as Elizabeth caught sight of him. She froze for a split second as her bright blue eyes shined in relief. His lips tilted in a small smile as she quickly dodged a dagger and continued her pursuit. Ryle surveyed the numbers and accepted the victory of the clearing as they narrowed in on the remaining few Southern guards. "My troops will pull back and aide in the citadel." Ryle stated. "Finish here and do the same." He barked to Clifton. Clifton nodded and watched his brother and his troops pull out and leave the clearing. His troops remained. Isaac remained. Elizabeth remained.

"I fear your usefulness has worn out, Prince Isaac." Prince Eric baited. He brought his sword hilt against Isaac's temple, the prince of the West falling to his knees as his vision blurred. Elizabeth lunged towards him, throwing her body in front of Isaac and blocking Prince Eric's final blow with her sword, the force rocking her back on her ankles. The prince growled as he back handed her across the face and heaved her aside. Again, Princess Elizabeth had saved Isaac and bought him more time. He mentally thanked her as he spotted Prince Clifton fighting his way towards him to come to his aide. Isaac grasped his sword firmly in his right hand and as Prince Eric extended his reach above his head, Isaac plunged upward with all the strength he had left, his shoulders ramming into the Southern prince as his sword emerged on the other side of the man's body. Eric's body jerked from the attack and Isaac withdrew his blade as the prince collapsed. Elizabeth froze at the sight. Prince Clifton stared as Isaac hoisted himself to his feet, leaning heavily upon his sword as a cane. He staggered from loss of strength. "He is done." He growled as he spit a mouthful of blood onto the earth. "We need to head back to the castle. If guards are rushing the citadel it is only a matter of time before they reach the inner courts."

Elizabeth dropped her sword and rushed towards Isaac, wrapping her arms around his neck in a tight embrace. He lightly patted her back with a light laugh of surprise. He met Clifton's appreciative nod with one of his own and released her. Elizabeth remained by his side as she turned to face Clifton. Love shined in her gaze as she smiled at him. Blood streaked her face and clothes, the injury on her arm still bled slowly, but she had never looked more beautiful to him. Clifton's guard emerged. "My Lord, we have cleared the area. The men headed back to the horses and will be riding for the citadel from the Southern direction as ordered."

"Good. See to it then." Clifton responded. The guard bowed quickly as he rushed through the trees.

Elizabeth spotted Edward on the other side of the boundary with several of his Uniters clearing away the bodies of the slaughtered Southern guards that had crossed over. No doubt, hiding them from Lancer's watchful eyes.

"We must get you back to the castle, Princess." Clifton stated warmly.

"Indeed." Elizabeth beamed. As she began to step forward a grunt coursed through the air as a swish from a blade swiped Elizabeth's left leg from underneath her. She crumbled in a cry as Isaac spun around to find Prince Eric clinging to life and gripping his sword with a bloody fist. A menacing smirk made his eyes dark as he used his last breath to take down the Princess of the North. Isaac, growling, plunged his sword into the prince's heart as Clifton rushed to Elizabeth's side. Pulling her into his arms, Clifton knelt beside her. Her calf bled profusely, and Clifton's stomach twisted at the sight of the damage. Isaac finished off the Southern prince and knelt to help as well.

"Elizabeth, just... hold still." Clifton managed as he struggled to maintain a hold on her as she thrived in pain. Isaac slid down towards her feet and gripped her ankles his eyes surveying the damage to her leg. He glanced up and caught Clifton's worried gaze and shook his head. Tears clouded Clifton's vision as he brushed her hair back from her face. He glanced towards the boundary line and saw Edward staring back at him. *The boundary*, he thought. If he sent her across the veil she would heal. Clifton turned to Isaac. "We send her across the line." He began lifting Elizabeth into his arms as she struggled to remain conscious.

"No. We cannot." Isaac stated rushing beside him.

"The Lands will heal her!" Clifton barked. "If we send her across, she will live."

"If we get her to the castle now, she can live here too."

"That is too big a risk." Clifton stated as he neared the boundary line. He pointed to Edward and back to Elizabeth's leg. Edward shook his head no. Isaac motioned towards him in a toss of his hand. "See, her own brother is telling you no."

Clifton eased her to the ground again and lightly cupped her face. "Elizabeth," he softly patted her cheeks and her eyes flickered open.

"You cannot do this!" Isaac pleaded. "Her sister, her father. They would be devastated."

"Her death would be more devastating." Clifton barked.

Clifton lightly kissed Elizabeth's hand as she reached up to hold his hand. He kissed her knuckles as tears slipped down his cheeks. "You must cross, my love. You will heal."

Elizabeth shook her head. "No. No, I cannot. Please, Clifton. No." Her voice was weak and her face pale as she struggled to maintain consciousness.

"You have to my love... your leg." He gripped her hand as she sat up and leaned against him. Her eyes traveled to her mangled leg and then to Isaac's worried gaze. Isaac shook his head no. She turned to Edward who echoed the Western prince's sentiments.

"No, Clifton. I will not cross."

"But you could die." Clifton stated.

"Then we hurry. I wish to be with you. I do not want to cross." Her words began to slur, as her body grew faint. "Please, Elizabeth." Clifton begged softly as he kissed her temple. She gripped the lapels of his tunic as he leaned over her. "I wish to stay with you."

He watched as her eyes closed and her body went lax. He quickly checked her wrist for a pulse and found it faint.

"We must hurry." He stated, as he began to stand. "I will fetch my horse. Guard her." He ordered Isaac. Isaac nodded and quickly began to make a tourniquet with his belt. He cinched it tightly above her knee and wrapped his tunic over her wound, pulling the sleeves into a knot, to try and stop the bleeding. He heard Clifton return and glanced up as Prince Clifton held the reins of two horses. "We ride along the tree line towards the stables. We will have more cover that way." Clifton stated.

"My father's troops should be arriving from the West at any moment. The Western side would be safer." Isaac countered.

Clifton nodded. "Fine, but we—" His words were silenced by a sword piercing through his back and out the front of his chest. A ragged groan escaped Clifton's lips. Isaac's eyes widened as the sword disappeared and Clifton fell to his knees. Isaac pulled his dagger and flung it at the Southern guard standing over Clifton's body, piercing the man's heart. Growling, he finished the man off by plunging his sword through his chest. Retrieving both weapons, he knelt beside Clifton as he panted for breath, his chest pouring crimson over the ground. Isaac glanced up at Edward who began pointing over Isaac's shoulder. Isaac turned to find two more guards making their way through the trees. He turned back to Clifton and began dragging him towards the boundary line. *He could not save them both*, he thought. And Clifton would not make it back to the castle in his condition. He gripped the prince's shoulders as he thrust his upper body over the line and motioned for Edward to pull him from the other side. Edward knelt and made easy work of retrieving Clifton's body and spreading him out on his side of the line. Isaac turned, took a deep breath, mustered what little strength he had left and began battling the two Southern guards.

∞

Edward knelt next to Prince Clifton and tapped his cheek. The prince's sharp green gaze opened, and he panted in shock as he ran a hand over his chest. His entire body tingled. Clifton looked up and found the calm and steady gaze of Prince Edward. "I-I crossed?"

"Yes, my Lord. Prince Isaac sent you across the boundary to save you. Lie still, your wound will heal in a moment."

Clifton sank his head back to the ground and waited until the tightening in his chest seized and the throb in his right shoulder disappeared. He took a deep breath and sat up quickly. "This can't happen." He pushed to his feet and felt Edward help him rise. "Elizabeth... she did not wish to cross. She wanted to stay with me, be with me. This can't happen." He barked in panic as he watched Prince Isaac battle the two guards on the other side. "This is what it feels like? To be helpless?" He looked to Edward and Edward nodded. "I do what I can."

"Yes. Thank you. I did not wish to sound ungrateful for what you have been doing. But how can I just stay over here when..." Clifton's words faded as he scurried the ground to find his weapons.

"Turn." Edward yelled through the veil though he knew no sound would reach the other side. His gaze carried through the boundary. Clifton glanced up to see what the prince referred to and his gaze hardened. "No!" He screamed as a Southern guard made his way towards Elizabeth's still body, sword at the ready. Clifton grabbed his sword from the ground and screamed, racing towards the boundary line. Edward tried to restrain him knowing he would only be shocked back several yards, but the prince plunged forcefully through the veil without even a shimmer. Clifton landed on top of the guard on the other side and tackled him to the ground. Edward stood with mouth agape at the sight. The prince could cross.

Prince Isaac turned around at the scuffle and stopped, his face full of equal confusion as he lowered his sword and watched Clifton kill the guard and stand. His body completely healed.

"You can cross?!" Isaac belted as he looked to a stunned Prince Edward. Edward pointed to Elizabeth and the horse for them to hurry.

Clifton rushed to Elizabeth's side and scooped her up.

"Carry her back." He ordered. Isaac flew into his saddle and reached down to accept the injured princess. "You can cross?!" He repeated.

"I will be along shortly. Speak of this to no one."

"You find me when you reach the castle." Isaac stated firmly. "We report this together."

Clifton nodded and slapped a hand to the horse's hide and watched as Isaac rode away.

∞

King Eamon watched as Ryle and his troops emerged within the village and rushed to the aide of the Northern guards. He reined in his stallion as his gaze travelled to the West and he caught sight of King Anthony and a full army of Western soldiers. A smile broke out on his worn face and he held up his sword in salute. Anthony mirrored his action as a sea of red swarmed through the village. Black tunics grew sparser as the East, West, and North united in their efforts to protect the Realm.

Eamon brought his horse to the gate of the castle and dismounted as an attendant accepted his reins and saw to his steed. He rushed inside to find Princess Melody tending to the wounded. She smiled when she spotted him.

"Your father has arrived, my dear, just in the nick of time."

Relief washed over her face and she brought him a goblet of water. "You are a sight for sore eyes, my Lord. An encouraging sight."

"The Southern army is retreating. What little forces they have left will be gone within half an hour or so. Success is ours."

"That is good news indeed, my Lord." Melody replied. Her gaze made quick work over his appearance to check for injury. Pleased she saw none, she lightly placed her hand on his arm and squeezed before walking away and continuing her duties. Eamon's gaze surveyed the room and he caught sight of Princess Alayna as she rushed by. Rejuvenated with hydration, Eamon turned back around and stepped outside onto the castle steps. Standing upon the parapet he watched as the colors of the Realm clashed upon the fields before him and the sounds of war began to fade. He thought of Clifton and Ryle and prayed they made it safely back to the castle. He watched the sun begin to set, the colors of the radiant sky casting shadows over a bloodied Earth. He had seen many battles in his days, but this one he knew would forever plague his mind.

"My Lord, your son calls for aide on the Eastern ridge." Eamon turned to find his captain holding the reins of their horses. Without hesitation, he vaulted into his saddle and rode out to aide Ryle in his victory.

∞

Alayna rushed through the main hall carrying a load of linens for several wounded soldiers as her father entered the room. He eased himself into his throne and Tomas provided him with drink and food.

"Father, I thought you would be resting." Alayna scolded as she rushed to his side.

"I am fine dear. Anymore news?"

She shook her head. "No. Though I aim to hear word from Samuel soon." She pressed the back of her hand to her father's forehead and felt for a fever. Relief washed through her as he reached up and grabbed her hand. "I am fine." He restated warmly. She listened to his breathing, pleased to find the wheezing had subsided. She heard the shuffle of boots as Samuel burst into the room and slid to a halt before them.

"Prince Samuel?" Alayna asked curious as to his form of entry until her gaze looked over his shoulder and saw Prince Isaac stumbling into the castle carrying her sister.

Alayna and King Granton rushed forward.

"W-what happened?" Alayna asked, eyeing the blood-soaked tunic wrapped around her leg and the deep gash in her sister's arm.

Prince Isaac's face, bruised, swollen, and bloody, showed no signs of conversing as he struggled lifting one foot in front of the other.

"Get her in here." Granton ordered, pointing to the dining hall in the next room. He waved his hand and Isaac gently laid Elizabeth on the tabletop. "Gretchen, fetch some water and linen strips! Renee, we need blankets!" Granton ordered. He lightly shoved Isaac into one of the chairs and watched as the young man's chest heaved in exhaustion.

Samuel stood in awe and awaited direction. King Granton caught the young man's gaze and directed him to a chair as well. "Samuel, I need you to hold down Elizabeth's right leg, okay?"

Samuel nodded and gently placed his hands on the Princess's uninjured leg as King Granton unwrapped Isaac's bloody tunic from his daughter's calf. He grimaced as he pulled it back. Alayna gasped and began to cry as she ordered Tomas to fetch the healer. "Leave it, Father. We must wait for assistance."

"We cannot leave it, Alayna, or infection will spread and she will catch fever."

Isaac stood and removed his sword from his belt. Alayna's eyes widened in horror. "No! No, we cannot do this, Father! Please?!"

Granton turned to Alayna and gripped her face in his hands. His stern blue eyes peered into the panicked brown gaze of his daughter. "Alayna, I need you to be strong. Your sister will die if we do not do this." Granton released her and turned to Mary who rushed into the room at the news of Elizabeth's return.

"Mary, take Princess Alayna to the main hall." Mary nodded and allowed Alayna to grip her arm for stability as she struggled leaving her sister behind.

Granton turned back and looked at the pale face of Prince Samuel. "Are you able to do this son?"

Samuel nodded, a green tinge working its way into his cheeks. Isaac studied him carefully. "He is fine, my Lord." Isaac answered for the young man. Samuel looked to Isaac's dark gaze and nodded, trying to mirror the Western prince's confidence.

"Hold tight to her other leg, Samuel." Isaac stated. He looked to King Granton who held Elizabeth's shoulders against the table. Isaac took a deep breath and raised his sword over his head and brought it down with brunt force. Elizabeth's leg separated at the knee in a clean cut. Samuel immediately turned and vomited on the floor at the sight of the hemorrhaging stub. Granton quickly grabbed linens as Isaac retied the tourniquet.

The healer rushed into the room at the sound of the amputation and swiftly took over King Granton's position as the king eased into a chair to catch his own breath. The king lightly patted Samuel's back as the boy sat with his head between his knees. Isaac continued aiding the healer, Granton impressed with his strength and service. When the healer had cauterized Elizabeth's leg, he turned towards King Granton. "We must not move her until the bandages have set. Then we must lay her somewhere comfortable, my Lord."

Granton nodded. "We will ready her chambers." He turned and spotted Tomas and waved him forward. "Find Mary and have her ready Elizabeth's chambers."

Tomas bowed and exited quickly. Granton studied Isaac closely. "Do you have any injuries, Prince Isaac?"

Isaac's stoic brown gaze that had been staring at the princess finally drifted up and he shook his head. "I am fine, my Lord. Nothing a good rest will not cure."

"You saved my Elizabeth's life. I am forever in your debt." Granton's voice choked as he fought back tears in his throat.

Isaac's eyes became glassy as he shook his head and cleared his throat. "No, my Lord. She saved mine."

Granton's brows rose slightly as the prince swiped a hand over his face and stood. "I must see if I am needed in the ranks."

Granton waved his hand. "Sit, Prince Isaac." Isaac stared at the king and slowly eased back into the chair. "You have done enough for today. Your body is tired and needs its rest. Your battle has been fought."

Isaac's gaze dropped to his hands until he heard a gasp as his sister rushed into the room. Melody dropped to her knees beside him, cupping his face in her hands as she cried with joy. She hugged him tightly around the neck, Isaac lightly patting her arm in response. She pulled away and quickly began swiping a damp cloth over his face. Isaac smirked and gently pulled her hand away from his face. "I am fine, Melody. Please."

She stopped and sat next to him. "What happened, Isaac?"

Isaac shifted uncomfortably in his chair. "Much, Melody. Much has happened. But I do not wish to speak of it just yet. I await Prince Clifton's return before we speak of such matters."

"Prince Clifton? He's alive?" Melody asked with hope in her voice.

"Yes, he is very much alive." Isaac stated.

"Oh, thank goodness!" Melody squeezed his hand. "We will have victory soon. King Eamon stated so just a few minutes ago. Father has arrived with troops from the West and all will be over soon."

Granton perked up at that news and sent up a silent prayer of thanks. Isaac nodded. "Good. Why don't you see to Samuel, sister? He could use some tonic."

Melody cast a worried look to Samuel and quickly helped him to his feet as she escorted him out of the room.

"She has served well." Granton complimented.

"I am glad." Isaac replied. "I am truly sorry, my Lord, for the princess." Isaac's gaze saddened as he glanced back to Elizabeth's still figure lying on the table.

"You mustn't be. You brought her home."

Isaac shook his head. "It was my fault though." He admitted softly, guilt slumping his shoulders. "I thought I had killed him."

"Who?"

"Prince Eric." Isaac stated.

Granton's eyes widened. "Prince Eric did this?"

"Yes, my Lord. It took us all off guard I am afraid. Prince Clifton tried to get Elizabeth to cross the boundary, to send her to Edward so she could heal, but she wished to remain on this side."

Granton's heart ached for his youngest daughter but swelled in pride at her courage. "Was Edward there?"

"Yes. He fought for us as well. We would have been severely outnumbered if he had not helped."

"Did he cross?" Granton asked.

"No. He cannot cross, my Lord. We pushed soldiers over to him as often as we could. It was actually Elizabeth's idea, smart one really."

"Indeed." Granton replied.

"She is a skilled swordsman, my Lord." Isaac complimented.

"That seems to be the consensus. I have read her box of letters and Edward speaks highly of her skills as well." Granton explained.

"She saved my life today… twice." Isaac admitted in disbelief.

"And you have saved hers." Granton added.

Isaac's mouth was grim as he studied Elizabeth's leg. He felt a comforting hand on his shoulder as an attendant offered him a goblet of water. She flashed him a charming smile and he recognized the woman as one of his stairwell maidens. He nodded his thanks but did not return her flirtatious nature and took a sip of his water. Granton watched him closely, realizing the days' events had quite hopefully altered the prince's usual ways. Though his eyes were haunted, Prince Isaac's demeanor spoke of maturity. Character was defined on the battlefield, Granton knew that to be true.

"You think you have the strength to carry her?" Granton asked, nodding towards Elizabeth.

Isaac stood, his body aching from head to toe, but he gently slipped his hands under Elizabeth's small frame and lifted her into his arms. Granton slowly followed him as they made their way slowly up the stairs to her chambers.

Mary awaited them at the door and rushed them to the bed. "Give me a few minutes to wash her and change her, my Lord."

Isaac eased Elizabeth's body onto the bed and stepped outside with King Granton. "You are probably anxious to see your Father." Granton stated. "Please, feel free to seek him out."

Isaac nodded at the dismissal and bowed. "Thank you, my Lord."

∞

Clifton stared at Edward across the line and ran a hand over his chest where his wound had previously just been. Edward stood just as perplexed. Clifton stepped towards the boundary again and Edward waved his hands for him to stop. Clifton nodded. He had to see if it were his emotions at the time of his crossing that allowed him to cross or if he were just able. He felt the slight hum in his toes as his boots crossed through the veil and he emerged on the other side.

Baffled, Edward reached forward and hugged him in a brotherly hug. "Welcome, brother."

Clifton took a deep breath, the crisp clean air filling his lungs.

"You healed?" Edward asked, swiping a hand over the hole in the front of Clifton's tunic.

"Yes. Fully. It is an odd sensation."

"I bet." Edward grinned. "How did you do it, Prince Clifton? How did you cross?"

"I do not know." Clifton answered honestly. "I just… did. Is there a trick? Or a hole?"

Edward shook his head. "No."

Several people emerged on the edges of the forest and Edward waved them forward in greeting. "Don't be scared, my friends. This is Prince Clifton of the Eastern Kingdom. He is our friend and ally."

Eyes widened in surprise and Cecilia stepped forward. "It is a pleasure, your Grace." She curtsied and slid an arm around Edward's waist.

"This is my Cecilia." Edward stated proudly.

Recognition dawned on Clifton's face and he smiled. "Ah, Cecilia, yes, I have heard much about you from Elizabeth."

Cecilia smiled. "Will she be alright, my Lord?"

"Aye, I pray so. Prince Isaac was to take her back to the castle. I must head back soon myself. The South has been defeated." Clifton answered.

Edward stepped forward and draped his arm over Clifton's shoulders and walked him away from the group back towards the veil of the boundary. "We must figure this out, prince. Why you are able to cross. Why Lancer is able to cross. What is the connection?"

"I do not know, your Grace, but I agree. We must figure this out. Have you been within Lancer's personal chambers again?"

"No, not yet, but I aim to tonight. He expects me to tonight." Edward replied. "I must say it is quite… eerie."

"I imagine so." Clifton studied the prince closely. He stood healthy, strong, and young. "You have not aged a day?" The question slipped out before he could restrain it, and Prince Edward chuckled. "No. I am the same age now as I was then. Odd, I know." They walked another turn of the clearing and then reached Clifton's spot of entry once more.

"I shall return once things calm down. Find out what you can from Lancer, and I will do my best to work on my end. A connection is there, we just have to unmask it." Clifton stated.

Edward shook his hand. "Take care of my sister, Prince Clifton. She adores you almost as much as you do her." He winked at Clifton and at the slight blush that crept up the man's neck. "Yes. I will most definitely see to her care, my Lord."

"And tell my father—" Edward paused and sighed, running a hand through onyx hair the same shade as Elizabeth's. "Well I do not know what to tell him other than I am sorry to have caused him pain, if I did."

"Aye. I believe you will find your father a forgiving man, Prince Edward." Clifton stepped towards the line and ran his hand through the fog of the boundary. Taking a deep breath, he stepped forward and into Elizabeth's clearing. He turned and nodded in farewell as he mounted his horse and vanished from view.

Edward accepted the comfort from Cecilia as she rubbed a hand over his back. "He will return, my love." She stated quietly.

Edward lightly kissed the top of her head and released her. "I must go to Lancer now and report the Southern guards crossed over. I will also be entering his reflection chamber tonight."

"Do not let the darkness take you." Cecilia pleaded up at him, her sapphire eyes full of worry.

"I will fight it, my love, especially now that we know it is not needed in order to cross the boundary. Now, away with you. Hide. I shall return soon." Edward clicked his reins and headed in the direction of Lancer's castle.

∞

Edward rushed into his chambers and shut the door, quickly washing away the blood on his face and hands and changing into a fresh tunic. He hid his satchel within his wardrobe and ran a hand through his hair. As he opened his door, Lancer stood on the other side with a quizzical expression.

"My Lord." Edward fumbled nervously. "I did not realize you were coming to see me."

"Aye, indeed." Lancer stood waiting for Edward to step aside and when he didn't, Lancer rolled his eyes and playfully slapped Edward's jaw. "Are you not going to let me in?"

"Oh, of course. Please." He gestured with a wave of his hand and Lancer waltzed inside.

"I thought we discussed your need for color in here, Edward. Seriously how do you live in such plainness?"

"I have yet to have the time, my Lord, but I will mark it as a priority." Edward stated. "I am afraid I was just about to come find you, my Lord."

"Really? What for? More exciting news?" Lancer's eyes sparkled at the prospect.

"Yes, quite a lot actually." Edward replied curtly as he motioned for Lancer to sit. "I fear the South has been defeated."

"No surprise there." Lancer mumbled in annoyance as he waited anxiously for Edward to continue, his foot tapping incessantly on the floor.

"Yes, well, several Southern guards crossed the boundary again." Edward held up his hands to ward off Lancer's comments. "Don't worry, I took care of them. All are dead."

"Very good."

"I must say, however, that Prince Eric is dead. I watched Prince Isaac of the West kill him with my own eyes."

"Is that so?" Lancer asked in amusement. "I bet that did not sit well with the king of the South." Lancer mused on a laugh.

"I am not sure, my Lord. Although, I do wish to explore the current status of the Southern Kingdom. From what I have seen and heard, my Lord, the battle was a bloody one and the South has been annihilated. I wish to see for myself. I wish to cross and see if perhaps the Lands can now simply take over what is left of the Southern Kingdom. There should be no resistance and I feel it may be of great use to us."

"You wish to cross?" Lancer asked pointedly, his eyes narrowing at Edward.

"Yes, my Lord."

"Oh Edward." Lancer sighed and pinched the bridge of his nose. "You realize if you want to cross you must embrace the power, right?"

"I do." Edward lied.

"And you are willing to embrace the power?"

"Yes." He lied again.

"Then we shall try tonight." Lancer stated. "Prepare to sacrifice of yourself, Edward."

"Is that all that is required of me?" Edward asked.

"I believe so." Lancer replied on a shrug. "But there are some things I do not even know the answer to, my friend."

They both stood silent a minute to contemplate the dilemma until Lancer broke the silence. "Meet me at the door in an hour."

Edward smiled and bowed gratefully. "Yes, my Lord. Thank you."

Lancer nodded in approval and walked out leaving Edward alone with his thoughts. His gaze roamed around his room and he sat on the edge of his bed. "Please let me cross." He whispered to the air.

∞

A celebration took hold of the Northern Kingdom as festivities of a battle won swept through the villages. The castle bustled with music and joy as food was served in the dining and main hall. King Eamon, King Anthony, Prince Ryle, Prince Isaac, Prince Samuel, and Princess Melody sat at the table awaiting King Granton. He emerged at the doorway with Alayna, the princess' tear stained face causing Ryle to sit up straighter in his chair. Granton sat in his designated spot and nodded his welcome. He reached for his glass. "It is with great honor and pride that I share my meal with you all tonight. The Realm is strong despite the uprising of the South. I thank you all for your aide, your friendship, and now your fellowship. Hail the victorious." He raised his glass as everyone raised theirs in response and echoed the sentiment.

Alayna watched Prince Isaac pick at his food, his gaze constantly fluttering to the spot on the table stained by the color of her sister's blood. No doubt, the prince haunted himself with his gruesome task from earlier. She found Ryle's understanding gaze and offered a weak smile as she saw the pain in his own eyes at the loss of his brother, who had yet to return. *Elizabeth and Clifton*, she thought sadly. Young and in love and neither able to join in the celebrations of victory for the Realm they both cherished. The thought saddened her heart and she fought for control of her emotions.

Princess Melody gasped quietly and reached for her brother's hand. Shaking Isaac's attention away from the tabletop she nodded towards the door at Prince Clifton, standing firmly on his feet, his emerald gaze sharp and direct. Prince Isaac stood abruptly, drawing everyone's attention to his face and then to the man he studied.

King Eamon and Ryle immediately left the table and ran to Clifton, embracing him and patting him on the back as they welcomed him into the room. Clifton's gaze sought Isaac again and he walked over to the Western prince and placed his hand upon his shoulder. Isaac did the same. "This, my friends, is my brother."

King Anthony's eyes widened in surprise and then proudly smiled as the two princes embraced in a brotherly hug. "How is she?" Clifton asked Isaac. Isaac shook his head, the words bitter in his mouth as he thought of poor Princess Elizabeth.

Clifton's face fell, and he glanced to King Granton and Alayna's sad faces. "Sh-she's dead?" Clifton asked quietly.

They shook their heads and relief washed over his features. "Then where is she?" He asked louder.

"She is resting." King Granton answered.

"I must see her." Clifton stated, turning to make his way towards the stairs.

"Halt son!" Eamon called after him. Clifton turned back around. "She is resting. You must rest as well, see to your injuries." As Eamon made the comment his brow furrowed as he surveyed his son's health. "What *happened* to your injuries, Cliff?" He asked in confusion.

Clifton's gaze found Isaac's and he slid into an open chair, resting his hands on top of the table. "I am healed."

"Healed?" Eamon asked in disbelief. "But you took an arrow to the shoulder, and by the looks of it a sword to the chest." He motioned to the shredded front of Clifton's bloody tunic.

"Yes, I did."

"But how?" Eamon continued.

Sighing, Clifton glanced around the table at the curious glances and he looked to Isaac again.

Isaac nodded. King Granton noted the exchange between the two princes with curiosity.

"I crossed the boundary line."

Gasps circled around the table and Granton stood, his chair teetering behind him. "Dare to repeat yourself." He ordered.

Clifton ran a hand through his shaggy hair nervously as he glanced up. "I can cross the boundary line, my Lord."

"How?" Granton barked.

"I do not know."

"How do you not know when you have done it?!"

Eamon held up a calming hand towards Granton that was ignored.

"Did you see my son? Did you see Edward?"

"Yes, your Grace. Your son is alive and well."

"And?" Granton prodded.

"And he sends his regards."

Granton fell back into his chair and placed a hand over his heart, his breathing unstable. Alayna leaned towards him and lightly squeezed his arm. "Careful, Father."

"So how did this happen?" King Anthony asked, as he looked to his own son's lack of surprise.

"I was... stabbed." Clifton motioned to the front of his tunic. "There was no saving me. Princess Elizabeth lay dying, and I lay dying. The princess wished to stay in the Realm. It was her last wish before she passed out. Prince Isaac continued to battle the remaining guards after I fell. When he secured the clearing, he did not have time to bring us both back. He pushed me over the boundary line to heal. Prince Edward saw to me immediately." Clifton finished.

King Eamon looked to Isaac. "I am forever in your debt, Prince Isaac."

Isaac shook his head. "No, my Lord. You are not."

"But how did you know you could cross back?" Alayna asked, her voice carrying over the whispers around the table.

"I didn't. I saw another guard trying to sneak upon Elizabeth's body as Prince Isaac battled more guards and I just— I just ran at him." Clifton's eyes were distant as if he relived the moment, and confusion laced his voice as he continued. "It was... incredible. When I first crossed over, my body healed within a minute or two. I felt stronger than I have ever been. When I saw Elizabeth vulnerable, there was no thought of whether the boundary could hold me back or not. I just... crossed."

"I brought the princess back," Isaac picked up, "because Prince Clifton wished to remain behind at the boundary. I'm assuming to test his crossing again." Isaac turned to Clifton as the prince nodded.

"Yes, I crossed back over easily. Spoke with Edward more and crossed back to the side of the Realm just as easily."

"This is incredible." Granton whispered to himself.

"This is what we have been looking for." Prince Ryle chimed in and looked to his brother. "If Cliff can cross, then there must be others that can also. There must be a trick."

"No, there is no trick." Clifton supplied. "Though Prince Edward stated his plan of entering Lancer's reflection chamber again tonight to see what he could unfold. He is convinced the key lies within that room."

Granton shook his head in disbelief, his heart heavy. "Well, there is much more to discuss. For now, let us be grateful for everyone's safe return." He raised his glass towards Clifton and then took a sip.

Elizabeth shifted, her body aching, her throat scratchy. She blinked, the soft lantern light shrouding her room in shadows. "M-Mary?" Her voice sounded as if she had swallowed a handful of rocks.

"Princess Elizabeth?!" Mary rushed to her side and quickly set about tilting up her head for a sip of water. Easing her head back against the pillows, she offered a small smile.

"It is good to have you back with us, my Lady. We have all been so worried." Mary lightly brushed Elizabeth's bangs out of her eyes as she brushed the back of her hand against Elizabeth's forehead checking for a fever.

"Isaac?"

"Safe, my Lady."

"Clifton?"

"Also safe." Mary beamed. "All of you are home safe."

Elizabeth shifted to her elbows and began to push herself into a sitting position. Mary helped her rise and adjusted her pillows accordingly. "Are you hungry, my Lady? Or thirsty? Are you warm enough?"

Elizabeth placed a stilling hand on Mary's. "I am fine for now, Mary."

"Alright." Mary readjusted Elizabeth's blankets to make use of her nervous hands.

Elizabeth leaned her head back against the feathered softness of her pillows and sighed. "Mary?"

"Yes, Miss Elizabeth?"

"Will you fetch the prince for me?"

Mary smiled. "Of course, my Lady. Prince Clifton has been eager to see you since his arrival."

"Not Clifton." Elizabeth stated and turned to her attendant with sad eyes.

"Oh?" Mary asked.

"Isaac, please." Elizabeth stated softly.

"Yes, my Lady." Mary curtsied and hurried out the door.

∞

Alayna's head popped up at the sight of Mary entering the dining hall, her gaze flashing around the table in search of someone.

"Mary?"

Mary curtsied to the room.

"Is my sister awake?" Alayna asked with a hopeful glance.

Mary nodded and held up her hands as several stood to rush out of the room. "She is quite tired, my Lady."

Clifton rose from his chair and Mary quickly waved him back to it. "No, my Lord. She asks…" Mary paused knowing Prince Clifton would be upset with the request.

"She asks?" Alayna prodded.

"For Prince Isaac, your Grace."

Clifton's heart lurched in his chest with disappointment. He looked to the equally surprised Prince of the West and Isaac rose. "Me? Why?"

"I do not know, my Lord." Mary stated. "I am just here to fetch you."

He turned towards King Granton for permission. The king nodded. He then turned to Clifton. Swallowing his wounded pride and heart, Clifton nodded grimly. Isaac stood. "I shall return with a full report."

Alayna offered an encouraging smile to the prince, sensing his awkwardness and shock to her sister's request. Isaac covered the floor to Mary in quick strides and everyone heard the echo of his boots on the stairs as he ascended towards Elizabeth's chambers.

"Don't worry, Cliff." Prince Ryle stated in a low voice.

"Who said I was worried?" Clifton grumbled under his breath.

"Your face." Ryle stated with a smirk. Clifton shot him an annoyed glare before taking a sip of his drink. "She will call for me in time. I just have to be patient."

"That is right." King Granton stated, embarrassment flashed over the two princes' faces at their being overheard by the king. "Elizabeth will call for all of us in her own time." He finished.

Granton lightly squeezed Alayna's hand and smiled at her, knowing full well she was disappointed not to be Elizabeth's first request as well.

∞

Isaac entered Elizabeth's chambers and made his way slowly to the side of her bed. She looked small and frail beneath the heavy coverings. Her black hair splayed across the cream pillows in silky waves. Her face was bruised, but her regal bone structure and delicate brows made her a picturesque sight.

"My Lady?" Mary whispered, lightly touching Elizabeth's hand.

Elizabeth's eyes opened, and she smiled at the sight of Isaac. She reached for him and he slid to sit on the edge of her bedside as she gripped his hand. "I am pleased to see you." She stated.

"And I you. You had us worried." Isaac stated. He gently held her hand in his and his brow furrowed. "Why did you ask for me, Elizabeth?" He asked bluntly, his voice low and his eyes haunted.

"I wanted to thank you." She shifted, and Mary situated her pillows.

Isaac scoffed at her response. "Thank me? I'm the reason you are lying in this bed." He gritted his teeth at the statement as disappointment and shame filled his heart. He dropped his chin to his chest to hide the emotions warring across his face. Elizabeth gently brushed the hair on his forehead aside as she tried to peer underneath it to see his eyes. "You are right."

His head snapped up at her statement. "You are the reason I'm lying here alive." She added to the end. "I would not be alive if it weren't for you."

Isaac shook his head and dropped her hand as he stood to pace. "No. Stop. Do you not remember what happened?!" He asked in frustration. "I stabbed Prince Eric. I thought he was dead. If I had double-checked… if I had made sure…" he ran a hand over his jaw and sighed. "I should have made sure, then he would not have been able to attack you the way he did. Then maybe you'd—" He motioned to her leg. "Then maybe you would still have your leg."

Elizabeth pushed herself up to a better sitting position and sighed as she ran a hand over her lap to smooth her blankets. "Yes, it is quite disappointing to lose part of my leg… but I suppose it pales in comparison to the loss of my life. Whatever you think you did or did not do, Prince Isaac, you might as well become comfortable with the praise I offer you. For I will not revoke it." Isaac walked back over to her bedside and sat. She squeezed his hand. "You fought bravely."

"And so did you. You were better than I thought you would be."

She grinned proudly. "I would not have been if you had not been clever in disposing of my overskirts."

They both chuckled softly as they replayed the day's events in their minds. Isaac's smile faded slowly, and he turned to face her. Her blue eyes studied him carefully. "Your prince is disappointed you fetched me over him." He felt her fingers lightly tap the top of his hand as she avoided his gaze. He tilted her chin up with his finger and narrowed his gaze to try and read her thoughts. "You going to tell me your secrets, princess?"

She shook her head making him laugh. "What if I promise not to repeat them?"

She tilted her head and her gaze squinted in disbelief at his words making him laugh harder causing her lips to twitch into a smile. "Ah, there it is." He lightly tapped a finger to the dimple in her left cheek.

"It will sound vain." Elizabeth stated in disgust.

"Ah, now look who you are talking to, princess. You think I will have a problem with vanity?" Isaac asked in jest making Elizabeth roll her eyes. Smiling, Isaac leaned back against the bedpost; his legs strode out on top of her blankets facing her. They sat opposite one another for a moment in silence, an easy quiet passing between them.

"I still feel it." She stated quietly. His brow rising in interest.

"My leg." She clarified. "I still feel it. I swear I had an itch on my little toe earlier." She grinned at the thought and he lightly tapped the toes of her remaining foot.

"I have heard that is quite common a feeling with people who lose a limb." Isaac shared.

"Mary seems to think she can find me a crutch of some sort so that I may walk soon."

"Ah, Mary…" Isaac smiled. "She spoils you." He winked at Elizabeth and she nodded. "Yes, she does."

Her smile slowly faded, and her vision began to blur as her mind wandered elsewhere. He watched as her chin quivered. "Do you think…" her voice trailed off as she tried to stifle back her tears. "Do you think Prince Clifton will find me…"

Isaac then realized Elizabeth's fear. She feared Prince Clifton would not love her due to her, what she believed, new deformity.

"My princess," Isaac's eyes softened with sympathy as he swung his feet to the floor and moved closer to her and enveloped her in a hug. He felt the warm tears soak through his shirt as she sobbed. "Clifton loves you, Elizabeth. And he will love you still. You are the same person."

She shook her head and pulled back to look up at him. "I am not the same. I feel so different. I wished to be beautiful on my wedding day, to wear a beautiful dress and walk— walk down to him. How can I walk to him, Isaac? How can I feel beautiful when my body is marred by such evil?"

Isaac brushed his thumbs over her cheeks and shook his head. "You put those thoughts out of your mind. You cannot think such things, Elizabeth. You are beautiful. You are strong. That is what Clifton sees. He does not see your injury any more than I do."

She swiped a hand over her cheek to wipe away her tears. "Like I said, I know it is but vanity that makes me feel this way, which in turn makes me even more disgusted with myself, I'm afraid." Elizabeth admitted truthfully.

Isaac chuckled. "You, afraid? Never." He winked at her as a smile tugged at the corner of her mouth. "Nonetheless, your secret is safe with me, Elizabeth."

"And yours with me." She stated, clearing her throat of her tears.

"Mine? Pray, what secret do I have?" Isaac asked as he stood to exit.

"That you're a good man." Elizabeth replied. She watched as he took a deep breath, her words shaking him to his core. "But don't worry,

Prince Isaac. Your secret is safe with me." She smiled at him as he nodded.

A small smirk tilted his lips. "Yes, well, we would hate to ruin my reputation." He bowed and then quietly exited. Elizabeth smiled comfortably as she leaned back against her pillows and sighed. Yes, Prince Isaac was a good man, whether he chose to believe it or not. She then turned to Mary and nodded. "Send up whomever wishes to come see me." Mary, smiling, excitedly exited the room.

∞

Edward felt the blood dripping from his hand as he stood in the darkness of Lancer's reflection chamber. He sensed the man's presence but heard nothing. He did not wish for the power to consume him, yet he wished to understand it. Then he felt it. The slight tug on his heart. The slight pull at his thoughts. Whispers of fog curled around his ankles. Black fog, he knew. The sconces on the wall lit and before him stood Lancer covered in the black smoke. His eyes, completely darkened, looked hollow and Edward took a deep breath to calm his nerves.

"You must embrace the power." Lancer's voice was low, abnormally low. Menacing. Threatening. He stood with arms outstretched as Edward's mind rang with the pounding of his heart, tortuous screams, and anguished cries. He placed his palms on either side of his head and tried to focus on Lancer's words, but he couldn't. His chest felt tight and he wished he could free himself from the sudden confinement.

"The oath was sealed by my blood merging with the darkness." Lancer explained. "It is my blood that holds the veil of the Land of Unfading Beauty. MY BLOOD that sustains this Land." His voice bounced off of the walls and pierced Edward's mind and echoed through him. He felt himself falling to his knees. "You must sacrifice of yourself, Edward." Lancer explained calmly. "My blood is your blood." He felt the sharp stab of the sword as it pierced through his chest and out his back. Gasping, he felt the tremors take over, the nerves in his body snapping and cratering. Lancer laughed as he withdrew the sword and dripped the blood from his own wounded hand into the open wound on Edward's chest.

"Your blood and my blood, Edward." Lancer repeated. "Do you feel it? Do you feel the power rushing through your veins, beating from your heart? Embrace it, Edward." Lancer's voice became distant as Edward struggled to maintain consciousness. Why was he not healing? He wondered. Why were his hands going numb? His feet? He felt his cheek land against the cold stone floor and his body began to shudder.

"The transformation is almost complete, Edward." Lancer's voice echoed off the walls and the lights enflamed and shot towards the ceiling. The blackness faded and all that remained was Edward's blood oozing over the floor and Lancer kneeling beside him. Lancer placed a hand over the hole in Edward's back and Edward's body began to heal. Within minutes, the room was still, the firelights steady, and Edward began to push himself off of the floor. Edward ran a hand over the front of his chest and felt no pain. *Incredible*, he thought.

He caught Lancer's large smile and ran a hand through his hair as he struggled for words.

"How do you feel?" Lancer asked.

"Good." Edward answered. "I-I must admit I was scared there for a second, my Lord. I thought I was to die."

Laughing, Lancer slapped Edward on the back in his usual friendly pat. "No, Edward. I have plans for you. It would not do me much good to kill you then, would it?"

"Aye, I guess not. What plans do you have for me?"

"You wish to cross to the Southern Kingdom do you not?"

"Yes, to see what is left." Edward replied.

"Then you will cross and do just that. There should be no problem now that my blood runs through your veins."

That thought had Edward inwardly cringing. Was he forever poisoned now that Lancer had spilled his blood within him? He prayed not.

"Is it just your blood I need in order to cross?" Edward asked curiously, wondering how Prince Clifton would have obtained the ability if that were the reason.

"Yes." Lancer answered. "The darkness you see in my chamber can only come from me. It was I who gave my blood and swore an oath of servitude to it. So naturally anyone who shares my blood shall have some of my abilities."

"And how many others have you shared your blood with?" Edward looked at Lancer as they made their way out of the main entrance of the castle and over towards the stables.

"Why, none, of course." Lancer replied truthfully. "It is not something I give freely, Edward. I was just told to give it to you, which is why you now have it."

"Who told you to share your blood with me?" Edward asked.

Lancer looked at him with a narrowed gaze and studied him closely. "You still do not know?"

"I am just confused." Clarified Edward.

"The darkness. The power. It speaks to me, to my soul."

"Of course." Edward stated. "I see. Well I count myself most fortunate for your favor, my Lord."

Lancer smiled and closed his eyes allowing the sun to shine upon his face. He sighed as he breathed in his surroundings. "Why don't you go make plans for your journey to the Southern Kingdom, Edward? You and I will meet again at dinner to discuss."

Edward bowed as he walked away towards the stables. He needed to leave a letter for Prince Clifton at the line. There was much to tell.

CHAPTER 11

The door to Elizabeth's chambers opened and several smiling faces entered. She spotted her father and welcomed him with a wide smile. He lightly kissed her hair as Alayna sat beside her and gently squeezed her hand. King Eamon appeared in the doorway and Elizabeth's nerves began to work their way into her heart. He nodded with a pleased smile on his face and entered into the room. Behind him stood Clifton, with Ryle bringing up the rear. Clifton stared at her, their eyes meeting and holding. Elizabeth held her breath and nervously flashed a glance towards Prince Isaac as he stood by his father and sister. He nodded in encouragement as she turned back to Clifton. She shrugged her shoulders as if to say, "Here I am." The slight movement sent the prince into a hurried pace to her bedside as he cupped her face in his hands and brought her into a fierce hug. He roamed his gaze over her face in relief, as if he did not believe what he saw. Elizabeth let out a nervous laugh, as her eyes grew glassy. She then spotted the red stain on the front of his tunic and placed her hand over it. Concern etched her face as Clifton broke into a smile. "There is much to tell you, princess." He laid his hand on hers as she rested it on his heart. His thumb brushed her knuckles and Elizabeth relaxed into a smile.

"You look well, princess." Prince Ryle complimented as he stepped into the room. "No worse for wear." He winked at her as he leaned against her bedpost.

"She is perfect." Clifton replied softly, soaking in the image of Elizabeth alive and well. His gaze shifted towards the slight curves of her legs beneath the bed covers. He noticed one of her legs was shorter than the other. He gently placed his hand on her foot and her eyes found his. He spotted her unshed tears as his gaze traveled to where her other foot should be and back to her face. His eyes were calm and kind. "You are well?" He asked, praying the amputation had not caused a fever or infection.

"Yes. Prince Isaac saw to me faithfully." She added, praising the prince of the West with gratitude. Clifton smiled, and he laid his hand upon hers as he sat on the edge of the bed.

"Tell me of the war. Is it over?" Elizabeth asked the room, her gaze traveling from one person to the next.

King Granton smiled. "I think we will let Prince Clifton fill you on the details." Granton nodded at Clifton as the prince flashed an appreciative smile. King Granton began waving people out the door to give Elizabeth and Clifton time alone. When the door closed, Mary brought Elizabeth a sip of water before tending to chores around the room. Clifton lightly laid his hand on top of Elizabeth's bandaged leg. "I am sorry this had to happen." He stated softly, disappointment in his voice.

Elizabeth inhaled a deep breath as she braced herself for the rejection she knew would follow.

"If I had gotten to the boundary sooner, perhaps this could have been prevented." Clifton continued.

Elizabeth shook her head. "No. You were where you needed to be, protecting your kingdom."

"I should have protected you." Clifton countered.

"You did. You arrived at the perfect time. Prince Isaac and I were grateful for you and Ryle." She squeezed his hand. "None of us could have seen this coming." She waved at her leg.

He slid to his knees on the floor beside her bed and held her hand to his forehead and then kissed the back of her hand. "I am still sorry, Elizabeth."

A faint smile tilted her lips. "You must not feel sorry for me, Prince Clifton. I will be fine. I am just grateful to be alive."

"And I am thankful for that as well. I do not wish to lose you, princess."

"Really?" Her eyes glossed over with tears of relief. His brow furrowed, and he tilted his head as he looked at her. "Why, of course. You are to be my wife. I care for you." His words trailed off as he glanced at the coverings over her legs and then back to her face. "I love you, Elizabeth."

A wide smile spread over her face as a tear slipped out of her eye. She laughed nervously as she swiped her other hand over her cheek. "Even if I only have one leg?"

"Even more so now, I believe." Clifton stated confidently. Elizabeth eyed him with doubt and he chuckled.

"You are a fighter, my love. A woman of strength. It is a great attribute and one I find quite appealing." He leaned forward and kissed the back of her hand once more and released her fingers.

"You have no idea how pleased I am to hear you speak those words, Clifton. I feared... well, I feared you would find my injury... unflattering."

Clifton shook his head. "You are an incredible woman, Elizabeth. It would take a lot more than a battle injury to keep me from marrying you." He winked at her and smiled at the small blush that stained her cheeks. He caught sight of Mary smiling out of the corner of his eye.

Elizabeth patted the edge of her bed for him to arise and sit beside her once more. He did, and she patted his arm. "Now, it is your turn. Tell me why you are sitting before me with not so much as a scratch upon you, when your tunic suggests there should be injuries." She requested.

Clifton took a deep breath. "I believe my news will surprise you, love."

"Try me."

He grinned at her response and nodded. "Well, when you passed out from your injury, Prince Isaac watched over you as I fetched our horses so that we may retreat back to the castle and have you attended. I returned, and as Isaac and I were speaking, I was stabbed from behind." He turned so she could see the hole in the back of his tunic as well. She gasped and leaned forward to run her hand over the torn fabric. "But there is no bandage." She stated in worry. "Are you alright?"

Clifton pulled her worried hand away from his back and held it between his. "Yes. I am more than fine. In fact, I am better than ever. See, when I was stabbed, Prince Isaac faced more guards pressing upon him. He could not make it back to the castle with both of us, Elizabeth. He had to choose to save one of us, or perhaps save us both with— a different method."

Her blue eyes were serious as she listened carefully to each word. "He shoved me over the boundary line so that I might heal and so he could bring you back here."

"What?" Elizabeth asked. "You crossed? How? For how long? Did you see Edward? How did you come back?"

Clifton chuckled at her rapid fire of questions. Elizabeth leaned back against her pillows in disbelief as she studied him. "I did cross. Your brother saw to me. He is a very kind man, Elizabeth. I was only there but a few minutes. When I healed, I was able to see you through the veil, lying on the ground while Isaac battled more guards. You were about to be attacked. I could not just stand there and watch, so I ran towards you. I passed through the boundary with ease and prevented the guard from killing you. I do not know how it happened or why I was able. That is something we are all trying to figure out, including your brother."

Elizabeth sat in shock. "You can cross." She stated quietly, pondering over her own words. "You can cross." She repeated. Her eyes darted to his again and she leaned forward her eyes surveying every inch of his face. "You are completely healed." Her words held disbelief at the sight before her. "I must speak with my father, and we must prepare a letter for Edward of news in regard to the outcome of the war here. I also want to know what he has learned from Lancer." Elizabeth turned back her covers, forgetting the unwelcome sight of her bandaged stub, she began to swing her legs over the side of the bed. "Mary, fetch me my robes." Her cream undershirts draped over her injury, hiding it from view, and Clifton chuckled. "Slow down now, love. You are healing. You need to rest. Your father and I have discussed what needs to take place, and the Council is preparing. But you— you need to heal." He tried to put a restraining hand on her arm as she shifted to stand and lean against her bedpost in await of Mary.

"Do not be absurd, prince. I am part of the Council myself. I do not wish to be left out of the loop when the timing is critical."

He smiled at her stubbornness. "Elizabeth," his voice was sweet as he eyed her in admiration. "You need to rest. Your injury is still healing. You could catch a fever if you overdo it. You are not out of the woods just yet."

"More reason for me to contribute as much as possible, just in case I take a turn for the worse." Elizabeth countered. "Mary, my robes." She ordered again.

Clifton stood and walked towards the door. "I guess if I cannot change your mind, I will leave you to dress. Have Mary fetch me from outside your doors when you are ready to go downstairs. I will be your chariot, my Lady." He winked at her as he eased her chamber door closed. Elizabeth smiled at his retreating back and welcomed the robes Mary gently placed over her shoulders and cinched around her waist. She watched as Mary placed a delicate slipper on her one foot and gently fluffed the bottoms of her skirts. "I believe you are ready, my Lady."

Elizabeth pushed off the bedpost to test her balance and hobbled with her arms stretched out on either side of her. Pain etched her forehead as she strained, her lips set in a firm line. A small welp of pain slipped from her lips and she finally leaned forward and rested against the bedpost once more.

"Patience, Miss Elizabeth." Mary stated quietly.

"Yes, well I think we both know that has never been my strong suit, Mary."

Mary nodded. "I will fetch Prince Clifton."

Clifton walked into the room and proudly smiled at Elizabeth's effort of standing on her own. "You will be running about the castle in no time, love."

She giggled as he scooped her into his arms with ease. "I hear there is a Council Meeting we are missing. Shall we?" He asked with a wink.

She nodded. "Yes. Carry me away, Prince Clifton."

He laughed as he stepped through the doors and headed in the direction of the Council Room.

∞

"If Clifton can cross, we need to figure out what it is that allowed him to do so." Ryle presented to the Council. His piercing blue eyes shot around the room. "Perhaps it was his emotions at the time of his crossing that allowed him to push through."

"No." Isaac replied. "If it were emotions, Prince Edward would have been able to cross back long ago."

"He has a point." King Eamon replied. "Edward stated that Lancer spoke of his blood being the key to the sustenance of the Unfading Lands. His blood holds the boundary line up." Eamon glanced down at his hands and then to his son. Ryle studied his father closely, his brows knitting together. His father was hiding something, he could feel it.

The doors to the room opened and Clifton stood carrying Princess Elizabeth.

"What on Earth?" Alayna gasped. "Prince Clifton, she should be resting." The scold was halted by Elizabeth's wide grin and wave. "No. I do not wish to rest. I wish to be a part of this Council. Father?" She looked to King Granton for permission.

"Only if you are feeling up to it, my dear."

"Of course I am." She answered promptly and pointed to an open chair for Clifton to ease her into. She sat next to King Anthony and King Eamon. Eamon reached over and lightly squeezed her hand in welcome.

"Now, what was the topic of discussion?" She asked.

"Lancer's blood connection to the boundary line." Ryle explained.

"Ah, yes. I assume all of you have read Edward's letters?" She asked, glancing to the kings in the room. They all nodded.

"Good." She replied. "And what have you all come to think?"

Ryle repeated their thoughts and she lightly tapped her chin as she thought.

"Father." Ryle called to King Eamon. "Want to share with us what is on your mind?"

Eamon's eyes bounced up in surprise at his son calling him out in front of the group. "Pardon?"

"You look as if you wish to say something." Ryle studied him with suspicion. "Care to share?"

King Eamon cleared his throat. "Not at the moment. There are still too many uncertainties."

Ryle's inner voice rang warning bells in his head. It was unlike his father to withhold information, and the unsettled feeling in the pit of his stomach told Ryle he needed to push the matter harder. "We are all just tossing out theories, Father. Please?" He waved his hand for his father to share.

Eamon glanced to Granton and ran a nervous hand over the front of his tunic to calm his racing heart. "I— well, I believe I may know of a connection— between Cliff and Lancer that could allow Clifton to cross."

Everyone stared at him on the edge of their seats, begging him to continue.

Clifton leaned forward and patiently waited.

"If Edward believes it is Lancer's blood that controls the boundary line and Unfading Lands, we may have a secret weapon in our favor." Eamon began. "If Lancer's blood is required in order to obtain the ability to cross the lines freely, then there are several people who may be able to do so."

"What are you saying?" Ryle asked, his voice dropping to a steely level of impatience.

"Lancer was once a normal man, son. He has… family within the Realm."

"Family who shares his blood. His bloodline." Granton stated, finishing the king's thought.

"But how does that tie to Cliff?" Ryle asked with a wave of his hand towards his brother. "Are you trying to tell me my brother is a blood relative of Lancer?"

King Eamon looked to Clifton and nodded. "Yes." He paused as several people gasped around the room. Clifton's eyes took on a hardness, laced with traces of uncertainty as he glanced at his father. "You both are." Eamon added.

Ryle's eyes widened, and he leaned forward, piercing his father with a firm gaze. "How?"

King Eamon glanced around the room. "I am sorry to have never shared this, but…"

Elizabeth reached over and squeezed his hand. "You are sharing it now, my Lord, and that is all that matters. Please continue."

He smiled at her sweetness and regret covered his face as he looked to his sons. "Lancer is your mother's brother." He stated calmly. "You share his blood through your mother's side. He is your uncle."

Ryle and Clifton both stared at their father in shock, as everyone at the table sat in silence. No one stirred as the awkwardness in the room created a stifling air.

"Welllll…." Prince Isaac interrupted the quiet. "That sure explains a lot."

King Anthony cast his son a look of warning that Isaac shrugged away. "So, we figured out why Prince Clifton can cross. We can assume Prince Ryle can cross. Any other relatives we can send over there?"

"Excuse me?" Ryle stated. "We are not crossing."

"Why not? Your brother did just fine. Perhaps a meeting with you and Edward is exactly what is needed. After all, future Captain of the Guard, I would think, militarily speaking, that you crossing to discuss matters with Edward may be quite beneficial."

"Easy for you to say." Ryle grumbled. "What happens if I cross and am not able to return?"

Isaac did not respond.

"Exactly." Ryle stated. "There are too many unknowns."

King Granton held up a hand to calm the tempers in the room. "The connection of blood relatives being able to cross makes the most sense. Perhaps we should mention this to Edward and hear his thoughts."

"I wish to write him a letter." Elizabeth stated. "Prince Clifton will take it to him for me."

"No." King Granton stated. "Prince Clifton and I will take it to him."

Alayna turned to her father. "Father, you are not well enough to ride. I highly…"

"It is decided." King Granton cut her off. "I wish to see my son. I know I am weak, but I wish to see Edward."

"Why do we not send you across, my king?" Isaac asked. Everyone turned, and King Anthony's eyes widened at his son's outburst. Granton studied him closely but with curiosity. Isaac lifted his hands at the grueling glares cast upon him and leaned forward. "Hear me out." He stated. "You are not feeling well, my king. And may I speak plainly?"

"Not sure what has stopped you from doing so in the past." Ryle barked.

Isaac acknowledged the prince with a forced smile of annoyance and then turned back to the king. Granton nodded. Isaac took a deep breath, knowing the words he spoke may offend the king. "My Lord… your health is… unstable."

Alayna straightened in her chair and her eyes narrowed as she poised herself ready to defend her father from Prince Isaac's assault.

"Would it be such a risk if we sent you across the boundary line? You would get to see your son. You would also be healed of your ailments. With Prince Clifton's ability to cross back and forth, you would still maintain open communication with the Realm while also being able to aid Prince Edward in the Unfading Lands."

"This is absurd." Ryle tossed out.

"I am not finished." Isaac stated in annoyance. "He would live. He will not live here. That is a certainty. Yes, Princess Alayna is to take the throne soon, but we could utilize the king's influence right under Lancer's nose. I think it is the least expected event to occur."

"But what of the strength of the Lands? Sending the King of the Realm over the lines will surely cause the boundary line to shift in great leaps." Eamon suggested.

"Not if his loyalties remain with the Realm." Isaac explained. "Do we really wish to lose our king? I do not mean to offend, princess, I believe you will be a worthy queen, but do you want to lose your father? We have an opportunity here, to conserve power and strength on our terms!" His voice rose in excitement. "Lancer believes the king is dying. If we send King Granton over the lines to Edward, Alayna will take the throne and Lancer will believe the king is dead. We could hide our biggest strength in the enemy's camp, and Lancer will never know."

"Meanwhile," Elizabeth chimed in with exuberance. "Edward and Father can establish an army of guards within the Lands that will aid the Realm when we wish to send troops across to defeat Lancer."

Isaac nodded at her in thanks and looked to King Granton. Granton shook his head and leaned back in his chair. The temptation was there, he thought. To live and not die. To cheat death and live a life with his son. A life he missed. Yet, he knew it was not the right decision. The Land of Unfading Beauty was evil. No good could come from using the Land's power to live longer. Life was meant to end. Death was inevitable. Granton embraced the life he had lived and the path of death he must take. Yes, he wished to spend more time with his daughters and Edward, but if his life were meant to end soon, he wished it to end naturally. He did not wish to use the evil and darkness of Lancer to his advantage. He wished for the Realm to conquer without the use of darkness.

"I will not cross." Granton stated. Elizabeth's hope of saving her father deflated.

"But Father, you could live." She pleaded.

He offered her a tender smile. "I know my dear. But the Lands are not to be trusted. I do not wish to use Lancer's evil for my personal gain. There is a time for everything, even death. I do not wish for the Realm to succumb to the use of darkness. I will remain within the Realm."

Isaac and Elizabeth exchanged disappointed glances, but both understood the king's position.

"That being said, I do believe there is truth in what Prince Isaac states. Prince Clifton can cross. We must utilize the open communication with Edward. This is a new advantage."

Prince Clifton nodded. "I will make daily visits to the boundary, my Lord."

"Yes." King Granton ordered, his eyes growing weary as he leaned heavily on the armrest of his chair. "Those who wish to prepare a letter for Edward may do so now. Prince Clifton and I will leave after breakfast in the morning to meet with him at the boundary. For now, we continue to celebrate our victory over the South, with a good night's rest." King Granton stood and he motioned for Clifton to help Elizabeth, who had grown severely quiet towards the end of the meeting due to the pain in her leg. She shifted uncomfortably in her chair.

Everyone stood to leave and Alayna looked to Elizabeth. "You need to take it easy, sister." She warned Elizabeth. "You will not heal if you demand to be present at every meeting."

"I wish to be present, Alayna. I refuse to be placed in solitary because I am weak. I can still serve." Elizabeth reached up as Clifton rounded the table and carefully lifted her into his arms.

"She is to go straight to her chambers, prince." Alayna ordered. "And no lingering. She needs her rest."

Clifton and Elizabeth both smirked at the scolding as Elizabeth laid her head on his shoulder. He could feel her tiredness and slowly made his way up the stairs.

∞

Prince Samuel sat at the bottom of the stairwell, his chin resting on his crossed arms as he leaned against his knees. He wished to join in on the Council meeting but knew he did not have a place within the Realm's Council just yet. He pondered over the death of his brother and struggled with feelings of loss and betrayal. His father. He sniffed back tears at the thought of his father's last breath. How must it have felt to be betrayed by his eldest son? Samuel's heart ached at the thought, and he hoped his father knew of his loyalty there at the end. His mind then wandered to the Northern guard that was held captive at his kingdom. His head perked up as he realized there would be no one there with the authority to free him... except for himself. He was the prince. Surely now that his brother was gone, he could go back to his kingdom and reestablish the Southern Kingdom. Perhaps Prince Ryle would assist him. He shook away the thought. No. No one would want a young man taking over an entire kingdom. No matter his rights to the throne, he was too young. King Granton would most likely place a steward over the throne until he became of age. Three years. Samuel sighed heavily at the disappointment. He glanced up as he heard footfalls on the stairs.

"Ah, Samuel." Prince Ryle smiled at the young prince, his former distrust now erased due to Samuel's loyal service. "You must get some rest, my friend. It has been an eventful day."

Samuel nodded. "Yes, my Lord."

Ryle stopped and eyed him curiously. "Is something wrong?"

Samuel shook his head. "No, my Lord. Just tired, I suppose."

"Hm." Ryle nodded taking Samuel at his word, though he could see something weighed on the boy's mind. "Well get some rest. Tomorrow King Granton and I wish to speak to you about your father's kingdom."

"Oh?"

"Yes, there is much to discuss." Ryle gave him a friendly pat on the back as he walked off. Samuel watched the confident prince stride through the main hall in the direction of his chambers. The future King of the East, Samuel thought. Would he ever compare to Prince Ryle? He became depressed at the thought of that comparison and turned at the slight touch to his elbow. Princess Melody smiled at him.

"I wondered if you might escort me to my chambers, my Lord?"

Samuel's shoulders relaxed, and he nodded. "Of course, my Lady." He allowed Melody to link her arm with his as he led her down the hall.

"You look as if you have lost your best friend, Prince Samuel. Are you sad over the loss of your brother?"

Samuel walked silently a few moments as he struggled with his answer. "Is it awful that I honestly do not know?"

"Not at all." Melody comforted.

"I fear I am struggling with my emotions over the loss of both my father and my brother. Both of them had corrupted views of the Realm, but they are still my family. What is to become of me now that they are gone?"

"I would think you would become king, my Lord." Melody stated without doubt.

Samuel took a shaky breath and laughed nervously. "I fear I am a long way from being ready for that position. I am not sure I ever will be ready."

"You are ready, Samuel. You risked your life for the Realm at the cost of your own loyalty to your kingdom. Nothing speaks of more honor than that." She praised him softly. They reached the door to her chambers and Prince Isaac opened the door to step out. His brow rose in curiosity at the sight of his sister on the arm of the young prince. A small smirk tilted his lips as they both bowed to him.

"Prince Isaac." Samuel stated humbly. He then released Melody's arm and bowed to her as well. "It was a pleasure, Princess Melody."

She curtsied and smiled. "Likewise, Prince Samuel."

Samuel watched as she entered the room, his gaze floating over Isaac's shoulder until he saw the princess no more. His brown gaze then fell upon the amused expression of her older brother and he fumbled. "Um, good night, my Lord." He blushed at the scrutiny and walked off.

Isaac stepped into the hall on a snicker and made his way to the portico. He wasn't quite sure where he was headed; all he knew was that he needed some air. Normally when he felt bogged down by a mood, he would find himself a lass and have some fun. Yet, that idea did not quite appeal to him at the moment. *Odd*, he thought. He never quite pictured himself not finding that idea appealing. His mouth straightened at the distasteful thought as he headed towards the stables. His mind replayed the events of the day. Was it really just this morning that the battles began? In a day's time, loyalties were tested and friendships were strengthened. He thought of Princess Elizabeth. *She was an honorable woman*, he thought. Full of fire and passion. What was he thinking throwing away his opportunity to wed a woman like that? He shook his head. They had fought together, a team. She was a skilled fighter and an even better friend. He found he valued her, and her opinion of him more than he valued his own father's. She saw through him. He should hope to never disappoint her again. Though he could not have her as his wife, Isaac knew she would forever be special to him. They had saved each other from death and perhaps their own pride. He eased himself down on a bench outside the stables and studied the surrounding landscape. It was dark, but his eyes could still make out the small flickers of lanterns throughout the kingdom and castle grounds. A kingdom, recovering from a fight, so that tomorrow's sun could bring about a new day of rebuilding. Sighing, he leaned his head back against the wooden boards of the stable house and closed his eyes. His body ached from the abuse of the day, and he was exhausted. Yet, he did not want to be within his chambers to rest. He found the castle stifling. His father's worried gaze smothered him. His sister's adoration smothered him. He did not deserve such praise or concern. He closed his eyes and listened to the sounds of the night until he drifted off to sleep.

∞

"You think it best to enter the main gate?" Edward asked Lancer as they trotted on horseback towards the boundary between the Unfading Lands and the Southern Kingdom.

"Yes. I want people to see us, Edward. We need to make our presence known." Lancer's shoulders bobbed up and down as his horse softly trotted.

"Are you sure I will be able to cross?" Edward asked as they neared the foggy veil. He saw the villagers tending to their land and homes, completely unaware of the darkness looming just beyond the boundary. Stalking them.

"Edward, really, must you question it again?" Lancer turned to him with a smirk. He was not annoyed at the questioning, but somewhat amused at Edward's innocence to what now ran through his veins.

"Come, bring your horse next to mine. We should cross together." Lancer waited until Edward's Triton lined up with his own. Lancer nodded and then proceeded. Edward felt the tingle as Triton's head made it through the veil. But when the fog reached Edward's hands, he felt an electrifying spark that shot him flying off the back of his horse and falling to the ground. Triton bucked at the sudden absence of his rider and turned back around towards Edward. Lancer faced Edward from the opposite side of the boundary and shook his head in disappointment. He crossed back over.

Edward's body ached from not only the fall but the absolute seizing that coursed through him at the impact. He still sat upon the meadow grass several yards from the boundary.

"It should have worked." Lancer stated. "We must try again. Get on your horse Edward."

"No." Edward replied, slowly rising to his feet. "That was painful, my Lord."

"Try again, Edward." Lancer ordered again, his face turning into a scowl.

Frustrated, Edward stormed over to the boundary line and walked into the fog, the ripple of light that shot through the veil sent him flying back and hitting his back against a tree. He slowly slumped to the ground, breathing heavily as his body tried to recover.

"Try again." Lancer stated.

Edward looked to him in disbelief. "You cannot be serious, my Lord? It will happen again, I assure you. My body cannot take another blow."

"You will heal. Try again." Lancer demanded again.

Edward rolled his eyes and stood to his feet. He thought of Prince Clifton, the emotion he must have felt at the time of his crossing. He was striving to save Elizabeth, out of love. *Perhaps if he thought of his family and Cecilia,* Edward thought. He took a deep breath as he ran towards the boundary line with a fierce scream. He immersed into the fog and felt the air rush out of his lungs as he was tossed back into the Lands and landed on his stomach, face down in the dirt.

Lancer laughed. "Well, I must say that was a new approach. We will try again another time, Edward. The Southern Kingdom can wait. It is really of no importance to us any way. Considering its defeat, I'm sure it is not at the top of King Granton's list either."

Edward brushed his hands over his knees as he walked towards Triton. Running a calming hand down his horse's snout, he softly patted his neck. Mounting into his saddle, he looked to Lancer. "I do not understand this, my Lord. Your blood should have worked."

"Perhaps it was not enough."

"But how much more can you sacrifice?"

"Not sure. I feel our attempts may be in vain." Lancer stated. "Don't worry though Edward, I still value your position in my guard and private council. I was never too pleased about you crossing back into the Realm in the first place. This just confirms my ill feeling." Lancer explained.

"I see."

"Don't be so disappointed, Edward. You are a great man meant for great things." Lancer praised.

"Yes, well, I believe I will take time to reflect upon that, my Lord. Do you wish for me to travel with you back to the castle, or may I dismiss myself?"

"You are dismissed. I believe I will visit my reflection chamber in your absence and see if there are other alternatives for us that we have yet to uncover."

"Very well. Good day." Edward nodded in farewell as he and Triton branched off from Lancer and headed the long way around the boundary line towards his clearing where he normally met Elizabeth. He wished he could see his sister but knew that the injuries she obtained during the battle would have left her in the care of the castle for quite some time.

As he ducked under the overhanging limbs of a willow, he emerged into his undisturbed and peaceful clearing. Slipping from his saddle, he grabbed his satchel and withdrew a piece of parchment. He would address a letter to Prince Clifton sharing the last few days' events. Perhaps his experiences would provide his friend some insight. As he walked towards his regular tree log, he stopped in his tracks. There beyond the veil of the boundary stood Prince Clifton with his father. Edward's heart pounded in his chest as he surveyed the older man in front of him. His father's face had aged considerably over the last five years. His once vibrant gaze was dim, and the lines of his face were etched deeply, beyond age, and into sickness. Despite the slumped shoulders and decaying frame, his father still held an air of regality that Edward found intimidating. Did he dare approach his father after all this time?

Clifton heard the king take a deep breath at the shock of seeing his youthful son round the corner of the trees in the Unfading Lands. Edward spotted them in equal surprise. Neither man moved an inch. Prince Clifton cleared his throat. "Perhaps, your Grace, we step a bit closer?"

King Granton moved robotically as Clifton lightly nudged him forward. Edward walked towards them as well, his steps slow and unsure.

Clifton smiled at him in greeting. "Where is that blasted rabbit?" He asked out loud as he glanced around the ground. He found Thatcher near the river and quickly snatched him. "If you wish to pass your letters to your son without me, you use this little guy, your Grace. Princess Elizabeth and Prince Edward have trained the rabbit to be their personal delivery service." Granton studied the small ball of fur and lightly stroked its head. "They use an animal?"

"Yes." Clifton replied. "Animals pass freely through the veil."

"I had heard such news." Granton replied.

Clifton placed the rabbit back to the ground and it scampered off into the reeds near the river. "However, today I volunteer to be your carrier." He extended his open palm and King Granton gently laid his folded piece of parchment into Clifton's hand.

"If you give me just a few moments, I will be right back."

Granton nodded silently, his wonder over the whole situation keeping him quiet. He watched as Clifton stepped to the edge of the boundary. Taking a deep breath, Clifton took a step over the line and entered the Lands. King Granton's eyes widened as he watched, and he slowly lowered himself to the large rock Elizabeth normally occupied.

Edward smiled in greeting as Clifton exhaled a relieved breath. "I must admit I was quite nervous to cross."

"Aye, I imagine so."

"Your father wished to give you a letter." Clifton stated and handed the parchment to Edward.

"I cannot believe he came to the boundary line." Edward stared at his father who studied them closely.

"Aye, he insisted he bring his letter personally, along with several others." Clifton reached into his tunic pocket and withdrew two more letters. "One from your sister Alayna, and of course, the other from Elizabeth."

Edward chuckled and ran a hand through his dark hair. "I am honored by all the responses. I must admit these surprise me. Not Elizabeth's, but Alayna and my father."

"He wishes to converse with you for a bit. Do you have the time?"

"Yes. I just left Lancer's company. I should be good for a few hours." Edward replied.

"Did you find out anymore news?"

"Some. He believes his blood is the answer to everything. He stabbed me last night and mixed our blood so that I may cross into the Realm to survey the damage of the Southern Kingdom. We attempted my crossing this morning and it failed." Edward ran a hand over his chest where he still felt the driving of Lancer's blade.

"You could not cross?" Clifton asked, his brow furrowed.

"No. I'm thinking it must not have been enough."

"I think you are correct." Clifton stated. "We also believed Lancer's blood held the key to crossing."

"But how does that explain you?" Edward asked with a wave of his hand at Clifton's figure.

"My father just confessed in last night's Council meeting that I am a blood relative of Lancer. He is my mother's brother and my uncle. We believe those in his bloodline have the ability to cross." Clifton answered.

Edward's eyes widened. "You are his kin?"

"Apparently so."

Edward paced around the clearing. "Does this mean your brother will have the ability to cross?"

"We believe so but are not willing to test his crossing unless absolutely necessary."

"Aye. Good idea. This is a wonder." Edward stood baffled and glanced towards his father once more. "I guess I should return my father's letter."

"Yes. I will leave him here for a bit. He wishes to stay. I must warn you that his health is not well, and the ride over has made him weak. I will return for him around noon." Clifton made his way back to the boundary line and turned. "He is not upset with you, Prince Edward, just so you know. I believe he wishes to make amends before his death."

Edward nodded, and his familiar blue eyes grew glassy. "I hate seeing him like this."

"We all do." Clifton replied. "He is a good man, a strong king."

"Long ago I would have disagreed with you, Prince Clifton. But I was young and selfish. I did not see what all I had in front of me."

"It happens to the best of us, prince." Clifton nodded towards him in assurance. "See you in a few hours. Oh, and I must sincerely ask that you write Elizabeth a letter. She would be a complete sore sort if I did not bring something back to her."

Edward chuckled and nodded. "Of course. Thank you, Clifton."

Edward watched as the prince stepped back through the fog and over towards his father.

"Well, is he well?" Granton asked curiously.

"Yes. Very. He says he has quite a few hours to spare, so you two should not be interrupted."

"Thank you, Prince Clifton." Granton roamed his gaze around the small clearing and spotted Elizabeth's arena and marks carved into the clay. "She really did have another life over here, didn't she?"

"Yes." Clifton smirked as he thought of the first time Elizabeth showed him her oasis. "This place is special to her."

"As are you." Granton stated, noting the small flush that crept up the prince's neck. "I do not wish to embarrass you, Prince Clifton, I just want to say thank you. I have spent many a night praying for a man who could love my Elizabeth for who she is. I am most grateful she found that with you."

Clifton tilted his head at the sentimental conversation and eyed the king carefully. "Are you feeling alright, my Lord?"

Granton chuckled but his lips held a sad smile. "Quite fine. Please, when you return for me, will you bring your father?"

Clifton eased to his knee before the king and studied him. "I will, but only if you are honest with me, my King."

Smirking and biting back a small laugh, Granton lightly patted him on his shoulder. "You are a good lad, aren't you? I am fine, my son. Please do not worry over me."

Clifton rose back to his feet and nodded. "Your son will be sending you a letter soon. I will send him Thatcher. Just be ready to catch the small creature when he sends him back over."

"Of course." Granton watched as Clifton sent the small rabbit across the line to Edward. He then bowed towards King Granton and slipped through the trees back towards his horse.

∞

"I wish to wear my cream corset and lace." Elizabeth demanded as she leaned against her pillows and crossed her arms in annoyance. She studied her sister at the foot of her bed and scowled.

"No." Alayna stated without even a glance up from her papers. "You will wear a new white corset and your dress skirts will be the pale blue of the Eastern Kingdom. The ribbons to tie will be white as well."

Elizabeth blew an air of frustration and her hair fluttered over her forehead. "Perhaps we should make sure I am able to walk before we plan my walk down the aisle, sister."

"You will be fine." Alayna looked up and smiled. "With father's health failing, I believe an urgency should be placed upon your wedding, sister."

"Yes, but I am not even fully recovered yet." Elizabeth countered.

"I know." Alayna sighed as she slipped from her looming position and sat on the edge of Elizabeth's bed. "But with the war against the South now over, King Eamon and his sons must return to their kingdom to assess the damage to their villages and rebuild. It is a perfect time for Prince Clifton and you to get married that way you can make the journey with them and be introduced to the Eastern Kingdom after such a bleak time. People will rejoice."

"I do not wish to leave just yet." Elizabeth replied. "Not with Father feeling the way he is and with our own kingdom out of sorts."

"The Realm and the kingdom have been through much lately. That is why I think a joyful event is necessary." Alayna explained.

"But what of Father? I wish to be here with him in his last few months. I could not bear it if I were gone and he passed." Elizabeth held her sister's sympathetic gaze and they both sat quietly, pondering over the thought of not having their father around.

"I do not wish to think on the subject." Alayna stated quietly.

"Me either." Elizabeth echoed. "But it will happen, Alayna. Are you ready to lead the Realm? Fully?"

"Is anyone ready for such a task?"

"I imagine not." Elizabeth replied in understanding.

Alayna studied her sister's wounded leg, the stump covered by the mauve blankets and coverings of Elizabeth's bed. "I believe we found a craftsman who can create you a false leg and foot." She reported.

Elizabeth's brow rose. "Oh?"

"Yes. He claims to have made them for members of the guard in the past. Mosiah attests to his honesty and praises his craftsmanship."

"So, I shall be walking around with a wooden peg as though I were a pirate." Elizabeth held her hand over one eye as she quirked her mouth in what she hoped was a piratey sneer. Alayna laughed. "Only if you wish to. I figure it will aid in your stability."

"Yes. I think it would be quite fun actually."

Alayna shook her head in bewilderment. "You are so strong, little sister. Sometimes I wonder if I should pass the throne to you."

Elizabeth shook her head. "No, thank you. It is all yours." Elizabeth winked. "Besides, perhaps you will soon have a prince of your own to share the burden with."

Alayna's smile slowly faded, and she stood. She adjusted her lavender skirts and picked up her parchments. "We shall see. Now, where were we? Oh yes, your dress."

Elizabeth groaned and then leaned back against her pillows and closed her eyes as Alayna continued drowning her in wedding details.

"Now, Princess Melody and Prince Isaac will stand with us. Melody with me and Isaac with Ryle." Alayna stated, making a small notation.

Elizabeth's eyes popped open. "Isaac." She stated.

Alayna glanced up. "What about him?"

"Have you seen him today?"

"No." Alayna stated. "But that is no surprise. Word around the castle is that he never made it back to his chambers last night. No doubt enjoying his victorious day with some… female entertainment."

Elizabeth shook her head. "No. That is not like him."

Alayna tilted her head and wrinkled her brow in disbelief.

"Well, not anymore." Elizabeth added. "Could you see if you can find him?"

"Whatever for?"

"I wish to ask him a favor." Elizabeth answered.

"Lizzy, the man is a cad. Yes, he saved your life, and I am forever grateful for that, but I do not wish for you to have fanciful thoughts of him making a turnaround. He is still the man he was."

"No, he isn't." Elizabeth replied.

"Yes, he is." Alayna countered firmly. "His disappearance last night is proof of that."

"You do not know him as I do. He has changed." Elizabeth defended the prince wholeheartedly. She knew Isaac had changed, had seen it with her own eyes.

"I believe you are wrong."

"Yes, well you were not there, Sister. You did not see the way he fought and the choices he had to make. Whether you choose not to believe, or whether he chooses to cover it up, Prince Isaac is an honorable man." Elizabeth's voice had grown louder in the heat of the moment and carried down the hall. "I stand by his newfound character."

"Quite loudly too." Prince Ryle's voice drifted into the room from the open doorway and had both women turning to him in surprise. "I hope I am not intruding on anything."

Alayna and Elizabeth replied but in opposition of one another. Alayna pierced Elizabeth with a firm gaze as she waved away her sister's negative response. "Please, Prince Ryle, join us. We were just discussing wedding plans for your brother and my opinionated sister." Alayna finished.

Elizabeth lightly tossed a decorative pillow her sister's direction, Alayna's mouth widening at the contact as she felt the silk cushion hit her cheek. She blushed under Prince Ryle's amused expression and cleared her throat as she stepped several paces away from Elizabeth's bed to avoid future assaults. "What brings you by, my Lord?" She asked.

Prince Ryle studied her carefully and then dropped his voice to barely above a whisper. "I wondered if your father had discussed my military wishes any further, my Queen."

"Oh." Alayna looked to Elizabeth's now dozing figure and motioned for him to follow her outside into the hall. Once the door closed behind them, she smiled warmly. "I do not believe the matter has been discussed with your father as of yet, but my father accepted Mosiah's resignation this morning. I believe the discussion will take place at tonight's Council meeting."

A relieved smile fluttered over his handsome face and he grabbed her hand in thanks, the contact making them both blush and separate quickly. "Apologies, my Queen."

She waved away the comment and then began walking towards the main stairwell. "I was just addressing your family's departure with my sister. I plan to have arrangements for her wedding complete today, so that she may accompany Prince Clifton back to your kingdom. I feel the occasion will offer a sense of hope to the people after such a war."

"Indeed it will. And how does Princess Elizabeth feel about being the future Queen of the East?" Ryle asked.

"I have yet to tell her." Alayna stated as she stepped off the last stair into the main hall.

"You have not told her that marriage to my brother will lead her to the throne?" Ryle's gaze narrowed as he studied Alayna.

"No. One step at a time, Prince Ryle. We have yet to even tell your father of your decision. I do not wish to worry or burden my sister until the matter is a certainty."

"Burden her?" Ryle asked. "You think she will not want to be Queen?"

"It has never been her desire." Alayna stated simply.

"But what of my brother? Would she back out of their marriage if he were to be announced future King?"

Alayna sighed and then stopped in her tracks. She placed a small hand on Ryle's arm. "I do not think Elizabeth would ever pass up the opportunity of marrying your brother, Prince Ryle. She loves him."

Relief washed over the man's face.

"All I am saying is that the idea might take some getting used to." Smiling softly, she squeezed his elbow before walking away. Ryle studied her figure as she left, the lavender skirts sashaying behind her. Elegant and regal. *A true queen*, he thought. A queen he would serve faithfully. He turned at the sound of boots entering the hall and found his brother walking towards him with a wide smile.

"You seem pleased this morning." Ryle commented as Clifton glanced around and spotted Alayna's retreating back. "I am. I have successfully left King Granton conversing with his son at the boundary, and both men were eager to talk. I think it is a very good morning. Which reminds me, King Granton wished for me to bring Father back with me when I returned to retrieve him."

"I believe he was in the conservatory with Anthony and Melody last I checked." Ryle offered.

Clifton smiled. "I may wander my way upstairs and tell Elizabeth the good news. She will be quite pleased, and mad as a hen to have missed out on it."

Ryle chuckled. "As much as I think she would enjoy your visit, you may hold off for a while, Cliff. I just left her chambers and she was sleeping."

Disappointment washed over Clifton's face. "Oh. Very well then."

Ryle laughed and slapped him on the shoulder. "You can see her later, brother. No need for the sour face."

Clifton grinned, and he shrugged. Placing a hand on his heart he sighed. "She does funny things to me, brother. I never thought I could be so happy."

"I am happy for you, as is everyone else. We all see the love between the two of you. It is one of the most encouraging topics during this dark time. It is also why Princess Alayna wishes to wed the two of you by week's end." Ryle explained.

Surprise fluttered over Clifton's face. "Week's end? Why so soon?"

"She feels the marriage will be uplifting to the people of the Realm and also an opportunity to transport Elizabeth back with us when we leave for the East."

"I see." Clifton rubbed a hand over his chin. "That does put a rush on things, now doesn't it?"

"Were you hoping to drag the engagement out longer?" Ryle asked with amusement.

"No. I mean… well, sort of. I had hoped Elizabeth would have enough time to fully heal before such an endeavor."

Nodding, Ryle began walking towards the conservatory. Clifton fell into step beside him. "I'm afraid that will not be the case, brother. I think this may just be the first surprise in store for you."

Clifton's brow rose as he pondered his brother's words. He sensed a tension in his brother's demeanor and wondered if Ryle were upset with him for something. Before he could lose himself to deep thoughts, they entered the conservatory to find their father.

"My boys!" Eamon greeted. "I see you two have awoken to find the day beautiful."

"Yes." Ryle stated as he found a seat next to Melody on one of the long sofas. He nodded in greeting as she continued working on a stitching pattern of some sort.

"Cliff, how is that future wife of yours?" Eamon asked cheerfully.

"Apparently resting. I have yet to see her this morning." Clifton eased into a chair opposite the two kings. "I spent the morning taking King Granton to the boundary line to visit with Edward."

Both kings looked at him in surprise.

"Granton rode out this morning?"

"Yes. He was weak, but he insisted." Clifton replied. "He also wished for me to bring you with me when I returned, Father."

Eamon and Anthony exchanged concerned glances. "Anthony will come too." His father stated firmly, booking no room for argument. "We should go now."

His father stood quickly. "Ryle, please fetch my attendant and tell him to ready our horses."

"Of course."

"Is something wrong, Father?" Clifton asked curiously as he sensed the urgency behind his father's actions and King Anthony's willingness to ride out at a moment's notice.

Clifton held up his hand, "Whoa now Father, I told King Granton I would return for him at noon."

"No, we ride now, Cliff. Hurry now and fetch your horse."

Eamon rushed by him towards the main entrance as his horse was brought around from the stables.

Henry still lurked at the front of the castle retrieving special attention from several children in the market square as Clifton bounded down the steps. He smiled as the kids looked up at him in surprise and adoration. He vaulted into his saddle and clicked his reins to quickly catch up to his father.

CHAPTER 12

Dear Father,

> My, is it good to see you! I fear I am at a loss for words in your presence. I have not read your letter as of yet, but will while you read this one.
>
> Much has happened the last few weeks. Elizabeth to be married. The South's uprising. The battle in the East. It is times like this the Realm is fortunate to have you as king. I do not wish to waste time with pleasantries of welcome and longing. We both know there are more dangerous topics of discussion. However, I wish to take a moment and soak you in. It has been a long five years, Father, and I do not wish to cover up the fact that I have missed you."

Edward watched as his father read his letter, the slight tremor in the king's lips proving he was moved by his son's words.

> I have heard of your failing health. Elizabeth keeps me informed, and now so does Prince Clifton. I hate to see you ill, Father. I trust that you have tried all methods of treatment for your condition, so I will not berate you on possibly seeking wisdom

elsewhere. I am sure with Alayna and Elizabeth hovering over you, their attention is enough at the moment.

Elizabeth tells me Alayna has begun to take the throne of the Realm. I am proud of her. I am proud that you have allowed her to do so. She will be a great queen. I also know that Prince Clifton and Elizabeth are to be wed soon. I cannot tell you how pleased I am to hear of this. He is a most splendid match for her. They will be very happy together and she will forever be loved.

And speaking of love, I had hoped to introduce you to my Cecilia, but she is currently with the other Uniters within the woods. I would say perhaps next time you visit you two can meet, but I sense this may be our only opportunity to share together. So perhaps in another life. She has made my time here in the Lands better than could be expected.

By now, you must have learned of my position with Lancer's guard. I assure you Father that my heart and loyalties will always remain with the Realm.

Granton looked up at his son and offered a sad smile. Not disappointed in his son, but disappointed that he had missed so much time getting to know the man before him. His son was an honorable man. He sniffed back the tears in his throat as he began to pen a response.

My dearest Edward,

I cannot tell you how it feels to gaze upon your face after so many years. A face, I must admit, that has plagued my mind every day and every night since your departure. I am sorry, my son. I would like to continue my apologies, but my first letter I wrote you that Prince Clifton handed to you, speaks more on that line. This letter I wish to just speak with you, a task I have longed for quite some time.

Yes, the last few weeks have been full of battle and war, but hope settled upon the horizon, the kingdoms united in a way I have never seen. Though Prince Eric of the South corrupted his purpose,

Prince Samuel, has emerged a most pleasing future king. He served us well over the last few days. He will also serve well under Alayna. Alayna will be a wonderful Queen of the Realm. She is ready for the position.

Despite Prince Eric's hopes of destroying the Realm, I fear his assaults only made us stronger. Our allies are close. I feel we can weather the next wave of storms successfully. I have read your letters to Elizabeth, and I know the bigger threat is Lancer. The Land of Unfading Beauty has been a silent threat for many years, and I know it is but a sleeping giant. I thank you for your insight and sacrifice to provide the Realm with information. But please be careful. In the next few months, your presence in the Lands will be of great importance to Alayna and the Realm's guards. A war is coming, Edward. I feel it within my soul. Your role is but just beginning. I am pleased with the newest revelation of Prince Clifton's ability to cross. Lancer's bloodline is strong and may be his very undoing. Utilize the friends you have in the Realm, Edward. Sacrifices will need to be made, lives will be lost, but the Lands must be defeated. Lancer must be destroyed. If the darkness and evil he possesses spreads any further, we will all come to ruin. It must be contained and destroyed.

King Granton slipped the parchment upon Thatcher's neck and watched as the brown ball of fur slipped across the veil straight towards Edward. He gasped and held a fist to his heart as a sharp spasm pierced through his body. His lungs tightened, and his breaths sputtered as he tried to calm the passing wave of pain. He spotted Edward's gaze of concern and waved his attention away and to the letter he held in his hands. Edward lifted his letter and read.

Granton eased onto the rock and rested. He felt the cold sweat dripping down his back and the heat of the morning sun filtering through the trees on his face. He watched as Edward read his words, his son, his handsome son. A leader, a guard, a Uniter. His lips twitched into a sad smile as his thoughts then carried to his daughters. He withdrew the letters from his emerald cape's pocket. One for Alayna and one for Elizabeth. He brushed his thumb over their names as his wheezing breath shuddered.

∞

"The East's horses must be groomed and ready for departure come tomorrow." Prince Ryle ordered the stableman. "We will be departing after the wedding of Prince Clifton and Princess Elizabeth." The lanky caretaker bowed and set about his duties as Prince Ryle stepped out of the stables to walk back to the castle. He stopped as he stumbled upon Prince Isaac leaning against the wooden planks of the structure, sound asleep. The prince had not bathed from the prior day's battles, and his hair lay matted from the morning's dew. Ryle knelt beside the man and lightly nudged his shoulder. Prince Isaac did not move. Concern bloomed in Ryle's crystal blue eyes as he nervously placed a hand to the man's neck to test for a pulse. His fingers found cold skin and he jerked back and fell to his behind as Prince Isaac jolted from his slumber. The prince reached for his blade out of habit as Ryle held up his hands in surrender. Isaac towered over him. "What are you doing?" He barked.

"My apologies, Prince Isaac. You looked… I was just making sure you had a pulse."

"You thought I was dead?" An amused smirk tilted the prince's lips as he extended a hand to help Ryle to his feet.

"Well you were sleeping as if you were and your whereabouts have been unknown since yesterday evening."

Isaac grunted in response. "I wished for some air last night. I must have fallen asleep and forgotten to make my way indoors."

"You mean you have been in this very spot since last night?"

"Yes." Isaac sheathed his sword and brushed his pant legs. "I must say, I do look a bit ragged. Perhaps I shall go bathe. I suppose I now see why you thought I was dead."

Ryle chuckled and nodded. "Yes, your appearance was quite sobering. I am pleased to find you alive and well."

"So, what have I missed so far this morning? It looks almost midday."

"Aye, it is. King Granton left early this morning with my brother for the boundary line to speak with Edward. My brother and both our fathers have gone to retrieve him. Other than that, the only other matters of the day are Princess Alayna planning Princess Elizabeth's wedding."

Isaac nodded. "And what of the villages? Are Mosiah and the guards handling the clean up?"

"Yes. I will be riding out shortly to assist."

"Well," Isaac inhaled a deep breath and stretched his back. "I guess that means a relaxing day for me. Everything is being handled already."

Ryle rolled his eyes at the prince's aloofness. Princess Alayna was right about him, his heart had not changed.

"If you should wish to seek out company, I know Princess Elizabeth wished to speak with you." Ryle stated. He then noted a swift change in the prince's face. Worry flashed in his dark eyes. "Is she alright? Did she catch fever?" He began pacing down the portico towards the castle.

"No." Prince Ryle stated, causing Isaac's steps to slow. "She just wished to talk with you, I believe."

"Oh..." Isaac's brow rested, and a small smile tilted the corner of his lips. "Well, I guess I will visit her chambers for a bit if she is not resting and see what is on her mind."

He turned to walk away, and Ryle grabbed his arm in a firm clasp. Isaac glanced down at the prince's restraint and then to his fierce gaze. "Problem?"

"The Princess' sudden interest in you causes worry to the future Queen, Prince Isaac. Should you have ill intent against her or my brother, I wish you to know where I stand." Ryle's voice held a threatening note and Isaac shrugged away from his grasp.

"Yes, well, your feelings are noted." Without providing a defense or even a reasoning, Isaac decided to let the prince stew about his evasiveness. He knew people doubted his character, but Elizabeth knew his heart. He bounded up the stairwell to her chamber door and knocked. Mary answered almost immediately and smiled in welcome. "My Lord."

Isaac bowed. "Mary." He greeted. "Is the princess up for company?"

Mary stepped back for him to enter and waved him ahead. "Miss Elizabeth, Prince Isaac is here to see you." Mary called into the room. Isaac's gaze adjusted to the dim lighting of lanterns in the room and he glanced around in search of Elizabeth. He noted the presence of a man seated in a chair by her fireplace. The man nodded in greeting.

"Isaac! I'm so glad you are here." Elizabeth's voice carried from behind her trifold changing boards and she poked her head around the side. "You are just in time."

His smile quirked and his brows rose. "In time for you changing? Why Princess, I did not realize we were to meet like this."

She rolled her eyes and laughed. "In your dreams, prince." She heard him laugh as she slowly eased herself from behind the boards. She stumbled slightly and gripped the side of the wooden frame as she emerged wearing her trousers.

"Ah, I see you have resorted back to your lesson attire." Isaac stated. He noted the pant leg of her left side rolled up to her knee and a series of leather straps connecting from her waist and shoulders and wrapped around a wooden frame of a half leg.

"Prince Isaac, I would like you to meet my new leg." Elizabeth motioned to the dark wood and giggled as she attempted to stand straight without holding the changing boards. She held her breath as the pain shot through her leg and up her spine. Isaac sensed her discomfort but knew her pride held back her gasp.

"It is a beauty." Prince Isaac complimented. "In fact, I believe you now have the prettiest legs I've ever seen."

Elizabeth laughed. "Coming from you, I take that as an extreme compliment." She teased playfully. He shrugged his shoulders and grinned.

She took a cautious step forward. Grimaced. Softly moaned in pain. "My wound is still not fully healed. It's rather tender. But Mary bandaged it with plenty of cushion."

"You do not need to rush this, Elizabeth." Isaac stepped forward and extended his arm. She gladly accepted and allowed him to lead her slowly around the room. The other man stood and surveyed her mobility. "He is the talented craftsman for my leg." Elizabeth motioned towards the man in a friendly gesture of appreciation.

"I see." Isaac stopped and unlinked her arm from his and released her. "Now you try it alone." He had made sure to leave her standing in the middle of the room, so she did not have a support system to catch her. Elizabeth stepped forward onto her wooden leg and quickly brought her next leg forward. It was a hobbled gait, but Isaac knew she would soon walk fluidly as if the wood was as much her leg as the real one. He nodded in approval and stepped back forward.

"Pretty soon you will be asking me to let you ride Lenora." Mary commented from across the room in pride.

"I wish to see my horse soon enough." Elizabeth added. "But I fear I must sit for a bit now. I am quite sore."

Isaac led her over to a sofa and eased her down. "Please sit, Isaac. I had hoped to see you."

"Aye, I bumped into Prince Ryle and he stated you wished to see me."

"Yes, I fear the next few days may be hectic with the wedding and all. Plus, my departure for the Eastern Kingdom." She looked around her room and sighed. "I love it here, it will be hard to leave."

"You will visit often, I am sure."

"Yes, but I know it will be hard to come as often as I wish. You leave for the West after the wedding as well."

He nodded. "Yes, it is time we head back to our own kingdom, I'm afraid."

"You will be missed." Elizabeth admitted.

Isaac snickered. "By you, perhaps. However, I feel most will be relieved by my absence."

"Yes, I am sure they will." Elizabeth reached over and squeezed his hand. "I hope, Prince Isaac, that you will come visit me in the East. I wish to maintain our friendship, as well as my friendship with your sister."

Isaac nodded and felt a tightness in his chest at her kindness. "As soon as you and the prince are settled, all you have to do is send word." He winked at her and she beamed, her blue eyes sparkling.

"Good. Selfishly, I wish we could all stay here and live together as one."

Isaac laughed. "You honestly think Prince Ryle and I could live together?"

Elizabeth grinned. "It would keep life interesting, wouldn't it?"

"You are an optimist, Elizabeth. It is one of the many characteristics I admire about you." Isaac admitted. "I trust you know that I will always be there for you and your family, no matter the cost or sacrifice."

Elizabeth tilted her head to the side as a sweet smile bloomed over her face. "I know."

They sat for a moment in silence as Mary bustled around the room. Isaac then slapped his hands to his knees. "Well, I guess I should leave you, Elizabeth. I have wasted most of my day with sleep, and I desire to bathe. I find I am quite odorous."

Elizabeth laughed. "Yes, I wondered why you had yet to change."

"Well I accidentally fell asleep at the stables last night."

"The stables?" She laughed and shook her head.

"Alone, mind you." He added with a smirk. "I was just too tired to make the trek back into the castle, I guess."

"Well please, do not let me keep you." Elizabeth eased to her feet and waved away his offer of help. "No, I will walk you to the door."

Nodding in approval, Isaac walked slowly beside her.

∞

Clifton dismounted at the edge of the clearing as his father and King Anthony did the same. He led them beyond the branches into the opening where the Rollings River rushed through and King Granton sat. "My King," Clifton began, "I am sorry to return early, but my father insisted he come immediately." Clifton stated as he walked towards the older gentleman. Clifton glanced towards the boundary line, Prince Edward's face full of worry. He then rushed to King Granton's side. The king's chin rested against his chest as if he had decided to take a rest. Clifton lightly nudged his shoulder and Granton's body began to tumble over. He caught the king around the shoulders.

"Father!" He yelled in panic as he eased King Granton's body to the ground.

King Eamon's distraction with Edward across the line quickly vanished when he saw the nature of his son's scream. He and Anthony rushed forward and knelt beside Granton.

"Come now, Granton." Eamon stated as he lightly slapped the man's pale cheeks.

"It is no use, Eamon." Anthony's voice was sad, and his eyes held worry.

"No. He will rise." Eamon argued as he lightly nudged the king once more. He then ran a thumb over Granton's eyelids, lifting the thin layer of skin to see his eyes. A sob escaped his lips as he let the lids drop closed.

"Is he dead?" Clifton asked, his own voice quavering at the thought.

"Yes." King Eamon leaned back on his haunches in defeat. He met the wide eyes of Edward and nodded, the young prince falling to his knees in anguish and his face falling to his hands.

"We must get him back to the castle." Anthony stated, easing his hands underneath Granton's body. Eamon quickly lifted from the other side. "Cliff, you must help us carry him."

Clifton stood in shock. King Granton was dead. He had led him to his death. He knew the king was too weak to make the journey, yet he brought him. Elizabeth would be devastated. She would surely not want to marry him after he killed her father.

"Clifton!" His father barked. "Come lad. We need your help."

Clifton turned towards Edward as the saddened prince watched his father being carried away. He motioned towards the ground beside the rock King Granton had sat and there laid two pieces of parchment. *Elizabeth and Alayna*, Clifton read. He tucked them into his tunic pocket and bowed towards Edward. Edward held a hand over his heart and clinched his hand in a fist. Clifton nodded his regards and disappeared through the trees. He reached his father's side in time to help lift King Granton's body over the side of his horse.

"I must say this is not how I wished for this to happen." Eamon stated quietly.

King Anthony echoed his sentiments. "We get him back to the castle. The Princess's will need a moment to say their goodbyes before we send him down the river."

"Down the river?" Clifton asked.

"In the ceremonial burial." Eamon replied. "But let us get him back before we discuss this any further." Clifton could tell his father's own sadness threatened to overcome him if they did not start moving. He jumped into his saddle and they slowly made their way back to the castle.

∞

Samuel watched as Prince Clifton's head emerged on the horizon along with the other kings. His eyes squinted as he noticed the extra body they carried with them and the significance of the emerald robe draped over him. His eyes widened as he jumped to his feet from his seat along the parapet and began yelling for Princess Alayna and Prince Ryle.

Coming to the front entrance, Ryle grabbed Samuel by the shoulders as the boy almost rushed passed him. "What is it, Samuel?"

The young man's eyes held unshed tears as he glanced up. "Your father returns, my Lord." Prince Ryle glanced up and spotted his family. His blue gaze then drifted to the limp body of King Granton. "Fetch the Queen, Samuel. Hurry!" He released the boy into a sprint and rushed his way down the front steps, intercepting his father on foot.

"What happened?!" He reached up and began hoisting the weight of the king on his shoulders. Clifton dismounted and helped his brother as King Anthony and King Eamon rushed them inside and out of sight of the market.

Once indoors, the brothers eased Granton's body onto a sofa in the conservatory as Alayna entered in a panic. As soon as her gaze spotted her father's body, a sob escaped her lips as she stumbled to her knees by his side. Ryle stepped forward, but his father placed a restraining hand on his chest. "Let her be." He whispered sadly.

"Father?!" Alayna shook his shoulders, knowing full well he had passed, but beside herself to allow him to. She grabbed his hand and pressed his palm to her cheek, the cold skin making the tears in her eyes spill forth faster. "M-my Lords," she turned, her tear streaked face breaking everyone's hearts as they all struggled with their emotions. "H-how did this happen?"

Clifton felt the shame swallow him whole as she looked at him for an answer.

"It was his time, Alayna." Eamon spoke softly. "He passed in peace."

"This cannot happen now." She begged as she looked back at her father's still body. Her shoulders began to shake as she leaned her head against Granton's shoulder.

"We must fetch Princess Elizabeth." Anthony stated.

Alayna's head popped up. "No, leave Elizabeth be."

"But she must be told." Anthony countered.

"She will be. I do not wish her to see my father this way."

"Alayna," Prince Ryle began, stepping towards her and speaking in a compassionate voice. "Elizabeth would want to be here."

Alayna turned away from his sweet gaze and ignored him.

"I will fetch her." Clifton stated. "I… need to be the one to tell her."

Eamon gripped his arm before he left. "This is not your fault, son."

Clifton shrugged his shoulders in defeat and slipped from his father's grasp. Eamon watched his son ascend the stairs weighted by guilt of the king's death. He prayed his son realized his act of taking Granton to see Edward was exactly what Granton wanted. Granton wished to see his son before he died, and he received his dying wish. His son helped the king. He did not kill him.

"We must prepare the tombs." Alayna wiped the back of her hand across her cheeks as she attempted to sniff back her tears.

"But my Lady, a river burning is custom." Anthony stated.

Alayna's eyes narrowed at the king and she stood. "I do not wish to burn my father, King Anthony, no matter the custom. We prepare the tombs. I will send Samuel to fetch the priest."

Ryle watched as Alayna exited the room, leaving her tears, her pain, and her worries lying with her father. She was Queen now, and the woman had erected a wall over her emotions in preparation for the role. He shook his head in disappointment as he watched her order Samuel to the chapel.

∞

Clifton knocked on Elizabeth's door and was surprised to see it swing back quickly and see her standing before him. He noted Prince Isaac standing next to her and his brow rose in curiosity.

"Ah, my prince," Elizabeth beamed. "I wondered when I would see you today. I must say, it makes my heart happy you have come." Elizabeth's smile faltered when she noted the stormy gaze of pain Clifton held.

"What is the matter?" She asked immediately, pulling his hand for him to enter. Isaac remained to listen.

"I am sorry, Elizabeth." He squeezed her hand in return as she walked him towards the sofa and sat beside him. She motioned for Isaac to sit across from them. She lightly ran a hand over his hair as he rested his face in his hands to gather courage to voice the issue at hand.

"Clifton?" She asked quietly. "What is it?"

He glanced up and his green eyes held sympathy and hurt. "I went to fetch your father from the boundary line. He wished to visit Edward this morning." He spotted Isaac straightening in his seat as if he knew the report already. He reached for her hands and held them in his own. "When I arrived—" he bit his bottom lip a moment to calm his emotions. "When I arrived, your father was… dead."

Elizabeth's eyes widened and tears immediately sprang to them. "W-what? No. You must be mistaken. M-my father— he is fine. He is well." Her words trailed off as tears began to spill down her cheeks and she glanced to Isaac. "D-did you know this?"

He shook his head.

"W-where is he?"

"Downstairs. In the conservatory." Clifton stated. Elizabeth slowly stood to her feet.

"Take me to him." She demanded.

Clifton stood and grabbed her hands in his, brushing his thumbs over her knuckles. "Princess Alayna did not wish for you to see him just yet."

"When have I ever cared what my sister thought?!" Elizabeth belted. "Take me to him now, Clifton."

He nodded, his mouth set in a firm line. He turned, and they made their way to the door. "Isaac, please come." Elizabeth stated over her shoulder as she limped towards the door.

Isaac quickly rushed towards her and swept her into his arms as Mary and Clifton rushed onward. The Eastern prince had yet to notice Elizabeth's temporary leg. They reached the bottom of the stairs and Isaac could see the pain in Elizabeth's gaze from her wound, but the stubborn woman wished to see her father. When they reached the conservatory, all eyes fell upon her. Equal shock to seeing a woman in trousers as well as to the wooden attachment strapped around her, the two kings watched as Isaac set her to her feet and she slowly made her way to her father's figure. It was then that Clifton noticed her false leg, the slight limp to her steps, and the watchful eye from the prince of the West. Elizabeth eased onto the edge of the sofa and placed her hand over her father's hands upon his chest. She studied his face and a watery smile fluttered over her own. "He is at peace now." She stated quietly. Looking up to the other kings, they both nodded. She swiped away her tears as she tenderly adjusted her father's collar and buttons. She then resituated his hands. She gently laid her head against his chest and wrapped her arms around him in a hug. She closed her eyes and imagined all the times he had returned it. His strong arms lifting her up into the air as a little girl. The firm squeeze he would hold on her until she giggled or squirmed free. She eased back up and lightly cupped his face in her hands. "Rest easy, Father."

She glanced up to find sad faces surrounding her and she smiled at the sweet friends that sheltered her. "You were all special to him, in your own way. Each of you brought something to his life, and for that I thank you. He truly was a blessed man to have friends who care so deeply."

She reached her hand up and Clifton stepped forward to help her to her feet. She flushed when she stumbled. "If my sister is about, I wish to speak with her." Elizabeth glanced to Ryle and the prince nodded before exiting. "King Eamon. King Anthony. I wish for you two gentlemen to oversee his burial, please. Alayna should not have to carry the burden."

The two kings bowed at her request and left the room.

"Mary, please cover him in linens until his body is transported." Mary nodded.

Sighing on a shaky breath, Elizabeth glanced up at Clifton. He lightly brushed her hair back behind her ear and leaned his forehead against hers. She softly closed her eyes.

"If you are alright, Princess. I will find my leave." Isaac stated quietly.

Elizabeth nodded. "Yes, Prince Isaac. Thank you."

He offered a faint smile as he turned to leave.

When they were alone, Elizabeth leaned against Clifton heavily. "I must sit."

Clifton quickly lifted her by the waist and carried her the few feet towards an empty chair. She sat readily and reached for his hand. He knelt in front of her and allowed her to trace a finger over the lines of his palm. "Clifton, I am sorry you had to be the one to bear the burden of my father's last wish."

His brow furrowed. "I'm sorry?"

"I see it in your eyes." Elizabeth stated, lifting her gaze to his. "You feel this is your fault, do you not?" His green eyes dropped back to their hands.

"Please?" Elizabeth asked, waiting until he peered up at her again. "You must know that my father knew it was his last moments. The ride did not kill him. The exertion did not kill him. It was his sickness that killed him. I do not wish for you to carry the burden of guilt, when there is none to be handed out."

Clifton bit back a sob as he nodded. "I am truly sorry for your loss, Elizabeth. I am… sad for you."

She smiled tenderly and cupped his face, her thumbs brushing his cheeks as she stared into his green meadowed gaze. "I know, and I thank you. I do not wish to be sad over my loss. I will miss him terribly, but I believe it would be selfish of me to wish him here when he suffered so. He is now able to rest. His soul is at peace, and his body no longer suffers. I find peace in that."

"Aye, and he would wish you to be joyful instead of sad." Clifton replied.

She nodded. "I worry for Alayna now, though. She will not take this well."

"She did not." Clifton stated.

"But she will come to terms with it. We all will. Father would not want us wallowing in loss. He would want us to look forward in love." Elizabeth glanced up as her sister entered the room with several attendants. She spotted Elizabeth and Clifton, her swollen eyes and cheeks speaking for her grieving heart. "I wish to bury him in the tombs." She stated, her tone seeking an argument.

Elizabeth nodded. "I think he would like that."

She saw her sister's hope for a fight deflate. "Very well. I guess I will see to the arrangements."

"I have asked King Eamon and King Anthony to see to them." Elizabeth stated. "You have other arrangements to plan, sister. I will see to this one."

Alayna stiffened her shoulders and began to retort, when Prince Ryle stepped behind her and rested his hand on her shoulder. "She accepts your help, Princess Elizabeth." He answered. Elizabeth watched as Alayna's lashing died out and she allowed Prince Ryle to escort her out of the room.

"He has a way with her." Elizabeth stated softly. "She listens to him and values him."

"Aye. I believe he feels the same." Clifton answered. He stood and extended his hand. "Perhaps, my incredible love, you may allow me the honor of escorting you back to your chambers so you may rest. I assume your new mobility has tired you out."

Elizabeth cast a nervous glance down at her leg. "It is quite hideous isn't it?"

"Not at all."

"You are being too kind, but I will accept it only because I am too tired and worn of spirit to combat you at the moment." Clifton smiled tenderly as he helped her to her feet and lifted her in his arms and carried her up the stairs.

The evening sky came and along with it a steady and unyielding rain. *Fitting*, Elizabeth thought, as she stared out the Council Room's window. Even the weather mourned her father's passing. She turned at the sound of the door as others filtered into the room. Alayna sat stiffly in her father's chair at the head of the table, and everyone found their seats. Elizabeth peeled her eyes away from the rain and smiled softly at Clifton's handsome face across from her.

"Good evening, Council." Alayna stated. "I know we all gather with heavy hearts tonight, but my father would have wished for us to continue on in his stead." She glanced around the room and surveyed all the different faces. Allies and friends.

Samuel sat awkwardly beside Prince Isaac. Alayna had asked him to join in on the meeting now that he represented the Southern Kingdom, a position she knew would invite questioning. "My father's funeral proceedings will be tomorrow afternoon in the main hall. The castle doors will be open for anyone in the kingdom to enter. Mosiah has assured me that the guard will be available to stand watch."

Elizabeth shifted uncomfortably as she adjusted one of the leather straps circled around her waist. Alayna briefly caught the motion and waited until her sister's fidgeting had subsided before continuing.

"I do not wish to prolong current topics of discussion. The East and West will return to their kingdoms at week's end as planned. The royal wedding will take place day after tomorrow as planned." King Anthony started to speak, and Alayna held up her hand to stop his words. "Other topics I wish to bring to the table are the matters of the Southern Kingdom and the current position of Realm Captain of the Royal Guard."

Eamon looked to Mosiah in surprise.

"I have relinquished my position as Captain, as previously planned and discussed the matter with King Granton and Princess Alayna prior to this meeting." Mosiah stated. "I will, however, remain on duty in the guard until a new leader is selected."

"And what of the Southern Kingdom?" King Anthony asked. "Prince Samuel is too young to take the throne. Should we not be searching for a steward?"

"And has anyone stepped forward in hopes of the position of Captain?" King Eamon inquired.

"I will address both of these issues, my Lords." Alayna stated confidently. "First, in regard to the South, I believe Prince Samuel should have the right to choose."

Everyone turned to look at Samuel, the young man's eyes widened in surprise and Elizabeth smiled at him.

"It is his right to claim the throne after his father and brother passed. If he feels he is ready, we will support him."

"Well?" Anthony pushed. "Are you ready to be king, little one?"

"I am fifteen." Samuel stated. "I am not a boy, nor am I a man. I understand I have much to learn in order to manage a kingdom, but I also know what it is I wish not to do. I do not wish to rule the South as my father and brother did. If the Queen should support me with an aid, I wish to fulfill my role as king as soon as possible and establish an amicable ally to the rest of the Realm."

Isaac slapped Samuel on the back in a brotherly pat and smiled at the kid. "I will assist you." He nominated.

"As will I." Clifton and Ryle stated at the same time.

Alayna and Elizabeth shared a smile of encouragement at the comradery around the room.

"It is settled then. We make plans for the coronation of our King of the South, King Samuel." Alayna nodded in resolution. "Now in matters of the Captain of the Guard." She began. "A request has been submitted before the former king and myself just recently, prior to the war between the kingdoms." Her gaze locked onto King Eamon as she spoke, and the man held upon her every word. "Prince Ryle of the Eastern Kingdom wishes to protect the Realm in the role as Captain."

Eamon's eyes widened as he turned to his son. "Speak now." His voice was calm, but his eyes held a restrained fire that had Ryle and Clifton both shifting in their seats.

"It is true. I approached King Granton and the future Queen just prior to the Eastern Kingdom's battle. I wish to relinquish my rights as future king to my brother." He turned to Clifton and placed his hand on his shoulder as he continued. "So that I may serve the Realm as protector of the throne."

Everyone fell silent as the weight of Ryle's decision carried throughout the room. Elizabeth studied King Eamon closely at his son's announcement. "We have prepared for your kingship since your infancy, Ryle. The kingdom expects you to be king." Eamon stated, his hand lightly tapping against the table as he spoke.

"I know Father, but I also know our kingdom will equally respect and serve Clifton as their future king as well. Trust that I have pondered my decision thoroughly."

King Eamon leaned back in his chair and rubbed a hand over his beard as he let the matter sink into his brain. "Have you even asked your brother if he would be willing to accept the throne?"

Ryle turned to his stunned younger brother and smiled. "I feel Cliff is more than ready when the time comes, and he will now have a strong queen to support him." Ryle nodded at Elizabeth. She inhaled deeply and waited for King Eamon's next statement.

"Well, Cliff?" Eamon asked. "Do you accept your brother's crown for kingship?"

Clifton looked to Elizabeth across the table, their eyes briefly holding as he wished to assess her feelings on the matter.

She nodded her blessing.

"I will." Clifton stated, his voice confident. He felt Ryle squeeze his shoulder in thanks as their father leaned back in his chair with a look of exasperation. "Well I guess that is settled then. Who am I to withhold protection to the royal crown?"

Alayna smiled. "All kingdoms in approval of the appointment of Prince Ryle of the Eastern Kingdom as the new Captain of the Royal Guard of the North and of the Realm, please raise your right hand."

Hands rose around the room and she smiled. "The matter is settled."

Mosiah nodded his approval.

"Now, my friends, are there any other requests or concerns?"

"I think there are many." Elizabeth replied. "We must not forget that during this time of grieving for the king, or the celebration of new leadership," she motioned towards Samuel, Ryle, and Alayna, "or the merging of two kingdoms," she motioned between herself and Clifton. "We have an underlying threat across that boundary line. We are misguided if we believe Lancer is not a threat. He is a lion on the prowl."

"I do not believe anyone has forgotten, sister." Alayna stated.

"I am just stating that all of these events that are currently happening do not need to blind us from the task at hand. Our task as leaders of the Realm is to protect the Realm. What are we doing right now, in this very moment, to counteract the strategies being plotted against us on the other side of the line?"

King Eamon held up his hand to calm Elizabeth. "I do not think taking time to grieve or to celebrate is diverting us away from Lancer's threat. Trust me, we are aware of his power and the darkness that resides in him. But the Realm cannot afford to go up against the Lands until we ourselves have recuperated from the battles and regained our strength and leadership in all kingdoms. We must remain patient, Princess Elizabeth."

Alayna squeezed Elizabeth's hand. "Patience has never been my sister's strong suit, your Grace."

Elizabeth agreed by nodding, causing several to smile at her honesty.

"But I believe King Eamon is right." Alayna announced. "In order to overcome the Lands, we must first prevent our own Realm from being overcome by the recent events."

"If I may?" Prince Isaac held up his finger and waited for Alayna to nod. "I think an importance needs to be placed upon Princess Elizabeth's concern."

"Isaac, we already established what the Realm will be doing." King Anthony scolded.

"Aye, I understand that, Father. But what I am trying to convey is that right now we are all gathered around this table together. We are here for one another and supportive. By the end of the week, however, we will all be venturing to our separate kingdoms and living life as we have always done. How long before we meet again? How long before we discuss the matters of the Unfading Lands? How long until Lancer sets a force against us? We need to establish a set time to reconvene before we all depart, or the Unfading Lands will fall behind us until it is too late."

"I agree." Samuel stated, his voice slightly edged with nerves as he contributed to the conversation.

"Yes." Clifton added. "Prince Edward was very open with me about his attempts at crossing the boundary. He and Lancer both attempted to cross into the Southern Kingdom because they believe it to be weak. Edward is still not able to cross, but Lancer passes freely. His eye is already on the Southern Kingdom. I, for one, am uneasy with that."

"Aye, me as well." Samuel quietly agreed.

"We all are." Alayna stated. "That is why Mosiah will be accompanying Prince Samuel back to the Southern Kingdom with a wave of ranks from the Royal Guard. Samuel will have protection while he reestablishes his kingdom. We will also be visiting back and forth to provide him with guidance. "Alayna replied.

"In regard to Lancer, I wish for Prince Clifton to maintain interactions with my brother across the boundary line. I am sure you two can establish a meeting place near the Eastern Kingdom. It is imperative that we utilize my brother and his forces. If Edward should confess a fear of an attack, we will then begin our preparations for war. Until then, our focus is to build up our strength during these times of change." Alayna stood in dismissal. "From now until the end of the week we have a funeral and a wedding. A time for grief and a time for joy. I wish you all a good evening." Alayna and Mosiah exited, and the rest of the room sat quietly for a few moments.

Prince Samuel stood and quietly pushed his chair under the table. Isaac reached out and grabbed his arm before he departed. "I will assist you whenever, my Lord. All you have to do is send word to the West."

A relieved smile washed over Samuel's face as he nodded. "Thank you, Prince Isaac."

"The East is at your assistance as well." King Eamon stood, his presence towering over the young king, but his smile welcoming. "Granton had high hopes for you, son. I know you will be an honorable king."

Samuel did not respond as the king passed by him and exited the room. He glanced to Elizabeth and she winked at him. "Well, I for one am starving, gentlemen. Shall we make our way down to the dining hall for some of Gretchen's delicious creations?" She eased to her feet.

Several agreements fluttered through the room as she stood. "Prin- I mean, King Samuel, will you please track down Princess Melody and bring her to the dining hall as well?"

"Yes, my Lady." He bowed and quickly exited. Clifton smiled at Elizabeth as she slipped her arm in his. "Do you have a plan circulating up there?" He lightly tapped her temple and she grinned. "I do not know what you mean, Prince Clifton." He chuckled softly as he trailed a finger down her soft cheek.

"You realize you marry one another in two days, do you not?" Ryle asked on a sigh of false annoyance.

"Aye, how could I forget?" Clifton beamed as he glanced down at Elizabeth's dazzling gaze.

"Then perhaps you two can move a bit faster and enjoy one another's soft eyes when others are not starving."

"How insulting your brother is, Clifton." Elizabeth jested. "To insist we rush ourselves when I only have the use of one leg."

Everyone stopped, and Ryle's face blanched at the thought of insulting the princess.

It was the slight quirk to her brow and sassiness to her lips that had Clifton bursting into laughter and surprising everyone. Elizabeth laughed as well as she patted Ryle's stunned face in passing.

Isaac and his father smirked at one another at the princess' humor and all made their way down the stairs to the dining room in equal uplifted spirits at Ryle's embarrassment.

CHAPTER 13

The next couple of days flew by in a blur and before she could blink, Elizabeth found herself standing before her mirror watching Mary tie ribbons in her hair for her wedding day. The pale blue dress was made of the finest silk she had ever brushed her hand against and she found the delicate stitching beautiful. Alayna had chosen every detail perfectly. She tilted her head as she surveyed herself in the mirror, her blue eyes blazed against her creamy skin, the blue of the dress aiding in their brightness. Blue eyes like her father. A sadness tugged at her heart as she thought of the day before and the outpouring of love from the people of the kingdom as they ventured into the castle to say their goodbyes to the king. She prayed today that they would be rejoicing instead of mourning. She felt her stomach flutter at the thought of marrying Clifton. His handsome face and unruly hair. Smiling, she straightened as Mary stepped to the side to survey her work. "Beautiful, my Lady. Absolutely beautiful."

"You think he will like it?" Elizabeth asked nervously, lightly touching the tips of her black hair. The cascade of curls that draped over her shoulders and down her back looked smooth as silk.

"We will not place your veil in your hair until we are near the main hall." Mary explained.

Elizabeth nodded, stunned at the image she made. A blushing bride, she thought, full of love and wonder and nerves.

A throat cleared, and she gasped as she turned thinking Clifton had come to sneak a peek at her. She relaxed, and a slow smile spread over her lips as she spotted Prince Isaac standing in his red formal tunic and white wolf's fur. "You look stunning, princess." He complimented.

"Do I?" Elizabeth asked, her worried smile making him laugh.

"Yes, but only if you stop fidgeting." He warned.

She accepted the arm he offered, and they made their way out the door.

"The crowd is set. The groom is waiting. The only thing left is you." Isaac stated as they made their way down the stairs. Mary followed closely behind.

As they neared the entrance to the main hall, King Anthony, King Eamon, Prince Samuel, and Prince Ryle awaited. They all smiled as she stepped to the front entrance. King Eamon beamed, his smile slightly faltering as tears of joy beckoned to fall. "My dear," he hugged her tightly. "You look gorgeous."

"Thank you." Elizabeth replied as Mary lightly pinned the cathedral length veil in her hair. Mary then stretched the thin lace out across the floor behind Elizabeth.

"Are you ready to be escorted down the aisle?" King Eamon asked, extending his arm.

Elizabeth glanced shyly at Isaac. "Actually, my Lord, I wondered if perhaps Prince Isaac could do the honor."

Isaac's brows rose along with the other men's.

King Eamon nodded. "Of course, my dear." He stepped out of the way and smiled just as the doors opened and music fluttered through the air. The two kings made their way down the aisle and towards the front where Alayna stood nearest the priest. Princess Melody stood along the steps to the left as Clifton awaited Elizabeth in the middle. Prince Ryle and Prince Samuel made their entrance and stood along the steps lining up towards Clifton. Ryle lightly patted his brother on the back as the music changed and Isaac stepped forward with Elizabeth on his arm. They waited at the back of the room until Mary waved them forward.

"Thank you, Prince Isaac, for escorting me on such a special day." Elizabeth whispered to him.

"I am honored you would ask me to." Isaac stated looking down on her. He winked at her as he began leading them down the aisle.

Alayna's brow rose at the sight of Isaac as Elizabeth's escort, but knew her sister and the prince of the West had formed an odd bond since their battle against the South. She watched as Elizabeth's pale blue dress shined and the white roses billowed from her hands. *She made a stunning bride*, Alayna thought. She moved elegantly, her limp almost nonexistent as she made her way towards them. She studied her future brother and grinned at the love shining on his face as he witnessed the sight of his gorgeous bride.

Clifton felt the breath leave his lungs and the entire room as Elizabeth stepped into the doorway. He heard nothing as his gaze roamed over her beautiful dress, the colors of his kingdom, the kingdom they would one day rule together. His eyes roamed from her feet to her face, and the small nervous smile she carried widened when their eyes met. He felt his chest swell in pride at the thought of being her husband. He caught the amused gaze of Prince Isaac as he slowly brought Elizabeth towards him.

When she reached the platform, the priest addressed the congregation. Elizabeth did not hear a word as she gazed at Clifton's bright green eyes and perfect smile. *He looked handsome*, she thought. His usual unkempt mane combed back away from his face.

His formal tunic crisp and clean. She sensed his nerves and knew they shared a similar feeling. She watched as Alayna lightly dabbed a tear away, and her gaze found the sweet smile of Prince Ryle as he stood proudly by his brother.

"And may you give this woman to this man." The priest waved for Prince Isaac to hand Elizabeth over. He slipped her arm from his and gently squeezed her hand, bowing on his knee as he kissed her knuckles. He then stood and gently placed her hand in Clifton's. The two men exchanged a look of confirmation. Isaac's challenge for Clifton to protect Elizabeth, and Clifton's acceptance. Elizabeth watched as Isaac found his place next to Ryle and then she turned her attention to Clifton. She repeated words, sonnets, prayers... she wasn't quite sure what all she said, all she knew was that she loved the man before her.

A cheer erupted in the crowd as the time came for Clifton to claim her as his wife. He leaned forward and lightly brushed his lips over hers, Elizabeth's hands finding the lapels of his tunic and holding him to her. Everyone cheered louder at her insistence for a longer kiss. Clifton kissed her again and a slow smile spread over his face as he felt her slide a small white stone into his palm.

They turned to face the guests and everyone cheered again as white rose petals rained down on them from the balconies. The music then began to play as they slowly made their way out of the castle and to the parapet where their marriage would be announced to the kingdom.

Elizabeth sighed as soon as the sunshine hit her face and she turned to find Clifton studying her closely.

"What are you thinking, prince?"

"That I may now stare at you for as long as I wish." He winked at her making her blush as he waved to the crowd. The villagers tossed well wishes and roses up onto the parapet as Elizabeth and Clifton greeted them with happy hearts. A new life had started, a new chapter for her. She knew life in the East would be different, but since the rise of the South and the ever-present threat of the Unfading Lands stormed into their lives, she knew the North would always be her home. They would return here in due time. All of them would return here. She turned as her sister stepped onto the parapet and in between them to bestow the royal blessing upon their marriage and to hug Elizabeth.

"I will miss you, sister." Alayna stated quietly as she squeezed Elizabeth to her in a tight embrace.

Elizabeth smiled and bit back her own tears as they giggled softly. "I will return soon enough."

"Aye, I know you will." Alayna slipped her arms from Elizabeth's shoulders and held her hands in front of her as Clifton stepped forward and bowed. Alayna waved away his formality as she hugged him tightly as well. When she slipped from his grasp he gently reached into his tunic pocket and withdrew a small folded piece of parchment bearing her name in her father's handwriting. "This is yours, my Queen." Clifton stated quietly. Alayna nervously took the letter and tucked it into her skirt.

"You two be careful. I will be anxiously awaiting the next reconvening of the Council. Should you need me before then, all you have to do is send word." Alayna soberly sought Elizabeth's gaze. Nodding, Elizabeth grinned. "I will be fine, Alayna. You take care of yourself."

Alayna nodded as well as Prince Ryle stepped out and shook his brother's hand in congratulations. "She will be well looked after." He promised, the light touch to Alayna's shoulder confirming Elizabeth's hopes he would stay behind. Her heart relieved itself of the worry of her sister being alone and she smiled at the thought of Alayna being looked after by Ryle.

"Well," King Eamon stepped beside his son and waved to the people as well. "It is time we take our leave." He turned to Alayna and hugged her. He pulled away from her slightly and looked into her calm gaze. "Take care my dear. If you should need anything, you know where to send for me."

Alayna nodded. "Thank you, King Eamon. Safe journeys."

"My boy." He reached around Prince Ryle's neck and pulled him into a firm embrace. "Take care of our Queen." Ryle nodded. "I will, Father." King Eamon squeezed Ryle's shoulder as his eyes clouded with unshed tears. He took a deep breath before releasing his son's shoulder.

The Eastern royal carriages pulled to the main entrance of the castle, the horses' bridles and the carriage covered in white roses and greenery. Clifton and Elizabeth made their way to the first carriage and they waved one last time before ducking inside. King Eamon bowed to King Anthony and his children and then turned and gave a final wave to his son and Alayna as he occupied the second carriage.

To the sound of hooves and shouts of joy, Princess Elizabeth of the North and of the Realm united with the Eastern Kingdom.

∞

Edward sat upon the log in his clearing and stared at the parchment in his hands. His father's handwriting bold and confident. The fluid strokes crossing the page conveyed words of love and leadership. He shot a gaze to the rocks across the line, to the place his father drew his last breath. He had watched as his father gave into his sickness. The ease in which he passed his last letter and then sat on the stone. He had waved at Edward. A final small tilt of the hand as he gently closed his eyes and welcomed death. Edward pinched the bridge of his nose to halt the tears.

There would be time for grieving later, he thought. For now, every ounce of his being would be used to destroy the boundary. If the boundary line did not exist, he would have been with his family, would have been with his father in those last moments. He stood and paced over the damp earth and tried to plan his next move. Lancer would give up on him soon if he did not embrace the power. He would not be able to cross by blood, but Edward knew Lancer would not relinquish his personal pursuit of Edward's loyalty.

He gripped the horn of his saddle and whipped his long leg over the side and into the stirrups. He needed to enter the reflection room on his own terms. He needed to see what lurked within its walls, without the distraction of Lancer's empty words. As he trotted up to the castle, he quickly dismounted and shrugged away the welcomes of guards and attendants. He was on a mission, and his mission was darkness. He traveled the halls, his boots echoing on the stone floor, until he reached the door of Lancer's reflection chamber. He glanced both directions and spotted no one. He then reached for the old iron handle and slipped inside. The room was dark, as was its usual condition. He stepped towards the middle of the room, his heart heavy, his thoughts whirling, and his hatred for the boundary line fueled his anger as he grabbed his sword and sliced the palm of his hand in a quick flourish. He did not feel the pain; he only felt anger. The rush of the heat in his veins had his heart pounding in his chest and the desperation of his emotions surfaced to an eruption. He screamed, a battle cry of anguish and ferocity.

"How dare you?!" He screamed into the darkness. "How dare you take away my father?! How dare you take away my family?! How dare you take away my life?!" His cries bounced off the walls and no one answered. The flames did not light. The room was silent. He fell to his knees and sobbed. How could he sit back and watch his family die? How was he to break down that boundary that separated him from his family? How was he to fight an invisible force? *Hatred versus hatred*, he thought. Oh, and he hated whatever force enabled the hold Lancer possessed on the boundary line.

Suddenly, the flames ignited, and the sconces burned bright around the room. Edward's gaze looked to the door in fear of Lancer emerging. Spotting no one, his gaze then traveled down to the black smoke emerging around his knees. His breathing hitched, his blue eyes darkened, and the pain in his heart from his loss, overcame his senses and he allowed his hatred for Lancer to consume him. He felt the sting, that first initial pinch of pain as his hand pulsed. He stretched out his arms and wailed to the ceiling. *Hatred was the key*, he realized. The key to embracing the power. The key to the Land of Unfading Beauty. The key that locked the boundary line and the key that would open it. For he reached out his blood-stained hand and watched as the blackness seeped into his wound. His allegiance to the Realm drove his hatred towards Lancer and the Lands. There would be no turning back, he knew. He would risk his blood, his very life, to save the Realm. His *father's* Realm. And he would do so with the very weapon Lancer believed him incapable of embracing. Hatred.

The war continues…

Darkness Divided, Part Two in The Unfading Lands Series

Where will YOUR allegiance lie?

ABOUT THE AUTHOR

Katharine E. Hamilton started her writing career nearly a decade ago by creating fun-filled stories that have taken children on imaginative adventures all around the world. By using her talents of imagery and suspense to illustrate the deep, underlying issue of good and evil within us all, Katharine extends the invitation for adventure to adults everywhere. She finds herself drawn time and again by the people behind her adventures and wishes to bring them to life in her stories.

She was born and raised in the state of Texas, where she currently resides on a ranch in the heart of brush country with her husband, Brad, her son, Everett, and their two furry friends, Tulip and Cash. She is a graduate of Texas A&M University, where she received a Bachelor's degree in History. She finds most of her stories share the love of the past combined with a twist of imagination.
She is thankful to her readers for allowing her the privilege to turn her dreams into a new adventure for us all.

All Titles by Katharine E. Hamilton

The Unfading Lands Series
The Unfading Lands
Darkness Divided
Redemption Rising

The Lighthearted Collection
Chicago's Best
Montgomery House
Beautiful Fury

Children's Books
The Adventurous Life of Laura Bell
Susie at Your Service
Sissy and Kat

Find out more about Katharine and her works at:

www.katharinehamilton.com

Social Media is a great way to connect with Katharine. Check her out on the following:

Facebook: Author Katharine E. Hamilton
Twitter: @AuthorKatharine
Instagram: AuthorKatharine

Email: khamiltonauthor@gmail.com

Made in the USA
Middletown, DE
30 December 2023

46028767R00205